THE HOUSE OF HIDDEN SECRETS

LAUREN WESTWOOD

B
Boldwood

First published in 2017 as *Finding Secrets*. Second edition published in 2022. This edition published in Great Britain in 2025 by Boldwood Books Ltd.

Copyright © Lauren Westwood, 2017

Cover Design by Emma Graves Design

Cover Images: Shutterstock

The moral right of Lauren Westwood to be identified as the author of this work has been asserted in accordance with the Copyright, Designs and Patents Act 1988.

All rights reserved. No part of this book may be reproduced in any form or by any electronic or mechanical means, including information storage and retrieval systems, without written permission from the author, except for the use of brief quotations in a book review. This book is a work of fiction and, except in the case of historical fact, any resemblance to actual persons, living or dead, is purely coincidental.

Every effort has been made to obtain the necessary permissions with reference to copyright material, both illustrative and quoted. We apologise for any omissions in this respect and will be pleased to make the appropriate acknowledgements in any future edition.

A CIP catalogue record for this book is available from the British Library.

Paperback ISBN 978-1-83678-007-6

Large Print ISBN 978-1-83678-008-3

Hardback ISBN 978-1-83678-006-9

Ebook ISBN 978-1-83678-009-0

Kindle ISBN 978-1-83678-010-6

Audio CD ISBN 978-1-83678-001-4

MP3 CD ISBN 978-1-83678-002-1

Digital audio download ISBN 978-1-83678-004-5

This book is printed on certified sustainable paper. Boldwood Books is dedicated to putting sustainability at the heart of our business. For more information please visit https://www.boldwoodbooks.com/about-us/sustainability/

Boldwood Books Ltd, 23 Bowerdean Street, London, SW6 3TN

www.boldwoodbooks.com

To Eve, Rose and Grace with love

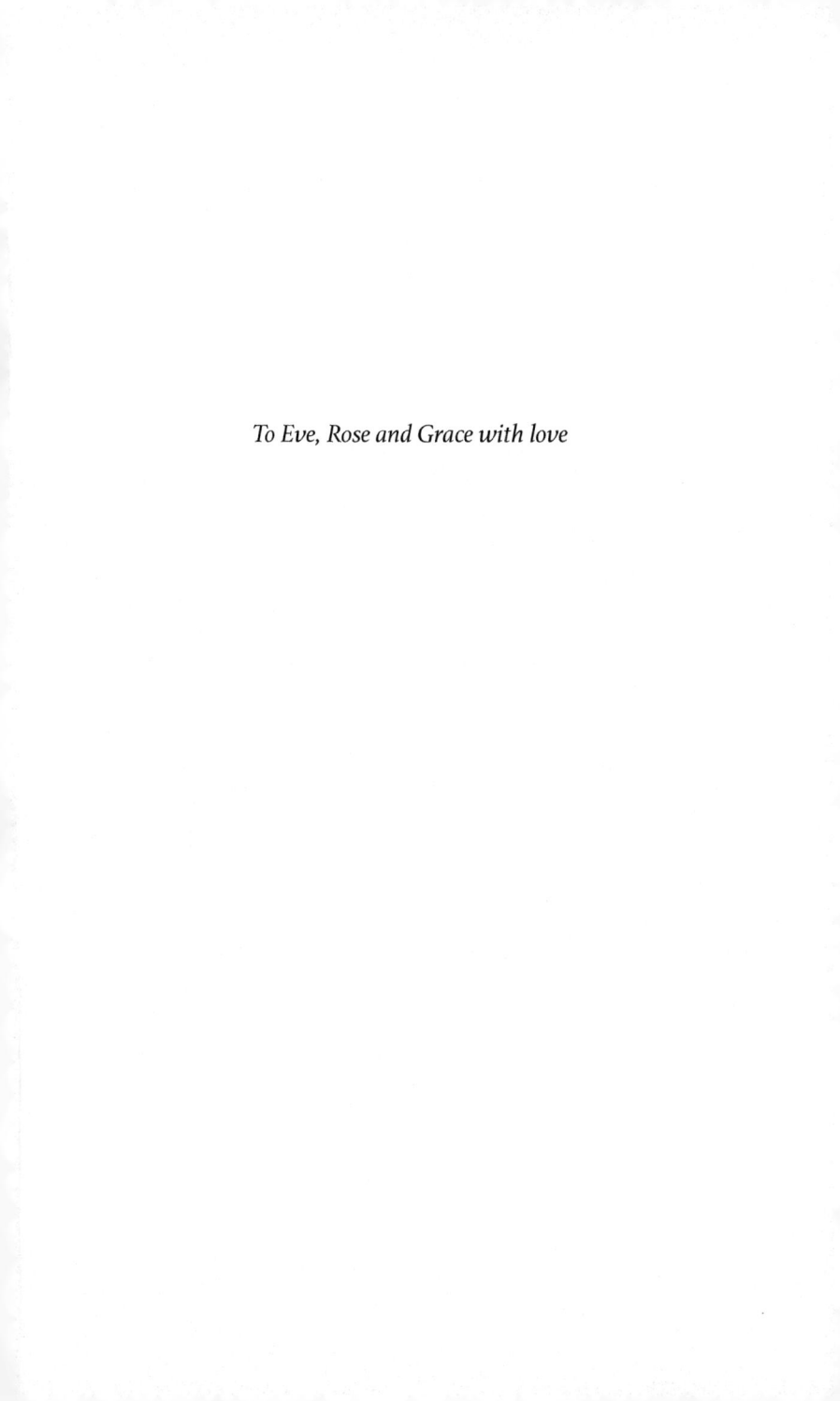

PROLOGUE
DIARY OF HAL 'BADGER' DAWKINS – 1940

London, 12 November 1940 11.30 p.m.

Tonight was the worst yet. The end of a world that doesn't end – it just keeps going. My ears still ring from the thunder of planes, the whine of the bombs, and the explosions that feel as if they might blow my head apart. And the screams – the dreadful, dreadful screams.

We were called out to a terrace in Holloway, near where I grew up. The big house at the top of Larkspur Gardens had suffered a direct hit. White-hot fear seared through me as we pulled up in front. Had the family escaped? Had she escaped?

There were casualties in the street, blackened and burned. Robbie, the damned photographer, was already at the scene filming the rubble and carnage. We loaded the ambulance with casualties, and my partner sped off to the hospital. I stayed behind to tend the wounded.

I waved my fists at the planes as they flew off into the night. My throat was thick with ash and dust and the metallic tang of blood. Smoke curled up from the bombed house towards a make-believe heaven and a God that doesn't exist.

But just then, snowflakes began to fall, pure and weightless from the sky. A child crawled out from underneath a heap of rubble. Her face and hair were streaked black; she shivered in a torn dress and thin coat. Looking up to the sky, she stuck out her tongue, letting the white crystals melt there.

Like the world was still a beautiful place.

PART I

'Watch with glittering eyes the whole world around you because the greatest secrets are always hidden in the most unlikely places.'

— ROALD DAHL

1

MALLOW COURT, BUCKINGHAMSHIRE

May 2000

It's the perfect day for a wedding. The wisteria twining around the arbour is in full bloom; the sprigs of white roses hand-tied with lavender silk ribbons have a hint of dew on their petals. The weather is warm with a slight breeze that ruffles the organza chair bows. Wisps of clouds decorate the sky like celestial confetti. Bees hum in the borders and an iridescent butterfly floats from flower to flower. Daisies and buttercups dot the field where the marquee has been erected amid grazing sheep.

Perfect.

Most importantly, from my perspective at least, the posh Portaloos, the five-tier cake, and the sushi chef from Nobu all arrived early this morning right on schedule, followed by a lorryload of chilled Pol Roger. As Winston Churchill once said of his favourite tipple: 'In victory, deserve it. In defeat, need it' – and I'm going to make sure that it's victory all the way. And luckily, when something did go wrong – the vicar coming down with stomach flu – I managed to sort a replacement quickly, thus keeping everything done and dusted.

And perfect.

'Damn it.' The bride-to-be cups her manicured hand and lights another Marlboro Light, flicking the match into the peonies. She looks at me with pure venom. 'You've ruined everything.'

I force a calm smile. At this moment, Miss Heath-Churchley looks very little like her full-page soft-focus photo in *Country Life* that won her the hand of Mr Ernest ('call-me-Ernie') Wright-Thursley. When she came round to the wedding fair, she showed me a laminated copy:

> Miss Celestina Heath-Churchley of Albright House, West Sussex. Eldest Daughter of Charles August Heath-Churchley, OBE, and Suzanna DuBois Heath-Churchley. Educated at Chichester Preparatory School and Cheltenham Ladies' College with a degree in Equine Business Studies.

It's literally kept me awake at night wondering how they're going to hyphenate their surnames – try saying Churchley-Thursley five times fast. And do Heath and Wright just drop out of the equation forever? You'd think that as the manager of an elegant stately home-cum-wedding venue, I'd know these things, but in this case I'm flummoxed.

'The vicar deeply regrets that he's taken ill...' I say for the umpteenth time. 'Fortunately, I was able to find a replacement on short notice. Your ceremony can proceed right on schedule.'

The soon-to-be-previous Miss Heath-Churchley – or Cee-Cee, as her bridesmaids call her – glares down her nose at me, taking in my faux-suede jacket, indigo jeans, and biker boots. Clearly, she has a sixth sense that I lack upper-class origins – or any origins whatsoever. Given my lack of breeding, I normally wouldn't have a problem telling her exactly where to take her two-hundred guests, her horse-drawn carriage, her string quartet, harpist *and* dance band, her carb-free canapés, and her photographer from *Tattler* and stick them. But instead I take a deep breath and remind myself that 'the customer is always right'. Because with a 400-year-old house that's one of the finest examples of Elizabethan architecture in the South East, complete with apocryphal royal visitors and a truly shocking annual maintenance bill, I have a responsibility to hold my tongue. Especially when 'Daddy' Heath-Churchley is paying an awfully big fee to hold Cee-Cee's wedding in the award-winning gardens.

'A woman vicar?' Cee-Cee practically spits. 'Who the *hell* has a woman vicar? Couldn't you at least find a real one?'

'She's a fully ordained member of the Church of England,' I say through my teeth. 'In fact, she's a senior chaplain – the sick vicar's *boss*.'

Which isn't *exactly* true, but she doesn't need to know that. Actually, the vicar is my friend Karen from uni, who got her doctorate in theology and then took holy orders because, in her words, 'there are so many eligible men'.

'But what will people think!' Cee-Cee moans.

'That you're right on trend,' I say. 'Women vicars are quite the thing now. Madonna and Guy Ritchie already have one booked.'

'Really?' She stamps out the cigarette with the toe of her white satin Manolo, obliterating it into the paper rose petals. 'And where the hell is Ernest?'

'I haven't seen him yet,' I say. 'Would you like me to ring the Golden Fleece and make sure he's had a wake-up call?'

'You'd better.'

'And I believe the vicar would like to meet with you both before the ceremony. Get to know you.'

'Whatever.' She raises three fingers in a 'W' shape. 'I'm off to have a bath. There'd better be hot water.' Standing up, she begins walking towards the coach house where she and her bridesmaids are staying. 'And make sure my things are moved to the bridal chamber.'

'Of course,' I say to her spray-tanned back. *Your highness.*

Catherine Fairchild, the owner of Mallow Court, warned me before the first wedding fair that most brides would want to be treated like royalty on their special day. It's not something I can relate to. I was never the kind of girl who liked pink flouncy dresses and simpering Disney princesses. My socialist dad was proud of me for that, though sometimes Mum despaired. Every once in a while, she would bring home a dressing up costume from the charity shop, only to find it later covered in mud and crumpled up in a ball in the corner of my room. I preferred being a pirate or a wizard (or, given my upbringing – a communist revolutionary) whenever dressing up was required.

Maybe it's ironic that I'm now in charge of a stately home where we hope to eventually hold ten to twelve weddings a year. I've earmarked the Heath-Churchley deposit for upgrading the guest loos. Cee-Cee's wedding is our first, so it's imperative that it goes off without a hitch. Looking on the bright side, if I can keep *her* satisfied, our future brides should be a piece of cake.

I make my way over to the marquee to check on the caterers. Inside, 'Mummy' Heath-Churchley, the maid of honour, and two bridesmaids are sampling the chocolate fountain and a bottle of Pol Roger.

'Has my stepson Christopher arrived yet?' Mrs H-C asks.

'I don't think so,' I say. 'But I'll look out for him.' Not that I've got a clue who he is, as to me, one posh toff looks the same as the next.

The mother of the bride pops the cork on another bottle. I take a final look around – everything looks shiny, polished, over-the-top, and expensive. Relieved, I return to the main house. The cool yellow stone glows in the morning sun, the light reflecting off hundreds of higgledy-piggledy mullioned windows. In a past life, someone like me would have been, at best, a servant at a house like this. But thanks to a first-class degree in Medieval Studies from Oxford, a well-connected tutor, and being at the right place at the right time, I'm the one in charge.

In a little under three years, I've helped Mrs Fairchild put the huge Elizabethan mansion that her father renovated after the war onto the map of stately homes. Between the well-scripted tours, the organic tearoom, the gift shop featuring traditional crafts and artisan beers, the adventure playground, corporate away days, and now the weddings, we're starting to turn a profit. And when our first wedding is finally over, I can turn my attentions back to my pet project: an exhibition called 'Clothing Through the Ages' to be held upstairs in the long gallery.

As I'm about to enter through the kitchen door, an orange and black Smart car zips around the crescent drive and screeches to a halt in the disabled parking space, sending gravel flying into the delphiniums. A woman in a dark trouser suit and white shirt jumps out, strawberry blonde curls bouncing at her shoulders.

'Karen!' I say, relieved to have a real-life flesh-and-blood vicar on site. 'I'm glad you're here.' I lower my voice. 'Though I'm not sure the bride is quite so chuffed.'

My friend waves her hand expansively. 'Never mind that,

Alex. First I've just got to tell you – I met the most amazing bloke last night. Big strapping lad, built like a shire horse. Didn't quite catch his name – Eddie, or Denny, or something.'

'I thought you'd turned over a new leaf.' I put my hands on my hips. 'What was it you said when you were ordained? "No more casual and meaningless encounters"; and that you were going to live "strictly by the Bible"?'

'Ahh, Alex,' she intones in her sermon voice. 'This was neither casual nor meaningless. And it was definitely biblical – like Adam and Eve in the Garden of Eden.'

I roll my eyes. 'Probably more like Sodom and Gomorrah.'

'Touché.'

'And where did you meet this "big strapping lad whose name you didn't quite catch"?'

'At the village pub.' Her brow furrows. 'The Golden Fleece. You should know as you booked the room.'

'Yeah – sorry about that. I'd have had you stay with me, but the shower's bust.'

'No worries,' she says. 'The night was a revelation. Let's just say that the dog collar has many uses, though not all of them are strictly sanctioned by the ecclesiastical texts.'

'You're incorrigible.'

'Yes, well…' She checks her watch. 'Let's get this show on the road. I should meet the bride and groom before I tie the noose for them…' She winks. 'I mean the knot.'

'The groom isn't here yet and the bride's having a bath, so would you like a cuppa?' I gesture towards the house.

'Isn't there any champagne?'

'Well, yes…'

'Come on, Alex.' She pulls my arm. 'Let's live a little.'

I allow myself to be dragged a few steps before standing my ground. 'No,' I say. 'It wouldn't look right. Besides, I've got—'

'Hey, you! Ms... What is it? Hart?'

I cringe at the dulcet tones of Cee-Cee yelling at me from the coach house. I mentally tick off everything that could be wrong: no hot water, a spider in the sink, bath gel the wrong scent...

'Where the hell is Ernie?' she whines. 'You said he was staying at some grotty old pub. And now he's missing.'

'Missing?'

'I rang Ant. He went up and checked his room. He's not there, and his bed hasn't been slept in.'

'Oh.' I swallow hard. 'He's... um... probably just on his way here.'

'Ernie?' Karen says, wide-eyed.

'Is *she* the woman vicar?' Cee-Cee glares.

A huge black SUV pulls up driven by Ant, the groom's best man. A half-dressed, fully dishevelled Ernie stumbles out of the passenger side holding an empty bottle of whisky.

'Darling...' he drawls, practically falling at Cee-Cee's feet.

'Where have you been, dearest?' she scolds in a little-girl voice. 'How naughty that you've been keeping me waiting. We're supposed to meet the vicar.' She wrinkles her nose. 'It's... *her*.'

Cee-Cee looks at Karen, gesturing with her pearlescent nails.

Karen looks at Ernie.

Ernie looks at Karen, letting out a little sputter.

Cee-Cee looks at Ernie...

Then Karen...

Then me.

Karen looks anywhere *but* at me.

'Umm, actually...' Karen says. 'We've met.'

Cee-Cee screams.

2

It takes over a year to plan a big society wedding. But it takes less than an afternoon to unwind one. Instead of 'I do's and church bells, Cee-Cee's shrieks are the order of the day.

'You bastard! How could you?'

I launch into action mode, shooing Karen into the house, barring the *Tattler* photographer from the area, and grabbing a broom when Cee-Cee starts smashing champagne glasses on the terrace. I manage to save a few glasses, pass them around to the members of the bridal party, and pour everyone a brandy.

'Cee-Cee, sweetie, it meant nothing – just one last fling. You know, like the one you had on your hen night with that bass guitarist...'

A squiffy Mrs Heath-Churchley brandishes a half-empty bottle at Ernie. 'How dare you do this to my daughter?'

I gesture to the Robbie Williams lookalike who's fronting the dance band; he grabs her arms before she can physically unman her son-in-law-not-to-be.

'And what will my husband say about cancelling this wedding again?'

I marshal together a few bridesmaids to help phone the wedding guests and cancel. I'm about to speak to the caterers when the mother of the bride's rage changes direction.

'And where's that slag of a vicar? I'm going to make sure she's... defrocked.'

Karen is nowhere to be seen. I return to the house and find her sprawled out on the sofa in the blue drawing room.

'I'm so sorry, Alex!' She gulps back tears and the last dregs of a bottle of Pol Roger nicked from the bar.

'You're sorry?' I seethe. 'Too bad your "revelation" didn't include the fact that your "big strapping lad" was the groom! You knew how important this was to me. It was our first wedding and it had to go right. Instead, it's a complete disaster!'

'I had no idea who he was.' She looks more remorseful than I've seen her. 'I should go out and apologise in person.' Her lips inch upwards into a momentary smile. 'Would it be awful if I asked Ernie for his number?'

She's joking – I think. 'You stay here,' I command.

'Fine. Get yourself a glass. We can have that long overdue chat you promised.'

'What?'

She looks hurt. 'Or did you invite me here *just* to marry your posh paying guests?'

Guilt pinches my chest. I was supposed to meet Karen last night at the pub, but just as I was leaving, Mrs Fairchild asked me to sit with her. She'd received a letter that had upset her, so I'd stayed at the main house until almost ten. By the time I'd got round to ringing Karen, she hadn't answered.

'We can catch up tonight,' I say. 'Since obviously the wedding won't be going late.'

She shakes her head. 'I can't stay. I've got a Venezuelan

bishop coming round tomorrow. It would have been nice to see you, but I guess you're too busy.'

'Well, sorry,' I say. 'Sorry I couldn't make it down the pub, so you *had* to screw the groom. Sorry that I wanted everything to go well. I'd earmarked the deposit to upgrade the guest loos. And now I'll have to face Mrs Fairchild and tell her about the awful cock-up.'

'Gosh, Alex.' Karen's blues eyes are round and wounded. 'You've changed. I mean… guest loos? When we were at uni, your mind was on "the sacred and profane in medieval architecture" and "historical mysteries surrounding the Ghent Altarpiece". I'd no idea that these other things had become so important.'

'That was a long time ago.'

In her eyes I see the reflection of my last year at uni, when she stood by me while I broke myself on the rock of a doomed love affair with Xavier, an Argentine poet who conveniently happened to be my neighbour, but (I later discovered) inconveniently happened to be married.

'How things change,' she says.

'Look, Karen,' I say. 'At the time, you told me that I needed to move on. So that's what I've done.'

'Have you, Alex? Because to me it looks like you're hiding away from the real world. I bet you never leave this place. Never have any fun.'

'They're not mutually exclusive.'

Karen and I have never shared a common idea of fun. From the moment we started rooming together at uni, I discovered that she liked parties, waking up with strangers, and drinking a raw egg with Worcester sauce for breakfast. Whereas I liked having small groups of friends over to discuss books, taking long, solitary walks along the river, and curling up in the window seat with a glass of wine and a mystery novel. Maybe it's because we were so different that we got along so well.

'I love it here,' I say, feeling defensive. 'I'm much closer to the real world than I ever was at uni. And in the real world – whether we're talking medieval times or right now – vicars don't sleep with the groom before the wedding.'

'I guess I'd better go, then.' She sets down the empty bottle.

'I guess you'd better. You can't drive in this state, so I'll find someone to give you a lift to the village.'

Standing up, she gives her dog collar a little tug. 'Look, Alex. I was out of line and I'm sorry. For my penance I shall compose a sermon along the lines of "we're all human, and sometimes we fall from grace".'

'I know, Karen. And I'm sorry too.' I sigh. 'I really miss you. It's just I've been so busy.'

'Busy is good, Alex, and it's obvious that you've worked wonders on this place. It's practically running itself. But are you going to be doing this forever? You may love it here, but are you really happy? I mean, it doesn't take Mother Teresa to see that you're lonely. You keep busy so you don't have to face real life.'

I shake my head. 'Can't I just enjoy what I've got? A steady job in a beautiful place. It may not be enough for you. But for me – things are good.'

'Are they, Alex?' She looks me deep in the eye. 'Are they really?'

'Yes.' But as the word leaves my mouth, I wonder if it's really true.

* * *

I resolve to put this awful day behind me and get back to normal. The wedding party gradually begins to disperse and the cleaning crew gets to work. I sneak away to my office: a cosy little room with wood panelling, a carved stone fireplace, and a window seat with red velvet cushions. A big oak desk takes up most of the room. I sit down and turn on my computer. There are emails to check, calls to return, invoices to pay, workmen to schedule, all of which I can do in my sleep. Admittedly, I *am* feeling a bit low. But surely, that will change when—

'Ahem.'

A hulking figure in a black tailcoat and bulging white cummerbund occupies the entirety of the doorway. I recognise Charles August Heath-Churchley, father-of-the-bride.

'Oh,' I say. 'Hello, sir.'

'You—' His jowls shake, Churchill style, when he rounds on me, his small eyes penetrating my inner armour. 'Who do you think you are, young lady?'

A loaded question, not that he's to know.

'Do you know what you've done today? The damage you've caused to one of the nation's oldest, proudest families?'

'I've caused?' I look at him aghast. 'With respect, sir, that's not fair. I can't be held responsible for the antics of the wedding party.' Even if the replacement vicar is my best friend, I don't add.

Venom leaks out as he laughs in my face. 'Not responsible? What are you then, the cleaner? The gift shop girl? Some little nobody? I thought you were the manager here. And in my book, the manager is responsible for *everything*.'

Cleaner? Gift shop girl? This man can probably trace his family back as far as the Neanderthals, but does that give him the right to insult me?

'I apologise that things haven't gone as planned,' I say. 'But I think we're done here.'

'Oh, we're not done,' he bellows. 'Not by a long way. I'll ring

Catherine and have you out on your ear, make no mistake.' He turns his broad, pin-striped backside to me and walks out.

'Go ahead, sir,' I mutter. 'Do your worst.'

I put my head in my hands. Despite my bravado, the whole awful business has ruined my day, and probably my whole month. Catherine – he'd called Mrs Fairchild by her first name like he knew her. Working here at Mallow Court is a lot more to me than just a job. Could he have enough clout to get me sacked?

No – that's silly. I straighten up, raking my fingers through my hair. Mrs Fairchild is not the type to be bullied by posh buffoons. Her father, Frank Bolton – aka the 'Knicker King' – was a working-class, self-made man.

I just need to go on as if nothing untoward has happened. After today, I'll never have to see anyone connected to the awful Heath-Churchley clan again. (Unless they happen to relist Cee-Cee as an eligible bacheloress in *Country Life* and I have the misfortune to catch a glimpse of it in a dentist's waiting room or something.)

Nor do I have to give Mr Heath-Churchley's slight a second thought. I'm an independent woman: I don't need roots, or family history, or a fancy name or anything else to be happy just as I am.

Little nobody...

I whistle tunelessly to block out the words. They don't matter, and I'll be fine later – tomorrow... or next week. Right now, however, a long-buried seed of self-doubt lies uncovered at the back of my mind. That it takes a lifetime to forge an identity from nothing, and less than ten seconds to tear it to shreds.

3

'Welcome to Mallow Court,' I say, my smile a little forced. It's a week since the wedding debacle, and I've yet to put it fully behind me. Though Mrs Fairchild has said nothing about sacking me, doubt continues to gnaw. Is Karen right? Have I put all my focus into my job to avoid thinking about my future? Maybe.

'I hope you'll enjoy today's tour through one of the loveliest Elizabethan houses in the South East.' I make eye contact with a few members of the American tour group. 'The house was built in 1604 by a wealthy wool merchant who was also—'

Someone's phone goes off. I stop my spiel, waiting patiently (if a little pained) for a man in a green bowling shirt to dig around his pocket, take out his phone, and answer it with a loud southern drawl: 'Hi, honey, how are the kids?'

A few people scowl in his direction; someone has the nerve to laugh.

He keeps talking. 'Yeah, we're seeing some old house now.'

I clear my throat, glowering at him. When I first started

working at Mallow Court, I wrote the script for the tours and gave all of them myself. Now, however, there are two other full-time guides. Usually, I find leading tours a welcome break from admin, and I enjoy meeting people who are interested in the house. But lately, I've been struggling to maintain my enthusiasm.

'Before I continue,' I say, 'I'd like to get a few ground rules straight. First, can I ask that you put your phones on mute…'

Thus follows a good thirty seconds of grumbling, rustling, digging, and beeping.

The man in the bowling shirt finally rejoins the group. 'Sorry, folks,' he says.

I ignore his apology while the last of the phones go back into pockets and handbags. An elderly man in a Red Sox baseball cap takes advantage of the chaos to remove his chewing gum from his mouth and stick it firmly to the bottom of a carved oak table.

'I'd also like to remind you that there's no eating or drinking inside the house.'

The old man grins at me through gapped front teeth and pops another tab of Orbit into his mouth. I sigh. Next to him, a pear-shaped lady in a 'Go ahead, make my day' T-shirt raises her hand.

'Yes?'

'But there's a tearoom, right? That's what the bus driver said. I want to buy some of that organic marmalade stuff for my daughter-in-law. And some artistic beer for me!'

'Of course,' I say. 'The tour will end at the tearoom and gift shop. Now, if we—'

Another woman raises her hand. 'And where's the ladies' room? The bathroom on the bus was just so stinky…' She shifts from side to side, managing to look desperate.

'Outside to the left. Now, please can you hold your questions. I promise I'll answer them as we go along.'

Another hand shoots up.

'Or at the end,' I say pointedly. 'Now, as I was saying...'

I gloss over the dates and identities of pale-faced subjects of old portraits. Lots of people who come to visit the house are interested in those things, but there's no use pretending that everyone is. Instead, I skip to the fun part.

'You might be interested to know about the current owner of the house. She's called Catherine Fairchild, and her father, Frank Bolton, was known as "the Knicker King". His company was famous for British-made ladies' underwear in the 1950s and 60s.'

A few amused tittles; it's the same with most groups.

'He was the first man in Britain to mass-produce the double gusset,' I say. 'For those of you who don't know what that is' – I raise my eyebrows mischievously – 'it's the business end of the knicker.'

Full on laughter now as a few underwear jokes are 'cracked'.

I move the group along to the billiard room, standing at the door as they go by. The last person is a tall man with light-brown-hair who must have been standing at the back. He's younger than the rest: early thirties, maybe. As he goes past, he stops momentarily and looks me in the eye. His are a most delicious shade of chocolate brown. An unexpected rush of heat shoots down my body.

'Umm,' I gabble, 'the next room is the billiard room.' Like that's not completely obvious given the huge table in the centre.

I stumble through my description of how billiards differ from pool, all the while aware of the tall man watching me and listening intently. As we're about to leave the room, he raises his hand.

'I have a question about Frank Bolton,' he says. His voice is deep, resonant, and definitely English.

'Yes?'

'Was it the ancestral home, or did he buy the house after the war?'

It's a perfectly valid question, but for a moment my mind goes blank. 'Mr Bolton purchased the house at auction in early 1945,' I say. 'It was quite rundown, and after the war, he began renovations to restore it to its former glory.'

'So how did Frank Bolton make his money?'

'Well...' I frown. 'It's like I said – knickers.'

'Before that, I mean. How did he make the money to found his underwear empire?'

I take a breath. It's a question that no one has asked before, and I get the feeling he's testing me. 'After the war, there were lots of opportunities for ambitious young men,' I say. 'Frank Bolton came from a humble East London background, but he was hardworking and determined. He was a self-made man.'

Though my answer sounds credible, in fact I have no idea how Frank Bolton raised enough capital to buy an underwear factory. The Americans nod appreciatively – they always like the idea of a self-made man.

I continue the tour but can't seem to find my stride. I transpose dates and forget the names of former residents, who they married, and the scandals they caused. We go swiftly through the rooms on the ground floor. I give gentle reminders not to touch the delicate fabrics or to sit on the antique chairs, on autopilot. All the while, I'm aware of the man at the back, lagging behind, taking everything in.

The tour ends upstairs in the state bedroom where a young Elizabeth I was rumoured to have spent the night on her way to Hatfield. When everyone has finished viewing the huge oak four-poster bed, the group clumps at the top of the back stairs. I invite them to explore the Tudor kitchens and visit the gift shop and tearoom below. Two people ask me if there's an elevator because their knees can't take the descent. I direct them to the tiny lift we had installed behind the panelling. When they're sorted, I turn back, looking for the tall, chocolate-eyed man. There's no sign of him. My adrenalin ebbs away, leaving a residue of disappointment. For all his questions, I was hoping that maybe he was interested in something *other* than the house, and that the spark of attraction was mutual.

I follow the last tour members to the gift shop, making small talk and overseeing purchases of marmalade, beer, tea towels, and herbal soap. One of the women asks me if I'm related to the house's owner, or 'to the manor born'. I wince a smile and tell her that 'I'm just the tour guide, nothing more.' Moving away, I continue looking for the tall man. But he has well and truly disappeared.

4

I feel oddly deflated after the tour. The tall man had seemed interested in the house and the family, but clearly had no interest in me – and why should he? I slip out of the gift shop and go to the disabled loo across the corridor, a cosy little room painted buttercream yellow, with a vase of lavender in the tiny window. I stare at my image in the mirror, trying to make sense of what I see.

I've always been tall, thin, and lacking much of a figure, but despite eating leftover baked goods from the café, my clothes look baggy. My shower was fixed earlier in the week so at least I'm clean, but my hair, copper-brown and usually cut in a sharp, chin-length bob, could use a trim. My skin is pale, lacking any kind of glow or lustre. I look older and wiser than my twenty-eight years, but not in a good way. Karen is right – in creating my own snug little world here at Mallow Court, I've let myself go.

I pinch my cheeks to add some colour, but it only leaves red marks. Where is the sharp, feisty Alex who did debate club at college and worked double shifts at the local Budgens to save money for uni? Where is the erudite Alex who got a first-class degree and fell in love with a poet? Where is the real-world, down-to-earth Alex who never cared if others came from wealthier families, had nicer houses, fancier cars, and pedigrees stretching back to the Norman Conquest?

The woman staring back at me in the mirror is a competent curator of an important historical building. But other than that, I don't really know her any more.

Leaning forward, I pluck at a stray eyelash. My eyes are greyish blue: in Xavier's words, the colour of the winter sea. The colour is unique in my family – I like to think it came from my birth mother. Not that I spend much time thinking about her. Dad has never made a secret of the fact that I was the product of a new age union: Dad met my birth mother while travelling around America protesting Nukes and following the Grateful Dead. When she died, he brought me home to England and eventually got married to Carol, who's the best mum ever.

But just beneath the surface, there's an itch I can't quite scratch. Every day, I extol the virtues of a house dating back to the time of Elizabeth I, and yet I can barely trace my own history back to the early 1970s. Half of my make-up is from a woman who I know nothing about, who came from a family I know nothing about. Half of me is a gaping wide hole that will never be filled with the roots of a family tree. Should I try to find out more? Will that somehow make me feel more complete?

I look out the tiny window to the garden in full bloom. Mallow Court is noted for its many garden rooms, each one bounded by tall hedges. Nearest the main house, the cottage garden is bursting with colour: white sweet pea, purple allium, pink foxglove, blue delphinium. Near the arch at the other side,

I glimpse Mrs Fairchild cutting lilacs for the vase in the great hall.

I wave to her but of course she can't see me. I've never envied her growing up at Mallow Court, but I do envy the fact that she knows exactly where she came from. She had a loving father whom she adored, two boisterous younger brothers, and a mother, Mabel, who was by all accounts a prime specimen of a wholesome, upstanding 1950s woman.

The question the attractive man asked pops back into my mind. How did the 'Knicker King' get the capital to found his underwear empire? Frank Bolton came from humble East London roots, but I don't know much more than that. Most visitors who come here are interested either in the history and architecture of the house, the spectacular gardens, or the valuable collection of antiques. Others simply get a chuckle out of the underwear anecdotes. That's more than enough genealogy for most people.

But the question is a valid one, and something I should know the answer to. I make a mental note to ask Mrs Fairchild to tell me more about her dad. But, right now, I feel the need to leave the idyllic hideaway of Mallow Court and breathe the grimy air of the real world for an afternoon. And though it's probably futile, I can pose a few questions about my murky heritage to the one person who might know.

I leave the loo and re-enter the gift shop, breathing in the smell of rose diffuser sticks, honey-scented candles, lavender drawer liners, and lily of the valley eau de toilette. While I prefer the smell of old books, I can see why the shop does a roaring trade. We have a selection of gifts for the gardener, educational toys and books for children, greeting cards, jewellery, hats, patterned wellie-boots, tea towels, and a good selection of potted plants and seeds – not to mention the marmalade and beer.

Edith, the assistant manager, has just finished ringing up a customer when I approach.

'I'm off to run an errand,' I say. 'Can you hold the fort?'

'Sure. Take your time.'

'Thanks. Are there any new candles in?'

'Ah.' She gives me a knowing look. 'Off to Abbots Langley then.'

'Well, it *is* his birthday on Sunday.'

'How about this one?' She leads me over to a shelf where there's a collection of candles in various floral scents. 'Green tea, vanilla, and verbena?' She hands me a little green candle in a glass votive.

I take a whiff. 'Yuck. It's perfect.'

* * *

I drive through country lanes and gradually widening roads, back to civilisation – in this case, the busy town of Hemel Hempstead and a little M25-adjacent village called Abbots Langley. I wind through the residential roads and pull up in front of the house where I grew up. The yellow brick house is of 1960s construction, with PVC windows and a glassed-in porch. The front garden is a mismatch of sickly-looking potted plants, climbing ivy, and a mint green Figaro with two flat tyres.

I don't bother with the front door; instead, I follow a narrow path at the side of the house. In stark contrast to the front of the house, the back garden is an immaculate oasis of calm – a spiritual garden in Balinese style with spaces delineated by leafy palms, stands of bamboo, and solar lanterns. There's a gravel Zen garden flanked by raised wooden decking, a meandering koi pond criss-crossed by twin arched bridges, and the garden shed has been converted to a large open-air structure with a fluted roof and a floor of rubber matting. It's here that I find Dad, his body bent in the middle, executing a perfect downward dog. Perfect except for two fingers on his right hand that are raised off the ground, holding a cigarette.

'Hi, Dad,' I say. 'How's it going?'

He lowers his knees and sits back on his haunches. He's wearing thigh-hugging cotton bottoms flared at the ankle. His chest is bare, revealing a virtual map of unfortunate tattoos – Chinese characters, a smudged version of the Indian goddess Shiva, her open arms now sprouting Dad's chest hair. He looks at me for a moment with his unreadable 'guru' face, then stands up, taking a long drag on the cigarette.

'It's not *going*, Alexandra. It's all about inner stillness – remember?' He holds his arms open and I go for a hug, enjoying the feel of his airy-fairy solidity.

'Did Buddha smoke roll-ups, Dad?' I say when we separate. 'I thought you were going to quit.'

He waves the cigarette expansively. 'Throughout the centuries, many men of great wisdom have experimented with substances to help them experience the divine. Native American shamans are well known for using hallucinogens in their rituals. Then there's the Christian religions that use wine as a symbol of transubstantiation. And don't forget John Lennon – a religion all on his own.'

'I won't.' You can't possibly grow up in the same household with Dad and forget John Lennon.

He stubs out the cigarette into a Raku bottle. 'And to what do I owe the pleasure of this visit, your highness?' He nods his head in a mock bow.

I laugh. Dad, of all people, knows very well that I'm no

princess. Instead of reading me fairy tales when I was little, he read snippets from Karl Marx, the *Bhagavad Gita*, and the *Guardian*. Mum, on the other hand, tried to overcompensate by taking me to every Disney film that came out. But Dad's non-traditional style won out. By the time I was old enough to form my own opinions, I decided that Cinderella needed to stand up to those mean stepsisters and tell them to empty their own chamber pots. And while Snow White may have had hair as black as ebony, skin as white as snow and lips like the red rose, she was also as thick as a plank.

Still, ever since I took the job at Mallow Court, Dad won't let me live it down. He thinks that by working for the *aristocracy* in a *temple of the oppressor*, I've crossed over enemy lines. In addition to being a pub manager by night and a private yoga instructor by day, Dad's the staunchest Labour supporter imaginable and is secretly waiting for a British version of Lenin to appear out of the northern hinterland. Although by the time I was in senior school everyone was waving the banner of Glasnost and Perestroika, for Dad, it was a sad day when the Berlin Wall fell and even he had to admit that communism – at least of the Soviet variety – was a historic failure.

'Come the revolution, daughter, you won't be laughing,' he says solemnly.

'OK, Dad. But until then, are you allowed a birthday gift?' I hold out the little package.

He unwraps it warily, like it's some kind of capitalist Pandora's box ready to snatch his soul. Removing the candle from the box, he holds it up to his nose and nods approvingly. 'An inspired blend of ancient ingredients. I'll burn it later today for my new PiYo hybrid class.'

'Great,' I say. 'Happy Birthday.'

He waves his hand. 'Birthdays are just another turn of the wheel of birth, death, and rebirth.'

'And speaking of which,' I say, 'I wanted to ask you some questions. About my mother.'

He lowers his body back down and swings into a side-plank position. 'Your mum's at work today and then she's got a dental appointment in Hemel. She should be back around half four, depending on traffic. You're welcome to make yourself a cuppa and wait for her.'

'Not Mum,' I clarify. 'My mother – my real mother.'

He looks at me for a long moment. 'Don't let your mum hear you say that, OK? "Real mother".' He shakes his head. 'It would break her heart.'

'Sorry – I meant "birth" mother. I know that Mum's my mother in every way that matters. But I want to know more about my biological origins. The woman who is half of who I am.'

Dad gets to his feet and straightens his arms, stretching into a mountain pose. 'What brought this on?'

'Nothing. But don't I have a right to know something about her?'

'I haven't kept her a secret, have I?' He shifts his balance to tree pose. 'You know almost as much as I do.'

'I don't see how that can be true. After all, it was you who...'

'Impregnated her?'

'I was going to say met her. Got to know her. Enough to, you know...'

'Impregnate her?'

'Well... yeah.'

Dad closes his eyes and I can hear his deep belly breathing. 'Those were different times,' he says. 'More people believed in the dream back then.'

'You mean it was a free-for-all?'

'She believed – your birth mother.'

'Believed what?'

He switches legs. 'She believed that class and social standing shouldn't matter. She was from a rich family, grew up in a nice home, but she didn't want those things. We may have missed Woodstock and the early Vietnam protests, but many of us believed in a better world. A world without hunger and war.'

I resist the urge to roll my eyes.

'You see this?' Opening his eyes, he points to a jumble of faded characters tattooed on his chest just below his heart. 'This is the name I knew her by: "Rainbow". I had it tattooed in Sanskrit. Her life was like a rainbow, brief but beautiful. You couldn't grab hold of her or possess her. And that was part of her beauty.'

'You say she came from a rich family? I don't think you've mentioned that before. What do you know about them?'

For a second, his mask of calm drops and he waivers on his leg. His core muscles visibly contract as he steadies himself and puts his foot back on the ground. 'Nothing. We didn't talk about things like that.' He shrugs. 'I'd tell you more if I could. We were both very young.'

'And how did she die?'

'You know this already,' he says. 'She was a fragile girl, and never in robust health. Not long after you were born, she drifted off to sleep and didn't wake up again. But that smile on her face – it was like an angel's.' He sighs. 'Nothing was the same after that. I didn't want to keep travelling around without her. So I brought you back here to put down roots. I met your mum, married her, and the rest is history. Your history. The *only* family history that matters.'

'I'm not sure about that.'

He lowers his hands to prayer. 'Even so.'

'And that's really all you know? You don't even have a photograph?'

'No, I don't. Other than up here.' He taps his head. 'Rainbow was a bright, flickering candle in a dark world. Her light went out, but not without leaving the world a better place.'

'How?'

'Well... there's you.' His smile disarms me, and I can see why half the housewives in greater Hemel Hempstead *and* Watford take his classes and have a crush on him, despite his many flaws. He grabs a crisp white towel from a wicker basket and wipes off his neck. 'You have her eyes,' he says. 'Her beautiful eyes, the colour of light rays breaking through storm clouds.'

Emotion swells like a wave in my chest. I turn away, looking at a clump of ornamental grass swaying in the wind.

Dad tosses the towel into a hamper and lights another cigarette. 'Can I tempt you to stay for the class, Alexandra?' He exhales a thin tendril of smoke and uses the cigarette to light the candle I brought. 'It might give you some inner peace.'

'No, thanks.' I hate yoga – always have, and probably always will. It's painful and boring in equal measure, and I'd rather relax in a nice hot bath.

'OK. I'm glad you stopped by.' Dad puts out the cigarette and we hug each other again.

'Me too.'

He flips through his CD collection and finds the pan pipes – my cue to leave. The sad truth is that I *do* seem to know almost as much as Dad about my birth mother. Today has been a waste of time.

On my way out, I have to flatten myself against the wall of

the house to let a trio of women pass. They glare at me like I'm a corrupting influence over their guru or something. 'God, he's good, isn't he?' I say. 'My pelvic floor sure got a workout.' Smiling, I walk off with a fake bow-legged limp.

* * *

In truth, I wasn't expecting to learn much from Dad. Part of me is disappointed, but I'm also relieved not to have uncovered any bombshells. I *am* lucky to have had a happy childhood and still have a good relationship with my parents. That's really all that matters.

Besides, the little I know about 'Rainbow' doesn't make me eager to learn more. I would probably have been a disappointment to 'a bright, flickering candle' who left her rich family for a 'higher calling'. New age peace and love have never been my thing, and it was partly in rebellion against Dad's world view that I decided to study medieval history. In the Middle Ages, society was strictly regimented. Women who gave birth out of wedlock were shunned, or worse, and most property was owned either by feudal lords or by the church. Nonetheless, I fell in love with Gothic architecture and churches, especially the glorious stained-glass windows designed to let in divine light, the tall spires challenging the sky. Religion had a strict set of rules, and there was none of this 'wheel of death and rebirth' nonsense. If you were good, you went to heaven; if you were bad, you rotted in hell. I'm glad I don't live back then, but there is something to be said for simplicity.

I drive through the gates of Mallow Court and up the long, tree-lined drive to the house. Thinking of it as my home fills me with a strong sense of guilt. I remember when I first took the job: Mum was excited and wanted a private tour of the house. I'd expected Dad to rail on about 'trickle-down economics' and the 'tyranny of the upper class', but instead, he'd been strangely silent. All he'd said then (and has repeated a number of times since) was, 'I didn't raise you to live like this.'

I park at the back of the coach house: a two-storey half-timbered building. A lot of it has been converted into wedding accommodation, but the top floor, through a door marked private and up a narrow oak staircase, is my flat. When Mrs Fairchild first offered me the job at Mallow Court, she told me I could convert the coach house loft if I wanted to live onsite. I took her up on it, and for three months while the works were in progress, I had a room in the main house. During that time, she and I grew fond of each other and used to sharing space. She'd asked me if I wanted to stay on, but I'd declined. The part of me who is Dad's daughter wasn't comfortable living in such an opulent house (not to mention one with an antique heating system and no power shower). Besides, I love having my own space and ample room for all my books.

As I unlock the door, the day's tension begins to ebb away. The main room is sharply eaved, but there are skylights on the ceiling that flood the room with natural light. Kicking off my boots, I flop onto the sofa and stare up at the pink-edged clouds passing above my head. A vision of the tall, brown-eyed man creeps, unbidden, into my mind. Sitting next to me on the sofa with a glass of wine in his hand, looking at my books, chatting about architecture and the house, and life in general. I know it's a future that's not going to happen – he wasn't even interested enough to buy a postcard in the gift shop.

But who knows? Maybe in the future there will be *someone* – a thought I haven't entertained for three long years.

I reach for a book, open it, stare at the words on the page, and close it again. Xavier is long gone, but I'm still trapped in a delicately wrought shell of my own making. But now, that shell has started to crack. And the chill wind of the unknown that's swirling just outside feels oddly refreshing.

5

13 NOVEMBER 1940 – 12 A.M.

I stood there and watched the girl, fear and relief battling in my chest. The snowflakes melted as they hit the ground. It was so quiet that I could hear the hum of the camera behind me as Robbie filmed the grisly scene. 'Turn that damn thing off,' I said. But of course he was just doing his job.

Another siren began to wail in the distance. The girl had a heart-shaped face and strawberry-blonde curls, now nearly black with soot. She stared up at me with round blue eyes that had seen more than any five-year-old's ever should. I knew those eyes. She put her thumb in her mouth and began to suck it.

'Are you hurt?' I asked.

She shook her head, looking small and scared. When I tried to draw her away from the rubble, she wouldn't budge. I knew then that someone else was inside.

'Is your mother in there?'

She nodded.

Hope deserted me as I crouched down and shone my torch in the hole. The girl had been hiding under the kitchen table – and underneath I could see a pair of legs wearing ladies' shoes. The legs were attached to a body, wearing a black dress and shawl. A silent wail rose up inside of me. 'Marina?' I croaked.

The foot moved. I pushed against the table with all my strength. Ash and rubble rained down, but somehow, I managed to lift the table and shove it to one side. There was a low groan of pain. She was alive.

But her right arm and half her face were missing.

'Mamochka?' The girl rushed forward.

'Stay back,' I said, but it was too late.

'No!' The little girl put a hand to her mouth. I tried to pull her back, but she leaned over her mother.

Her mother reached under the shawl around her neck. 'Take this, Dochka, and keep it safe. It's yours.' Something sparkled on a chain as she placed it in the girl's hand.

Her fingers stiffened and her body began to convulse. A moment later, she fell still.

6

I'm awakened at 5 a.m. by pigeons cooing in the rafters. I roll onto my back and open my eyes, fully expecting to be back to my old self, the unsettled feeling gone. But something has shifted inside me, like a glacier reshaping the landscape. *I'm happy*, I remind myself. *I know who I am; I have everything I want.*

In the rose light of morning, everything around me is familiar: my bedroom with the scrolled iron bed and a white matelassé bedspread. The varnished wooden floor is cold beneath my feet as I swing out of bed, groggy and in need of coffee. I'm out of milk, so I decide to brew a pot over at the main house. I'm due to give a tour later in the morning, and I want to do some work on the costume exhibition before the coach arrives.

I get ready and go outside. Although it's still very early, Mrs Fairchild is already outside in the kitchen garden, wearing her wide-brimmed straw hat, floral blouse, and gardening gloves.

She looks up from her weeding, startled for a second. I think of how preoccupied she's been lately and wonder what could be wrong. But when she smiles at me, my worries melt away. 'Morning, Alex,' she says. 'You're up early.'

'I couldn't sleep,' I say.

'Well, no matter.' She takes off one of her gloves and rubs her wrist. 'It's such a beautiful day. And this is the best time to be outside.'

I glance at the blue sky and the bright flowers of the garden. 'It is nice,' I say. 'And it will be even better after a coffee. Do you want one too?'

'I'm fine for now. I left a lemon drizzle cake in the staffroom. Do help yourself.'

'That's nice of you,' I say warmly.

She puts her glove back on and digs up a dandelion with her fork. 'What else is planned for the day?'

'We've got a couple of tour buses scheduled and a wedding couple coming to view the venue.'

'I'll make sure the flowers in the vases look tip-top.'

'They always do.' I smile. Mrs Fairchild always takes care to make sure the house not only looks lovely, but also smells good. She has a way with flowers – and with people.

'Thank you, child. It's nice of you to notice.'

'Sure. I'm off now. I need to do some work on the costume exhibition.'

Her smile wobbles. 'Yes. About that – I left a few bits and bobs I thought you might be interested in. Don't feel you have to use them. It's just some of my things from the Swinging Sixties.'

'Great, thanks.'

She tilts her head, staring closely at me. 'You look a little peaked, Alex. Is something wrong?'

'Oh, no.' I wave my hand nonchalantly. 'I'm fine.'

'I hope you're not still bothered about the Heath-Churchleys.'

I shudder at the name – the memory of being shouted down by Cee-Cee's father crashes over me. I can accept some blame for a cock-up on her special day. But accusing me of interfering with one of 'the oldest, proudest families' in England? He made it sound like they were royalty and I was a common criminal. I should have laughed in his face – why didn't I laugh in his face?

Little nobody.

Some days, my humble origins feel less like a chip on my shoulder and more like a steel girder.

'To be honest, I am a *little* bothered,' I admit. 'Mr Heath-Churchley said he was going to ask you to sack me. If there's an axe about to fall, can you let me know?' I risk a smile.

'Oh, Alex, you shouldn't be worried about that. Charles did ring me up. We had a nice chat and I set him straight. He's like a big bull – blowing all kinds of steam and bluster. But really, he's harmless.'

I raise a sceptical eyebrow.

'I told him we'd return his deposit. I hope that's OK. He's very disappointed that the wedding didn't go ahead. Especially since it isn't the first time.' Her blue eyes twinkle.

I've no idea what she's talking about, nor do I care. 'I'll send the cheque back today,' I say. 'I only wish the wild oats had all been sown before they entered our turf.'

'Please don't look so forlorn, Alex.'

'I just wanted the first wedding to go well. And the money would have been nice. I've had to put off the lads who were coming to do the loos.'

'But Alex, you shouldn't put off your projects.' Mrs Fairchild looks distressed. 'You only need to ask, and I'll give you the money.'

'That's not how it works – we're running a business, remember?' I sometimes get wound up that Mrs Fairchild has no concept of profit and loss. Her lifestyle is modest, despite living in a grand house, and she has enough money for her needs. Hence she doesn't always take my careful budgeting and book-balancing seriously. I suppose it's better than the alternative – having to scrimp and save and count squares of toilet roll and recycle tea bags. But it's my job to make sure the house earns its keep without charity or handouts, even from its owner.

'Point taken.' She makes a puppy dog face. 'But I don't mind putting in a little extra here and there. Birthdays and Christmas, you know.'

'And it's much appreciated. But let's see where I get with the wedding couple this afternoon.'

I start to walk off; I really *need* a coffee. And maybe something sweet: the lemon cake, or a leftover scone from the tearoom.

'You know, Alex…' Mrs Fairchild stops me again. 'Sometimes I think I did the wrong thing to bring you here.'

'What?' I whirl around. '*Have* I done something wrong?'

'Of course not,' she says brightly. 'I couldn't ask for a better manager. You know that.'

'Then what is it?'

'I know I'm an old busybody, but I heard what your friend Karen said. About your hiding yourself away here, and needing to get out more.'

I laugh freely. 'Karen and I have quite different lifestyles. She's the life of the party. I'm not. It doesn't mean I'm not happy.'

Mrs Fairchild taps the dried dirt from her fork. 'I was a lot like you, Alex. Believe it or not.'

'I don't believe it. You're so outgoing.'

She smiles distantly, like she's slipping into a memory. 'I was a shy girl once,' she says. 'I didn't want to call attention to myself.'

'You – shy?' Mrs Fairchild is *definitely* not shy. She's president of the local WI, assistant music director of the church choir, and although there's a team of gardeners that come in once a week, she spends most days working out in the garden when the tourists are around, so she can 'meet nice people and have a chat' – usually about the best way to deal with bindweed, or how to keep a stone path free from moss. Whereas the parts of the job I enjoy most are researching the house, managing the staff (most of whom I consider to be my friends), and generally the parts that don't require too much contact with the visitors.

'Yes,' she says. 'I was shy, at least until I met George Fairchild. We were married for over forty years. But in order to meet him, I had to leave this house. I was a debutante in London.'

'Well, I'm definitely not doing that!' I try to picture myself with shoulder-length ringlets, a floaty white dress, and elbow-length gloves rather than my usual boots/jeans/blazer ensemble – it makes me laugh.

'I suppose it seems silly to the modern generation,' she says. 'But I did it because my dad wanted it for me. I loved him so much.' She falters. 'He always tried his best to make me happy.'

'I'm sorry, Mrs Fairchild, I didn't mean to be flippant.'

In truth, I find it a bit unsettling how raw her father's – Frank Bolton's – death is to Mrs Fairchild even though it happened decades ago. When she speaks of him, it's like she's been transported back in time to when she was 'Daddy's little girl'. It makes things a bit awkward, especially when a fair few tourists come solely to hear our 'Knicker King' quips and have a laugh about double gussets.

'No matter,' she says. 'But take it from an old goat: your friend is right. It would do you good to get out more.'

'Everyone seems to have a lot of ideas about what I *should* be doing.' I cross my arms.

'Your friends just want the best for you.'

'So what do you suggest? That I go on a singles cruise? Join a dating service? Sign up for ballroom dancing?'

'Probably. But I know you won't.' She picks up her fork and continues weeding.

I look fondly at the old woman – saviour of my bacon after the grubby situation with Xavier. When we split up, everything connected to the university made me sick to my stomach and I decided to abandon my doctorate. For a few months I was like a leaky boat without a rudder, with no direction and no idea what to do with my life. I'd sunk so low that there seemed only one thing for it – I'd get a job. The problem was that despite all my years of higher education, I had no idea how to go about it.

The career centre seemed an obvious place to start. The woman at the desk eyed me warily, like I'd just blown in on a freak wind from Mars. When I gave her my CV, she wrinkled her nose like there was a bad smell.

'Have you tried *The Lady*?' she said.

I left her office hanging my head. She'd made it clear that a first-class degree in medieval studies was worth exactly jack squat in the 'real world'.

Dutifully, I checked *The Lady*. There were jobs for nannies and secretaries and housekeepers. Cocooned as I'd been in my ivory tower like a bookish, auburn-bobbed Rapunzel, the real world seemed like a frightening place. What was I going to do with my life (and why on earth hadn't the question occurred to me before?)? It's not as if I was independently wealthy. It's not as if my grants covered anything more than basic living expenses.

Like so many other young academics, I'd expected to get a job teaching history at a university, or perhaps a sixth form college or girl's school. But my recent tutelage in a broken heart had made me eager to leave academia; and besides, there was nothing remotely like that in *The Lady*.

The fact that I'd drawn a blank made me even more determined. I next went to my academic advisor and said the grubby words: 'I want to get a job.'

To my surprise, he didn't look at me like I had two heads. 'Good for you,' he said.

'Can you help?'

'Let me ask around.'

As a student of history, I'm not supposed to believe in things like karma or a divine plan. Things happen mainly due to a chain of events that leads one on to another. Nations rise and fall, wars are won and lost, and social changes occur largely due to factors that can be studied, analysed, and explained. Which is why, when my advisor called me in the very next day and laid a letter on the desk in front of him, I dared not hope that my ship had come in.

'I'm going to recommend you for this position,' he said. 'That is, if you're interested.'

'Great. I'll take it,' I said, before adding as an afterthought: 'Can I ask what it is?'

'An important benefactress of the university is planning to open her house up to the public. Rickety old Elizabethan place. A couple hundred years out for you, maybe, but I'm sure you'll find the plumbing and heating system to be positively medieval.'

'Elizabethan is fine,' I said. 'As you say, what's a couple hundred years?' The fact that the job involved history at all seemed like icing on the cake.

'She wants to run tours of the house and garden – probably needs the money to keep the place watertight – I've no idea. But she's looking for a manager.'

'A manager?'

'Someone to do the legwork. Tart the place up, deal with the legal hoops – fire alarms, disabled access, permits and whatnot. You'll hire the tour guides, set up the tearoom and gift shop. All sorts, really.'

A manager. Although I'd never considered doing such a thing, and naturally wondered if I *could* do it, it seemed like a worthwhile challenge. And if nothing else, it would be a change of scenery.

'It sounds great.'

'Yes, well...' He took out a handkerchief and blew his nose like a first chair trumpet. 'Let's just say you happened to be in the right place at the right time.'

And so I was. Looking back almost three years later, I still wonder: was it karma, a divine plan – or just good luck? As I packed my things to leave the university, I concluded that either way, surely it couldn't be worse than pulling pints or telemarketing.

And when I saw Mallow Court for the first time, I stopped caring...

That first time, it was a day not unlike today: the sun was out, wispy white clouds decorated the sky, and I came upon Mrs Fairchild at the edge of the lake garden wearing a broad hat and floral-patterned blouse. She'd been on her knees weeding a bed of primulas amid a forest of silver birches, her back to me. 'Hello,' I'd said, trying not to startle her. She'd turned around and looked up, her face going pale for a moment like she'd seen a ghost. But immediately, she'd stood and greeted me, all smiles. 'I'm glad you're here, Alex,' she'd said as we shook hands. 'Very glad.' She blinked rapidly, her eyes watering. I suppose it was because it was a windy day and there was lots of pollen in the air.

In any case, over the course of the next few days and weeks, chats over cups of tea, brainstorming as we walked together through the house and grounds, and her suggesting that I convert the flat in the coach house so that I could 'walk to work', I'd felt welcome and valued. I also felt a strong connection to the house that I couldn't explain. I wasn't daunted by its size or its age. I quickly came to know its ins and outs and quirks almost like it was an old friend.

The house was actually in pretty good nick, and Mrs Fairchild wasn't short of cash. Instead, she was eager to *share* the house with outsiders – so that people could appreciate the house she'd been *blessed* to inherit.

I suspected that Mrs Fairchild could have got on with many of the jobs herself. She had plenty of contacts with local tradesmen, a decent accountant, and lots of ideas. Whereas I'd never 'managed' anything before, and while I threw myself into learning the job, I suspect that in those early weeks I didn't totally earn my keep. Nonetheless, the job was just what I needed at the time. What I still need now. So why is everyone telling me that my future lies elsewhere?

Mrs Fairchild looks at me like she can read my thoughts. 'Oh, go on now, Alex. No sulking.' She unloops a tendril of bindweed. 'You know I love having you here and you're the best thing that could ever have happened to this place. But just remember, at some point, you need to look after number one. I don't want you to waste away here now that the business is up and running.'

'But I'm not.' I stare at her. 'I have lots of ideas, and I love the house and—'

'I know you do.' She pats my arm affectionately. 'And you'll always find another project here as well as an open door. In fact...' She trails off, and suddenly the worried look I've noticed lately is back.

'Is everything OK?'

'Yes, of course. I'm fine – it's you we were talking about.'

'But there's really nothing wrong.'

'I'd hate to see you end up alone, Alex. Take it from me, it's not all it's cracked up to be. Even at my age, life is much more exciting with someone special in it.'

There's a sudden twinkle in her eye; a flush to her cheeks. An unlikely possibility strikes me. 'You sound like...'

No. It's impossible.

'Like I've met someone?'

I stare at her. 'Have you?'

'Well, it's early days.' Her face is suddenly all aglow. 'We'll see. But as for you, my dear, remember – when your ship comes in, you don't want to be heading to the airport.'

I shake my head, a little overwhelmed. 'Actually, I'm not a fan of planes or boats, Mrs Fairchild. I'm *walking* inside now to make that coffee.'

7

Alone in the quiet of the house, I drink two cups of coffee and eat a piece of lemon drizzle cake, my mind spinning. Mrs Fairchild is *seeing* someone? Who could she have met, and where? It may be early days, but if she's mentioning it, it means it can't be *that* early. If I wasn't Edith's boss, we might have had a good gossip about it. Or I could tell Karen – except we haven't spoken since the Churchley-Thursley debacle. I try calling her, but the phone goes to voicemail and I don't leave a message.

I tidy up the kitchen, ruminating that it's Karen's fault that even Mrs Fairchild thinks I need to 'get out more'. How annoying! A vision flashes into my mind of the tall man with the chocolate brown eyes, and I feel an unwelcome frisson. If Mrs Fairchild has a new 'distraction', I'd best stay unattached and able to hold the fort.

I head upstairs to work on the costume exhibition before the first tour. It will be staged in the long gallery on the first floor of the house. As I climb up the main staircase, I run my hand over the smooth oak of the banister, marvelling at the lifelike quality of the carved fruit and leaves, acorns and roses. The dark wooden panelling and deep red of the stairway carpet runner is enveloping, womb-like. The landing at the top of the stairs branches into three corridors. I take the one to the left. A few metres on, the hallway is cordoned off with a floor-to-ceiling piece of plastic sheeting and a sign marked 'Exhibition under construction'.

I dip under the plastic. Even filled with naked mannequins, crates, display cases and information boards, the long gallery is a stunning space. The ceiling is a confection of white plaster, with the curving arms of geometrical shapes framing bosses with the family crest, Tudor roses, fruits of the sea and the forest, and emblems of the four seasons. Diamond-pane windows set into the panelling stretch the whole length of the hall on one side, letting in a flood of light even on dull days. I can picture the ladies of old taking their exercise, strolling up and down in gowns of rich velvet and brocade, their hair pulled back in French caps and snoods set with seed pearls. Serene and lovely: embroidering by the fireplace, playing the harp or bowed psalter, reciting prayers and poetry from a book of hours, their voices and laughter echoing through the space.

The exhibition of 'Clothing Through the Ages' was my brainchild. It seemed a perfect way to bring the house to life and provide a focal point to draw in visitors in the busy summer months. I called up an old friend from my degree programme who works at the V&A, who fortunately agreed to help.

Turning it into reality, however, has taken some doing. Although Mallow Court contains a wealth of antiques and valuable heirlooms, it doesn't have a security system to match, and we had to upgrade it before the V&A would loan out their treasured textiles. The woman who brought the boxes and crates had looked none too impressed when I told her the alarm system hadn't yet been fitted. After convincing her the items would be safe in my care, she carefully supervised the unloading of every mannequin and case of clothing, and I had to double- and triple-sign the inventory forms. Today, I plan to finalise the pieces we're using, write a draft of the tour leaflet, and find some interesting titbits for the *de rigueure* children's treasure hunt.

On one of the Savonarola chairs, I notice a pile of clothing that wasn't there before. It's not in the microfibre, breathable, moth-proof slip covers of the V&A pieces, but in plastic drycleaning wrappers on wire hangers. These must be the things that Mrs Fairchild left for me to look at.

The top piece is a fitted mini-dress in a rainbow-coloured paisley pattern that looks like something from 'Lucy in the Sky with Diamonds'. I try to picture a young Catherine ('Cat'?) sporting the dress with patent leather boots and a psychedelic headband. I slip the dress over the head of one of the mannequins. 'You look cool,' I say. 'Or is it "far out"?' She smiles her vacant, painted smile.

The next piece is a boucle coat with a black and grey houndstooth pattern. I touch the leather collar and the watersmooth satin lining. The lining appears to be hand-stitched inside – a couture piece. The label reads 'Chanel'.

Immediately, I withdraw my hand, feeling guilty for not wearing the gloves left by the V&A woman. The pieces from the museum are old and lovely, but to me, the Chanel coat is even more special. Hopefully I can convince Mrs Fairchild to give me some spicy, real-life anecdotes of wearing it on the town in London: maybe to a Beatles gig or the West-End premiere of *Hair!*

The next few pieces are more great examples of their era: a lace fifties-style wedding dress with an Audrey Hepburn collar, two early seventies paisley silk skirts, and an Yves St Laurent skirt suit. It's an interesting insight into Mrs Fairchild's past, and I'm a little surprised at how stylish she must have been. Since I've known her, she's worn mostly gardening attire. Not that I'm one to talk: my wardrobe consists mostly of tops, jeans, and blazers. Nonetheless, I have a strong urge to try on some of Mrs Fairchild's things. What had she said? – 'In many ways, I was like you.'

I remove my blazer and pick up the Chanel coat. 'You didn't see me doing this,' I say sternly to the line of mannequins. I put the coat on; the lining is soft and fluid against my skin, the wool warm and enveloping. It's a perfect fit. I do up the leather tie around my waist and walk to the end of the long room.

I pretend I'm Catherine Fairchild in the early 1960s on a day trip to London, walking up Bond Street staring at the beautiful clothing in the shop windows. The coat would be in the window of a little boutique. Instantly, she knows it's perfect, and, in a cold house like Mallow Court, practical too.

At the end of the room there's a narrow mirror above a small inlaid table. I look at myself in the glass; it's like I'm a different person. I do a little twirl and shove my hands in the pockets. My right hand touches a crisp piece of paper and underneath, a soft piece of cloth with something hard and oval-shaped inside.

I take it out. The cloth is a small black velvet bag with a drawstring. There's a note pinned to the velvet scribbled in Mrs Fairchild's writing: *For Alex?*

Instantly, I'm intrigued. It's as if Mrs Fairchild *knew* I would love the coat most of all. I open the bag and remove a locket on a silver chain; lozenge-shaped, about the length of my thumb. The metal is tarnished to almost black, but it looks like silver. The locket is weighty and solid, and feels oddly warm nestled in my hand. The top is decorated with delicate blue forget-me-nots in silver and enamel, with tiny crystals that sparkle in the light. I turn it over, looking for an inscription. The back is chased with a pattern of flowers and leaves, but there's nothing else. On the long side of the oval is a catch. It's a little stiff, but eventually I work it open.

A tiny bird made of paper-thin silver mesh pops up. It stands about two inches high on a silver perch, and each of the tiny feathers on its wings are set with crystals or glass coloured like rubies, sapphires, emeralds, and diamonds. There's a soft whirring sound, and slowly, the bird begins to rotate. I gasp. It's so beautiful and delicate – there must be a tiny battery inside making it move. The bird's lower beak moves on impossibly tiny hinges like it's singing, but no sound comes out. It rotates halfway around in its case and then stops. The mechanism continues to click and whir like it's stuck. I close the case halfway and watch as the bird folds up like a miniature children's pop-up book. I open the locket again. The bird winds back to its starting position and begins its half circle rotation. I watch, mesmerised. It's such an odd, quirky little piece of jewellery, but charming too.

I unpin the note that says *For Alex?* Most likely, Mrs Fairchild wrote the note to remind herself to ask if I wanted to use the piece for the exhibition. Mystery solved.

I return to the other end of the room and put Mrs Fairchild's clothing with the other pieces I've chosen. Maybe after the exhibition she'll let me have the coat. Especially now that she's jumped on the 'Alex-must-get-out-more' bandwagon. Wearing it, I almost want to leave my cosy lair and rejoin the world again. Almost. I put my blazer back on and slip the jewelled bird into my pocket for safekeeping.

8

13 NOVEMBER 1940 – 12.15 A.M.

I covered Marina's face with her shawl and turned away, swallowing back the bitter rush of bile. I had to be strong now – I had to think.

'Did you know her?' Robbie said, putting down his camera.

I shook my head – it was easier that way.

'Damn shame,' he said, shaking his head as he walked off. 'It's a devil's lottery.'

I took the girl over to the kerb across the street, away from the body of her mother. As the snow floated around us, the world seemed stuck in slow motion. I spread out my coat for us both to sit on. The thing in her hand sparkled in the darkness as her blackened fingers opened a catch. I watched, transfixed as a bird made of silver and precious jewels danced in her hand. It was the most exquisite thing I'd ever seen. The girl laughed, delighted with the trinket. But then, the bird stopped moving. Frowning, she tapped it like it was broken. I stared at her, wondering...

9

When I emerge from the long gallery, my tour is waiting in the great hall. It's a group of sixth-formers who spend most of the time whispering and chatting and aren't the slightest bit interested in the house.

By the time I've ushered them to the café, it's nearly lunchtime. I take a quick walk outside hoping to ask Mrs Fairchild about the locket, but I don't see her in any of the usual places. When I return to the house, I notice that the rope cordoning off the Rose Drawing Room is down; the room is too small for more than a look-in by the tour groups, and normally it's not used. Still, it's one of my favourite rooms. The walls are panelled in warm oak, and the curtains and soft furnishings are tastefully done in oatmeal damask and soft rose brocades. There's a log fire set in the fireplace ready to be lit on the first day of autumn with two high-backed armchairs in front.

From one of the chairs, a paper rustles.

'Oh!' I cry.

Mrs Fairchild stands up from the chair, her face unusually

pale and drawn. There's a piece of paper in her hand. She folds it quickly, stuffing it in the pocket of her cardigan.

'Sorry to startle you,' she says.

'No worries.' I look down at the piece of paper – a letter maybe? – in her hand. 'Are you OK?'

'Yes, fine,' she says too quickly. She glances at the empty vase on a table next to the sofa. 'Just wondering if you'd like dahlias for that vase or white roses?'

'Whatever you think is best.'

'I'll get to it.' She sidles past me and leaves the room.

How odd, I think as I replace the cord across the door.

* * *

After a second tour, I have lunch with Edith in the staffroom, sampling the day's leftovers from the café and sharing a bottle of organic elderflower and lime pressé. To my surprise, Edith, too, seems concerned about Mrs Fairchild. 'While you were doing your tour, she came to the shop and said she was leaving. She's off to visit a sick friend and will be gone a few days.'

'What?' I sit forward. 'She didn't mention that when I spoke to her.'

'I didn't want to pry,' Edith says. 'She seemed a little... off.'

'I'm sure she's fine.' I decide it's best to hide my concern. Mrs Fairchild normally acts like a kind of surrogate grandmother to me and the whole staff. She's normally so sunny: one of those people who never seems to have their feathers ruffled. Until recently, that is. Lately, she has seemed more guarded and evasive, and I never would have suspected that she had a new romantic interest – not one that made her happy, at any rate. And the piece of paper that she put in her pocket? Was it a letter containing bad news? Like Edith, I don't like to pry, but maybe I should have. I wish I'd remembered to ask her about the jewelled bird when I saw her earlier. I finger the trinket in my pocket. Learning more about it will have to wait.

After that, bad luck is the order of the day. On my final tour, an elderly woman takes ill in the billiard room. I move the others on and go to the gift shop for help. By the time I return, the woman is sitting on one of the fragile needlepoint chairs, having helped herself to a large slug of brandy from the cut-crystal decanter next to the cue rack. She's tipsy and loud as I escort her out to the coach, apparently having made a full recovery.

Meanwhile, the wedding couple arrives at the same time the men come to install the security system. By the time I'm done showing the couple around, the security people have wreaked havoc – running wires and cables everywhere, creating trip hazards, and causing the mains circuit to overload. The café appliances and credit card machines go down, and there are no lights in important places like the loos. Meanwhile, a couple comes in for a self-guided tour with a massive dog in tow that leaves muddy footprints everywhere.

'Oh, but we thought the house was "dog-friendly",' the woman says indignantly when I ask them to remove the dog.

'You're welcome to leave him outside,' I say, my teeth clenched.

'Obviously not – he's a wolfhound with a *pedigree*.'

That word again. I give her my best 'little nobody' look and point to the door. The woman huffs, jerks the dog's leash with one hand, her husband's arm with the other, and storms out.

The little crises get sorted, but the chaos has thrown me off my game. Especially when the security man offers me his card and says, 'Call me and let's go for a beer.' I mumble thanks and shove it in my pocket. My hand touches the velvet bag with the locket, and when the man is gone, I take it out.

It truly is a work of art. I admire the delicate lattice of forget-me-nots, seed pearls, and crystals on the case. It must be from the 1950s – I've seen lots of costume jewellery at antique fairs with bright paste jewels. Granted, none were as exquisite as this. I decide to put it on the mannequin with the fit-and-flare wedding dress. Maybe Mrs Fairchild wore the locket for her wedding to George Fairchild? I wish she was here so I could ask her.

At the end of the day, the cleaning crew arrives and Edith and I close up the gift shop, putting the day's takings in the stockroom safe and boxing up the extra food for a local charity.

'By the way,' Edith says as we're finishing up, 'there was a man here today – he acted kind of odd.'

'Odd? What do you mean?'

'He's been here before. I've noticed him once or twice.'

'That's not unusual, is it? Maybe he lives nearby.'

'It's just that today I was helping a customer carry in some pots of roses to the till. I was gone for a minute at most. When I came back inside, he was in the stockroom.'

I frown. 'What was he doing there?'

'He said he was looking for the loos. Which might have made sense if he was a first-timer.'

'And if there wasn't a big sign pointing to the toilets,' I add dryly. 'Did you notice anything missing?'

'No.'

'If you see him again, let me know.' I wipe the till with a dust rag, then stop as a thought occurs. 'What did he look like?' I say. A pair of chocolate brown eyes invade my thoughts, along with a flickering flame of hope.

'He had white hair and tanned skin – a bit wrinkly around

the eyes. I think he was Mrs Fairchild's age, maybe older. Mid-seventies?'

Not *him*. Disappointment oozes through me. 'Keep an eye out if you see him again. And hopefully, the new alarm will help deter any funny business.'

I go with Edith while she gets her handbag. 'You seeing Paul tonight?' I ask out of politeness. Paul is Edith's newish boyfriend who also happens to be a police officer. He pulled her over for a bust taillight, and the rest is history.

'Yes.' She blushes. 'He's taking me to a new French restaurant in Oxford.'

'Great. Have a drink for me.'

'Thanks. I will.' She glances at me hesitantly. 'And should I ask if he has any single friends?'

Not Edith as well!

'Please don't,' I say.

'OK, sorry.'

'It's fine.' I sigh. 'I'm happy with things as they are.'

'It's just that sometimes you look—'

I hold up my hand. '*I'm* fine.'

'Bored,' she finishes.

'Well,' I say, 'I guess that's a patch on lonely or desperate, which is what Mrs Fairchild and everyone else seems to think.'

Edith shakes her head. 'You're a really cool person, Alex. You'll never be desperate.'

'I'll keep that in mind.' I take out the security man's card and toss it discreetly in the drawer under the till, along with the cards from other workmen who have asked me out in the past.

I walk Edith to the front door, which is now rigged with the new alarm. The box is hidden out of sight in the vestibule. Together, Edith and I puzzle over the instructions and I type in the code to set it.

'You've got thirty seconds to go out,' I say.

'Right. See you tomorrow.'

Edith leaves and I set the new alarm just to make sure I know how. I take off my blazer and leave it near the alarm box. I'm planning to stay at the main house to do some work on the exhibition and coming back for my jacket will remind me to disable it when I go out of the house. I'm about to return to the stockroom to get some pens and a notepad when I hear a noise from inside. I feel a little squeamish and annoyed. No matter how much I spend annually on pest control, we never quite get rid of the mice.

I take a pad of paper from the shop instead, and on my way out I visit the disabled loo across the corridor. As I'm washing my hands, I hear another noise just outside the door followed by a click. Definitely not a mouse...

I undo the latch and turn the knob.

Nothing happens.

10

This can't be happening. I try the knob again but the door won't open. In addition to the latch on the inside, the door locks with a key from the outside, and the key is kept above the door lintel when we have to close the loo off for maintenance. Sloppy... but it's always been that way. But who could have locked the door?

In the corridor outside, I hear the thud of footsteps.

'Hey!' I cry. I kneel down and check the keyhole. Sure enough, the hole is dark, the key jammed inside. The strange man Edith mentioned and the noise in the back of the stockroom takes on a whole new significance. Someone's inside the house; someone followed me to the loo and locked me inside!

I take a breath, trying to stay calm. Maybe it was just a straggler who stayed past closing time and then wanted to create a distraction so they could leave. Or maybe he (I'm convinced it's a he) hid away, planning to steal something. Mrs Fairchild's things, or, God forbid, the V&A items?

I press my ear to the door. The house is silent. I spend thirty seconds hammering on the door and shouting 'help', not because I expect anyone to come to my rescue, but because that's what you *do* in these situations. I next analyse the small window set high in the wall above the toilet. If I was some kind of contortionist, I might be able to lever myself up and squeeze through, somersaulting into the 'old rose' bushes underneath. Obviously a non-starter, but I'm running out of options. As much as I love Mallow Court, the thought of spending the night in the disabled loo while an intruder is running rampant is not a pleasant prospect.

I open the window wide enough to satisfy myself that it's not a realistic means of escape. Immediately, there's a loud shrieking sound. I cover my ears, but my whole head is ringing with the noise. It's the new alarm. I totally forgot that they rigged up the windows as well as the exit doors. Though in this case, maybe it's a good thing. The alarm is wired directly to the security company, and any trip should bring them here in force. I sit on the loo lid and check my watch. The response time is supposed to be twenty minutes. I put my hand in the pocket of my jeans and grip the smooth case of the jewelled locket. The silver warms quickly against my skin. The intruder might have time to steal a few things, but I'm glad I have the bird with me.

The alarm stops wailing for a few seconds, though my ears keep ringing. It starts and stops intermittently, and I feel like I'm locked in a cell being tortured. Eventually, the sound of a lone siren coming from outside jangles my thoughts. My rescue brigade has arrived! Maybe if it's the same bloke from earlier, we can go for that beer. Anything to get out of here.

'Help!' I yell through the small window.

There's no response, but all of a sudden a loud *thunk* comes from the front of the house. I hope they're being gentle with the ancient oak door! The alarm shrieks for a final time, the sound replaced by that of heavy footsteps.

'Over here,' I call out. 'I'm in the loo.'

A burst of muffled voices; something bumps against the door. The wood strains against the hinges. 'There's a key,' I cry. 'Just turn the key – you don't need to break it down.'

The knob turns. I'm free.

'Thank you so much,' I say to the—

Oh.

I swallow hard. Three policemen in riot helmets and bullet-proof vests are standing before me, brandishing night sticks.

'Hi,' I say. 'I'm glad to see you're taking our security so seriously.'

A fourth man steps forward, thrusting a battered ID in my face. Detective Inspector something-or-other. He holds up my jacket, which I'd left by the door when Edith left. 'Is this yours?' he says sternly.

'Yes,' I say. 'My phone is in the pocket. If I'd had it, then I could have rung someone...'

'And this?' He holds up a brown envelope. 'Catherine Bolton' is scrawled across it in blue biro, the writing shaky and crab-like.

'No, that's not mine. It must be for Mrs Fairchild. Bolton's her maiden name—'

'Do you acknowledge that it was in plain sight on top of your jacket?'

'No. I've never seen it before.'

'Take her to the car,' the DI says.

'Wait,' I say, standing my ground. 'There's obviously some mistake. I'm the manager here. Someone locked me in the loo.'

'We had a call from a Catherine Fairchild, the owner of this house. She reported that an intruder had broken in. Are you Catherine Fairchild?'

'No, of course not. She's not here.'

'So where is she?'

'I... I don't know. But—'

'Turn around against the wall, please, and put your hands behind your back.'

'Excuse me?'

'We're taking you to the station under caution for trespass.' One of the officers steps forward and forcibly turns me to the wall. Another one takes out a pair of handcuffs.

'Wait!' I panic. 'You don't need those.'

'Take her to the car.'

'But – I live here!' I make a last-ditch plea to stop this nonsense.

The detective raises an eyebrow. 'Is this your driving licence?' He holds up what is obviously my driving licence.

'Yes.'

'And your residence is Ivy Cottage, Abbots Langley?'

'That's my parents' house. I've been meaning to change my address with DVLA. But I've never managed to get around to it.'

'Take her to the car,' the DI repeats. 'And you search the house.' He points to one of the armed men. 'Find this Catherine Fairchild and make sure she's all right.'

'But she's not here! I mean – I could call her...' I exhale in futility. 'Except, she doesn't have a mobile, and I'm not exactly sure where she is.'

The DI silences me with a look and a tsk. Feeling like a common criminal, I hang my head and allow myself to be escorted out to the police car.

11

I can't believe this is really happening. From the back of a police car, the familiar world that blurs by outside the window looks hostile and forbidding. I've done nothing wrong; why can't they just accept that? My skin crawls like eyes are peering at me through twitching curtains as we drive through the village. At least they haven't put the siren back on.

The nearest police station is in Aylesbury. When we arrive, the officer ushers me in through the back door and down a grey corridor towards an imposing wooden desk. I feel like Josef K in Kafka's *The Trial*, arrested without knowing why. Except, I do know why. Someone framed me.

The officer escorts me to the duty sergeant, who takes my details and confiscates my mobile.

'I'd like to make a phone call,' I say. 'I'm entitled to that, right?'

The sergeant shrugs and passes me back my mobile. My hand is shaking as I scroll through my contacts. I wish I knew who Mrs Fairchild is staying with so I could ring her and sort it out, but I don't. I scroll down, pausing at Karen's number. She's a vicar of the Church of England; her voice will carry sway. But she lives too far away to come bail me out. I find Edith's number. She'll back me up, and maybe her boyfriend can put an end to this ridiculous nonsense. I ring her mobile but it goes to voicemail. I hang up without leaving a message. The duty sergeant smiles smugly and holds out his hand for my phone. I relinquish it, the reality of my situation beginning to hit home.

A female officer escorts me to an interview room. She gives me a quick pat-down, immediately finding the velvet bag with the jewelled locket.

'What's this?'

I raise my chin indignantly. 'It's part of the costume exhibition I'm curating at Mallow Court in conjunction with the V&A.'

'What's it doing in your pocket, then?'

'Well, it's kind of a long story—'

She cuts me off with a raised hand. 'Save it.' She puts the locket in a plastic evidence bag, tossing it in the tray along with my mobile and handbag. 'Someone will be in to take your statement shortly.' She points to a moulded plastic chair on one side of a table. 'Sit.'

I sit. The female officer goes out with my things and returns a few minutes later with a polystyrene cup of coffee. She sets it on the table in front of me and leaves again. I take a sip and sputter – it's lukewarm and bitter. With a sigh, I push the cup away and settle in for the long haul.

The tiny room is painted a soul-crushing shade of greygreen. On one wall is a large dark window that hides anyone on the other side who might be watching. I'm fairly sure no one is watching – the station seems too short-staffed for anyone to take an interest in a lowly loo-breaker like me.

I get up and do two laps of the room, and sit back down

again. The minutes tick by; or maybe it's hours. They've taken my phone and I don't have my watch. Clearly it's some kind of plan to break me down. And that's fine – I'm ready to break. But no one comes.

How many other people have sat in this room under false pretences? How many hours, days, weeks, and years of productive human time have been sucked away into these depressing walls? How many cups of undrinkable coffee forced down, how many environmentally unfriendly polystyrene cups tossed out? How many endless, pointless thoughts, self-debates, and 'if only's generated?

Suddenly, the door handle clicks. I'm half-expecting a man in a trench coat and Homburg hat, come to inject me with Sodium Pentothal, or maybe a sadistic priest to read me my last rites. At the very least, a bored-looking policeman come to tell me that, unfortunately, his boss has been held up, and hopefully I don't 'mind' waiting a little longer.

Instead, I stare up at eyes that are as dark and brown as melted chocolate. Eyes that I recognise from the back of a tour of elderly Americans. They disturbed and intrigued me then, and now, I want to stand up and take a running swan dive into them.

'Ms Hart,' he says in the same sonorous voice that enquired about the origin of the 'knicker fortune'. 'I'm sorry there's been this mistake. I've spoken to DI Anderson, and you're free to go.'

I stand up, feeling limp and gooey, and generally disorientated. The fear that I've been holding inside rushes through my body like a passing fast train.

'It's about time,' I say. My eyes meld with his as I point to the cup on the table. 'One more sip of that and I'll be suing for police brutality.'

The man laughs. 'I'd definitely have taken your case.'

He stands at the door, and I walk past him out into the piss-yellow corridor. I'm aware of him watching me as I pause and look in both directions, unsure which way leads to the quickest exit.

'It's this way.' He points to my right. His hand is inches from mine, and I can feel a burning sensation in my skin at his nearness. And as eager as I am to leave before anyone changes their mind and throws me in a cell, I can't let this chance slip away.

'Who are you?' I say.

'Sorry, rude of me. I'm Timothy Edwards. You can call me Tim.' He holds out his hand. I put my hands on my hips.

'OK, Tim. How do you happen to be here?'

Two officers turn down the corridor. He leans close enough to me that his breath tickles my hair. 'Happy to tell you everything. But can I buy you a real coffee?'

'That would be nice.'

'Great. I know a little place just around the corner.'

12

I collect my possessions and follow my rescuer out of the station. He takes me to a chippie-slash-kebab shop round the corner that, from the look of the hoodlums occupying many of the tables, seems to be doing a rollicking post-arrest trade.

He buys us each a coffee and we sit down at a table by the window.

'Thanks for helping me.' I take a long drink that warms my whole body. 'Sorry if I sounded ungrateful before.'

'That's quite all right, Ms Hart.' His eyes hold a twinkle of amusement.

'It's Alex.'

'Alex.' He smiles. 'Seriously, I just happened to be in the right place at the right time.'

'Oh?'

'I was there to visit a client – a repeat offender, I'm afraid.' He spreads his hands apologetically. 'I'm a barrister. I'd just finished with my client when I walked down the corridor and spotted you in the interview room. Of course, I recognised you...' He stares at me and I blush. 'So I asked the sergeant why you were there. He told me, and I set him straight. I said I'd taken a delightful tour of your stately home and that you were no intruder.'

'Thanks. I'm not sure exactly what happened. But I think I was set up.' I tell him about being locked in the loo and the anonymous call to the police from a 'Catherine Fairchild'.

He raises a startled eyebrow. 'Someone actually locked you in? Did they take anything?'

'I'm not sure. But they left something behind.' I tell him about the envelope addressed to 'Catherine Bolton' left on top of my jacket. 'It must be from someone from her past,' I say. 'Bolton is her maiden name.'

'How bizarre,' he says. 'You should probably get the police round to check the house.'

'No,' I say firmly. 'I'll follow up with the security company. They're getting paid to sort things out.'

Tim gets us each a refill. I watch him place the order, admiring his tall frame, smart suit, and neatly cut hair. 'Do you live around here?' I ask when he returns.

'Actually, no. I live in London. I do most of my work at the Crown Court. So it really was a lucky coincidence that I was here.'

'That's for sure.' I take a ladylike sip of my coffee. 'And what about the tour of the house that you were on? Why did you ask those questions about Frank Bolton?'

'Ah, so you do remember me.' He looks like a satisfied cat.

'Of course. I definitely remember people who ask questions I can't answer.'

'You did all right. "There were lots of opportunities available after the war for an ambitious young man",' he quotes. 'It certainly impressed the Americans. It's always nice to hear about a self-made man who came from nowhere and eventually managed to buy a stately home. It gives hope to the rest of us who aren't "to the manor born".'

'Like me, then.'

He gives me a look of mock-surprise. 'Surely not. You're so well-spoken. I've been trying to place your accent – is it Oxford or Cambridge?'

'OK... I admit, it's Oxford.' I feel a little defensive. 'I did my degree there.'

'I'm not surprised, as you're working in that fancy house and all.'

'It's not like that.'

'So you didn't grow up eating your baby mush from a silver spoon?' It's clearly meant to be a joke, but I don't laugh.

'I grew up in a semi in Hertfordshire. Mum's an accountant. Dad's a yoga instructor.'

'Really? What kind?'

'Hatha,' I reply automatically. Everyone tends to ask this, though few people know the difference.

'And do you partake?'

'No.' I shake my head. 'My idea of chilling out is a glass of wine and a book. Not that I get much free time. I like my job, so I work a lot.'

'Hmm.' He leans forward. 'Sounds like you don't get out much.'

'So I'm told. But is that really so bad?'

'No.' His eyes smoulder. 'Some of my favourite activities involve staying in.'

Before I can process the frisson between us, the moment is spoiled by the ringing of his phone. He takes it out of his pocket, looking annoyed. I don't mean to overhear, but I can tell it's a woman, her voice sounding croaky and frantic.

'Yes, OK,' he says. 'I said I'd come by tonight, and I will.' He checks his watch. 'I'm leaving now. Watch *Newsnight* till I get there.'

There's more haranguing and a few seconds later, he hangs up, looking sheepish.

'Sorry,' he says. 'Duty calls. My gran's been having nightmares lately.'

'Of course. No worries.' I feel absurdly relieved that the caller wasn't a wife or girlfriend.

He takes a final sip of his coffee and stands up. 'Let me drop you home on my way.'

'It's not necessary. I can get a taxi.'

'Really, Alex. I'd feel better if I knew you were safe.'

I like it when he says my name. 'OK.'

We leave the chippie together and walk a few blocks to his car: a swish silver BMW. He drives me back to Mallow Court and we reach the gates just as a car from the security company is pulling out. Tim stops and I roll down the window. 'Is everything OK?' I ask the man.

'Yes,' he says. 'We've checked the house and reset the alarm. I'll send someone round first thing tomorrow to speak with you.'

'Thanks,' I say.

Tim drives me to the front of the house. In the moonlight, the silhouette of the roofline is jagged and forbidding.

As I get out of the car, his forehead creases with concern. 'Are you sure you'll be safe?'

'Yes.' Inside, I'm warring with myself – part of me wants to invite him in, have a drink, see what happens. Another part of me is relieved that he's due at his gran's.

'Here.' He takes a business card from his pocket. 'Give me a call once you're inside.'

'OK. Thanks.'

'And Alex, I'd love to have your number. We can go out for a proper drink – or maybe dinner in London?'

'Yes, I'd like that.'

I give him my number and go up to my flat. Nothing is out of order, and I phone to give him the all-clear. I pour myself glass of red wine, contemplating how my ordeal might have a happy ending after all. Karen would be proud of me. I could ring her, but decide that just for tonight, I'll keep my newfound plans for 'getting out more' under my hat.

* * *

I spend the next day dealing with the fallout from my bizarre experience. First, I do a walkthrough of the main house to see if I can spot anything missing. There's nothing obvious. I'm relived too that Mrs Fairchild has left a message on the answerphone saying she'll be back tomorrow. The message ends without her leaving a number. I pick up the envelope addressed to 'Catherine Bolton' and hold it up to the light. It's made of thick paper, and I can't see through it. I'm tempted to open it; by locking me in the loo, someone has made it my business. But before I can do so, I'm called away by the security team, so I leave the letter on Mrs Fairchild's writing desk.

The security people check the house and find nothing. Perhaps it was a one-off incident, maybe a prank, though I still have no idea who would do such a thing, or why. To be on the safe side, I have the crew install a few cameras in obvious places to deter any after-hours mischief. Then I gather the staff together, stressing the need to be vigilant.

'Gosh, Alex, I feel terrible that I left you alone last night,' Edith says.

'You couldn't have known. It was a freak thing.'

'Could it have been the man I saw earlier?'

'Maybe. Is there anything else you remember about him?'

'Not really.' She laughs awkwardly. 'Now that I'm with Paul, I don't really notice other men.'

'That's nice.' Unhelpful, but nice.

'And what do we tell Mrs Fairchild?' Edith asks.

This is something I've puzzled over. 'We'll have to tell her that someone was snooping around and to be on her guard. But I think she'll be safe. Whoever it was probably took advantage of the fact that she was away.'

'So it was planned?' Edith's voice holds a note of fear.

'Maybe. But the security team has checked everything. We've taken action.'

'I could get Paul to come around.'

'No police,' I say firmly. 'Not until I talk to Mrs Fairchild.' I decide not to tell Edith about the envelope left by the intruder. 'Let's keep this under wraps for now.'

'OK, boss.' Edith's face pinches into a rare frown.

* * *

That evening, Tim rings me. Hearing his voice sparks my adrenalin. 'Just checking that everything's OK,' he says.

'It's fine.' I smile down the phone, grateful for his concern.

'And are you there alone, or has the Knicker King's daughter returned home yet?'

'She'll be home tomorrow. I'm not quite sure what I'm going to tell her.'

'I understand. Anyway, I wanted to invite you for a drink in London on Friday evening. I'd love to see you again.'

'Friday?' The years of being 'off the market' press heavily on my shoulders. Do I play hard-to-get? Tell him I'm busy? Before I can decide, I hear myself saying: 'Friday is fine.'

'Great. I can see you after court. I'll text you someplace to meet.'

'Perfect.' I hang up the phone feeling nervous, then stupidly excited, then nervous again.

I take the velvet bag with the locket out of my pocket, where it seems to have taken up permanent residence, and undo the catch. 'I'll take you to London and have you looked at by a jeweller,' I say as the bird pops up on its perch and begins its slow half-rotation. Its beak opens and closes on impossibly fine hinges, like it has a secret to tell me. But try as I might, I can't quite hear what it has to say.

13

13 NOVEMBER 1940 – 12.17 A.M.

Just then, another ambulance roared up. Flea, who I've known all my life, jumped out.

'What a goddamn mess!' he yelled to his partner. 'Looks like Jerry's given this place a proper kick up the backside.'

'Shhh.' I pointed down at the girl. 'Mind your tongue, will you?'

'Righto, Badger. Poor poppet.' He patted the girl on the head, his gaze fixing on the jewelled locket in her hand. For a moment, his eyes seemed to sparkle with lust at the colours of the jewels. He looked away and glanced over at the body of the woman. 'God, Badger,' he said, 'it's not her, is it?'

I felt a barely controllable urge to punch him. 'Yes,' I said. 'It is.'

14

When I return to the house the next day, Mrs Fairchild is getting out of a taxi.

'Alex!' She greets me with an enthusiastic hug and a kiss on the cheek. 'How are you?'

'I'm fine, Mrs Fairchild. But you left so suddenly. I was worried.'

'Sorry about that,' she says. 'It was a last-minute thing, but I did let Edith know. I needed some fresh air – and to get away from here for a few days. So I went over Bath way to visit a friend.'

I pick up her overnight bag and carry it inside the house. We walk together to her little private kitchen next to the staffroom. 'And did your uh... friend... have a nice time too?'

'Of course.' She ignores my insinuation. 'My *friend* Marianne and her sister Gwen have a nice cottage in a village there. It's always nice to catch up with the old crowd.'

'Sounds good. But when Edith told me you'd gone, I thought maybe it was with your new man. The one you mentioned.'

'Understood.' She chuckles. 'But when you get to be my age, you don't have to drive to Lover's Lane for a fumble in the back of Daddy's car. And anyway, I knew you'd be here to hold the fort.'

'Um, yes. About that…' I take a breath. 'We had a slight hiccup while you were away.'

I go over to the writing desk and hand her the envelope addressed to her. Just for an instant, her calm expression cracks. She recovers quickly, but I can tell she's bothered. If only I'd opened the envelope before giving it to her!

'What's this?'

'I'm not sure. Someone left it here for you after hours. And locked me in the loo while they were at it.'

'No! Are you all right, Alex?'

'Yes. But whoever it was must have hidden in the stockroom after hours. Luckily the alarm went off. Which reminds me, I need to show you how to use it.'

'Yes, fine.' She turns away, clearly unsettled.

'Mrs Fairchild?' I speak quietly. 'I can tell that something's wrong. Please, I want to help.'

'Nothing's wrong,' she says sharply.

I take a step back. In the three years that I've known her, she's never once raised her voice to me.

Instantly, her face registers shock. 'I'm sorry, Alex. I didn't mean to speak to you like that. It's just, the idea of an "uninvited guest" makes me nervous. You know I love having the house open to the public, and we've never had any problems. But you could have been in danger.'

'I don't think so. I think it was just an isolated incident.' *I hope so*, I don't add.

'I'm so grateful that you were here to handle it,' she says.

'You're doing a stellar job, Alex. As always.' She slips the envelope into the pocket of her cardigan. 'Now, I must get on with the garden. The weeds must be having a field day, if you'll excuse the pun.' She walks over to the door and puts on her gardening clogs. It's obvious that she's not about to trust me with any confidences.

'There's just one more thing.' I pull out the locket, holding it up for her to see. The silver is warm and smooth in my hand, almost like a living thing. 'I found your note – and this.'

She stares at the locket like it's a hypnotist's crystal. Her blue eyes grow wide, her lids heavy. 'Oh, that. I forgot I left it.'

I can tell she's lying. But why? I hold out the locket to her. 'Do you want it back? It's a lovely piece.'

Her hand trembles as she reaches towards the locket but doesn't take it. 'No, I don't want it.' She lowers her hand. 'It's just a trinket I've had ever since I was a girl. A child's toy.'

'Really? I've never seen anything like it.'

'I thought you might like to see it.'

'Thanks.' Everything about her manner is off, but I press on. 'If you tell me more about it, then I can do a write-up and put it in the exhibition along with your lovely clothing.'

'No,' she says firmly. 'I don't want it on display. It has sentimental value, but that's all. My father gave it to me. It was just after the war. I don't like to think about those times.'

'I understand.' Though I don't, really. Why would she have put it with the costume exhibition things if she didn't want it displayed? And the connection to the war... I glance at her through lowered lids and do the maths. It's never really occurred to me that Mrs Fairchild was alive during the war. To me, she's always seemed more like late fifties than late sixties. I want to question her further, but her face seems distant and shuttered.

'Anyway, maybe you can put it back in my jewellery box? Locked up?'

'Of course.' I keep hold of it, strangely reluctant to let go. 'Although, I am going down to London on Friday. I could take it to a jeweller and get it cleaned. Maybe find someone who could tell me something about it?'

'You'll be wasting your time, but go ahead. I know a man you can take it to. His workshop is at Hatton Garden. I don't know his address, but anyone round there can direct you. Just ask for the Clockmaker.'

'The Clockmaker?'

She pretends not to hear me as she moves briskly to the door. 'Must be getting on,' she says. With a final glance at the silver locket in my hand, she purses her lips and goes outside.

15

Normally I'd say that whatever's bothering Mrs Fairchild is none of my business. If she wants my help, she can always ask. But the 'uninvited guest' has made it my problem. Mrs Fairchild has seemed preoccupied for a few weeks, even before the failed wedding. I should have realised that something was wrong back when she asked me to sit with her in the evenings. And that day in the drawing room when I saw her tucking away a piece of paper into her pocket – was that related? Is she being blackmailed? The idea that Mrs Fairchild could have given anyone grounds for blackmail strikes me as ludicrous. But I also wonder why she left the jewelled locket for me to discover only to be so evasive about it. I enjoy a good mystery as much as the next person, but as I sit on the train to London, the unanswered questions rattle worryingly inside my brain.

The little towns blur by as the train speeds towards the capital. I clasp the velvet bag inside my pocket. Personally, I've never been into wearing jewellery, and other than a few gifts for Mum over the years, I've never bought anything fancy or expensive. Even I've heard of Hatton Garden, however – it's a street near

Chancery Lane that's the centre of the London jewellery and diamond trade.

I take the *A to Z* out of my handbag and check the map again. After Hatton Garden, I'm supposed to meet up with Tim at a wine bar near the Crown Court. My stomach flips at the thought of going on a proper date. I have no idea what to do or say. But as a barrister, he must talk for a living, so hopefully he can fill the silence.

As the train pulls into Euston Station, I'm hit by a wave of panic. I *love* London, I remind myself. Every year when I was a girl, my parents took me to see a panto at Christmas and then on to Hamleys. Jammed into the crush of shoppers, Dad would pull me aside and indoctrinate me about the shameful decadence of Western culture, scoffing at the children fighting over Power Rangers and Cabbage Patch Dolls. Mum would secretly sneak upstairs to buy me a Barbie doll or a stuffed toy. For me it was the best time of the year.

When I got older, Mum used to sometimes take me to Oxford Street to buy summer clothes. Dad would skulk along behind, regaling us with horror stories about how my denim shorts were probably made by five-year-old children in a Bangladeshi sweatshop, and that the manufacture of my trainers was contributing to the melting of the polar ice caps. Even so, I loved London and secretly vowed that someday I'd have a little flat near the British Library. My dream was to spend my days reading books, my nights frequenting eclectic coffee houses, and my weekends visiting free museums and galleries. I came close when Karen offered me a room in her flat after uni. But by then I'd met Xavier and was bent on staying on at Oxford. By the time the relationship went balls up, Karen had moved to Essex.

As I step off the train, my ears are assaulted by the vast echo of sounds. Men and women wearing suits and carrying briefcases rush past me, and I deliberately slow down to let them pass. I take the escalator down to the Tube, my eyes flicking over posters for films, musicals, and the new Tate Modern. For some reason, all I can think about is Mrs Fairchild and the fact that when she was a girl, Tube stations were used as air raid shelters. How awful it must it have been to experience the rush of panic when the sirens began to wail, the frightful irritation of having to leave meals uneaten, valuables unattended; children pulled by the hand out of their homes without having used the toilet or finished their schoolwork. Grabbing the ugly, alien-looking gas masks down off the coat rack pegs and rushing to the shelter at all hours.

I hug the right side of the escalator. How did people overcome the claustrophobia of the queue to get down the narrow stairs? Did their eyes gloss over the posters reminding that 'loose lips sink ships', 'make do and mend', and to 'keep calm and carry on'? And how did it feel, that peculiar mix of fear, boredom, and Blitz Spirit? Films often depict people in the shelters bonded together – singing, knitting, and sewing, playing with the children, all the while keeping a cool head, a stiff upper lip and that indomitable 'never say die' British mindset.

But was that the truth? What did it feel like as the ground shook with the explosions? What was it like to wonder if you'd have a home when you emerged, or if your cat would make it, or what happened to the elderly neighbour who didn't answer when you knocked? Maybe he was in the bath or maybe he'd gone out. Or maybe he had the wireless turned up so loud that he didn't hear the sirens, and even now, his life had been snuffed out. And for a little girl like Catherine Fairchild – or Catherine Bolton, as she was back then – the things she'd seen and endured must have caused deep, if well-disguised, scars.

I feel panicked in the crush of people on the train and in the tunnels when I change trains at Tottenham Court Road. By the time we reach Chancery Lane, my whole body is in a cold sweat. I push my way off the train, trying to stay calm. This shouldn't be hard – everyone's doing it. But away from the rarified atmosphere of Mallow Court, I want to jump out of my skin. I grasp the stair railing and pull myself upwards. No one stops to ask if I'm OK. This is London, after all.

Finally, I emerge into a circle of grey-white sky. I breathe in the dense air of bus exhaust and cloying humidity, glad to be above ground. I join the flow of pedestrians walking down Holborn towards the Inns of Court. The architecture in this part of London is a fascinating mix of Victorian, Gothic, brutalist, and modern office blocks. At New Fetter Lane, I cross the street and turn down the unassuming little lane that is one of the premier jewellery and diamond centres of the world.

Displayed in each brightly lit shop window is a fortune in sparkling stones and finely crafted silver and gold jewellery. The further I walk, the less I know what I'm doing. Nothing I see resembles my little 'trinket', as Mrs Fairchild called it, and there's no sign of any clockmaker.

Eventually, I come to a shop that sells jewellery-making tools and findings. It looks less imposing than the retail jewellers, so I go inside to the till where an old man is reading the *Racing Post* while idly fingering an unlit cigarette.

'Can I help you, luv?' he says.

'I'm looking for The Clockmaker.' Saying it makes me feel foolish. Of course he won't know—

'Oh, aye.' He raises a busy white eyebrow.

'Really? You know who I'm talking about?'

"Course, luv. It's just around the corner.' He waves with his cigarette. 'Little alleyway back of Churchley and Sons.'

The words suck away all sense of relief. *Churchley & Sons*. It can't be the same Churchley as in my ill-fated wedding couple, can it?

'You got that, luv?'

'Just around the corner,' I repeat. 'Thank you. You've been very helpful.'

'Ta, luv.'

Feeling light-headed, I leave the shop and find that 'around the corner' proves to be anything but 'just'. I get lost in the warren of backstreets and alleyways that curve in odd directions. I ask two more people who tell me that it's 'just around the corner' and that 'I can't miss it'.

I can miss it, and do, until I realise it's right in front of me. Unlike the small shops along the street, it's actually a huge facade of white marble that looks more like a government ministry than a shop. The entrance is flanked by white pillars with a pediment on top, and the only sign is a brass plate saying 'Churchley & Sons, Fine Art Auctioneers' and a golden bell. I consider ringing the bell and running away, like we used to do as kids to uptight neighbours. But I spot the security cameras above the door and decide not to risk any further police attention.

And luckily, I'm not interested in Churchley & Sons anyway, but somewhere around the back. Like Alice down the rabbit hole, I plunge down the alley at the side of the building and end up in a loading bay. That's when I hear it. A sound: regular and steady, yet somehow jumbled. Across the loading bay is a brick building with a few tags of graffiti. A door in the wall is standing partly ajar. The sound is coming from inside.

I go through the door into a narrow corridor with another

door at the end. Suddenly, all hell breaks loose. Bells – I've set off an alarm! Memories of the police station come rushing back. I'm about to run away when the alarms make another sound: 'cuckoo, cuckoo'. There's a chorus of four chimes, and everything begins to cuckoo at once.

Clocks! Lots of them! I've definitely found the place.

'Hello?' I call out.

There's no answer. I go through the door at the end of the corridor and find myself in the most bizarre workshop I've ever seen. There are mountains of clocks: clocks on walls, clocks on shelves, a forest of grandfather clocks, clocks in various states of dishabille on a long workbench, their intricate metal innards carefully laid out. There are carriage clocks and funky alarm clocks, digital clocks, and a whole wall of cuckoo clocks. Everything is jumbled and the wooden floor is covered with fine metal dust and boxes of tools and piles of papers, books, and diagrams. I feel like I've stepped back in time, or maybe forward. One by one, the clocks stop chiming, whirring, buzzing, and cuckooing, and fall back into a steady drone of ticking. Rhythmic, yet completely out of time. For the first time in what seems like days, I grin.

From a corner of the room, a throat clears.

I jump, still startled from the clocks going berserk. Turning around, I see a desk, piled high with stacks of books and papers. I peer into the dim light, expecting to see a wizened old man with wild white hair, a monocle, and a leather apron, straight out of Dickens. But the man who stands up from behind the desk is anything but...

He's tall – very tall – with a rangy but strong-looking body. His hair is dark brown and comes almost to his shoulders, curling a little at the bottom. His chin is covered with a stubbly beard, but his cheekbones and facial features are well-defined.

He looks to be in his early thirties. He's wearing faded jeans and a Pink Floyd *The Dark Side of the Moon* T-shirt. But the thing that draws my attention is his eyes. They're pale and blue – almost luminous as they lock with mine.

He gazes at me silently with a half-smile on his face, bringing his long fingers to his chin in consideration. 'I was going to say carriage clock,' he says. 'But maybe pocket watch. Hmmm, strange. Usually I can tell right away.'

'Sorry?'

'What you're looking for.'

'I'm not actually here to buy a clock,' I say.

'That's what they all say.' He winks conspiratorially. 'But I've found that there's usually something here for just about everyone. Look at this.' He picks up something off the desk. It's a Mickey Mouse watch on a red leather strap. 'Walt Disney gave this to Julie Andrews when she starred in *Mary Poppins*.'

'Really?'

'Yes, look here. There's a mark.' He points to a scratch in the metal so tiny that I barely notice it. 'It says: "Thank you for the magic, Love Walt".'

'I never would have known,' I say.

'And here.' He strides over to a shelf and takes down an ugly-looking black box. 'This is one of the earliest clock radios ever made. A Casio.' He holds it out. 'It's not really digital. It has plastic numbers that flip around.'

'I had one of those in my bedroom as a kid,' I say. 'I'd forgotten all about it.'

He chuckles. 'I had one too. Funny how time flies.'

'I guess you would know.'

'You'd think, wouldn't you?' His eyes catch the light and glint like a pale moon as he puts the clock back on the shelf. 'But actually, when I'm in here working, it's the one place where

I really do lose track. Time is passing all around me, but I don't even notice it.'

'That is odd.'

'But you aren't here to talk about time, and you aren't here to buy a clock. So...' He considers me. 'Do you mind if I ask – why are you here?'

'I don't mind,' I say with a laugh. The roomful of clocks and the man himself are so odd that I feel strangely at ease. I've never been very interested in clocks – I expect most people aren't – except as useful devices to tell me whether I'm early, late, or just being stood up. But in this place, clocks seem intrinsically interesting.

I take the velvet bag out of my handbag and set it on the worktable. My hands fumble as I untie the cords and withdraw the locket. I watch his face: first impressions tell a true story. He picks up the heavy silver lozenge, the chain coiling over his long fingers. His brows draw close together. Something flickers in his eyes: disbelief.

He flicks open the catch. The bird pops out and begins its slow mechanical rotation, silently moving its delicate beak, the crystals on its feathers sparkling in the light of his work lamp. He stares at it, clearly fascinated. It's like he's forgotten that I'm there. He snaps the locket shut and opens it again, still mesmerised.

'Amazing.' He stares at the bird, all trace of amusement gone from his face. 'Where did this come from?'

'It belongs to a friend. I'd like to have it cleaned. But I'm also hoping to find out something about it.'

'I'm not sure I can help you with that,' he says. 'I haven't seen anything like it before.'

'Oh.' I can't quite hide my disappointment.

He moves behind his worktable and turns on a bright magnifying light. 'I think it ought to be able to sing,' he says.

'Sing?'

He searches around on the desk, picking up one tool after another. Finally, he settles on a thin sharp probe, like a dental instrument. He holds the locket under the light and prods delicately at the metal joint that makes up the bird's throat.

'Something's stopping it from turning all the way around,' he says. 'And, if I'm not mistaken, there's a music box inside.' He looks up. 'Do you mind if I have a fiddle about? I won't damage it, I promise.'

'Um, sure. That's why I'm here.'

He holds up a magnifying glass and peers down the bird's throat, probing with the wire instrument.

I lean in closer until our heads are almost touching. His dark hair falls in a curtain over his eyes and I can't see his face, but I watch his adept fingers as they search the bird's throat.

'It's swallowed something.' He speaks with the gravity of a veterinarian trying to help an injured animal. 'It's jamming the tiny wheels and gears inside.'

He passes me the glass and I peer into it. Close up, the mechanism seems even more complex. But because I don't know what I'm looking for, I can't tell what's out of place.

He takes another tool from the leather roll: a tiny pair of pliers that wouldn't look out of place in a doll's toolbox.

'There's something wedged inside,' he says. 'Maybe a child once tried to feed the bird?'

'Maybe.'

Was Mrs Fairchild that child? Seeing the mechanism through the glass has led me to question once again whether this really is just a child's trinket. To my, albeit untrained, eye, it looks like a delicate work of art.

The Clockmaker's hand is rock steady as he performs the necessary surgery. It seems to take a very long time. I hold my breath, willing it all to go well.

'There. Got it!' Gingerly, he pulls on the object that he's hooked with the pliers. Something flashes gold in the light and he sets a piece of metal onto the table.

'A key!'

'Yes.' The Clockmaker continues to perform post-operative work on the bird. He goes through a succession of miniature screwdrivers and probes, checking the joints, dabbing oil on with a paintbrush, and tightening unbelievably tiny screws.

I pick up the gold key and turn it over in my hands. It's tiny – just over a centimetre long, with a trefoil design at one end and notches at the other. It reminds me of the key I had to my pre-teen diary – pink faux-leopard skin with a gold lock – where I wrote down all of my precious twelve-year-old secrets. Or perhaps it's the key to a jewellery box? I hold it up close and peer at it. There are a few scratches on the notched end of the metal, but no other markings.

'That should do it,' the Clockmaker says, grinning proudly. 'Watch this.' The bird folds up on its tiny hinges and he snaps the locket shut. He opens it again. The bird springs to life on its perch and begins its slow rotation. Instead of stopping halfway around, the bird continues in a complete circle. The hinges on its beak move, and this time, there's a delicate tinkling sound as the music box inside begins to play. I gaze at the small object in the hand of the Clockmaker, mesmerised by its delicate perfection.

'Wonderful, isn't it?' His face is lit by the pure delight of a child looking into the window of a toyshop at Christmas. Warmth spreads inside me. He senses me looking at him and smiles, but neither of us speaks for a long moment. That silence, as much as anything, makes an impression on me. Finally, when the tune comes to an end and the bird falls still, he snaps the locket shut.

'Thank you,' I say. 'I never knew it could sing.'

He dabs a bit of oil on the outer hinges. 'I wonder what the song is.'

'I could ask Mrs Fairchild; she's the owner.' I sigh. 'But I'm not sure she'll know.'

'Fairchild, did you say? That name sounds... familiar.' His face darkens. 'Where did you say this came from again?'

'I didn't.' All of a sudden, it's like a heavy curtain has descended between us. 'The owner lives in a house called Mallow Court. Up near Aylesbury.'

'Mallow Court.' He again strokes his chin, considering. 'You know, I've definitely heard of that place. In fact—'

But I never do learn what 'in fact' he's heard, because just then, a door flanked by two grandfather clocks opens at the side of the room. An attractive blonde woman comes into the room, wearing a smart skirt suit and high heels. 'Chris...' she says, a teasing smile on her face. 'You know you've got a meeting with — Oh, sorry...' Seeing me, she cuts off. 'Sorry, Mr Heath-Churchley – I didn't know you had a customer.'

Heath-Churchley.

'No worries, Agatha,' he says. 'But can you tell Dad I'll be up later? I'm in the middle of something.'

Dad! My mouth gapes open in stunned horror. Maybe it should have been obvious given the location of the shop, but I can't believe that the Clockmaker, of all people, happens to be a member of my bogey family.

The woman purses her high-gloss lips and looks at me in disdain. The Clockmaker turns back to the locket, but I snatch it away, along with the key, and shove them both into the velvet bag.

'Sorry, but I've got to go.' Despite being surrounded by clocks, I check my wrist for a watch that isn't there. 'Thank you for your time, Mr... um... Heath-Churchley. I can show myself out.'

I turn and make for the door.

'Wait a minute,' he says. 'Please.'

I whirl around, frantically digging in my handbag for my purse. Money – he must want money for the work he did. 'Of course,' I say. 'I'll pay now. How much?'

'No. That's not it.' He looks positively wounded. Silly me – the rich never like to talk about money. 'I mean, I don't even know your name.'

'It's Alex.' I'm too flustered to come up with a fake name at the drop of a hat. 'Thanks again for your help. If you do want payment, then send an invoice to Mallow Court.'

I reach the door and duck out into the alleyway just as the clocks begin to chime the half hour. The cuckoos pop out and I hear their sound echoing behind me, sounding like 'stupid, stupid, stupid...'

Which is nothing short of the truth.

16

I walk quickly away from the workshop, vaguely retracing my steps through the warren of streets. It's as if I've emerged from a cosy, magical world into a grim new reality. The sky is dark and a few raindrops begin to fall. I don't have an umbrella, and it only takes half a block before the sky opens up and rain pours down with biblical force.

I lower my head and run, but the rain soaks through my jacket. It fills me with a cold, wet gloom. Why didn't I just stay where I was and wait out the storm? Does it really matter that the Clockmaker is a Heath-Churchley? Just because 'Daddy' was awful to me, and the wedding disaster still haunts me as my first real failure as the manager at Mallow Court, does it follow that the sins of the father must be visited on the son?

But the more I think about it, the more indignation I feel. The Clockmaker may be holed up in his quaint little workshop, but it's still attached to 'Daddy's' auction house. He hasn't exactly struck out on his own. Not when there's an attractive PA who probably has an intercom at her desk but decides to seek him out in person. He may be eccentric, but he's still a man – and rich and posh at that.

And what's more... Mrs Fairchild knew! She suggested I take the bird to 'The Clockmaker'; she sent me straight into the jaws of the lion. Incensed, I storm to the Tube. Just as I'm about to descend into the bowels of subterranean London, my phone rings. It's Tim. In the strange world of wind-up clocks and mechanisms that don't run on batteries, I'd almost forgotten the reason I came to London in the first place. For a second, I consider rejecting the call – I'm soaked and in no fit state for man or beast. Instead, I barge my way into the recessed doorway of a wigmaker's shop and answer breathlessly on the sixth ring.

'Hi, Alex, you haven't forgotten me, I hope.' His voice is deep and resonant. And given where I am, I wonder what he would look like in his barrister's wig – and nothing else.

'How could I forget my "get out of jail free" card?'

'Not only free, but I'm going to buy you a proper drink. If you're still up for it.'

'Absolutely,' I say. 'I'm on my way.'

* * *

I catch a glimpse of my reflection in the window of the wine bar – I look like a drowned rat that's crawled out from one of London's underground sewers. I'm about to turn around and walk away, but already Tim has spotted me; he comes over to the door and ushers me inside.

'It's lovely to see you again, Alex.' He leans in and kisses me on the cheek, his lips just brushing the corner of mine. I shiver – he's quite handsome; and besides, it's been a while since anyone bothered to kiss me.

'You too.' I take in his perfect suit, clean-shaven square jaw and light brown hair that's shiny and tousled from the rain. If anything, he's almost *too* good-looking. Who knew that was possible? Surely a man like him would be better off with an equally well-groomed woman, like the Heath-Churchley PA, rather than someone like me.

'How was your journey?' he says.

'It was fine, and thanks for inviting me. It hasn't been the best day. Forgot my umbrella – as you can see.'

'I like the slicked-back look.' He tucks a stray strand of wet hair behind my ear. I lean in and let myself be warmed by the lustrous brown of his eyes. 'But let's get a drink in you right away. Hopefully things will improve.'

'They already have,' I flirt back effortlessly.

He flags down a server and I order a large glass of Zinfandel. I still haven't worked out how much I should tell him. The fact is, we've only met once – twice if you count the house tour. Before he can ask me what I've been up to, I jump in first.

'So, how was court today?'

'Fine.' His nose twitches. 'It was the usual stuff. An old lady was suing the council because she slipped and fell on the library steps. She wanted her day in court, more to complain about the reduced opening hours and the fact that they don't have the two latest Jackie Collins books than about the access issues.'

'Really?'

'Really.'

'So did you win? I take it you represented the council?'

'Oh, I won, all right. I usually do. But I wasn't representing the council. I got my client a settlement for £150 plus expenses: train fare to court and a bun at the station. Now she can buy Jackie's latest – maybe even a signed copy.'

I smile. 'Sounds like a fair result. And it's refreshing to meet someone who's standing up for the underdog.'

'Oh, that's me, all right,' he says. 'Widows, orphans – the more downtrodden the better.'

I detect a touch of cynicism but forget it immediately when he puts his hand on mine.

'It all sounds very... philanthropic,' I say, my fingers tingling.

'What a word!' he says. 'Another old chestnut from – where did you say? Cambridge?'

'Oxford.' I withdraw a fraction.

'Ah, that's right.'

'What of it?' I joke. 'I mean, you're a barrister. Hardly a job for your average bluestocking.'

'I suppose not. But I am most definitely from humble origins.'

'So you said before. And where exactly is that?'

'East London.' There's a hint of pride in his voice.

'Which part?' In the years I spent in suburbia followed by my time in 'the city of dreaming spires', I've met very few people from what could be classed as the rougher areas of London. And looking at Tim Edwards, I wouldn't have pinned him on the map as coming from there.

'Near Holloway. A little street of semis that in its heyday used to be a Georgian terrace.'

'Used to be?'

'It was mostly destroyed in the Blitz. Then in the sixties, some sadistic architect with a passion for concrete and pebble-dash got his hands dirty. Gran's lived in the same road her whole life.'

'How interesting.' I think back to my Tube ride earlier when I was wondering how people survived the Blitz. I've barely given it a thought before, and now, twice in one day.

'A lot of the elderly people I represent were alive in those days,' Tim says. 'Believe it or not, even after all these years, there are still quite a few wrongs that need putting right.'

His face hardens momentarily, and I'm not quite sure what to say.

* * *

In the end, I have a drink too many and the inevitable moment arrives when the bar gets crowded, several groups are eyeing our table, and it's time to fish or cut bait. I'm warmed by the wine and laughing at Tim's anecdotes about his crusades for the underdog. Suit or no, it's an attractive quality in a man. Then there's those eyes…

I lean on his arm as we make our way to the door of the pub. My mind tells me I should leave. It's much too soon to go with him to 'see his flat', 'have a nightcap', or 'let one thing lead to another'. My body, however, is looking to take a leaf out of Karen's book—

'I've had a lovely time,' he says, kissing me on the cheek. 'I hope we can do it again soon.'

'Me too,' I say. All my 'will I, won't I?'s disappear in a cloud of bus exhaust. That's it, then, the evening's over – early by all accounts. 'Thanks for the drink,' I say. 'And the company.'

An SUV speeds through a puddle, splashing me. But by now, I'm already sobered up.

'I've got a big case on Monday that I need to prepare for,' he explains, obviously sensing my disappointment. 'No rest for the wicked.'

'I should get home too.' I lift my arm to hail a taxi. 'Good luck with your case.'

'Thanks. And maybe we could do dinner next weekend?'

Instantly I brighten. I know I'm supposed to play hard-to-get and that there are rules for these situations. But I don't know them, and I've never liked playing games. 'I'd like that,' I say.

'Great. Because there's someone I'd like you to meet.'

'Oh?'

'My gran.'

I give a flippant little laugh. 'I'm flattered. But isn't it a little soon?'

'Maybe. But I've got the feeling, Alex, that she'll want to meet you sooner or later.'

17

When I wake up the next morning, I'm still tired and a little groggy from my evening out. The velvet bag is on the bedside table next to me; I take out the locket and open the clasp. The bird rotates in a full circle, its beak moving in time with the tinkling melody. The tune is sweet and brisk, like a folk song, and yet there's an undertone of sadness there also. If I knew what the tune was, maybe I could discover where the locket came from.

And then there's the golden key. I tip it out of the bag into my hand. Another mystery. 'What do you open?' I mutter, turning it over. It's obvious where I need to start looking for answers...

Mrs Fairchild.

I think back to the years we've known each other. Over time, I've come to see her as so much more than an employer. She's a friend and confidante. A sort of adopted grandmother. A woman who's always willing to sit down and chat over a pot of tea and a plate of scones or a Victoria sponge, and always open and approachable. Until recently.

Now, something thick and stifling has come between us. I want to move it aside, show her that I'm here for her and am willing to listen and help any way I can. How can I get her to confide in me? And why did she throw me to the wolves – the Heath-Churchley family – when she knew what had passed between us?

I glance at the note on the bedside table: *For Alex?* It seems innocent enough, but clearly something painful lies beneath the surface. The last thing I want to do is make it worse… I'll need to tread carefully.

I tuck the jewelled bird and the key back into the velvet bag. I'll lock them away in Mrs Fairchild's jewellery box where she keeps her engagement ring and other jewellery that her husband, George, gave to her over the years. Though, as I slip the bag into my pocket, I have to admit that it's been comforting carrying the locket around with me like a talisman…

I check my diary: three tours scheduled for today, with one guide on holiday, so I'll be stepping in, unfortunately. Until I get to the bottom of things, house tours feel like an unwanted distraction.

On my mobile, I find a text from Tim Edwards saying that he had a great time last night, and is looking forward to dinner next week. In the light of day, I still feel intrigued by my 'champion of the underdog', though something about the way the evening ended left me a little deflated. Dinner, though, will give me something to look forward to, so I text a smiley face back and write the date in my diary. There's also another text: an apologetic message from Karen sent last night. I put the coffee on and give her a call. She answers on the sixth ring, sleepy and cross. But when she hears it's me, she revives a little.

'Alex! I'm glad you called,' she says. 'I've been praying and meditating over what happened. I really am sorry.'

I smile down the phone. 'I know. And I forgive you. What's done is done.'

'Good,' she says. 'Because I've concluded that if God wanted me to be a nun, he wouldn't have set up the C of E.'

'He didn't – Henry the Eighth did.'

'Technicalities...'

'Whatever. But listen – I've taken on board what you said about my needing to get out more.'

I give her the lowdown on Tim, holding the phone away from my ear so that her grand *whoop!* and *Go Girl!* doesn't deafen me.

'But we parted ways quite early,' I add. 'Should I be worried?'

'Not a bit. It means he likes you a lot.'

'But why me?'

'No idea.' She gives a mock snort. 'But just go with it.'

Glad of her approval, I give her the short version of other events: from being locked in the loo, to the way that Mrs Fairchild is acting. As per usual, Karen glosses over most of it. 'It sounds like a prank,' she says when I describe the call to the police from someone pretending to be Catherine Fairchild.

'But what about the envelope and the letter? Do you think someone could be blackmailing her?'

'Do you really think Mrs Fairchild is hiding some deep dark secret?'

'No. But how well do I really know her?'

'You're a good judge of character. I mean – we're friends. Right?'

I detect a note of remorse in her voice. 'Yeah,' I say. 'We are. And I'm sorry I got so mad.'

She laughs. 'By the powers vested in me by the church, I pronounce that we're both forgiven. Deal?'

'Deal. But listen, there's something else too.'

I tell her about the jewelled locket and my visit to the Clockmaker. I don't mention that he was attractive, though in a quirky, unconventional way.

'So what is this locket? Could he tell you anything about it?'

'I don't know. I ended up leaving in a hurry.' I rush to the punchline. 'Turns out, he's a Heath-Churchley.'

'No! The sins of the vicar visited on the flock.'

'Something like that.'

'Did he know who you were?'

'I don't think so. I panicked and left before he could figure it out. I didn't want "Daddy" to know I'd been there.' I sigh. 'I need to do something, though. I'm sure that whatever's bothering Mrs Fairchild has something to do with that locket. Otherwise, why would she have left it with the exhibition things, and then not want me to use it?'

'Don't take this the wrong way,' she says, 'but it sounds like you've been reading too much Miss Marple.'

'No I haven't. It *is* important... I'm sure.'

On other end of the phone, I hear a man's voice.

'Karen,' I say, 'is there someone there with you?'

'Whatever gave you that—' She gives a high-pitched giggle. 'Stop that – go back to sleep.'

'I'm going now,' I grumble.

'Good idea,' she says. 'If the locket is that important, then you'd better get to work.'

I hang up the phone, unsure whether to be in awe of Karen's exploits or downright disgusted. In any case, she can do what she likes, but *I'm* going to make myself useful. When I'm dressed and ready, I go to the main house. As I pass the Elizabethan dining room, I notice that a few place settings along the banqueting table have been moved, and a glass is tipped over and broken. I detour into the room and go to the long table that's set with a tableaux of fake food. I wrap the broken glass up in a cloth napkin and replace it with another glass from the sideboard. As I'm about to leave the room, I notice a single sheet of paper lying on a chair near the fireplace. Although this is one of the main rooms on the tour, Mrs Fairchild likes to sit in here sometimes because it's opposite the modern kitchen. She must have left the paper behind. I go to move it so it won't get lost when the next tour goes tramping through. Certainly, I don't mean to pry into Mrs Fairchild's private business, but I notice that the paper is a page photocopied from a notebook or journal. The writing is small and cramped and definitely not hers.

Giving in to my natural inclination to be nosy, I begin to read. It's a single entry of a diary dated November 1940. My heart seizes up. An ambulance driver sees a girl crawl from the rubble of a bombed housing terrace. She lifts her head and catches snowflakes on her tongue. The image is beautiful and heart-breaking all at once.

But at the bottom of the paper is an angry scrawl in blue biro – the same as on the envelope I found. *I know what he did!* it says.

'Alex?'

Mrs Fairchild enters the room carrying her knitting bag. She looks down at the paper in my hands. I brace myself as a cloud drifts across her face.

'Sorry.' I quickly hold out the paper. 'A tour is due in half an hour. I think you left this.'

'Thank you.' She takes the paper, folds it, and tucks it into the pocket of her cardigan. Then she turns to leave.

Afraid the moment will be lost, I speak in a low voice:

'Please, Mrs Fairchild, I want to help. You know I do. And I think you want me to.'

She stops walking and turns to me, her face sunny as if nothing's wrong. 'I keep forgetting where I've left things. It happens when you get old.'

'What is the jewelled bird, Mrs Fairchild?'

She runs her hand over the carved wooden door frame. 'It's just a locket,' she says after a moment. 'A pretty piece of jewellery.'

Time is ticking, and my tour will be arriving soon. I put my hands on my hips. 'Tell me...' I say.

Still hesitating, she looks at my face, but I have the feeling that she isn't seeing me. She's lost in another place and time altogether.

'It was mine and I lost it,' she says. 'But Frank Bolton gave it back to me. He came for me in the orphanage.'

'An orphanage? Are you the girl in the diary entry?'

My question seems to teleport her back into the room with me.

'Yes,' she says. 'I was orphaned in the Blitz, in a raid on East London. My mother was killed, but I managed to crawl out of the wreckage.'

'You're an orphan?' Shock reverberates through me. I never would have guessed in a million years. As far as I – and the world – know, she's the daughter of Frank Bolton, the Knicker King. 'I had no idea.'

'I don't like to talk about it, as I'm sure you can understand.'

I nod, aching with empathy. Technically, I'm not an orphan because I have a dad, even if I never knew my birth mother. But growing up, I sometimes used to wonder about her the same way an orphan would.

'And in fact, there *is* nothing to talk about,' she adds. 'It was so long ago. Frank Bolton was the only father I've ever needed. When he collected me from the orphanage that day, he said everything would be fine. And it was. I was his daughter in every way that mattered. I was happy.' Her smile is wistful. 'As for who my blood relatives are, I've long come to grips with the fact that I'll never know.'

'I'm sorry,' I say lamely.

'There's nothing to be sorry about. Young people these days have different ideas – modern ideas. If you're adopted, then you go in search of your birth parents as a rite of passage. But it wasn't like that in my day.' She squares her shoulders. 'We had orphanages and matrons, not foster homes and social workers. You learned to keep your head down and know your place. And if you were lucky enough to be adopted – and extremely lucky to be adopted by good people who raised you as their own – then you didn't ask questions. You didn't look a gift horse in the mouth.'

'I understand.'

'And remember,' she continues, 'we didn't have fancy computers or the worldwide web. The orphanages often had no records at all. And there were thousands of children orphaned during the Blitz. I wasn't the only pebble on the beach. Even if I wanted to, I couldn't discover the truth.'

'I see.'

She lets out a long sigh and leans against the door frame. 'I know you do, Alex. Nonetheless, there are some people out there who refuse to let sleeping dogs lie.'

'Is that what the message meant – the one at the bottom?' *I know what he did!* Angry words, but what do they mean?

Mrs Fairchild's face goes pale. 'I've no idea what that means. It's probably just some prank. Just like the uninvited guest locking you in the loo.'

'Surely a prankster wouldn't have access to Frank's diary—'

'It's not Frank's diary,' Mrs Fairchild clarifies with a frown. 'It's the diary of the ambulance driver who pulled me from the wreckage – a man called Hal Dawkins. His nickname was "Badger". There was a photocopy of the inscription inside the front cover. It must be with the other pages.'

'You've been sent other entries? Is that why you've been—?'

'Alex? Are you there? The tour bus has arrived.'

I curse under my breath as Edith appears at the door.

Mrs Fairchild looks relieved that our conversation is at an end. She glances out the window; a large silver coach has disgorged a group of Japanese tourists, their leader hefting a Burberry umbrella to guide them to the front of the house.

'Thanks,' I say to Edith. 'Would you mind showing them into the great hall? I'll be there in a minute.'

I turn back to Mrs Fairchild, determined not to give up quite yet. 'You said the locket was yours and that Frank Bolton gave it "back" to you. What did you mean?'

Mrs Fairchild looks momentarily confused. 'My mother had it,' she says. 'She gave it to me as she was dying and told me to keep it safe. But then... I lost it. I don't know how, but I did.'

'Well, it's great that you got it back.' I remove the velvet bag from my pocket. 'I'll lock it up in your jewellery box. I took it to London yesterday and showed it to the Clockmaker as you suggested. Who' – I feign nonchalance – 'incidentally happened to be a Heath-Churchley.'

She flashes a guilty smile. 'You caught me out. I didn't tell you beforehand so as not to deter you. The H-Cs are old family friends. I recalled that the son fixed clocks; he has an international reputation for it, apparently. I met him a few times when he was young. Always seemed like a nice chap.'

'Well, anyway, I managed to locate him, and he had a look.' I take the locket out of the bag. 'Turns out it's actually a music box. It was broken and he fixed it.'

'Broken?' She stares at the locket in my hand like she's seeing it for the first time. 'Yes, it was broken – that's right, I remember.' The shutters drop down over her face and I know she won't share the memory.

'There was a key shoved inside.'

'A key? To what?'

'I was hoping you might know.'

'No. I'm afraid I don't.'

Her response is disappointing, but I believe her. I open the clasp on the locket. The bird pops up on its metal perch and begins its slow dance around in a circle. The impossibly tiny hinges on its beak move, the jewels catch the light, and it 'sings' its song like the tinkling of bells.

Mrs Fairchild's cornflower blue eyes grow wider and rounder, following the bird like she's in a trance. Almost uncannily, the years seem to melt off her face. A sound comes from her throat – a low hum. She closes her eyes. As the music box plays, she opens her mouth and words come out. Words to a song in a foreign language that I don't understand. But the melody is sweet and simple, like a lullaby. Suddenly, she opens her eyes and gasps. 'Put that away!' She cups her hand over mine and snaps the bird back into its silver cage. Her eyes are alight with a strange fire. 'Mamochka?' she says, grabbing my arm.

'Mrs Fairchild?' I whisper.

Her eyes roll upwards and she sags against me. I just manage to drag her to a chair where she collapses in a dead faint.

'Help!' I call out, rushing to the door. 'I need help!' I can hear the footsteps of the tour group, the hum of their voices, and shutters snapping on cameras.

Edith rushes over. When she sees Mrs Fairchild draped on the chair, her hand flies to her mouth. 'What happened?'

'She collapsed. Fainted, I think.'

'Should I call an ambulance?'

Behind Edith in the hall, I hear footsteps and worried voices.

'She's got some smelling salts in the kitchen drawer.'

'I'll get them,' Edith says.

I go back to Mrs Fairchild and smooth the silver hair back from her face. 'It's OK,' I whisper, though in truth I'm terrified to see her like this. 'Whatever's going on, we'll sort it out together.'

She murmurs something; my heart seizes up in anticipation of her speaking again in whatever language is programmed deep within her brain. But then her mouth clamps shut and the wrinkles deepen around her lips.

Edith returns holding out a little green vial. I open the bottle and hold it under Mrs Fairchild's nose, turning away myself to avoid the overpowering odour of ammonia. She breathes in; her nose twitches. She begins to stir just as the lady with the Burberry umbrella enters the room, followed by a clump of tourists. There are a few exclamations in Japanese, and all of a sudden, the click of a camera.

'No photos please!' I rush over to try to move the crowd out the door. But halfway there, my foot catches the edge of the rug and I go sprawling to the floor. The room explodes with the light of photo flashes and the exclamations of gleeful tourists getting way more excitement than they bargained for on their tour of an old English house.

PART II

'Only when the clock stops does time come to life.'

— WILLIAM FAULKNER, THE SOUND AND THE FURY

18

13 NOVEMBER 1940 – 12.25 A.M.

Flea and his partner loaded the ambulance with the rest of the bodies. The girl started to shiver, going into shock. 'Stay here,' I said to her. I went to the front of the ambulance and rummaged around for a spare blanket. I found one, coarse and crumpled, behind the passenger seat and pulled it out. When I turned back, Flea was bending over the girl's mother, his fingers groping her hand.

'What are you doing?' I said sharply.

'Nothing, mate.' Flea stood up, quickly slipping his hand in his pocket. 'Just checking for a pulse.'

We stared at each other and I saw something unexpected. Cruelty. Though I'd known him all my life, it was as if I was seeing him for the first time. He took a cigarette out of his pocket and lit it. The moment passed.

'Go on then,' he said. 'Help us finish loading up.'

I went back to the girl and put the blanket around her shoulder. Her face was blank as she hugged her knees to her chest. Then I helped Flea load Marina's body into the ambulance. Had she been wearing a ring – the plain gold one she often wore so no one would question her having a child? Her fingers were bare and bloated now. I pretended that her blown-apart limbs were just waxworks in a museum. That the explosions in the distance were fireworks set off for Bonfire Night. I went about my work as an actor in a pantomime. One of those Greek tragedies where everyone goes crazy and ends up killing each other.

When the ambulance was loaded, Flea stood ready to slam the door. 'You want a ride back to base, Badger?'

'No,' I said. 'I've got to get the girl to safety.'

'Take her to Sadie's,' Flea said. 'She loves taking in strays. Cats usually. But in this case, she might make an exception.'

I nodded. As much as I wished there was another option, it would have to do for tonight. My bedsit was no place for a little girl, and I knew she should have a woman to comfort her. Flea's landlady – a big, mumsy Northerner – would do.

Flea got into the ambulance, his eyes lingering again on the locket around the girl's neck. As they sped off leaving only me and her, I felt her eyes burning question marks into my skin: What will become of me? Will you leave me too? Why did you save me when there's nothing left?

19

I manage to prop Mrs Fairchild on the sofa by the fireplace and revive her with a cup of tea. I ask Edith to sit with her, out of fear that seeing me might cause a relapse. When I catch up with the tour group, a few people whisper and point, and though I try to salvage my dignity, it's a lost cause. I lead the group through the house as quickly as possible. When the last stragglers are dispatched into the gift shop, I go back to the dining room, but Mrs Fairchild is gone. 'She went to her room,' Edith tells me. 'I said that one of us would check on her after lunch.'

'Thanks,' I say.

Edith and I return to the gift shop and help out Katie, the girl minding the till, with the customers. When the tour bus finally leaves, I go to look in on Mrs Fairchild, but her door is shut and there's no answer when I knock. Disappointed, I go outside to the garden and find a quiet bench under the grape arbour. I ring Karen and tell her what happened. 'The song sparked a memory in her,' I say. 'She started singing in a foreign language.'

'Weird,' Karen says. 'What language was it?'

'I don't know. Polish? Russian? I'm afraid to ask. She's still in shock.'

'Well, I guess if you can't ask her, you'll need to go back to Plan B.'

'Plan B?'

'You have to go and ask you-know-who,' she says. 'And make sure to keep me posted.'

You-know-who. As much as I hate to admit it, Karen's right.

* * *

First thing the next day, I go over to the house to check on Mrs Fairchild. Edith tells me that she has a migraine and doesn't want to see anyone, which I take to mean she doesn't want to see *me*. I arrange for the staff to check on her periodically, then catch the train to London.

I retrace my steps from last time, wending my way through the narrow streets to the strange little workshop behind the auctioneers. Heath-Churchley or no, I need to see the Clockmaker.

I arrive at five minutes past the hour, so this time there's no fanfare of chimes to herald my entrance, just a background ticking like a distant hive of bees. It's strangely comforting to find the man I've come to see alone in his workshop just the same as before.

Instead of announcing myself, I stand at the door watching him work. Over his strange light-blue eyes, he has on a pair of industrial goggles; his tall frame is stooped over as he heats a piece of metal with a blowtorch. When the metal glows red, he shapes it with a tiny instrument, then quenches the metal in a vat. The liquid makes a sizzling sound and steam rises up. It's such an odd trade for a posh public schoolboy, but watching him work with precision and focus, he's obviously in his element. Dad always used to say that 'the apple never falls far from the tree', but to me he seems different from the other members of his family I've had the misfortune to meet.

He removes the metal from the bath and drops it into another vat. He turns a knob to heat the liquid and puts down his tongs. Then he turns in my direction, like he's known all along that I've been watching.

'Hi, Alex.' He removes his goggles and pushes his dark hair off his face. 'I was hoping you'd come back.'

'Hi.' I'm unexpectedly pleased that he's remembered my name. 'I'm sorry I ran out last time. It's just—'

'You discovered my dubious family connections,' he says with a smile. 'Before I could even introduce myself properly. I'm Chris, or' – he straightens up with exaggerated stiffness – 'Christopher, if you ask my father.'

'Unfortunately, your father is not my greatest fan.' I outline the circumstances under which we had the misfortune to meet. I tell him exactly what his father called me, and about his threat to have me 'out on my ear'. Raw emotion wells up – I shouldn't care what some buffoon said to me in a fit of anger, but my peasant skin isn't as thick as I like to think. All the while I'm speaking, he continues to work, his face creasing deeper and deeper into a frown.

'But you haven't been sacked, right?'

'No. Luckily my boss, Catherine Fairchild, is too sensible to be bullied.'

'OK, that's good.' To my surprise, he starts to chuckle. 'Poor you. I know it isn't funny, but that's the way it is with my father – you either have to laugh or cry.'

'I wanted to tell him where to go.'

'You should have!'

'I couldn't though. Throughout the whole debacle, I was only doing my job. I thought I was helping out by getting the substitute vicar.' I shake my head. 'Little did I know.'

'What a cock-up all around, no pun intended. I can just picture Cee-Cee's face. Getting her comeuppance can't have been pleasant.'

'What do you mean?'

'The wedding was supposed to have happened last year. Until Cee-Cee hooked up with someone on her hen night. They cancelled a week before, rather than on the day. But the result was the same.'

'Another cock-up.' I give a little laugh.

'I'm afraid so. My baby half-sister isn't exactly a nun. What *must* you think of us?'

I wave a hand. 'Well, if your family is that "old and proud", I suppose you can do what you like. But I didn't know she was your *half*-sister.'

'Same father, different mother,' he clarifies. 'My mum was from another stodgy old family – the Stanleys. They were connected with the Heath-Churchleys through the auction house. Cee-Cee's mum was Dad's bit on the side. Dad and Mum divorced and he married Cee-Cee's mum. My mum's remarried too. She lives in the south of France.'

'Complicated,' I say. 'But come to think of it, the mother of the bride did mention a stepson. Were you supposed to be at the wedding?'

'Yes,' he says. 'Cee-Cee and I aren't close, but we're still family. I got a phone call saying that the wedding was off just as I was about to leave London.'

'Well, at least it wasn't a wasted trip.'

He tidies up the tools on his desk, still looking amused. 'Yes, but now we've all got to go even further afield. Since you've seen so much of my family's dirty laundry, Alex, you might be interested to know that the wedding's back on.'

'What? You're kidding.'

He grins. 'Now that the wild oats are well and truly sown, they can get down to the business of being Mr and Mrs Churchley-Thursley. Try saying that five times fast.'

I laugh. 'It's good to hear they worked things out, I guess.'

'Third time's a charm, hopefully. Though Dad isn't going to spring for a venue like yours again. It's a registry office and reception at the family pile in Scotland.'

'Such a shame.' I pull a face in mock sympathy.

'I suppose it is. Though I don't go in for those things anyway.' He indicates around him. 'As you can guess, I'm a bit of a black sheep.' He looks a little pleased. I can't quite figure him out, but in spite of everything, he makes me feel at ease. 'But enough about sordid family details. I don't suppose you came all the way here to talk about Cee-Cee's wedding. At least, I hope not.'

If Tim had said the same thing, I'd have taken it as flirtatious innuendo. But from Chris, I interpret it for what it is – interest in the locket.

'I brought this again.' I take the jewelled bird out of its bag and lay it on his worktable under the light. 'I need to find out more. Mrs Fairchild told me it was just a "trinket". A "child's toy". She can't – or won't – tell me much else.'

He picks up the locket and turns it over in his fingers, once again looking almost mesmerised by the glittering jewels, the enamel and the filigree work. He flips the locket open with his thumb. The jewelled bird sings its song once through, and he closes it. 'A child's toy,' he muses. 'Maybe.'

My spirits droop. 'If that's all it is, then I don't want to waste your time...'

'Ah.' He glances at me, his eyes sparkling. 'But the question is, who was the child?'

'What do you mean?'

He sets the locket back on the table and moves over to his desk, an antique table at the edge of the room covered with towers of books and papers.

'Have you heard of the House of Fabergé?' He takes a book from the top of the stack. It's bookmarked in several places with yellow stickies.

'As in the Russian Easter eggs?'

'That's the one.' He sets the book in front of me. It's hardbound with a blue and gold jewelled egg on the cover. 'They were most famous for eggs. But really the eggs were just the tip of the iceberg.' He flips the book open to the first sticky. There's a picture of a splendid gold and enamel clock. 'They did jewellery, of course, but also clocks and music boxes. Read the description.'

He points to the text under the photo and I read the passage aloud:

'The Charlottenburg Clock featured an intricate gold and enamel dial with tiny gold-leaf edged scales that fanned out into a sunburst. Inside, the brass clockworks were elaborately chased and could be seen upon opening the clock face. However, its most notable feature was its internal glockenspiel works, which featured a menagerie of clockwork animals and birds.'

Birds! I flip through the next few pages. 'Is there a picture?'

'Sadly not. Many of Fabergé's most priceless pieces were lost in the Russian Revolution and the World Wars.' He sighs. 'The Charlottenburg Clock was one of the casualties, I'm afraid.'

'That is sad,' I say. 'But this description' – I point to the passage – 'sounds very promising. Do you think this bird could have been made by the House of Fabergé?' My heart thumps harder against my ribs.

'Maybe.' His voice is measured, but his eyes have a cool fire in them. He's excited too.

I turn to the next tabbed page. There's no photo, but a block of text has been bracketed in the margin. I skim the passage – it's all about notable forgeries and fakes of everything from Fabergé Easter eggs to jewels that belonged to the Romanovs.

'Oh,' I say, deflating. 'You think it's a fake, then?'

'No, that's not it.' He flips through the book and his fingers accidently brush mine. 'It's just that we can't be certain, can we? Not without examining it thoroughly. We'd be looking for a mark, if there is one, and then we'd also need to establish its provenance.'

'How would we do that?'

He picks up the locket again and holds it close to his face, examining the enamel work and tiny jewelled forget-me-nots on the case. 'It's important to be able to trace the "story" of the piece. Who owned it, where it came from, how it ended up where it did.'

I exhale dejectedly. 'That could be a problem. I'm not sure Mrs Fairchild knows very much. It might have belonged to her mother, but then Frank Bolton reunited her with it in an orphanage.'

'Frank Bolton?'

'He was the owner of Mallow Court. He made his money in women's knickers after the war. He adopted Catherine after she was orphaned in the Blitz.' He's clearly eager for any information I might have, and vice versa. But a seed of guilt has sprouted in my chest. Mrs Fairchild is in a fragile state, and it doesn't seem right that I share her confidences without her permission. 'That's really all I know,' I say.

'The lack of provenance complicates matters. But if you like, I could examine the locket. Its internal workings are due a good cleaning and oiling anyway. What I did before was just a start. If I find a mark, then you can take it from there.'

'And if there's no mark?'

'It's still a fine piece of jewellery.'

'OK,' I say, 'that sounds reasonable. So does that mean I have to, umm... leave it with you?'

'I assure you that I'm a consummate professional.' He makes his voice sound extra-posh. 'And I can give you a receipt for it that carries the weighty reputation of the Churchley and Sons name on the letterhead.'

'Well in that case,' I say with a grin, 'OK.'

'Great. Now, if only I can find it.'

While he shuffles papers around on his desk looking for the letterhead, I have a nose around the workshop. The range of flotsam and jetsam extends well beyond just clocks. There are two RCA vinyl record turntables, a 1940s radio, and a reel-to-reel film projector like we had at primary school. 'What are all these things?' I ask. 'Are you a collector?'

'Not really,' he says. 'They're broken bits I've picked up here and there. I've fixed most of them, but haven't got round to selling them.' He smiles wryly, giving me the distinct impression that he probably never will get around to it. 'The truth is, I like to take things apart and put them back together. I can just about manage the electronics they made up to about the late eighties. After that, it's more about computers than mechanics. Not my thing, I'm afraid.'

I laugh, realising that I haven't spotted a laptop or even a clunky old desktop computer. There's something unprepossessing – and quite charming – about that fact.

'Ah, here it is, we're in luck.' He pulls out an engraved folder of rich cream letterhead with 'Churchley & Sons' embossed in black writing. He scribbles something on the paper, tears the sheet off, and hands it to me.

Without looking at it, I fold it and shove it in my bag. 'Thanks,' I say, 'and will you ring me when—'

We both jump as the telephone on his desk – circa 1980s with a dial and twisty cord – rings loudly. Chris looks at me apologetically.

'Go ahead,' I say.

He goes over and answers the phone. I pretend to look around, but I keep my eyes and ears on him as he speaks to someone called Sidney.

'Oh, that's not good.' He holds the receiver away from his ear a fraction. 'No, sorry.'

The voice on the other end rises in pitch. It's clearly a woman.

'I'll need to check,' he says, hesitating.

More animated talk on the other end.

'OK, great. I'll leave here in about an hour. I should make the six o'clock ferry, depending on traffic.'

I resist the urge to cover my ears or walk out of the room. The phone call has broken the spell of this odd little world.

With a sigh, he hangs up the phone.

'I should let you get on.' I pick up my handbag, trying not to look at him or the locket I'm leaving behind in his care.

'Sorry about that,' he says. 'I've got a family thing at a friend's place on the Isle of Wight. She's worried about my dad and stepmum arriving before me, so I need to leave soon.'

'Fine. You go. Um...' I point to the locket. 'Do you want me to bring it back another time?'

He looks wistfully at the silver lozenge. 'I'll put it in the safe,' he says. 'It will save you another trip.'

A bitter and unwelcome tang of disappointment floods my mouth. A woman is removing this man from his clocks to have a cosy little 'family thing' on the Isle of Wight. Undoubtedly in a huge Victorian retreat with a Grecian-shaped swimming pool and its own private ballroom. And the jewelled bird, which had so fascinated him just minutes ago, will have to spend a night or two in the safe. And I... I will return to Mallow Court, curl up on my sofa with a glass of wine and a book, like I've done so many times before – like I've been *happy* doing so many times before.

'Fine, whatever.' I wave my hand dismissively.

He pushes his dark hair back, seemingly confused by my brusqueness. 'I'll call you as soon as I have some results. To be honest, I'd rather be here working on it.'

'I'm sure.' I shrug.

The clocks begin to chime in unison as I turn to leave. The cacophony hurts my ears, and just like last time, I can't wait to be gone.

20

As I walk to the Tube station, I keep thinking about 'Sidney-from-the-Isle-of-Wight'. I could look her up in *Country Life*. There's probably a lovely soft-focus full-page advert of an 'eligible young lady'. Or maybe a 'taken' one. Perhaps there's another Heath-Churchley wedding in the offing – maybe I should have tried to sell Mallow Court as a venue. The thought makes me a little nauseous.

On the Tube, I stare at the people around me, annoyed with myself. I have a perverse image of Christopher Heath-Churchley going up the walk to the pebble-dashed semi in Abbots Langley. He'd be wearing jeans and a band T-shirt, stretching out his long legs as he sits in the yoga studio while Dad pours him a pot of green tea and Mum fusses over bringing him a plate of sausages cooked with kale. He and Dad would probably talk each other's ears off. Until Dad learned of his pedigree. Then it would be 'off with his head'. So the fact that it will never happen is just as well.

I then imagine Tim Edwards in the same situation. A champion of widows, orphans, and the underdog. Right up Dad's street. Somehow, though, I can't see him sitting quite so easily in the yoga studio – it must be that each time I've seen him, he's been wearing a suit. There's something a bit too polished, almost too perfect about him. Still, it could happen, I think.

The train home is delayed, so I get a coffee and a bun at the station. As I'm taking out my purse to pay, I find the receipt from Churchley & Sons that I'd stuck in my bag. I unfold it while I'm waiting. The writing is practically illegible, but I make out the words: *Jewelled bird mechanical locket, possibly Russian, late 19th century.*

Excitement grips me. Could the locket really be a Fabergé? Part of me wishes that I'd shared with Chris everything I know. I could have told him about Mrs Fairchild singing a song in a foreign language, almost like she was in a trance. Could the language be Russian? Possibly. But surely, that must be a coincidence.

By the time I arrive back at Mallow Court, the house is closed for the day and the staff have all left except for Edith. She tells me that Mrs Fairchild has been eating and drinking normally but has kept mainly to her room. That troubles me, as Mrs Fairchild rarely ever spends time in her room. When Edith is gone, I go up to see her. The bedroom door is shut, and I can just make out the sound of her heavy, even breathing. Disappointed, I decide not to wake her and return to my flat.

The red light on the message machine is flashing. Hope soars in my chest. Has the Clockmaker discovered something else? But of course not. He's off with Sidney, and probably on the train to Southampton right now. Except (silly me) of course he wouldn't take the train. Instead, he'll be driving down the M3 to the ferry in some fancy sports car – a Porsche, maybe – with the top down and the radio blasting Pink Floyd. My blood simmers with indignation. For all his ripped jeans and band shirts, Chris Heath-Churchley is a fraud.

The message turns out to be from Tim. His deep voice vibrates a chord deep in my abdomen and I instantly feel a little bit better – quite a lot better, actually.

'Hi, Alex,' he says, 'I hope you're well. Would you like to have dinner on Friday? Give me a ring when you can.' The message clicks off.

'Friday will be just fine,' I say aloud. Funny how keen I suddenly am to 'get out more'.

I decide to ring Tim back but it goes to voicemail. I leave a message saying yes to dinner, though I can hear Karen's voice in my head haranguing me for not playing harder to get. But the 'rules' don't interest me. Xavier and I never bothered with anything like rules. A memory rises to the surface: Xavier's silky voice calling me his *amo*, running his fingers over my naked thigh as we made love *al aire libre*. But the memory brings the pain and anger flooding back. Unknown to me, while we were engaged in extracurricular activities, Xavier's wife was at home in Argentina, getting the nursery ready for their firstborn child. Just as well that I'm shot of him.

I bring my mind back to Tim. Admittedly, things feel a bit less *organic* than they did with Xavier. But maybe that's not a bad thing.

Tim rings back while I'm still stewing in my juices, and we make plans for Friday. He offers to come up to Mallow Court, but I volunteer to come to London instead. Let him deal with the awkwardness of putting me on a train – or not – at the end of the evening. At least he doesn't mention me meeting his gran again.

For the rest of the evening, I flip aimlessly through the channels on the television, oddly unable to enjoy having a night in by myself. When I finally go to bed, my dreams are marred by chocolate eyes, ticking clocks, and the key to something that is just out of reach.

21

13 NOVEMBER 1940 – 12.30 A.M.

'Come on, let's get you inside. It's not far.'

The girl got to her feet and staggered a few steps. I worried that I might have to carry her the whole way. Robbie came back, his camera slung over his shoulder.

'You need help?' he asked. 'A lift somewhere?'

'Nah,' I said. 'I'm taking her to a mate's house. His landlady will look after her. It's just down the road.'

Nodding, he tugged the strap on his camera. 'Got some good footage tonight. Of you and your partners: our brave British ambulance crew.'

Something in the way he said it made my hackles rise. 'Why bother?' I snapped. 'Who wants to see pictures of this shit?'

'Someday, someone might.' He walked off into the night.

The cold seared my skin as we walked together without speaking, her tiny hand in mine. I recalled what I saw – Flea, bending over the body, putting something in his pocket. I feel certain that he wasn't just checking her pulse. I'd heard rumours of looting: kids stealing coins from the gas meters, thieves lifting military medals and anything else they could get their hands on. It was despicable. As if *we weren't all suffering enough. But I've known Flea since childhood – he's an upstanding member of the ambulance crew – a public servant. I'd trust him with my life. Out here in the horror and the chaos, the mind can play tricks on you. I must have misinterpreted what I saw.*

The snow had stopped completely by the time we reached the dark terrace of workmen's cottages. In the kitchen window I could make out a tiny crack of light visible under the black-out curtains. I must remind Sadie to tape it up or else she'll get a visit from the constable. But I was relieved to see the light. Good old Sadie – she could always be counted on for a late-night supper of beans on toast and the kettle still warm. The girl would be safe here.

'This is the place,' I said. 'Let's go inside and have a hot drink and something to eat.'

It was as if she didn't hear me. Her eyes were huge and glassy – like she was still back at the top of Larkspur Gardens, playing with a jewelled locket and catching snowflakes on her tongue.

As I untangled her hand from mine and adjusted the blanket on her shoulders, I firmly tucked the pendant on its silver chain into the neck of her dress. 'Your mother would have wanted you to keep it safe,' I said. 'Best keep it out of sight.'

22

Still half asleep the next morning, I crawl out from under the duvet and automatically reach for the jewelled locket, thinking it's on my nightstand. I have a moment of panic when I discover it isn't there. But of course I left it with Chris, which leads me to unpleasant thoughts of Daddy Heath-Churchley, Cee-Cee, and Sidney-from-the-Isle-of-Wight. But as the sun floods through the skylight, the clouds drift from my brain. What does any of that matter when the locket might turn out to be a Fabergé?

When I've showered and dressed, I go to check on Mrs Fairchild before the day's visitors arrive. The kitchen garden is awash with summer colour: sweet peas, calendulas, dahlia, peonies. There's also sound everywhere: pigeons cooing from the rafters, bees buzzing in the lavender, birds singing, the crunch of gravel under my feet. On the other side of the hedge I hear the sound of thwack, thwack, thwack and catch a glimpse of Mrs Fairchild's wide brimmed hat. I'm relieved to see that she's up and about and going about her gardening as usual.

'Good morning,' I call out loudly.

The thwacking sound stops, and just for an instant, everything seems still. Then, Mrs Fairchild waves her shears at me from behind a topiary peacock.

'Hello,' she calls out. 'Lovely morning. I'm just off to the garden centre to get some more aphid spray.' She gestures around her at the beds of old roses that frame the edges of the garden. 'These roses aren't thanking me for taking a day off sick.'

I stand in the gateway under the clematis arch. 'Are you feeling better, Mrs Fairchild? I was really worried.'

She sits down on an iron bench and pats the seat next to her. 'I'm fine, Alex. Really.'

'Good.' I sit next to her, enjoying the sun on my face. But Mrs Fairchild's cheeks seem very pale.

'I know it may not be the best time,' I say, 'but there are some things I've been wondering about. Some questions that I wanted to ask you. When you're up to it, I mean.'

'Go on then,' she says, keeping a stiff upper lip – literally. 'You deserve to know more. Ask your questions. Though, you may not like the answers.'

'Maybe not. But I feel responsible for what happened. When I showed you the locket, you seemed... very upset. You obviously recognised the tune that the music box played and started singing in a foreign language. Then, you fainted.'

'Did I?' She flicks at the dirt under her nails.

'What was the language? Was it Russian?'

She looks down at her fingers; at the edging of the lawn; at the wisps of cloud in the sky. Everywhere but at me. 'Yes. It was.'

'You said a word too – *Mamochka*. Does that mean mother? Was your mother Russian?'

'I suppose she was. Though I never really thought of her as my mother.' She frowns. 'Frank Bolton got married shortly after the war ended. His wife, Mabel, was my mum, though she didn't give birth to me.'

'I know the feeling.'

Mrs Fairchild fidgets uncomfortably on the bench.

'Can you tell me everything you remember about your birth mother?' I say. 'It might help me find out more about the locket.'

'I don't remember much. I was very young when she died in the bombings. Four, maybe. Or five.'

'What was she like?'

'I remember a kitchen,' she says, staring into the middle distance. 'The wallpaper was yellow with stripes. Green stripes. She was standing at the stove. I tiptoed in behind her. She'd left the bird on the table. I was so excited because she'd never let me touch it, or any of her special things that she kept under her bed. The bird was fragile and precious – I don't remember her telling me that, but I knew it. The chain clanked on the table as I picked it up. She jolted at the noise, and turned and screamed. The hot water in the pan flew towards me.'

'How awful.'

'She said something – I don't know the words now, but back then I understood. She thought that the bad people had found her.'

'Who were they?'

'I don't know.' She inclines her head.

'What happened next?'

'I screamed, and she realised it was me. She dipped my burned arm into a tub of cold water so that it wouldn't scar. She was scolding me, and fussing over me, and crying all at the same time. She wrapped a strip of tea towel around my hand, here.' She traces a blue vein in her wrist. 'But I was still scared. Because I loved her. She was' – she closes her eyes, searching deep in her mind for the word – 'Mamochka.'

I reach out and take her hand. Her eyes remain closed, but she doesn't pull away.

'Mamochka was always afraid,' she continues. 'That much I remember very clearly. Always looking over her shoulder and jumping at shadows. We lived in a basement. Next to the yellow kitchen. She didn't like to leave. Sometimes she had to go out to the shops, or up to the street for deliveries. She hated that.'

'But you don't know why she was afraid?'

'No, I don't.' Her eyes open suddenly and she withdraws her hand. 'As I said, I was very young. I remember the sirens – to me they sounded like the screech of a giant, flying dragon. We had to huddle in the dark. In the wine cellar or under the kitchen table. I couldn't look at my books or play with my doll. I was supposed to go to sleep, but how could I? All that racket above us outside. The house shaking and shuddering. Night after night. I wanted to make Mamochka proud by being brave, but really, I was scared.'

'I'm so sorry.' The words sound hollow and impotent. 'It must have been such a terrible time – terrible in a way that people of my generation can't even imagine.'

'Yes, that's true.'

'And what about the locket? Where did your mother get it?'

'I don't know.' She looks momentarily confused. 'It was a pretty, shiny thing. She had a wooden box of pretty things under her bed that I wasn't supposed to touch. But I loved the bird best. I wanted to play with it, but she wouldn't let me. She'd slap my hand if I tried. Later, not long before she died, the tune stopped playing. She told me it was broken and that I should forget about it.'

'Did you ever see a gold key?' I say, hoping to encourage her.

'No, I don't think so. Unless the box under her bed had a key? I don't remember much of anything. Just impressions. The only thing that's real to me from that time is the bird and Mamochka singing. I didn't remember it. Not until you opened the locket and the bird sang that song.' She begins to hum, but doesn't sing the foreign words. 'That's when it all started to come back: the yellow kitchen, the screeching dragon, the sting of the hot water. I guess I blocked it out, the way people do.'

'Yes. That's common, I think.'

She sighs again. 'There was another kitchen,' she says. 'With a big woman who talked funny. She had a lot of cats. I don't know who she was, to be honest. All I remember is that her kitchen was very brown. The wallpaper, the furniture, the floor. And there was a clock that looked like Mamochka's box. I remember that the bread tasted like sawdust and the beans were very runny. I didn't like them. But I didn't want to say.'

'And Mamochka wasn't there?'

'She was dead.' She wipes a tear from her eye. 'When I was in the brown kitchen, Mamochka was dead.'

I remain silent, hoping she'll tell me more.

'I sat at the table in the brown kitchen and cried. I'd lost it, you see. I'd lost the bird.' She stares at the wall. 'I know I had it. There in the snow, I had it. But then, it was gone.'

'Did someone take it?'

She ignores my question. 'Mamochka told me to keep it safe. With her last breath, she wanted me to keep the bird safe. I suppose...' She presses a hand to her temple like the memory hurts. 'It was so long ago.'

'It's OK,' I say gently.

'The big woman contacted two other people – a man and a woman. They took me away in a big black car to the orphanage. It was so cold, and I missed those runny beans on toast.' She shudders. 'And the bird. Most of all, I missed the bird.'

When she finally looks up, her eyes are bloodshot and

haunted. Sixty years later, and the memories are still raw. And maybe for someone else, too? Could that explain why someone is haunting her with the past? Though nothing in her story gives me even the slightest clue as to what she could be blamed for.

'What happened next?' I urge.

'It was horrible there,' she says. 'There were so many of us. We slept in tiny camp beds, and it was freezing. There was no coal, and no heat; and the food, well, you couldn't really call it food. I've no idea how long I was there. Days? Weeks, maybe? And then miraculously' – her face blooms – '*he* was there. Frank Bolton. Someone pushed me down on the playground outside. I skinned my knee and I was crying. I ran to the matron's office. A man was there. He had light hair and a nice smile. He looked jolly, like Father Christmas. He winked at me and held his hands behind his back. "Pick one," he said. So I did.' She giggles like a girl. 'The first hand was empty. I felt so sad. But then, he told me to try again. I picked the other hand. And just like that, he held out the bird.'

'But how did he get it?'

'He said, "This belongs to you, right?" He winked again. I was crying and laughing, all at the same time. He knelt down and took me in his arms. He smelled like chicory and carbolic soap. So... safe.' She smiles angelically. 'He put the bird around my neck and said that everything would be all right. That I'd never have to worry about anything again. And it was true. He gave me a good life – a happy life.'

'I'm so glad.'

Wiping her eyes, she stands up and walks towards the tall wrought-iron gate. I can see how upset she is, and I hate that I'm making things worse with my questions. But she was the one

The House of Hidden Secrets

who set me on the trail of the jewelled bird. She's the reason I'm doing this.

'Why you?' I say.

She stops walking. 'What's that?'

'I'm sure you were an adorable five-year-old,' I say, 'but there were thousands of orphaned children. And Frank Bolton had a wife and, later on, two sons. It wasn't as if he couldn't have children of his own. Why did he adopt you?'

She stands absolutely still, staring straight ahead at her exit route. Slowly, she turns to face me. 'Maybe the question *you* need to ask is: why you? Why would I put you, Alex Hart, manager of Mallow Court, on to the trail of the jewelled bird?'

She's caught me off guard. 'I don't know.'

'Look at me, Alex.' Her blue eyes are wide and earnest. 'Look very hard. I promised that I wouldn't tell you directly, but now...' A fresh line of tears snakes down her cheek. 'It will be painful to hear, but you deserve to know.'

I stare at the old woman – my employer, but also my friend – standing in her beloved garden. Her happiest place. The last three years rewind themselves in my head. From the day my advisor told me about the manager position to our first meeting, to all the conversations we've had. The laughs we've shared, the problems big and small that we've tackled together – the daily intertwining of our lives here at Mallow Court. The breath leaves my chest like I've been flattened by a very large bus. Too late, I raise my hands in crash position, as if to somehow ward off the shock.

'You're my... my...'

'Yes, Alex. I'm your grandmother.'

23

My mouth makes a wide 'O' but no sound comes out.

'It's true.' She takes a tentative step towards me, dabbing her eyes with a tissue. 'I'm the mother of your real mother, Robin. I wanted to tell you so many times before. But I couldn't. So I decided to give you the bird – the only thing I have left of *my* mother. I knew you'd ask questions and want to discover the truth about our family. Because family is so important. I never really understood that until I lost my Robin.'

She reaches out her hand. I take it, feeling the warmth as her blood courses through her veins. *My blood.*

'Tell me,' I whisper hoarsely.

She stares up at the passing clouds, marshalling her strength. 'Robin was a free spirit,' she says. 'Practically from the minute she was born. She was a sickly baby, and I worried about her. She resented that, and we never saw eye to eye on much of anything.' She sighs. 'Robin was a modern girl, whereas I was very traditional. I mean' – she lets go of my hand and gestures around her – 'we lived here.'

I stagger over to the bench and collapse onto it, clutching the arm for dear life.

'When Robin turned seventeen, she couldn't wait to leave home. I gritted my teeth and let her enrol on an art course in London. I thought that would be enough, but it was just the tip of the iceberg. She fell in with a "bad crowd" – at least, that's what George and I thought of them. It was like the sixties all over again, but without the innocence. They had the long beads and flowing hair, and the drugs too. But they were anti this and anti that. Protesting, travelling around. She certainly wasn't studying art.'

I stare at a bee buzzing in white roses, trying to take in what she's saying.

'Next thing I knew, the postmarks on her letters came from America. She'd started going by the name "Rainbow" and become a groupie following after some band – the Grateful Dead. She told me not to contact her, and that she and her friends were founding a commune. They wanted to live a pure life in a peaceful, classless society. They were going to sever all contact with "warmongers" in the outside world.' She shakes her head. 'My first instinct was to get on a plane and go find her, but George persuaded me not to. He thought I was too protective – that we needed to let her "sow her wild oats" and whatnot.' She sighs. 'There was a part of me that hated him for that.'

'She... died?'

'Yes.' She bows her head. 'She died because she didn't have proper medical attention when giving birth. She had an internal haemorrhage. As a child, she used to get tired and bruise easily. But I had no idea that having a baby would... you know...'

'I killed her.'

The words escape my mouth and echo around the hidden

garden, screaming into the cracks in the paving stones, poisoning the air, the trees, the flowers, every molecule of beauty around me. 'I killed my mum.'

'No, dearest Alex.' Mrs Fairchild sits down at the other end of the bench, giving me space. 'It was a dreadful mistake made by others – by Robin, by my husband, by me.' She shudders. 'She should have been in hospital, not that horrible... place. But hindsight is twenty-twenty.'

I put my head in my hands.

'And your dad feels it most keenly of all.'

'My dad?' Anger boils up inside me. 'So he *has* known the whole time.'

She lays a hand on my shoulders. 'Please, Alex. I don't want to drive a wedge between you and him. Not now of all times when the whole family has to stick together.'

'So he's the reason I wasn't told?'

'He made it clear that it was his place to tell you, or not. I respected that. But maybe we were all wrong, I don't know.'

'*Maybe* you were wrong?' I stand up, my hand shaking with the urge to rip out a rose bush by the roots and dash it onto the path. I settle for kicking the stone wall behind me. Hard. The sting in my toe feels good. 'How do you think I've felt all these years, not knowing? When the answer was right in front of me all along.'

'He and Carol were doing what they thought was best for you.' Her voice holds a pleading note. 'He didn't want you to blame yourself for her death. He also wanted to make sure you had a loving family – him and Carol, plus all their aunts, uncles and cousins. You didn't need the burden of being different.'

'It sounds like his misguided mumbo-jumbo.' Every vein and artery in my body is sizzling with anger – at Dad. At the lies I've been told and the truth that's been withheld until now. I close my eyes and try to picture a calm, peaceful place. But the first thing that comes to mind is a family trip to the seaside when I was eight, building a sandcastle with Mum while Dad did tai-chi about twenty feet away. I open my eyes. The woman in front of me looks suddenly much older than I've ever seen her before. Good old sunny, friendly Mrs Fairchild. A woman I'm proud to know and proud to be... working for.

'And this job? Was that a sham too? It wasn't a manager that you wanted. It was me.'

'Is that so wrong?' Her face is stricken. 'I was heartbroken when I lost my daughter, and I never wanted to lose you. But at the time, you dad convinced me to stay out of your life. I agreed and he kept me informed about you. We spoke on the phone, and occasionally he sent me photos. You have Robin's eyes.' She gulps. 'And later, when you were at Oxford, I was *so* proud. When I learned you were having problems with your young man, I worried that you'd go off to Argentina. And who knows what would have happened.'

'I wouldn't have done that.'

'I needed a manager for the estate.' She spreads her hands. 'All I did was make sure my letter ended up on the right desk at your university department.'

'So why now?' I say. 'Why keep silent for so long and then spill the beans?'

'Your dad called me and said you'd been asking questions. It was the same day I received the second diary entry. And then, there was the "uninvited guest". I don't know what it all means, but there's trouble brewing – I can feel it. I told your dad that enough was enough. You have a right to know the truth. And as soon as the words were out of my mouth, I knew I should have done it years ago.'

I slump back on the bench, my heart ripping in two. All the

questions. All the lies. And yet, does it matter? This woman next to me is my blood relative. My grandmother. She's told me the truth. Finally, belatedly. She's given me that, and so much more along the way.

I lean over and put my arms around her. She moves closer, not speaking. I appreciate the silence. There are too many chattering ghosts, too many screaming questions. Too many accusations, recriminations, and confessions. And all the while, the bees fly from flower to flower, a bird pecks at the cracks in the path, leaves rustle as a squirrel jumps from a tree and runs along the top of the wall. Life, in other words, goes on.

Mrs Fairchild rests her head against mine. A common pulse beats, cementing the connection between us. Her blood is in my veins, my blood in hers. Right now, for this one unexpected moment, nothing else matters.

24

She leaves me there – we both know I need some time alone. A whirlpool of emotions threatens to pull me under. There's joy in finding a connection with a person I already have strong feelings for, and sorrow at what Mrs Fairchild – my grandmother – has suffered over the years hiding her pain behind a sunny smile. And then there's the revelations I've received. All this time, I'd thought I would gain something by learning the truth, but instead, I feel like I've lost myself. The half-truths make it worse: the little titbits of information I've been drip-fed over the years – the fact that 'Rainbow' was my dad's new age soulmate, the fact that they couldn't be bothered with things as patriarchal as surnames, and the fact that my mother died 'shortly after my birth'. I can only surmise that I was told these things to sate my curiosity just enough to stop me asking more questions.

It's infuriating and wrong – and there's one person I can blame.

I jump in my car and drive as fast as I dare to Abbots Langley and the pebble-dashed semi that in another lifetime I called home.

Unfortunately, I arrive at a bad time. I pull into the road and have to park five houses away because all the nearer spaces are taken. Two women in full yoga regalia are rushing round the side of the house carrying rolled up mats. It's Dad's late afternoon Hatha class. And I'm just in time.

I get out of the car and stalk around the side of the house. As I approach the 'spiritual garden' at the back, I can hear the calming music, pan pipes and sitars, that Dad plays for the warm-up, and smell the sandalwood incense. It makes me want to throw up.

My boots crunch through the pebbles of the meandering path. I cross the little bridge with the koi fish underneath and arrive at the entrance of the outdoor pagoda. Underneath the flat, spreading roof, at least twenty people – mostly women, but also a few men – are lying on their mats doing belly breathing. At the front of the area on a small dais, Dad is lying on his mat. 'Breathe in,' he's saying. 'Bring the air from your mouth all the way down to the centre of your abdomen.'

I breathe in deeply. The extra oxygen fuels the anger inside me like bellows to a fire.

'Breathe out. Slowly, shhhhh.'

I exhale sharply, clenching my fists at my side.

'Let the spirit flow through you.'

I purse my lips. No one notices as I walk over to where the CD player is plugged in. The sitar makes a flowing riff, and a flute takes over the melody.

'Focus on your belly breathing. The tension is leaving your body.'

'No it bloody well isn't!' I jerk the cord out of the wall.

There's a collective gasp as all heads turn towards me and a few people scooch up onto their elbows. Instead of sitars, the sound of the nearby motorway invades the spiritual garden.

Dad moves into a lotus position, lacing his hands. We stare at each other for a few seconds. He knows that I know...

'Do we have to do this now, Alexandra?'

'I'm afraid so.' I put my hands on my hips. 'I'm happy to go into the house if you want. I wouldn't want your "followers" to learn that you're a big fraud.'

'OK.' Dad drops the 'spiritual voice'. 'Shania' – his eyebrows raise as he looks to a lithesome woman in the middle of the group – 'would you mind taking the class?'

'No problem,' the woman says. But by now, a few people are already sitting up and whispering together.

Dad gets to his feet. 'Shall we go for a walk in the garden? I always find it calming.'

'Whatever.' I follow him along the path.

We walk a short distance and he pauses on the footbridge. 'The bamboo is doing well, isn't it?' he says. 'Do you remember when we planted it together?'

'I do. It was ten years ago during the Easter holidays. Add that to another eighteen years, and you'll get my whole life. Which equals the amount of time you've been lying to me.' My breath is angry and shallow. 'All that time, Dad. You lied to me about my birth mother and my real grandmother – whom you knew about all along.'

He leans over the railing and looks down at the colourful koi fish. He's still doing his deep belly breathing, damn him.

I trot out the trump card. 'I mean, is that what Buddha would have done?'

From behind me, a sentence drifts into my ear: '...Didn't know she was adopted.' I hadn't realised that I'd been speaking quite so loud. And while yoga bores me to tears, I hadn't realised that the class was quite so eager for distractions.

Dad seems catatonic, so I turn back towards the roofed area.

'I'm not adopted,' I snap, looking for the culprit among the acolytes. 'He's my real dad. But he's been spinning a yarn all these years about some new age hippie fling and that he didn't know my birth mother's last name.' I inhale. 'He failed to mention that he's been in regular contact with my maternal grandmother, and didn't bother to tell me that she even existed.' I put my hands on my hips.

Dad lays a hand on my shoulder, startling me. 'Would it help if I said I'm sorry?'

'It might. Not that that will give me back all those years.'

A silver-haired woman glares at my dad. 'How could you do that? She can't get in touch with her spiritual self if she doesn't know the truth.'

A few other people murmur their assent.

'It wasn't like that.' Dad spreads his hands, his northern accent coming to the fore. 'I just wanted her to have a "normal" family – Carol and me, and our relatives. Is that so wrong?'

'She had a right to know,' another woman says.

'I don't know,' someone at the back chimes in. 'It sounds like he had his reasons.'

'I think children should be told everything and allowed to decide for themselves,' a grey-haired lady says.

'We did tell her.' Dad rubs his neck as his tension threatens the peaceful space. 'She knew that her birth mother died.'

'But not that I killed her!' I shout. 'That she died giving birth to me.'

'That's precisely why we didn't—' Dad protests, but he's cut off by the gaggle of his followers.

'Is there any of that ginkgo tea? The poor child can surely use a cuppa...'

Dad sits down on his dais; his normally relaxed hand trembles a little, like he's craving a cigarette. I know I am – and I don't even smoke. Two of the women get up and lead me to a table where there's a Japanese tea pot and a forest of little Raku cups. Except for one woman rolled up like a pretzel and two men chatting about whether relegated Watford will be promoted again, the others get up and follow suit, chattering and socialising. Class dismissed.

I take two teacups and go over to Dad, sitting down beside him. I hand him a cup, and then take a swig of the foul-tasting, bitter liquid.

'I thought I was doing the right thing for you – and for Mum,' he says.

'Yeah, I know. You always think Mum needs protecting. But what about Mrs Fairchild: Grandma Catherine? Doesn't she count?'

'She's your birth grandma,' he says. 'She wasn't a part of our lives any more than your birth mother was. Not really. Not for the important moments – like when you fell off your bicycle and needed stitches; or when you got chickenpox and were off school for a week; or needed cups of cocoa brought when you were studying for your A levels.'

'She might have wanted to be.'

He shakes his head grimly. 'Is that what you wanted, then – to visit her in that big fancy house and have her buy you expensive toys? Make a fuss over you, treat you like some kind of princess? And then drop you home in her fancy car with the leather seats, so you could return to your tiny house and your tiny bedroom, and beans on toast for your tea?'

'Come on, Dad. This isn't about a class struggle. It's about right and wrong. My grandmother lost her daughter. She was grieving. Then you took away her only grandchild. That was wrong.'

'Maybe.' Dad bows his head. 'I just thought our lives would

all be simpler – less cluttered, and more authentic – without you having to carry all that baggage. We were happy. You were happy... *are* happy.'

'Authentic! What a load of tosh.'

'I did what I thought was best.' His voice has an unusually desperate edge. 'I'm sorry if it was the wrong thing.' He reaches out and removes my teacup from my trembling hand. Then he leans over and folds me in his arms.

The chatting ebbs and a few of his followers make audible sighs, like their spiritual leader has just made a remarkable display of selflessness. Whatever. My tears begin to flow and are absorbed by the thick organic cotton of his T-shirt.

'I love you, Alex,' he whispers into my ear. 'I probably don't say that enough, but it's true.'

'Me too, Dad.' Disentangling myself, I wipe my eyes with a tissue. Despite Dad's bluster and mumbo-jumbo, he meant to do the right thing. His version, anyway. 'I'll call you, OK?'

'Yeah.'

I walk over to the CD player and plug the music back in. The sitar and pan pipes take over where they left off. 'Sorry to disrupt your class,' I say to the clump of students gathered around.

'Oh, no problem, dear,' the silver-haired woman says. 'My core will thank you for it tomorrow.'

25

I feel a little better after busting up the yoga class – there's nothing like kicking the stones in a spiritual garden to stir things up when you're feeling low. I return to my car and sit there for a long time, staring at the familiar street, the familiar houses, the setting for my familiar life growing up in a loving, if slightly eccentric, middle-class family. Dad's right, I don't regret my childhood or my life. It's my grandmother that I feel for. Whereas I lacked someone I didn't know existed, she lacked someone that she did.

And there's another person that my newfound knowledge is likely to hurt – Mum. I turn on the engine and crawl through rush-hour traffic to that dubious experiment in urban planning, Hemel Hempstead, or 'Hemel' to the locals. It's already five o'clock by the time I pull into the car park of the building where she works as an accountant for an insurance company. I worry for a second that I will have missed her, but then I catch sight of her ginger updo and the floral rainy-day coat from Boden that I bought her for her birthday. She's chatting and laughing with a friend, and I consider driving off and just letting her get on with her day. Dad can tell her, or not, about what happened.

But I open the door and get out of the car. Whatever Dad might decide, *I've* decided that she deserves to know.

'Mum,' I call out, waving my hand. 'Hi.'

'Alex.' Her face clouds over. 'Are you OK?'

'Yes, Mum,' I say. 'I mean, I'm not sick or anything.'

'Good.' She lets out a long sigh of relief. I feel guilty for worrying her. Two years ago, Mum had a breast cancer scare that luckily turned out to be nothing. Since then, she worries whenever I get even a mild cold.

'Can I talk to you?'

'Sure.' Mum says goodbye to her friend and turns back to me. 'Shall we go home?' she says. 'I've got a nut roast ready to go in the oven.'

'No thanks, Mum.' I've always hated nut roast. 'Is there anything here we can grab?'

'Well,' she says briskly, 'there's the chippy.'

'OK. I'll buy.'

We walk together back out to the main road near the train station. I can smell the chippy miles before we reach it, and my stomach rumbles in anticipation. Mum natters brightly about her work – the cake stall for the summer fete, a new hire in finance ('so good-looking – and single, I think'), a top she thought I might like in Fat Face. Although we have very little in common, I've always thought of Mum as one of the best people in the whole world. She's open and honest, and homely, and, in a word, *normal*. She reads the *Daily Mail* and *Hello!*, likes cooking but hates ironing, watches *Eastenders* and *Emmerdale*, hates herbal (including ginkgo) tea. She prefers step aerobics to yoga, and couldn't tell a Gothic arch from the Arc de Triomphe. She votes for any candidate she likes the look of, regardless of political party. It's not much of a stretch to believe that she's not my biological mother.

'So, Alex, how's your job going?' she says as we stand in line to order (chips and mushy peas for her, a large cod and no chips for me).

'Fine.' I tell her about the costume exhibition and the increase in tours we've had lately. She asks me if we're still stocking old rose hand cream in the shop.

I promise to bring her some next time just as Dad rings her mobile and talks for what seems a long time. She glances up at me a few times, but her face gives nothing away.

'I understand,' she says finally, ending the call with a sigh. I stare down at the initials carved into the wooden table, wishing that I hadn't come here and didn't have to cause her pain.

'You've known all along, haven't you, Mum?' I say quietly.

'You may think that your dad is to blame,' she says. 'That he's the reason we didn't tell you everything. But that's not true. He's not one for secrets. It goes against everything he believes in. He did it to protect me.'

'But why? Did you think I wouldn't love you? Did you think I'd love a dead woman more just because she gave birth to me?'

'I don't know.' She stares down at her nails. 'Yes, I suppose that is what I thought.'

'But that's crazy.' Our food arrives, but neither of us touch our plates.

'Is it?' Her eyes fill with tears. 'I couldn't take the risk. You see, Alex, I couldn't have children of my own. You were – are – everything to me. And I was madly in love with your dad. He was so arty and creative, and full of ideas. Then there was the whole Kama Sutra thing.'

'Too much information.'

She blobs a lake of ketchup onto her plate and stabs a chip

into it. 'But the best thing about meeting your father was the fact that he had you. We were a complete package; a ready-made family. He was open and honest with me about what happened to your birth mother, but neither of us thought you needed to be hurt by it.'

'The fact that I killed her?'

'No, Alex!' Mum reaches out and grabs my hand. 'She died of a health condition. Having a baby caused an internal bleed. Your dad and his lot didn't have a clue. A transfusion might have saved her if she'd been in hospital. But she wasn't.'

I swallow back a sob. For my birth mother, I feel a remote kind of sadness for someone I've never met, and never will meet. Whereas Mum's pain is on display right in front of me.

I move to her side of the booth and put my arm around her. Tears flow down her face like droplets of rain on a window.

'We should have told you everything – that you had a grandmother who was alive. But the idea of it opened a hole in the pit of my stomach. I didn't want her around looking at me and judging me. Knowing I could never be as good as her daughter. Thinking that I wasn't fit to raise her granddaughter.'

'No one could ever think that!' I say. 'Not ever. And certainly not Mrs Fairchild. She was sad about losing her daughter, but she would have respected you and Dad, I'm sure of it.'

She takes a tissue from her pocket and dabs her eyes. 'I know, and you're right.' Turning to me, she grabs my hand in earnest. 'Oh, Alex, can you ever forgive me for what I did? The fact is, I would do it again in a heartbeat. You're my daughter.'

'And you're my mum; of course I forgive you – and Dad, for that matter.' I lean in and rest my head against her cheek. 'I just wish you would have trusted me, that's all.'

'Yes. We should have done. Probably. It's just that I…'

'…couldn't take the risk?'

'Exactly.'

I kiss her cheek and return to my side of the booth. I eat my cod; she dips her chips in the pool of ketchup. 'So what happens now?' I say.

'Take some time to think. Then, I'll be happy to answer any questions you have.'

'Actually, I've got some questions that need answering now. There are some things I've learned about Catherine Fairchild.' I tell Mum that she was orphaned in the Blitz and adopted by Frank Bolton.

'Adopted! I never would have guessed. I remember meeting her when you started working at the house. She's so proper and well-spoken. She oozes class and good breeding.'

'I think that comes from attending a posh school.'

'Yes, maybe,' Mum concedes. 'In that case, it sounds like she was very lucky. There must have been so many children orphaned in the Blitz. It was nice of Frank Bolton to adopt her.'

'Yes. Very nice...' I hesitate.

'You think there's more to it?'

'I don't know. A few odd things have happened lately.' I tell her about the envelopes being left by the 'uninvited guest', omitting the part about me being locked in the loo and then arrested.

'That is worrying.'

'I read one of the letters,' I say. 'It was a diary entry. From the war – during the Blitz.'

'Really? And you don't know who's sending these diary entries? Or why?'

'No, I've no idea.' I tell her about the locket, wishing I had it to show her, but it's still with the Clockmaker in his safe. I recount Mrs Fairchild's 'episode' when I showed her the newly restored musical bird and she fainted.

'How awful.' Mum's brow furrows in concern. 'So what are you going to do?'

'Get to the bottom of it.' I trace my fingers over the carved initials in the wood. 'And learn more about my birth family, if that's OK with you?'

'Oh, honey, of course it is.' She purses her lips. 'I just worry, that's all.'

'I know, Mum.' I take her hand across the table and give it a squeeze. 'It's a lot to take in. But I want to find out more about the locket and Catherine Fairchild's mother.'

Mum withdraws her hand and fiddles with her wedding ring, lost in thought. 'I might be able to help,' she says. 'But it's a long shot.'

'What?' I lean forward.

'I could speak to someone in our life insurance department at work. They've got people who trace family medical histories. Granted, not that far back, but...' She shrugs. 'I could make a few calls.'

'Really?'

'It may well come to nothing.'

We both get up from the table. 'You never know, Mum,' I say. 'And in this case, I think it's worth the risk...' I give her a long hug and a kiss on the cheek.

26

I promise Mum that I'll drop in for Sunday lunch and give Dad a call in a day or two to help him heal his wounded chakra. When I return to Mallow Court, the lights are off and Mrs Fairchild has left a note saying that she's gone to choir practice. I collapse on the sofa, too tired to think but with my mind racing.

I stare up at the skylight and the silver-grey clouds, aching inside over the things I've learned. I feel desperately sorry for the birth mother I'll never know, and for Mrs Fairchild – my grandmother (it will take me a while to get used to thinking of her in those terms) who broke the silence and contacted me (though, I'm still miffed that it wasn't solely my skills as a manager that she wanted). And Mallow Court – I now understand why I felt a deep affinity to the house from the moment I saw it. It's a part of me too.

But as Mum said, I'll need some time to process the past so I can focus on the future. And both of those require getting to the bottom of the anonymous diary entries and stopping whoever is harassing Mrs Fairchild.

My grandmother's memories were a jumble, but she vividly described Mamochka living in fear of something or someone in a little flat next to the yellow kitchen.

Then, between the yellow kitchen and the orphanage, Mrs Fairchild mentioned a brown kitchen. Maybe a foster family? The common thread appears to be the jewelled bird: a pretty 'trinket' which was given to Catherine by her dying mother. The locket then disappeared for a short time, until Frank Bolton returned it to the girl in the orphanage. How did Frank end up with the locket? And why did he adopt her?

The questions spin around in my head, colliding with the raw emotions of the last few days. Whatever the truth is about Catherine Fairchild, it's my truth too. She's my grandmother. My grandma...

* * *

I must have dozed off because the next thing I know, I'm jarred awake by my phone ringing. It takes me a second to realise that I'm safe and sound in my flat. In my dream I was running away from a storm of fire, bombs exploding all around me, a black cloud of rubble flying through the air. My brow is drenched with sweat.

Moving in slow motion, I reach for the phone on the table. 'Hello,' I say groggily.

'Alex? Is that you?'

'Yes.' The terror of the dream melts away. 'Hello, Tim.'

'I hope you haven't forgotten about dinner – if tomorrow night's still good for you?'

'Yes, it's fine.' In truth, with everything that's been going on, it had slipped my mind. But now, butterflies flit in my stomach like I'm talking to a teenage crush.

'Good. Shall we say seven? I know a great little French restaurant.'

We make plans for the following evening. Despite my recent personal earthquake, I still feel excitement at the prospect. Seeing Tim will be a perfect escape from the tumult in my life. He's a safe, upstanding member of the community with good values *and* very attractive. Meeting him at the police station was surely pure luck – or maybe it was karma – but either way, I plan on enjoying myself.

I end the call and go to have a bath. As I'm running the water and steam is rising up into my face, the phone rings again. My towel falls to the floor as I hurry out of the bathroom to get to the phone. I reach it on the sixth ring and pick up breathlessly.

'Alex? It's Chris Heath-Churchley here.'

Hearing his voice makes me suddenly aware that I'm standing there stark naked.

'Hi, Chris,' I manage.

'Sorry to call so late. But I may have found something. Could you come by tomorrow? It may well be nothing. The thing is, I just don't know.'

'Would three o'clock work?'

'Yeah, fine.' His voice is sharp with tension. 'See you then.'

The line goes dead in my hands.

* * *

Chris's call was unsettling, and the next morning, I wake up wondering what he's found. It goes right out of my head, however, when I go to the main house and notice a brown envelope lying on the doormat addressed to 'Catherine Bolton'. I feel a sickening sense of violation – someone must have come here in the night and left it. The security cameras only cover the inside of the house, so there's no telling who it was. I pick it up and flip it over to see if I can open it without tearing it. The glue is stuck together so I start to tear the top of the long edge—

The door opens in front of me. It's Mrs Fairchild – Grandmother, I remind myself – in full gardening regalia. She looks every inch the carefree retiree out to spend a pleasant morning among the roses and dahlias. Except for her eyes, which look dark and sunken like she hasn't slept.

'Good morning,' I say, feeling a bit awkward and unsure what to call her.

'Hello, Alex. Did you sleep well?' Her smile seems forced. Before I can answer, she points to the envelope in my hands. 'Is that for me?'

'It was left on the mat.' Reluctantly, I hold it out to her.

'Thank you.' She takes it from me, her eyes snagging on the torn edge, and puts it in her trouser pocket.

'No problem. Oh, and by the way, I told him off.'

'Your dad?'

'Yes.'

She brushes my arm with her fingers. 'I'm sorry to have caused you pain, Alex. But it's been eating away at me for a long time. And until I get to the bottom of things, I thought it best you knew the truth.'

'It's fine. And I'd like to help.'

'I know,' she says. 'But right now, I need a little bit of time. The past is difficult enough. It all feels very raw. I hope you understand.'

'Um, sure.' I do understand, but I also feel disappointed.

'Good. I'll get on with the weeding then. It's supposed to rain later.' With that, she walks off, her rubber clogs crunching along the gravel path.

My instincts tell me to run after her and insist she enlighten me about the envelope and whatever's inside it – more journal entries, I assume. But after several years of being her employee, I don't feel comfortable pulling the 'granddaughter card'. Instead, I get on with my work, checking the answerphone messages in the estate office. There are several wedding enquiries, and a woman ringing about a scarf given to her by a 'dear friend from Australia' lost somewhere in the garden. For lack of any other purpose, I go back outside to look for the scarf.

It's a pleasant day – a bit hazy with a light breeze. I head down by the river and along the paths of the woodland walk, losing myself in the copse of birches and beeches. I think about all the people who've lived at Mallow Court and walked here before me. Frank Bolton was the first one of his line to live here, so even if I was related to him by blood – which, because my grandmother is adopted, I'm not – I couldn't claim kinship with past denizens. Although I've found an important link to my own heritage, the chain is disappointingly short.

There's no sign of the scarf by the lake, so I return to the main gardens. I find Mrs Fairchild in the rose garden, sitting on a bench under an arched yew hedge. Her trousers are dirty at the knees and she's clearly been at work. Now, however, she's gone very still, staring off into space. In her lap is a piece of paper.

'Mrs Fairchild?' I say softly.

'Alex.' She folds the paper swiftly in half. 'Sorry, I was miles away.'

'I'm looking for a scarf that someone lost. White with blue poppies – it has sentimental value.'

'I haven't seen it.' She gazes at me like I'm a complete stranger rather than her newly claimed granddaughter.

I know I ought to respect her solitude, but it hurts that she's not letting me help. 'We need to put a stop to this,' I say, pointing to the paper. 'We can't have people turning up and leaving envelopes where they aren't meant to be.'

I'm half-hoping that she'll hold it out to me. Let me get involved and make it go away. Granddaughter or not, I'm a trusted employee and I'd never betray a confidence.

Instead, she tucks the paper away in her pocket.

With a long sigh, I turn to leave.

'Wait, Alex.'

When I turn back, she's smiling in the old way like when we were just employer and employee and there was no long shadow between us.

'I think you're right,' she says.

I cross my arms. 'Fine. But you'll need to fill me in or I'm going to have to take action.'

'OK. You win.'

I move closer and stand before her.

'Someone has been sending me anonymous letters,' she says. 'Diary entries that relate to my childhood during the war. All that remembering – not to mention the changed circumstances between you and me – has been very difficult.'

'It's been hard for me too.' I manage a smile. 'But good too.'

She stands up from the bench, her eyes moist. 'Would it be OK if I...?' She holds out her arms and I go into them. She squeezes me tightly. I can feel the rise and fall of her chest, the beating of her heart. She smells of floral soap with a hint of linseed oil.

'I love you, Alex,' she whispers. 'I've always loved you. I just wish I'd told you sooner.'

'I... I love you too, Grandma.'

She pauses for a fraction of a second – then her worried face blooms into a smile. 'I've waited a long time to be called that,' she says. 'I didn't want to pressure you. But if you could learn to see me that way, then I'd be so grateful.'

'I do see you that way. Deep down, I think I've felt it all along.'

'Oh, Alex.' She kisses my cheeks and wipes her eyes. For now, the shadow has passed, but I sense it still lingering in the wings.

We come apart. As much as I want to maintain this new closeness, there are questions I need to ask. I walk over to one of the rose bushes and breathe in the vibrant scent.

'Do you have any idea who's sending the diary entries?'

'No. I figure someone found the diary and decided to make mischief. I can't imagine it's more than that.'

She's still holding something back, but it's a start. 'OK,' I say. 'But if there are any more envelopes, or intruders coming round to leave them on the doorstep, then I'll have to get the police involved.'

'Actually,' she says, 'I already have.'

'What?'

'My "friend".' She gives me a little wink. 'The one I told you about? He's a former DI with the police. I've told him what's going on and he's going to help.'

'Oh.' I'm a little hurt that she got him involved before me. 'And does this "friend" have a name?'

'It's David.' Saying his name takes ten years off her face.

'How did you meet him?'

'He's retired now, and recently moved up here from London. He gave a talk at a WI meeting about elder safety. He walked me home afterwards, and the rest, as they say, is history.'

'That's great.' I swallow back a dollop of jealousy. Having just found my biological grandmother, I'm reluctant to share her so soon.

'He said he may be able to find out who's doing it.'

'Good. And… what about the locket?'

'What about it?'

'Do the diary entries mention it? Chris the Clockmaker told me that it might be more than just a toy or a trinket. He thought it might be valuable.' Remembering his strange phone call, I frown.

Mrs Fairchild picks up her trowel. 'I highly doubt it. But you're welcome to find out what you can. It's yours, after all.' She rests her hand on my arm. 'My mother gave it to me when she died, and I would have given it to my daughter if I'd had the chance. Like a family heirloom.' Her smiles fades. 'I came upon it when I was looking through some of my old things for your costume exhibition. I always loved it, but the memories were painful too, so I kept it packed away. But when I saw it again, I wanted you to have it. I hoped you might find out the truth. But then the diary entries started coming, and things seemed too complicated.'

'I understand.' I put my hand on hers as emotion swells in my chest. Maybe it's because my grandmother never got the chance to give the locket to her daughter. Or maybe it's because the truth has come to light and now she's passed it on to me.

27

13 NOVEMBER 1940 – 1.30 A.M.

'Poor lamb,' Sadie said. The kitchen was brown and homely, smelling of overcooked meat and feral cat. 'Put her by the fire and let's get a hot drink in her.'

I ushered the girl over to the table. On the wall was a wooden clock that I hadn't seen before. I stared at the brass pendulums as they swung back and forth, blurring before my tired eyes like shooting stars. Sadie came over to me.

'You did right to bring her here,' she said to me. 'We'll make her nice and comfortable on the sofa. Though, she can't stay – she'll have to go to the church. Be evacuated with the others.'

I nodded. Of course she couldn't stay. But I didn't want her going to an orphanage either. 'Can you give me a few days?' I asked.

'Yeah. Poor mite.'

'You seen Flea tonight?' I said.

She snorted. 'I ain't seen him in weeks except at breakfast. He's out all night. Working – so he says.' She lowered her voice. 'But I'm not sure I believe him.'

'What do you mean?' The image of him bending over the dead woman had lodged itself in my mind, refusing to budge.

She leaned closer to me. I braced myself for the words I didn't want to hear. 'He's got a lady friend out Hackney way,' she whispered. 'I think she might be up the duff.'

'Oh.' My knees felt weak with relief. I knew Sadie was a good judge of character. She'd never let Flea live here if he was... up to something. I had to stop imagining things. Like the rest of us, Flea was just out here doing his bit.

'He pays his rent on time, so who am I to judge?' she said. 'What about you, Badger? You well?'

'As can be expected. You?'

I sat back, only half-listening, as she launched into a lengthy account of her son, Miles, who was 'out flying missions against them Jerrys'. I know she thinks the boys from the neighbourhood – me, Flea and Spider – aren't pulling our weight because we're not in the RAF. I thought of the blackened bodies in the street. They will rise again in my dreams until I wake up screaming. And I was glad she didn't know the truth about what I've seen.

The girl quickly became groggy and I carried her over to the sofa. As I tucked her under the crocheted blanket, I saw the silver chain around her neck. I thought of Flea's face as he laid eyes on it – her one small treasure. I pulled the blanket up to her chin. Sadie was here – she'd be safe. And I could trust Flea with my life... But could I trust him with this?

No. I couldn't.

'Good night,' I whispered, but the girl was already asleep. Gently, I reached under the blanket and undid the clasp. She didn't even stir.

I kissed her on the forehead and slipped the jewelled bird into my pocket.

28

I leave the garden having been gifted a jewelled locket of unknown provenance, and very little in the way of reassurance. For all her denials, the diary entries clearly *are* bothering my grandmother. Even if her policeman friend can sort things out, I worry that already, damage has been done.

I tick off my morning tasks: doing the final proof of my guide for the costume exhibition, touching base with the PR firm hired to do the publicity, and contacting suppliers who are providing food and drink for the grand opening. At lunchtime, I muddle my way through a speech on Elizabethan architecture to a local history group. Fortunately, most of them seem more focused on putting away the authentic 'meat feast' than on my talk, so I don't have to field too many questions or think about the rest of the day – my meeting with Chris followed by the dinner date with Tim.

I get the train to London Euston, feeling uncomfortable in my 'date' clothes: a floaty silk chiffon skirt in emerald green that Karen made me buy in the sales, a black sleeveless vest and waterfall cardigan. And my boots: black patent with pointy toes – I couldn't face a dinner date without boots made for walking.

When I reach Chancery Lane and wind my way through the maze of little streets off Hatton Garden, I worry again about what Chris has found out. Maybe he's discovered something bad – that the locket is a fake or that it's not a Fabergé at all. Even before the locket was gifted to me, I'd wanted to believe that it was more than just a cheap trinket – that it might be something really special. That its origins could provide a vital clue to finding out more about Mrs Fairchild's mother and our family history.

Though part of me can't help but wonder – will we all be better off if I succeed?

...Or if I fail?

* * *

Outside the door of the Clockmaker's workshop, I stand and listen to the hum of ticking clocks.

The quarter-past-the-hour cotillion heralds my entrance as I walk inside. One by one, the bells and chimes create a chaos of sound, and eventually fall silent. The ticking sound that replaces them is steady and rhythmic, like the beating of a mechanical heart.

I don't see Chris – where is he?

A sharp laugh filters in through the door that leads to the auction house. It's open a crack, and a yellow rectangle of light spills into the workshop. A man, and a woman. Chris – and the blonde PA? Or Sidney? Or are they one and the same?

I don't care. Clenching my fists at my side, I march up to the door. 'Chris?' I call out loudly.

The laughter stops. I fling open the door. A different blonde woman is standing in a corridor holding a tray of teacups. She glances in my direction and I draw back. Heavier footsteps come towards me. I hurry back to the centre of the workshop and stand in front of the workbench like I've been there all along.

'Sorry to disturb you,' I say with sarcasm. 'I thought we had an appointment.'

'Yes, we do.' Chris comes into the room. He's wearing loose-fitting jeans and a 'Nine Inch Nails – Head Like a Hole World Tour' T-shirt. I assess his face – good-looking in a sensitive way, but with the geeky air of a boy who plays with toys all day. Not the kind of man you'd expect to be quite so popular with the ladies.

'Did you have a good time with Sidney?' I can't stop myself from asking.

'It was OK.' He seems a little amused by the question. 'How about you?'

'No, I've never met her.'

'Good one.' He laughs. Going over to his desk, he flips through his papers. 'Have you been well, Alex?' He looks up, studying me. 'You look very nice.'

'Thanks. But actually, I've been better. Just a few family issues, you know.'

'I'm no stranger to those, believe me.' He picks up a notebook from the desk. 'Do you want to sit down? I'm guessing you want to hear what I've discovered.'

'I'm surprised you've even had time to look at it,' I say, sitting down in the orange vinyl visitor chair.

'I came back early from the Isle of Wight,' he says. 'I couldn't wait to get started.'

'Oh. So no engagement then?' The words are out of my mouth before I'm even aware of having spoken them.

'Sorry? What do you mean?'

I lower my eyes, mortified by own presumption. 'Well, you, Sidney, her family, your family. A romantic place like the Isle of Wight...' I pause. 'But of course, it's none of my business.'

A slow smile creeps over his face. 'It's nothing like that. Sidney's a family friend.'

'Oh.' As I'm trying to fathom why I feel so relieved, he pulls out a piece of paper and a sheaf of photographs.

'I took the locket apart and had a good look. It's a remarkable thing – so intricate and well-made. A true piece of art.'

'What did you find?'

'Nothing.' His eyes are strangely bright. 'I found nothing. No mark – nothing at all.'

'Oh.' Disappointment creeps into my voice. 'That's bad, isn't it?'

'Not necessarily.' He hands me the photos one by one. To me, most of it looks like parts from a machine catalogue – close-ups of tiny gears and wheels. 'The fact that it doesn't have a mark in any of the usual places might be very significant. But it's too early to know yet.'

'Didn't you say before that no mark was a bad thing?'

'I did, but that was when I thought that the bird might be a Fabergé workshop piece. Those always have a mark.'

'So it's not a Fabergé?'

'I said it's not a Fabergé workshop piece.'

'I'm not following.' I hand the photos back, feeling a little exasperated.

He opens a book – a different book on Fabergé than the one he showed me before – and points to a highlighted passage. I bend down and read it.

> Although most Fabergé workshop pieces bore a Workmaster mark, the finest pieces produced in the workshop often bore no mark. These were the pieces commissioned by the Tsar and the Romanov family themselves, often to give as gifts to special friends or family members.

I look up at him in disbelief. 'The Romanov family? Surely you can't think—'

'We can't be certain. Lack of a mark could mean it's not a Fabergé at all – there is that possibility.'

'How can we ever find out one way or the other?'

'We may never know for sure. That's how it is with art and antiques. All we can do is find out if the rest of the pieces of the puzzle fit together. But if you want my opinion...' His face erupts into a grin.

The Clockmaker believes that the jewelled bird might have once been a special piece commissioned by the Romanov family!

'God.' I feel suddenly breathless. 'Could it really be true?'

'I haven't had a chance to do much research,' he admits. 'Just on the marks. There were many different marks depending on who produced a piece, and where. I don't know a lot about Imperial Russia in the early twentieth century. I believe the Tsar was Nicholas II and his wife was Alexandra.'

'There were several children too,' I say. 'And a lot of cousins, aunts and uncles. It was a dynasty. The Tsar and his immediate family were murdered by the Bolsheviks during the revolution. I'm not sure about all the others.'

'Sounds like you know a lot about it.'

'Just general knowledge, really. But there is one other thing...'

I tell him about my grandmother and her strange trance

when she heard the bird 'singing'. 'She sang a song in a foreign language,' I say. 'I couldn't understand a word of it. But she told me later that it was a song Mamochka used to sing.'

'Mamochka? Is that Russian for mother?'

'Yes.'

We stare at each other, eyes wide. The unspoken possibilities crackle in the air between us.

29

When Chris hands me back the velvet bag, I can't resist taking the locket out and looking at it. He's cleaned and polished every millimetre of the silver gilt setting, and the inset gems sparkle under the bright light of his desk lamp. How could I ever have mistaken it for a cheap trinket?

'I'm almost afraid to touch it,' I say, nesting it in my palm.

'Let's not get ahead of ourselves,' he says. But I can sense that he too has done just that. 'Remember, until its provenance is proved for certain, it's just a pretty piece of jewellery, not a priceless treasure. Though the gemstones and gold are valuable in their own right.'

We both watch as I open the case and the bird 'sings'. It looks precious and magical, like a mythical creature out of a fairy tale, and the sound of the tiny music box is clear and bell-like. We both drift into a kind of trance, held in thrall by this tiny object. When the bird has finished its rotation, I shut the case. Without warning, the troubles and anxiety that have been plaguing me come rushing back. My grandmother, the diary entries, the 'uninvited guest'. My upcoming dinner date with Tim. Involuntarily, I shudder.

'Are you OK, Alex?' Chris reaches towards me. I can feel the energy in his fingers, but at the last second, he pulls back.

'Yes, I...' I stammer, feeling disarmed. 'It's just a lot to take in. I suppose I'd better let you get on. And I have some errands in London to do this afternoon.'

A shadow of disappointment crosses his face. I ignore the little voice whispering in the corner of my mind that actually, I'd much rather stay.

'Maybe I'd better leave the bird with you for now,' I say, 'to keep it safe?'

'Fine with me, but are you sure?'

'Yes.' I'm sure that if he keeps the bird for me, then at least I'll have a reason to come back here again.

'I'll put it back in the safe,' he says. 'Do you want another receipt?'

I stare at the locket; in a way, I'm longing for a receipt on his weighty letterhead, stating that the bird is 'possibly Imperial Russian'.

'No,' I say. 'I trust you. But can we keep this quiet for now?'

'Of course. Scout's honour.' He clasps his fist to his chest.

I study him narrowly. 'You were never a boy scout.'

He makes a face like I've wounded him, barely holding back laughter. 'No. But I always wanted to be.'

He opens the door for me.

'I'll do some research and see what I can find out about the Imperial Family,' I say.

'Good. I'll keep digging on my end about Fabergé.'

'OK, Chris. I'll see you soon.'

He looks at me, his crystal blue eyes unreadable. 'I'll look forward to it,' he says.

So will I, I think as I walk up to Clerkenwell Road and hop on a bus to the British Library. I've got several hours before my dinner with Tim, and I'm dying to find a connection between the jewelled bird, Fabergé, and the Russian royal line. Luckily, I still have a valid reader pass from my student days. When I enter the building, I'm awestruck by the huge rotunda of the main reading room, surrounded by floor-to-ceiling bookshelves. Apparently there are over 400 miles of shelves in the place, and as much as I'd love to do so, I've no time to explore them all.

In the main catalogue, there are hundreds of books on the Romanovs and thousands on the history of Russia. I pick three at random.

Two and a half hours later, I have my original three books open on my table, along with a dozen others. My hand is tired from writing notes, and I'd kill for a coffee. But other than that, I've barely noticed the time passing.

I've discovered that Nicholas and Alexandra, the last Tsar and Tsarina of Russia, had five children. Alexei, the only son and heir, was a sickly boy who suffered from a disease called haemophilia. Anastasia is perhaps the most famous child, as there were rumours that she survived the murder of her family, and even some pretenders who cropped up over the years. The less famous siblings are Olga, Tatiana, and Maria.

In 1918, the entire family was taken to Ekaterinburg in Siberia and placed under house arrest. In the middle of the night, they were taken out into the yard where they faced a firing squad.

One particularly macabre account records that the bullets aimed at Alexei originally ricocheted off him because he had gems sewed into his clothing that acted like armour. But alas, it wasn't enough. His killers had plenty of wherewithal to pump him full of more bullets, until one hit its deadly target.

It's all very tragic, and I feel a rush of sympathy for the family, especially the children, who were murdered. Fleetingly, I wonder how much Dad knows about all the blood shed on behalf of the 'glorious' red crusade.

I reread the notes I took on the other Romanovs who managed to survive the revolution and escape Russia. Surprisingly, there are literally hundreds of ancestors and descendants still out there. Even Prince Phillip's grandmother was a Romanov who settled in Greece after her escape. But for the last Tsar and his immediate family, there was no escape.

I stare at the shelves of books wondering how on earth Mrs Fairchild ended up with a piece of jewellery that might – and it's a long shot – have belonged to a member of the Russian royal family? Despite Chris's enthusiasm, it seems impossible. More impossible still is proving anything one way or the other.

I leave the library feeling a bit deflated. In all probability, this quest I've embarked on will turn out to be a wild goose chase. I spare a thought for the jewelled bird, bedded down for the night in the safe. As for Chris himself, he's probably left his workshop for another 'non-date' with another 'just-a-family-friend'.

The stuffy, exhaust-blackened air of a hot summer evening gradually brings me back to my senses. I jettison Chris H-C from my mind and catch a bus down High Holborn towards Shoreditch, where I'm scheduled to meet Tim Edwards. I plan to keep all the recent goings-on to myself and focus on enjoying a night out with an attractive man. As I get off the bus, my stomach feels light and fluttery at the potential for what this evening might – or might not – hold.

30

'Well, I must say, you look fantastic!'

I feel a tiny bit perturbed because Tim's comment immediately puts me off guard, and I know I'm blushing. He seems to mean it though, and I'm glad that he appreciates the effort I made.

'Thanks. So do you.'

Instead of the usual suit, Tim is dressed in a pair of khaki trousers with a razor-sharp crease, and a pink Oxford shirt. The pink sets off the dark brown of his eyes – which I'm sure is deliberate.

He laughs and brushes my hand with his finger. The touch resonates up my arm. 'I hope you're hungry. I've booked a great little French Bistro. It's called La Bouteille Rouge. It's brand new.'

'I'm sure I can find my appetite somewhere,' I say teasingly.

We walk together down the high street. It's lined with cranes and buildings under construction, and the pavements are teeming with young, trendy professionals and arty types. Being neither arty nor trendy, I feel out of place.

'Alex?' I realise too late that Tim is speaking to me about something – the weather? The sky has turned a threatening shade of steel grey, and drops of rain begin to speckle the pavement in front of me.

'I don't really mind the rain.' I stab blindly for a response to what is apparently the wrong question.

'Oh, well, that's good.' He frowns.

The restaurant is intimate and delightful, with dripping candles set in old wine bottles on the table, and bread with garlic-flavoured olive oil. But for some reason, I can't relax. Tim orders a nice bottle of wine: Côte de Nuit, I think. I drink two glasses in quick succession. Tim skilfully keeps the conversation going, but he seems a bit tense. I try to pay closer attention as he talks about his hobbies: rock climbing, windsurfing, and five-a-side football. My sense of dismay grows, as I know nothing about those things. But just as I've given up trying to think of something to say, he changes the subject.

'Have there been any more visits from your intruder?'

'No,' I say. 'Though, someone's been leaving letters for Mrs Fairchild that are upsetting her. Diary entries.'

'Diary entries?' Surprise flickers across his face. 'Whose diary?'

'An ambulance driver from during the war. He rescued Mrs Fairchild from a bombed-out building when she was a small girl. The memories are painful, and it's making her upset. I thought someone might be blackmailing her.'

'Has she done anything to interest a blackmailer?'

'Not that I know of.'

He pours the last of the wine from the bottle. 'Good. Though, I suppose there are some unanswered questions about her father.'

'Her father?' I sit forward. 'You mean Frank Bolton?'

'Of course.'

'He's actually her adoptive father. She was orphaned. But what do you mean?'

'Hey, relax, I was only joking,' he says. 'I was remembering our first meeting; when I asked that question on the tour?'

'Oh, right.' I laugh too, scolding myself internally. I really need to lighten up and try to enjoy the evening. Tim deserves that, surely.

He flags down the waiter and orders two coffees. Then, leaning forward, he brushes a strand of hair back behind my ear, letting his finger trail along my cheek. I smile, wondering what he intends for the rest of the evening. Out of superstition, I bought a day return ticket in the hopes the return part would end up being wasted. But I find him surprisingly hard to read. One minute he's flirty, and the next he's feeling the need to educate me or ask uncomfortable questions. Not something I take kindly to, if I'm honest. Then he melts me all over again with those eyes.

'So, Alex...' He leans even closer. 'Would you like to go for a walk?'

'A walk?' I swiftly realign my expectations. A walk isn't exactly a taxi ride to a nice hotel, but it could be the one thing that leads to another. 'Around here?'

'Yes.'

'OK.' I don't normally think of Shoreditch when planning a romantic evening stroll, but I'm willing to be persuaded. We leave the restaurant and I wait for him to take my hand, but he doesn't.

'Where are we going?' I say.

'You'll see.' His smile broadens.

Something in his manner raises a tiny spectre of worry.

Instead of walking towards the trendy bustle of Hoxton

Square, we head down the busy road towards Holloway. I look at the buildings we pass. At street level, most of them are down-at-heel takeaways, drycleaners, and betting shops. Above street level are brick flats, mostly sixties and seventies by the look of them. From what little I know of modern London history, East London was hit hard by the Luftwaffe during the Blitz. It's a shame they couldn't have rebuilt it with a little more architectural sensitivity.

'This area was levelled during the war,' Tim says, as if reading my mind.

'It looks like it's never really recovered.'

'Why do you say that?'

I fear I've offended him. 'It just looks a bit... um... eclectic.'

'I suppose it's beneath what you're used to, but this is where I grew up.' He sounds like a little boy being bullied. 'I thought you might like to see it.'

'I didn't mean to offend you, sorry.'

'It's OK. I'm just a London boy through and through.' Finally, he takes my hand. 'Anyway, it's not much further.'

Several blocks on, he steers me into a dark residential road with a road sign saying 'Larkspur Gardens'. The first few houses look old – Georgian. Then, as if part of the terrace was surgically removed, the rest of the road is a long line of red-brick semis.

'This way,' he says. 'We're the last house on the right.'

I stop walking. '*We?*'

'Sorry, I should have warned you. It's Gran's house. She really wants to meet you.'

He's all charm and polish again, whereas I feel like a caged animal.

'Your gran? Really?' I fake a laugh, caught off guard. 'I don't want to impose.' I make a show of checking my watch. 'I mean, it's late. It wouldn't be right.'

My hand still in his, he draws me closer, his eyes warm and melting. 'Come on, Alex. I've told her all about you. Just come in for a cuppa.' He leans down and brushes my lips softly with his. Adrenalin surges through my body, waking up long-sleeping parts. 'And after that, we'll see, shall we?' His breath tickles my ears. Then he takes a very small, but very disappointing, step back.

'Oh, all right.' I hate myself for giving in. But what harm can it possibly do to have a cuppa with his gran?

31

My feet grow increasingly leaden as we near the end of the road. The house is tiny – the two semis together look like a small house that's been chopped in two. On his gran's side of the sickly hedge separating the two halves, there's only the door and a small window on the ground floor, and an upper floor with the same footprint. In front, there's a huge wheelie bin and a recycling crate that's overflowing with empty wine bottles; Tim's gran must enjoy a tipple or three. The net curtains are drawn, and I can hear the sound of a TV. The green paint on the door is flaking off, and there's a *No Junk Mail* sticker above the mail slot. Tim walks up to the door and bends down to get a key from under a pot of dead geraniums. He unlocks the door and gestures for me to go inside. Somehow, because the place looks so unwelcoming, I know I can't back out.

'Gran,' Tim calls out. 'We're here.'

We go into a tiny hallway, barely wide enough for Tim to walk straight in without knocking coats off the wall rack. The house smells of cigarette smoke and deep-fried chips. In another room, the TV switches off.

'Wait here.' He goes through a door into the front room, closing it behind him. 'I brought Alex,' I hear him say.

All of a sudden, I have a strong urge to bolt.

The reply is muffled, but I hear Tim say: 'Now Gran, you said you'd be on your best behaviour—'

'Bring her in – I want to meet Catherine's granddaughter,' an elderly female voice says. My pulse jolts. It's a set-up – just like when I was locked in the loo and then arrested. I have a sickly notion that it might all be related.

Tim comes out a moment later, all smiles. 'Sorry,' he says in a low voice. 'I just wanted to remind her that you were coming.'

'I heard what she said. She knows I'm Catherine's granddaughter. How does she know that? I mean... *I* didn't even know that until yesterday.'

'Really?' For the first time, he looks concerned. He reaches out to pat my arm. I flinch. 'Catherine and my gran are old friends,' he says.

'Old friends?' I hiss. 'You should have told me.'

'I'm sure Gran can tell you more. Why don't I go make some tea?'

I steady myself against the wall, trying to calm my breathing. The anonymous envelopes, the diary entries, and the 'uninvited guest' have made me jumpy and suspicious. And now, a relative stranger and his grandmother seem to know more about me than I do myself. But maybe I'm overreacting. Maybe Catherine and this woman are old friends and she rang and told her what happened. It's possible. I stare at Tim's handsome face. His brow is furrowed in worry. Either he's a very good actor or else I'm completely off base in suspecting him of anything. Still, the situation is making me very uncomfortable.

'Really, this isn't necessary,' I say. 'In fact, I think I'll get a taxi back to the station. The trains only go every hour—'

'Tim?' the old woman calls out.

'Just a minute, Gran.' He spreads his hands in a pleading gesture. 'Just say hello... please.'

He's backed me into a corner and we both know it. It would be rude to just walk out on an elderly lady, and if she really is a friend of Mrs Fairchild's then I ought to pop in and say hello.

'Some date,' I mutter under my breath as I walk into the lounge.

A woman is sitting on the sofa covered up with a well-worn afghan rug. Her black hair is streaked with grey, and she's wearing a purple velvet tracksuit and a pair of flip-flops – something I can't imagine Catherine or any of her WI friends wearing. Her face is a map of wrinkles, and her nose has a reddish tinge of burst capillaries. Still, I have the feeling that she might not be quite as old as she looks.

The room is shabby, crowded with a brown three-piece suite and a giant television. On one wall is a shelf full of knickknacks, and next to the sofa is a small table and a bookcase. There are overflowing ashtrays on every available surface. The only colour in the room is a large framed photograph of Tim in a robe and mortarboard smiling smugly, holding his law diploma against a backdrop of Lincoln's Inn.

'Hello.' I force a smile. 'Mrs—'

'Edwards.' The woman looks up at me with deep-set eyes the same chocolate-brown colour as her grandson's. But instead of looking warm and melting, hers look murky and unfriendly. Her hands quaver as she holds a cigarette to her mouth and lights it with a plastic lighter. Her lips purse around her cigarette as she considers me. 'Have a seat,' she says.

I sit on the saggy brown armchair nearest the door, in case I need to bolt. 'Nice photograph,' I say, pointing to the photo of Tim.

The House of Hidden Secrets

She blows out a thin column of smoke. 'He was the first one in the family to make good.'

I don't even attempt to respond. I know Tim said he was from a humble background, but there's an undercurrent of desperation and hostility here that I hadn't expected.

She ashes the cigarette and gives a rasping cough. 'Graduated top of his class, he did. No one expected that, I can tell you.'

'It's impressive that he represents people in need.'

'People in need,' she snorts. 'That's his mistake. Never try to help people in need – won't get you anything but grief.'

'I suppose it can be a bit thankless.' *Where is Tim to rescue me? How long does it take to boil a kettle?*

'Thankless! Yes – *you* could say that, Catherine's granddaughter.'

Her tone sends a chill through me. I stand up, itching to leave. Tim's gran seems to be a few cards short of a full deck. Is he trying to test me – to see if I can tolerate his family before things go too far? It's a test I'm going to fail.

'I think I should go see how Tim is coming with that tea.'

'Sit down,' she says sharply.

I'm so startled that I do as she says.

'Most people think it was a long time ago,' she says. 'I was only a bun in the oven when it all happened. I didn't even meet Catherine till much later – when her dad forced her to come back to the old neighbourhood and look down on the rest of us. But it was a long hard shadow over my whole life, let me tell you. And my daughter's life, and Tim's life too.'

'I'm sorry, I have no idea what you're talking about.' I stop bothering to sound polite.

She stubs out the cigarette and stares at me intently. 'My

father was a good man,' she says. 'A hero. He drove an ambulance during the Blitz.'

'Oh?' I feel an icy stab of concern. 'That sounds very noble.'

'Yes, it was noble. He saved lives. People were screaming, burning, maimed. The bombs whined overhead, and most people went to the shelters. But my father didn't. He was out there in the midst of it all, risking his life to save others and documenting all of it. And where did it get him? Where did it get him, I ask you?'

'I have no idea.'

'It got him arrested, that's what. They sent him to the Front where he got a bullet in the back for his troubles.'

'Really?'

'Here, look.' She levers up and takes a black leather-bound book from the shelf next to the sofa. It's an old photo album. I catch a glimpse of baby pictures in colour – most likely Tim. But instead of showing me photos of him naked in the bath or with Superman pants on his head, she flips to the back of the album where some old newspaper clippings are pasted on with flaking glue. The first clipping shows a heavy-set man with a mop of chestnut hair being led away in handcuffs. The date on the clipping is 1950 and the title reads: 'Wartime looting cover-up exposed'.

Feeling the weight of her eyes on me, I skim the article. According to the report, Winston Churchill himself hushed up arrests of looters during the Blitz in order to maintain public morale and the 'Blitz Spirit'. The article speaks of a man who was arrested in late 1940 for looting, but his case never went to trial. His name is Harold Dawkins.

'Dawkins?' The name sounds familiar but I can't place it.

'Hal Dawkins. My father,' the old woman says.

I continue to look down at the paper so I don't have to look at her. 'I'm not quite sure I understand.'

'No?' She grabs the book away from me like I'm unworthy to be granted access to her precious memories. 'What exactly don't you understand? My father was arrested but never tried. He couldn't put up a defence to prove that he was innocent. Instead, they hushed it up. Sent him to the Front; and he was killed.'

She shakes another cigarette from the pack and lights it.

'He never lived to see his child born – me.' She flips over another page. There's a short telegram pasted there, regretfully informing the next of kin of Harold A. Dawkins that he was killed in the line of duty.

I try to imagine how it would feel to receive something like this about my own father. Unwittingly, my eyes fill with tears.

'So now you begin to see.' Mrs Edwards sniffs. 'My mum fell apart because of the whole nasty business. It ruined all our lives. But it won't ruin Tim's life. He's made good, I tell you.'

I swallow hard. 'It all sounds very tragic, and I'm sorry for the loss your family suffered. But why are you telling me this?'

'Tim says you're a nice girl. That you know nothing.' She flips the scrapbook to the last page and sits back.

I stare at the grainy black and white photo on the page. It shows three men in ambulance service uniforms standing together, arms around each other's shoulders. The man on the end is holding a bottle of beer – and I recognise Hal Dawkins from the other photographs in the album. But it's the man in the middle that I look at. A man I recognise from numerous photographs kept in pride of place at Mallow Court. The beloved adoptive father of Catherine Fairchild…

Frank Bolton.

Somewhere deep inside of me, a light goes out. I force

myself to look up at the old woman, to see the truth imprinted behind her eyes – her version of it, anyway.

'Yes,' she says, 'that's Frank Bolton.'

'And?' I struggle to keep my voice level.

She shakes her head. 'Everyone loved my father, Hal. He was a laugh – not to mention good-looking and smart. Always willing to lend a hand for a bit of graft, or spot a round of drinks with the last of his wages. He and Frank might have grown up together on the wrong side of the tracks, but my father was on the up and up. And Frank, well, he was jealous. He was one of those quiet types who kept his head down like a worm in the dirt. He could have been a clerk at the factory or maybe a civil servant. But instead, he stood on the shoulders of giants – my father – and heaved himself out of the muck. All the way to that fancy house in the country that Catherine's so proud of.'

'He made something of himself. What's wrong with that?'

She laughs, barring a set of yellow-stained teeth. 'My father had one flaw. He thought his charm would see him through anything. So when the chips began to fall, he didn't take it seriously enough. When Frank accused him, people listened.'

'So you're saying that Frank accused your father of looting?'

'Aye.' Her lip curls upwards as she stabs a gnarled finger at Frank Bolton's image. 'My father died for a crime he didn't commit. And your grandmother – the *lovely* Catherine – she's been living off the back of it ever since.'

'I don't believe you.' I grip the grungy sides of the chair.

She shakes her head. 'You may be a nice girl, but you seem a little thick. It was despicable what they did. Frank, and others like him. Stealing from people's homes when he was supposed to be saving lives. When people got home from the shelter, everything was gone – art, jewellery, money, even clothing. But who could they complain to? Nobody wanted to hear that the

Blitz Spirit was a big load of cock and bull. Certainly not the police.' She laughs bitterly. 'And it got worse too. Looting from corpses – even from people who weren't dead yet – and helping them on their way.'

All my muscles tense up at once. I want to laugh in this woman's face. Get up and leave, slamming the door behind me at the indignity of her accusations. But instead, I sit there, rigid.

'And Frank's other friend' – she points to the third man in the picture – 'he was posh. His family had friends in high places. Handy when it came to disposing of things.'

'You have no proof of any of this, do you?'

When she smiles, her crooked teeth make her look like a witch. 'You don't know what I have and what I don't have now, do you, girl? You'd better ask Catherine – she might tell you differently. My father, you see, he fancied himself a bit of a scribbler. He loved keeping his journals.'

'How dare you!' I push away the photo album and catapult up from the sofa. 'You're the one who's trying to frighten Mrs Fairchild. I've seen what you've sent her. Entries from a diary – your father's diary, I suppose – with nasty little notes scribbled in the margins. That's harassment.'

'I'm just letting Catherine know what's what.' She cackles a laugh. 'Now who's looking down on who?'

'Mrs Fairchild doesn't deserve any of this – and neither do I.' In two strides I'm at the door. 'I've heard enough. Goodbye.'

The old woman continues to laugh as I rush out of the room. My way is blocked by a smiling Tim in the hallway, carrying a tray.

'Cup of tea?'

* * *

I push past him and run out into the night. Behind me, I can hear Tim shouting at his gran. 'What did you say to her? I thought you just wanted to have a chat?'

Tim yells out the door as I run: 'Alex? Alex!'

I double my pace, petrified that he's going to chase after me. I pull out my phone – if he follows me, I'll have to ring – I don't know! – 999. I'll tell them that I've been brought to East London under false pretences or something. I rush around the corner of the road and practically ram into someone walking the other way. 'Oh!' I call out, my arms wheeling to stay on my feet. The other person has no such problem. It's an old man with a walker. His gnarled hands grip the handles and he doesn't even waver. There's a small dog at his feet that starts barking its head off at me.

'Down, Winston,' the man commands. The dog gives one last yap for good measure.

'Sorry,' I say. 'I wasn't looking where I was going.'

The old man gives a concerned tsk. 'You should be looking up there.' He points a crooked finger at the sky. 'Bomber's moon – that's what we called it.'

I look up at the full moon that's come out from behind a dark bank of cloud. Suddenly, my eyes begin to swim and I can almost see the dark silhouettes of planes blocking out the light, come to kill, maim, and wreak havoc on London.

'You were there?'

As if sensing my distress, the dog lets out a whimper. Is it me, or is everyone in this neighbourhood just plain bonkers?

'Oh aye. Flew a Spitfire – beautiful little plane. And I was born and raised on this street. Whenever there's a moon like this, Winston and I come and keep an eye out. I'm not about to let Jerry force me out of my rightful house and home. No, ma'am. Miles Pepperharrow – that's me – is going nowhere.'

I lean down and pat Winston on the head. 'Sounds sensible, Mr Pepperharrow,' I say. 'But *I* need to get somewhere. Any idea where I can get a taxi?'

He points in the opposite direction from Shoreditch. 'Try two blocks over. It's a busy road. Lots of 'em about.'

'Thanks,' I say, hoping he means taxis. 'You and Winston take care now.'

'We will, young lady,' the old man says. 'We most certainly will.'

PART III

There will come soft rains and the smell of the
 ground,
And swallows circling with their shimmering
 sound;
And frogs in the pool singing at night,
And wild plum-trees in tremulous white;
Robins will wear their feathery fire
Whistling their whims on a low fence-wire;
And not one will know of the war, not one
Will care at last when it is done.

— SARA TEASDALE, 'FLAME AND SHADOW'

32

13 NOVEMBER 1940 – 3.30 A.M.

I left Sadie's house and started walking. The snow had melted into soggy puddles and clouds covered the full moon. I wandered back up the road thinking of what I'd seen, and why tonight it affected me more than before. But of course I knew why. Marina. I tried to distance myself, forget her name. Forget that I knew her. It was casual, after all. But the girl... those eyes. The truth in them staring at me like a mirror...

I put my hand in my pocket and touched the locket. It was heavy and warm, almost like a life force in itself. I knew I was right to take it and keep it safe for her. I'd give it back... I could trust myself.

Though my shift was over, I walked back to the ambulance dispatch. Two men were huddled around the table drinking cups of bitter chicory. 'Evening,' I said. One of them grumbled a reply. As I put the kettle on again, I heard uneven footsteps outside. A man walked in – not Flea, but Robbie with his camera.

'What are you doing here?' I said.

'Nice to see you too,' he responded. 'I'll have a cup of tea since the kettle's on.' He put something on the table. 'Brought you this,' he said.

It was a black and white photograph. It seems like a lifetime ago that he was here taking photos of 'our brave ambulance crew' for a newspaper article. The photo showed me, and Flea and Spider, looking years younger. Looking happy. The living embodiment of 'Blitz Spirit'. And now Spider's family home is a pile of rubble – the poor bastard's still on his shift and won't even know it yet. And Flea... well...

'It's for you,' he said. 'I made some copies. Keep it to show your kids someday, and your grandkids. Show them that you did your bit.'

'Yeah.' *I tucked the photo into my pocket.* 'Like you, you mean.'

He shook his head. 'Bum leg. Even your lot wouldn't have me.'

He turned to leave. The kettle began to spit and hiss.

'Wait a minute, Robbie,' *I said.* 'What else have you seen?'

He shrugged. 'Enough.'

'Sit down,' *I said.* 'Tell me.'

33

Frank Bolton. 'Knicker King', philanthropist, pillar of society and saviour of a crumbling Elizabethan house called Mallow Court. Frank Bolton. The beloved adoptive father of Catherine, my birth grandmother.

Though he's not related by blood, he's still the trunk of my newly discovered family tree. But does he also have a secret side to his dossier – a dark side that's remained hidden over almost sixty years? Is he the kind of man who would capitalise on the misfortune of others? The kind of man who would steal from innocent people during one of the darkest moments of history and then frame another man for it, issuing him with a death sentence in the process?

For my grandmother's sake, I don't want to believe it. But despite knowing the ins and outs of the country house he purchased and restored, I know very little about him. The question Tim asked that day on the tour resonates in my mind: How did he make the money to buy the factory? I'd made up an answer on the spot – 'The war provided a lot of opportunities for an ambitious young man.' Little did I know then what kind of 'opportunities' may have arisen for Frank Bolton.

The taxi drops me at the station; I have to run to catch the last train. The carriage is stuffed full of people eating stinky Burger King food, and I stand near one of the doors, feeling sick to my stomach. I've worked so hard to turn Mallow Court into a business, make it my home, and find out the truth about my family – but could all of it be built on lies and criminal acts? And what about my grandmother? For over sixty years, Frank Bolton has been the rock on which her life was built. Even in death, she idolises him. How will she react if she even suspects the accusations being made against him by Mrs Edwards?

I think back to how upset and preoccupied she's been lately. The brown envelopes, the journal entries written by Hal Dawkins – they must be the 'proof' that Mrs Edwards spoke of. It's not Mrs Fairchild herself that's being blackmailed, but her family name, her respected adoptive father, and her right to be in the place she's called home for sixty years.

I clench my fists. How dare Mrs Edwards upset my grandmother like that?

But what if it's the truth?

The train disgorges me an hour later onto a dark platform where no one is about. In the dimly lit car park, every shadow holds a possible threat. My phone rings in my bag and the hairs prickle on the back of my neck. While I was on the train, Tim called several times, but I didn't answer. I hurry to my car and drive back to Mallow Court. Only when I'm back inside my flat with the door bolted do I listen to my voicemails.

Three are from Tim. My thumb hovers over the delete key, but I force myself to listen. The first message is breathless and frantic. 'Alex, it's me. I'm so sorry. Please, pick up and let me explain. Gran's a little unstable, as you probably guessed. She told me what she said to you. Really, I had no idea about any of it. Please, pick up – I—'

The message cuts off. I put the phone down, my heart slowing for the first time since I ran out of the house in Holloway. Could Tim be for real?

I listen to the next message.

'Please, Alex – I need to explain. Can we talk? I'll come to you. Tomorrow. Call me back.'

Tomorrow. Oh God. What can I do? I'll have to call him back and tell him not to come. To stay away from me—

Voicemail goes to the last message. This time it's just a click.

I turn on the TV to occupy my brain as it tries to make sense of everything and comes up woefully short. Mrs Edwards surely sent some of the diary entries by post – she as good as admitted it. But try as I might, I can't see her coming all the way to Mallow Court to leave an envelope on the doorstep. Did Tim do it for her? Was he the person who locked me in the loo, conveniently showing up later at the police station to play knight in shining armour to my damsel in distress?

I flip aimlessly through the channels, bypassing late-night game shows, shopping channels, and phone sex adverts. I settle on a documentary on the bombing of Dresden, which seems appropriate. In the lower right-hand corner is a little man – the sign language interpreter. The narrator is going on about tonnes of explosives and numbers of burning buildings. The interpreter seems to give up midway through and spreads his hands in a big 'boom' gesture. Then he stands back to 'watch' as the bombs fall, and there's footage of women and children rushing out of burning houses with as much as they can carry, and getting flattened by the sheer force of the firestorm. It's so awful, but I can't look away. I think not only of my grandmother but also of the man walking his dog – Mr Pepperharrow? I can't imagine living through what they did – the terrible fear, the pain of loss, the total and complete ruption in the fabric of normal life.

The narrator starts up again. 'In the end, the city was reduced to a smoking ruin.' The interpreter twiddles his fingers like smoke rising to the sky as the footage shows the devastation. I've had enough. I lie down in bed and turn off the lamp. But I keep my eyes open, staring at the light leaking around the edge of the curtains from the 'bomber's moon'.

* * *

I wake up in a tangle of damp sheets the next morning after tossing and turning with nightmares. Tension tightens in my chest as I get ready to go over to the main house. I desperately need to speak to my grandmother – though I'm at a loss as to what I'm going to say.

Her clogs aren't in their usual place by the door; I surmise she's already up and out. I go outside to look for her, but she's not in any of the usual places. Admittedly, it's a relief not to have to mention Mrs Edwards's allegations. In telling off the old woman for harassment, I hope I've put a stop to the brown envelopes and nasty accusations scribbled in the margins of an old journal. But the truth has a strange way of outing itself. The best thing I can do is develop my own arsenal of weapons against slander and lies. Returning to the house, I search up Frank Bolton on the internet.

The search generates a surprising number of results, mostly related to Frank as the chairman and CEO of Intimates Unlimited. A few of them chronicle the modest details of his early life. He was born in Warrington in 1915, and his family moved to East London when he was still a boy. His father was a warehouseman for a cloth manufacturer and his mum was a school teacher. By all accounts, Frank was a smart boy, if a touch reserved, and he got himself an apprenticeship in the business office of the clothing manufacturing company where his father worked. Just as he was working his way up the corporate ladder, war broke out. He was wounded in the shoulder early in the Norway Campaign in April 1939, and when he returned to London and the Blitz began, he became an ambulance driver.

This last piece of information chills my blood. The article confirms what I already know from the photo. Frank Bolton was an ambulance driver, just like Mrs Edwards had said. *But...* I remind myself sternly, that doesn't mean he did anything wrong. On the contrary – he risked his life to save others. Most likely, Frank Bolton was a hero.

The article then talks about his career in ladies' underwear. He purchased a disused factory at auction that made thermal underwear, elastic, and RAF uniforms. After the war, Bolton took advantage of new fashion trends and began making ladies' undergarments and nylon stockings. His unique selling point was the 'double gusset', which he marketed with racy adverts of hand-drawn pin-up girls. In the 1950s, there was a newfound focus on luxury goods that the average person could afford. What better than British-made lacy pants?

I stare at the tiny photo of his first factory. Frank Bolton sounds like a legitimate businessman who happened to be at the right place at the right time – a kind of Sir Alan Sugar for ladies' knickers. The article talks about Frank's marriage to a pin-up girl named Mabel and their two sons, Henry and Daniel. There's a brief mention of the house, Mallow Court, that he purchased, contents and all, in a dilapidated state. It also mentions an adopted daughter, but doesn't give her name.

I shut down the website, questions battering my head. Why

did Frank Bolton adopt a wartime orphan? Why did Catherine, and not his sons, inherit the house? And then there's the most pressing question of all... What do I do now?

One thing's for sure: I need to see all the diary entries that Mrs Fairchild has received so far. Even if they wouldn't stand up in a court of law, they could make things look bad for Frank Bolton. I need to lay all the pieces out in front of me and see what picture they form. Surely that's what a barrister like Tim would do.

Tim. My skin crawls as I think of the 'uninvited guest'. Stalking me from the stockroom, locking me in the downstairs loo; then, calling the police – or maybe having his gran make the call pretending to be Catherine Fairchild – and having me arrested. Conveniently turning up just in time to 'rescue' me; worming his way into my life with his deep voice, dark eyes, and the sob story about widows and orphans. What a fool I was to trust him.

I'm about to go out and look for my grandmother again when all of a sudden, gravel sprays and a silver car pulls up. The car nips into the disabled parking space, and Tim jumps out brandishing a bouquet of white lilies wrapped in cellophane. Speaking of the devil...

'Alex!' he says. 'I came as soon as I could. I need to explain—'

'You *need* to move that car.'

He has the nerve to laugh, obviously thinking that I'm joking. That in and of itself sets my hackles on edge. He takes a few steps towards me, holding out the flowers.

'I mean it,' I growl, keeping my hands at my side. 'I'll have it towed, and you along with it.'

'Alex, please. Let's get a coffee. I know you must be upset—'

'Upset? Really?' I barrage him with an outpouring of my

suspicions. From blackmailing an old lady about her family history to falsely imprisoning me and gaining my trust under dishonest pretences. 'And then, to top it off,' I shout, 'you put me through the ordeal of meeting your crackers gran!'

'Alex, pull yourself together.' He sets the lilies down on top of his car and puts his hands on my shoulders. I pull away. 'I *like* you, Alex. A lot. Why do you think I'm here?'

'I don't know,' I snap. 'Maybe to leave another unmarked envelope with an upsetting diary entry?'

'That's ridiculous.' His voice deepens like he's addressing a hostile witness. 'I haven't left any envelopes. I came to the house and took your tour because I was curious. Gran's had that photo album around for so long. She talked about Catherine Bolton like they were old friends – that's what I thought, anyway. So I wanted to learn more.'

'Why? So you could wreck an old woman's retirement?'

'Because Frank Bolton knew my great-grandfather, Hal,' he says. 'He's the only link I have to his past. His life was cut short, as you know, by the accusation of looting. He didn't get a trial – Winston Churchill himself hushed it up. Nowadays it would be seen as a miscarriage of justice. But back then, during those dark days... I guess there were reasons for it.'

'Do you think your great-grandfather was innocent?'

'I don't know.'

'So why now? Why bring it up after all these years?'

'Because it's only recently that Gran found proof. Her father's journal. Hal "Badger" Dawkins. She read through it and immediately saw that it supported her theory that he was innocent. And implicated Frank Bolton in the process. So now, she's got a real bee in her bonnet.'

'More like a hornet's nest. And where did she find this precious diary anyway?'

'She was sorting out some old boxes in the attic.' He scratches the non-existent stubble on his chin. 'I gather she found it in a box of her father's things.'

The fight flows from my body, leaving me limp. 'And what does she want with us? Money? Some kind of justice?' I round on him. 'Is she another one of your "widows and orphans" who are trying to right past wrongs?'

'No.' His voice softens. 'She's my gran. She may be a bit off sometimes, but I love her. I'm not going to lie – when she first told me the story, I did feel that a terrible injustice had been done to my family. But I also told her that it was most likely too late to do anything about it. I advised her to forget the whole thing. To let it go.'

'Well, you sure succeeded.'

He takes a step forward, reaching out to me again. I step back, but this time, when he persists in putting his hand on my arm, I don't jerk away.

'Gran did send a few of the diary entries through the post.' He hangs his head. 'She admitted that when she first saw the diary, inscribed with her father's name, and telling all about those terrible times, she wanted Catherine to know the whole upsetting truth. I'm really sorry, and I hope you won't hold it against her. But neither she nor I left anything here at the house, and for the record, I certainly didn't lock you in the loo.'

I draw back. 'But what about your being there at the police station? You can't expect me to believe that you just happened to be at the right place at the right time.'

I stare him down, sure that I've caught him out.

Instead, he starts to laugh. 'You're right – it wasn't a total coincidence.'

'No?'

'The truth is, I'm friendly with one of the police officers at the station. He's helped me on a couple of cases in the past, and though he's supposed to be retired now, he's still around a lot seeing his mates. After I did the house tour, we went down the pub for a drink. To the Golden Fleece – you know it?'

'I know it.' I press my lips in a line.

'We spent the whole afternoon catching up. I told him all about visiting Mallow Court and how I met this smashing tour guide – very sexy, in fact.'

I stare at him, my face growing hot.

'So when he heard about the arrest at Mallow Court, he put two and two together. He rang me, and I came to rescue you.'

I want to believe him. He takes me by the shoulders again and draws me close. He tilts my chin up with his finger and leans in, his lips brushing mine. Part of me wants to pull away, and part of me feels like jelly. I stand there, not quite responding, but not quite protesting either.

When finally we come up for air, he holds me at arm's length. 'I *really* like you, Alex. Please say you forgive me.'

'I forgive you.' The words stumble out of my mouth.

'Good. I won't keep you any longer – I'm due in court this afternoon. But I'll ring you later.'

'No... I mean... I don't know.'

He brushes a lock of hair back from my cheek. 'Sorry about the car,' he says with a sideways grin. 'Next time I'll take care to park properly.'

He picks up the lilies and thrusts them into my hand. I stand there watching until his car disappears in a cloud of gravel dust. He had an explanation for everything. But in actual fact, his assurances have made me even more unsettled.

If he's not responsible for what's been going on, then who is?

34

I put the flowers in a vase and go to look for my grandmother. She's nowhere to be found, and when I ask Edith, she reminds me that Mrs Fairchild is away for the whole day at the Hampton Court Flower Show. I sit Edith down and tell her about the revelation – that I'm Mrs Fairchild's granddaughter. I'm expecting her to be surprised, but in actual fact, she just nods her head.

'It explains a lot,' she says. 'The way you two are around each other. And I've always thought you looked a bit like her.'

'Really?'

'Yes.' She smiles. 'I'm so happy for you.'

'Thanks.' I decide to not mention the fear that my newfound contentment might be woefully short-lived.

Taking advantage of my grandmother's absence, I go up to her room to look for the diary entries. But the door is locked, and I feel too guilty to use the master key. Instead, I closet myself in the estate office, leaning against the desk with my head in my hands.

I think about Tim's visit, the memory of the kiss turning sour in my mouth. The attraction I felt for him has become irreparably blurred by the inky doubts that have crept in around the edges. Regardless of what he may believe himself, his gran has made accusations against Frank Bolton – terrible accusations. And Tim brought me round to meet her so she could throw them in my face.

The scholar in me tries to view things dispassionately: yes, there are mysteries, and I may never know the truth. Every student of history knows that 'truth' often consists solely of what is written down by the survivors. The historical record is biased and incomplete. And in this case, I've yet to see a shred of real evidence proving that Frank Bolton was anything other than an upstanding man. Or that Hal Dawkins, Tim's great-grandfather, was innocent of the crime for which he was accused. But assuming that the diary is a voice from the grave, I'll have to find some way to prove that Frank Bolton is innocent. If I don't, then my grandmother will suffer.

Despite the worries battering my head, I manage to get through the day's activities: PR for the costume exhibition, scheduling venue viewings, fishing a nappy out of a blocked loo, escorting a woman out of the Tudor kitchens for smoking a cigarette.

When the house is closed for the day, I go into the green salon where a number of old photos are displayed. The room was updated in the early 1900s by a rich American related to the Rockefellers. There's a stunningly ornate plaster ceiling, but other than that, the room is cosy rather than grand, papered in green silk with an embossed ivory leaf pattern and furnished with comfortable, if slightly saggy, William Morris print chairs and sofas.

At the rear of the room there's a huge Steinway Grand purchased by Frank Bolton as a present for his wife Mabel. Occasionally, we hold concerts in the great hall, and the piano is moved there by a specially hired crew. But it spends most of its life in this room, its lid a display area for Mrs Fairchild's photos. There are wedding photos, a photo of Robin as a baby, and a few of her as a smiling child with blonde hair. I've looked at these photos many times before, but never really *saw* them. *My mother*. I peer at her closely, noting that there's very little resemblance between us. Only the eyes… and I'm not quite sure how that makes me feel. There's also a photo of me taken as part of a group shot of the staff last Christmas. The rest of the surface of the enormous lid is filled with photos of Mrs Fairchild's beloved adoptive father, Frank Bolton.

The nearest photo shows Frank shaking hands with Tony Blair at a charity lunch for the blind. Frank must have been in his late sixties at the time, but even so, he's still a good-looking man. His hair is thick and white; his skin has a healthy tan. He's not a tall man, but he's well-built with a broad chest and shoulders. The main feature that I note, however, is the self-composed look on his face, the camera catching a blur of warmth in his blue eyes. According to my grandmother, his smiles were rare, and mostly reserved for his family. She said that he was a man who 'loved life'. From this photo, I can believe it.

One by one, I analyse the other photos of Frank. He's captured in many different settings: sitting at an easel in the garden, dressed up for a ball, giving a cheque to a charity for displaced coal miners. His upright demeanour never seems to waver. Either he has a clear conscience, or – worryingly, if the allegations against him are true – no conscience at all.

I set down the last photo, wiping my fingerprints off the frame with my shirt. There's nothing in Mrs Fairchild's shrine to indicate that her adoptive father might have had a dark and ruthless side: a side that allowed him to steal from others in order to amass a 'life-loving' fortune. But what about the photos she doesn't have on display, and Frank Bolton's own photos, papers and personal effects? I can't imagine that she's thrown them away. Where are they?

Something catches my eye on a little table next to the fireplace that's normally empty. It's another photo frame but this one is face down on the table, and I know it doesn't belong there.

I turn the frame over: it's a black and white image of Frank Bolton. He's wearing his ambulance uniform, his arms draped companionably around two other men. Hal Dawkins, and the unknown friend in the photo that Mrs Edwards showed me. It may well have been taken at the same time. I undo the little swivel hooks on the back of the frame and take the picture out. The paper is brittle and yellowing, but there's an attribution stamped on the photo: *Robert Copthorne, November 1940*.

November 1940 – the same month and year Hal Dawkins was arrested! I peer closer. Just below the date, I can just make out three words written in faint pencil: *Flea, Badger, Spider*.

I puzzle over the words. Could they be nicknames? I recall my grandmother telling me that the diary was inscribed as written by 'Badger' – Hal Dawkins. If – and it's a big *if* – I'm going to proceed under the assumption that Frank Bolton and Hal Dawkins are both innocent, then perhaps it's the third man who's guilty. What had Mrs Edwards said about him? *He had friends in high places.*

At the very least, I should find out who he is. I put the photo back in the frame and leave it face down on the table the way I found it.

35

The next day, I oversleep and don't get to the house until after ten. I'm stressed and agitated, and it doesn't help when Edith tracks me down and tells me there's a man here to see me.

'What man?' My heart takes a swan dive. Tim again? Back to see if I'm up for another round of 'kiss and make up'? I'm not, I realise. In theory, I've forgiven him. But his gran has opened a can of worms that I haven't managed to close. I can't trust him, so I can't take things further.

'I didn't get his name, but he's in the café.' Edith frowns at my lack of enthusiasm. 'He asked me what you liked and I told him coffee and scones. I hope that's OK?'

'Yes, thanks.' I can't be mad at Edith. Not when I haven't confided in her, or anyone, about what's happened. I'll get rid of him and then I'll call Karen, I decide. It will help to talk to someone neutral, even if there's bound to be a pep talk at the end of it.

'OK.' She gives me a little wink and heads back in the direction of the gift shop.

I comb my hair and apply a coat of lip gloss. Mum always

advised me to look my best when sending a man packing. I wish I knew exactly what to say to get the message across, but I'll have to trust myself to wing it.

The café is noisy and crowded, and a delightful scent of coffee and fresh-baked scones wafts in the air. I look around but don't see Tim. But when I catch a glimpse of the tall, leggy man sitting at a little corner table by the window, my stomach gives an excited flip. Although he's wearing his usual T-shirt (today it's The Rise and Fall of Ziggy Stardust and the Spiders from Mars) and jeans, seeing Christopher Heath-Churchley out of his workshop is a revelation. I let myself acknowledge for a fraction of a second how unique, and rather stunning, he is.

'Hi, Alex!' He stands up as I approach his table. 'I hope it's OK me turning up like this?'

'Of course.' I enjoy the bubbling feeling inside me as he kisses me casually on both cheeks. 'It's great to see you.'

'Do you have time for a coffee?' He holds up a silver number five that he must have got at the till. 'I took the liberty of ordering for two.'

'Yes, great.' I sit down, feeling better than I have in days.

Adele, the barista, comes over to the table carrying a tray. 'Here you are, sir.' She sets down the tray and gives me a surreptitious wink, which I ignore.

Chris unloads the tray. He pours us each a coffee and passes me the basket of fresh cinnamon scones. My favourite. I'm aware of his long legs stretching out close to mine.

'I was curious to see Mallow Court.' He cuts his scone in half, spreading it generously with butter. 'Though I wasn't quite sure I'd be welcome given my "family connections".'

'Your entrance fee is as good as anyone else's, I guess.'

We both laugh. Just being here in his presence, I feel light inside; at ease, except for a strong undercurrent of attraction.

Unwittingly, I realise how with Tim, there was always a faint air of judgement. He made me feel defensive about my education and my job. And regardless of his apologies and excuses, stories about meeting old friends down the pub, and wanting me to meet his gran for a cuppa, all along he was hiding things. Those chocolate eyes turned out to be deep, muddy quicksand.

I realise Chris has asked me a question. He's no longer laughing or smiling.

'Are you sure you're all right, Alex? Do you want me to leave?'

'No!' I say. Without thinking, I reach out and take his hand. When I realise what I've done, I withdraw it swiftly and sip my coffee. The liquid is dark and bitter; I forgot the milk and sugar. What *is* wrong with me? 'I'm sorry,' I say. 'It's just that some things have been going on here and I'm kind of stressed. Some of it goes with the job – I've been busy preparing for the costume exhibition. But there are other things too. I probably shouldn't say, but...'

I want to tell him; confide in him. It doesn't matter who his father is, or what schools he went to or what car he drives. As far as I know, he hasn't judged me on those things. It's *me* who hasn't looked beyond what's in a name, to the man my instinct says he is underneath. A good man. Someone that I'm going to trust.

'Someone is out to hurt Mrs Fairchild,' I say. 'My grandmother.'

I tell him everything, starting with how my parents hid the truth about my birth mother and grandmother from me. 'It was done for noble reasons,' I say, 'but the revelation has knocked me for six. I'm still getting to grips with it.'

He listens intently to my story, his face occasionally slipping into a frown.

'And now,' I continue, 'my grandmother has been receiving anonymous letters. Diary entries from back during the war.'

'Whose diary?'

'A man called Hal Dawkins. He was an ambulance driver who worked with her adoptive father, Frank Bolton. Hal Dawkins pulled Catherine out of the wreckage during the Blitz.' With an embarrassed sigh, I proceed to tell him about Tim (leaving out certain details such as my erstwhile attraction to him, and the kiss that had once seemed promising) and meeting his vindictive gran.

'So this Tim person brought you to this woman under false pretences?'

In the safety of his presence, I'm able to laugh about it for the first time. 'It was unbelievably awful,' I say. 'It was like' – I hesitate as a wicked thought enters my brain – 'like you introducing me to your dad and him realising that I'm the "little nobody" who ruined his daughter's wedding.'

'Yeah.' He laughs awkwardly. 'I get it.'

'She genuinely feels aggrieved. And if what she said is true, then I can understand why. But I was completely ambushed.' I shake my head. 'Tim claimed afterwards that he didn't know what she intended to say. He concocted a good story to explain all of it. But he admitted that his gran sent the diary entries to Mrs Fairchild. I can't get around that, can I?'

His pale eyes cloud with concern. 'I'd stay away from this Tim character, and his gran, if I was you.'

'Yeah. I'm going to.'

'But what exactly is she claiming?'

'She says that her father was framed for looting – a crime for which he paid the ultimate price.'

'But how does that implicate Frank Bolton?'

'She says Frank was the real looter and that the diary entries prove it. She said that Frank Bolton gave trumped-up evidence against Hal Dawkins and got him arrested.'

'Whew,' Chris whistles. 'Quite a business.'

'Yes.' Telling him my story, I feel unaccountably relieved. I sense that my troubles are in safe hands: skilled hands, that can make sense of the most delicate and complex machinery. Hands that can make a long mute mechanical bird begin to sing again. What had he told me that time in his workshop? 'I take things apart and put them back together again.' It's my turn to sit back, while he mulls over the information.

'It's a fascinating story,' he says. 'And tragic, no doubt. But there are lots of gaps and very little proof. We need to figure out where we can find more clues.'

My mind processes the crucial word: *we*. He's going to help me. I don't have to do this alone.

'I agree.' I smile broadly. 'But I'm not quite sure what to do next.'

'I've got a few ideas.' He pushes back his chair and stands up. 'Like for starters, I think we need another pot of that delicious coffee.'

* * *

Time is suspended as we sit at the table, drinking coffee and eating scones, bandying about theories and strategies. The tea shop becomes more and more crowded as lunchtime approaches, but only a small part of me is even aware that an outside world exists. The conversation gradually becomes a general 'getting-to-know-you' chat about our lives. I tell him about my mum, dad, and my middle-class upbringing. Gradually, the chip on my shoulder seems to shrink. Chris is fascinated by my dad's dual penchant for yoga and Karl Marx.

'He sounds totally unique,' he says. 'Which is so rare these days.'

'He's that, all right,' I say. 'What about your family?'

His grin fades. 'I've never had the best relationship with my father.' He slits open a scone, spreads the butter, and closes it up again before taking a bite. 'Even as a boy. The fact that I liked to take things apart and put them back together drove him to distraction.'

'I can imagine.' I shudder to recall my own limited acquaintance with Chris's dad.

'He would have liked it if I'd been interested in racing cars, or yachts, or airplanes – something that was, to him, more impressive and practical.'

'Oh, much more!'

'But clocks…' He grimaces. 'That went down like a lead balloon. He never cared much for my mum's family. But I got on with them. My great-granddad Jeremy was a real clockmaker, not just a repairman like me. He taught me everything I know.'

I mull this over. 'I don't see why your father has a problem with your work. You repair and value antiques and your workshop is right behind the auctioneers.'

'Dad did try to get me interested in the family business once upon a time. But for him, it's not about the art and antiques. It's about our fees. He couldn't care less what comes and goes through our doors.'

'But he must know it's important. Surely a lot of checking must go on to make sure the artworks are authentic.'

'Of course,' he says. 'Provenance is all important. It's the foundation of our sterling reputation. Without that reputation, we couldn't attract the big buyers and sellers. But in our case, we keep our fees slightly lower than the competition – your Christie's and Sotheby's and the like – by not doing our own in-house research. I guess you could say, we maintain our standards by only accepting the best: that is, pieces with genuine, untarnished provenance.'

'Unlike the jewelled bird.'

'Well...' He spreads his hands. 'Yes.'

'That's OK,' I say. 'It's a family heirloom, and not for sale. Mrs Fairchild said that she would have passed it to her daughter, Robin, who was my birth mother. But instead, she's given it to me.'

'It's a fascinating piece: an incredible work of mechanical art. Much more interesting, in my humble opinion, than your average Chippendale dining set or old master painting.'

'You really think so?'

'I'm here, aren't I?'

'And here I thought you were seeking the pleasure of my company.'

'And if I was, would that be... out of order?' His eyes lock with mine. I stare into their crystalline blue. For an instant, I'm transported to a magical place where the sun is shining, and I'm stretched out, warm and languid; utterly at peace. A hand reaches out and touches my skin. Every cell in my body seems to open up like a flower. I blink back to reality. Chris has leaned across the table and taken my hand, stroking it with a touch so light that I'm sure I'm imagining it. Almost – except for the shimmering sensation drifting through my body.

I put all my effort into remembering how to speak. 'Um... what was the question?' are the only words I can find.

The moment is shattered by the ringing of a phone. It takes me a good long second to realise that it's my phone, squawking in the pocket of my jacket. I grapple for it, hoping it rings off. It doesn't. I'm aware of Chris watching me as I check the screen. *Tim Edwards*. Of all the blasted inconvenient times...

I press mute. Chris shifts in his chair. 'I really should be going—'

'No,' I say. 'You don't have to go. We could…' What is it that normal people do? People who like each other a lot. At least, that's how it is on my side. There's no point in trying to pretend any more that my interest is purely casual, or professional. 'Go for a walk,' I venture. 'In the garden. It's a lovely—'

The phone rings again, cutting me off.

'Damn it.'

'Go ahead.' He sips the last of his coffee.

With a reluctant sigh, I answer. 'Yes?' I say, curtly.

'Alex…' Tim purrs, his voice deep. But instead of vibrating strings deep inside me, this time, I just feel annoyed. 'I wanted to check how you're doing.'

'I'm fine.' I glance up at Chris. He's taken out a mobile phone and is scrolling through his text messages.

'Listen,' he says. 'Can we go for a drink? I've read through the diary. What's there anyway. Some pages are torn out at the end.'

'Torn out?'

'Yeah. I asked Gran. She doesn't know anything about it. But I'm trying to find out more.'

'Please don't bother.' A sense of disquiet rises inside me. 'We'll never know the truth of what happened back then. I'm sorry for what happened to your gran's father, really, I am. It's so tragic. But right now, I need to focus on my family. We need to put this whole thing behind us and move on.'

'Are you sure about that, Alex?' His voice holds a veiled threat. I can sense his face morphing into something ugly at the other end of the phone. 'Sure you can "put it all behind you" just like that?'

'Well, if you've read the diary and there's anything else to say, then maybe you can send me an email.'

'No. I want to see you. I thought that we were... that we had...'

Sensing that I need 'rescuing', Chris clears his throat loudly.

'Who's there?' Tim says.

'I'm just about to start a tour. So actually, I have to go. Bye, Tim.' I end the call and sit back in the chair, feeling shaken.

Chris puts away his phone, looking concerned. 'Are you OK, Alex?'

I'm about to say I'm fine but then I catch myself. I'm not *fine*. Why should I lie and say otherwise?

'I don't think Tim's going to let sleeping dogs lie. And if word gets out about Frank Bolton being a criminal... I don't know what my grandmother will do.'

'But surely that kind of thing just adds colour to this place.'

'She won't see it that way.'

'So we're back full circle. How do we find out the truth about Frank Bolton?'

'Well, there's another man in the photograph Tim's gran showed me. It was Frank Bolton, Hal Dawkins, and someone else. The three of them are in another photo I found here in the house. There are some names written on the back. "Robert Copthorne" – he's the photographer, I think. And then "Flea", "Badger", and "Spider".'

'What odd names.'

'I'm guessing they were nicknames.'

Chris frowns. 'Can I see the photo?'

'Of course.'

On our way out of the café, Chris takes our tray to the counter. I'm only half aware of the noise and the fact that the café staff, Adele and Chloe, are giving me 'thumbs up' gestures.

The other half of me is aware of Chris's solid presence as he follows me down the corridor and through a door in the panelling that leads to another corridor.

'I'd like to see more of the house,' he says as we walk. 'It seems so quirky – if that's the right word.'

'Perfect.'

'Though not today, I'm afraid. I'm due back in London. There's an auction of nautical timepieces coming up and the catalogue is due at the printers tomorrow. I've still got a couple of pieces to have a look at.'

'Sure.' I enjoy thinking about Chris in his workshop taking apart clocks and putting them back together. Though, somewhat less if it's connected with his father's auction house. 'This won't take a moment. It's just in here.'

I take down the rope across the door and usher him into the green salon. Although he's undoubtedly grown up in a lovely house – or *houses* – I'm still pleased when he lets out a low whistle.

'What a lovely, cosy room.'

'It is. My grandmother loves the light in here. And' – I raise an eyebrow – 'looking at the photos of her father.'

'Quite the shrine to Frank Bolton,' Chris agrees.

I go over to the table where I left the photo and am disturbed to find that it isn't there.

'I left it here,' I say. 'Someone's moved it.' My grandmother? I haven't seen her this morning, but then again, I've been 'otherwise occupied'. I search the room but don't find the photograph anywhere. Part of me wonders whether this is the work of the 'uninvited guest'. The fact that I'm sure Tim couldn't have taken the photograph doesn't make me feel much better. 'Maybe I'm going mad.' I look miserably at Chris. 'I swear it was here yesterday.'

'No worries.' He checks the black Swatch on his wrist. 'I really should be off now – you don't mind, do you?'

I do mind – more than I'd like to admit. But of course I don't say so. Instead, I smile and assure him that it was lovely to see him, and that I hope he will indeed come round for a proper tour of the house.

'I will.' He smiles in a searching way that makes me blush.

'Great.'

I lead the way out of the green salon and into the corridor that leads to the great hall. The guide on duty at the front door raises a questioning eyebrow at me as we go past.

Chris stops and examines the carving on the panelling next to the entrance. 'Amazing place,' he says. 'You're very lucky.'

'Thanks.' I grin. 'Yes, I am.'

Outside the door, he stops, looking confused. 'I'm in the overflow car park,' he says. 'Which way is that?'

I point in the right direction.

'Ah, I remember now.' I can tell he's lingering. 'I'll call you – or you call me if you find that photo.'

'Sure.' I step forward a fraction. The air crackles between us. A family with two small children and a pram come up the path from the car park, chatting and laughing noisily. A moment later, the guide is outside waiting to greet them. The moment passes.

'Goodbye, Alex.' Chris turns and walks off down the path.

* * *

I watch as he drives away – instead of a swish Aston Martin or Jaguar, he's driving a sensible Audi estate. If I'm honest, I was hoping that he would kiss me. But how can I want that when only days ago, I thought I was falling for Tim Edwards? Now, the very idea makes me shudder. What *was* I thinking?

I'm forced to put everything aside and give an impromptu tour to a family and a few other people who arrive practically at the same time. As I give my spiel about the house, the other puzzling issues come back to the fore. Where is the photo I found? Did Mrs Fairchild take it – of course she must have. No big mystery.

'...And I was just wondering if you knew what year they installed the indoor toilet?' a woman on the tour is saying.

'Oh yes.' I wrench myself back to reality. 'It was 1945, the year Frank Bolton renovated the house. He and his wife Mabel couldn't stand the idea of "roughing it" in their own home.'

'It's a very lovely house,' the woman says. 'Frank Bolton sure was lucky.'

'Yes,' I say. 'That's one word for it.'

PART IV

We shall defend our island, whatever the cost may be, we shall fight on the beaches, we shall fight on the landing grounds, we shall fight in the fields and in the streets, we shall fight in the hills; we shall never surrender.

— WINSTON CHURCHILL

36

13 NOVEMBER 1940 – 3.50 A.M.

'I've seen them cut the fingers off a dead woman to get her diamond rings.' Robbie took a long drag on his cigarette. 'Or they'll find a dying bloke and "help him on his way", then take his wallet and watch.' He shrugged. 'Happens a lot.'

'But it's criminal!' His account made me feel unclean. I touched the trinket in my pocket, fiddling with it nervously. I planned to give it back, but someone could easily misinterpret what I'd done.

'It's war,' Robbie replied.

'That doesn't make it right.'

He blew out a ring of smoke. 'I've seen a lot of wars in a lot of places. I've seen acts of amazing courage and self-sacrifice – just like the posters say. But I've also seen it bring out the worst in people. Things happen in the dark, in the chaos.' He spreads his hands. 'It's survival of the fittest. And everything has a price.'

'And what do you do about it – these things that you've seen? In the dark and the chaos when you're holding your camera. Do you just stand there?'

He met my glare unflinching. 'I don't hand out medals, or put people in jail. You can judge me for that if you want. I bear witness through my camera. You may think that's not important. And you may be right...' He stubbed out the cigarette on the table. *'In fifty or a hundred years, I won't be around to know one way or the other. Neither will you.'*

I clenched my fists; I wanted to hurt him and stop his philosophising. Every night I'm out there risking myself to save others. Not just people's bodies, but their whole way of life. Isn't that what we're supposed to be fighting for?

I didn't realise I'd spoken aloud until he laughed in my face. I launched out of my chair to take him by the collar and give him a good shaking. But just then someone else stumbled into the room. It was Spider. And he was crying.

37

When the tour is finished, I go outside in search of Mrs Fairchild. In the time since we last spoke, everything has changed. There's been good news: discovering that the jewelled bird might *possibly* be a rare object of royal provenance; and bad news: pretty much everything else. There are more questions and few answers. And now, there's a new threat.

How much, if anything, does my grandmother know about the looting? How much of the diary has Mrs Edwards sent her? I replay Tim's call in my head and the thinly veiled threat: that we won't be able to 'put it all behind us' so easily. It's imperative that she lets me see all the evidence that she's been presented with so far. I also want to ask her about the photograph that's gone missing. One thing's for sure – we need to work together to prepare for whatever is coming.

I catch a glimpse of her wide-brimmed hat just outside the walled garden, at the edge of the lawn that stretches down to the lake. She's sitting on a bench watching a pair of swans glide along in the shimmering water.

And she's not alone.

A man is seated next to her. He's maybe five years older than she, with white hair and an athletic build. They both stand up and smile at each other. He gives her an old-fashioned kiss on the hand. She says something and he laughs, and a moment later, they're embracing. I should go away – I've no right to invade her privacy. She'll introduce me to her 'boyfriend' when she's ready. But instead of turning away, I remain where I am, just out of sight. I feel a powerful urge to protect her. She's suffered enough loss in her life, and I don't want her retirement to be marred by any more heartbreak.

Not that it will be. I watch as the embrace ends, and they laugh together over something he's said. They're clearly smitten with each other. And why not? My grandmother is an energetic, attractive older woman, and the personification of 'sixties is the new fifties'. Not to mention *wealthy*. That last point gives me pause.

I slip under the yew arbour and watch as the man turns and walks away down the footpath by the river that leads to the village. He throws a bread crust to the pair of swans and hops over the stile at the edge of the woods, disappearing from sight. My grandmother gathers up the remaining food and rubbish from their picnic and stuffs it into a wicker basket. I give it another minute and then approach her.

'Oh, there you are.' I pretend I've only just spotted her.

'Hi, Alex, dear,' she says. 'Lovely weather, isn't it?'

'Yes, it is.' She looks happier than she has in days. I make a point of not looking up at the gathering rain clouds. 'Did you enjoy the flower show yesterday?'

'I did.' Her smile is warm. 'I've filled the potting shed with new plants. They had some spectacular old roses. I was just about to go off and start planting them.'

'Great. And I wanted to let you know that Chloe is making

pasties.' My grandmother loves beef and onion pasties, and Chloe, who is originally from Cornwall, makes them perfectly. 'But I see you've already had lunch.'

'Yes. I was meeting a friend.'

'A friend?' I say. 'That's nice. Lovely day for it, as you say. Did she have far to come?'

It's a small victory when she takes the bait. 'Actually, it was a *he*.' Her schoolgirl grin says it all.

'Ah. Was it the policeman, by any chance?'

'It was. He's called David – I think I told you? If you'd come a little sooner, I would have introduced you.'

'So it's serious then?'

'Oh, no.' She gives a girlish laugh. 'It's just a bit of fun.' She closes the picnic basket.

'And what about the... *other matter*... that he was looking into? Did he get to the bottom of who's sending the diary entries?'

Her sunny face clouds over. 'No. Not yet. He's very concerned, of course. But since no one has made an actual threat, he's advised me to wait and see what happens. No new envelopes have come, have they?'

'No. But I need to see the diary entries you're received. As soon as possible. So I know what we've got to contend with.'

'But I don't have them.' She looks suddenly confused. 'I gave them to David. I forgot to ask for them back.'

'Oh.' A quiet anger seeps through me. Policeman or no, she's trusted this 'friend' – whom she's known for about five minutes – rather than me, her trusted employee and only granddaughter. I decide it's time to cut to the chase. 'Do you know a Sally Edwards, by any chance?'

'Edwards? Well, I don't know...'

'Her maiden name was Dawkins. Sally Dawkins.'

Her face betrays the answer. She sighs like she knows it. 'I do – did. We weren't friends. Not then, and not now. In truth, I hadn't thought of her in years.' She purses her lips like a piece of a puzzle has clicked in place. 'Until recently, that is.'

'You know it's her, right? Sending the diary entries?' I feel affronted by the wild goose chase my grandmother has led me on.

'No... I mean, I suspected it might be her.' Her lip curls in distaste. 'But like I told you, Alex, I have little memory of that time. Thinking what must have happened has been hard. Most of the entries were about the bombings and the rubble, and my time at the house with the brown kitchen. There's also some business about photographers and looters – but I have no memory of anything like that.' She shakes her head. 'I don't know why Sally would send them, but I have a feeling that she's holding something back. Like I've been told the punchline but haven't heard the joke. That damned woman!'

I've never heard my grandmother curse before. Sally Edwards's mean-spirited actions have clearly affected her more than she wants to let on. I'd been prepared to tell her everything I'd discovered so far, but now, I reconsider. My grandmother obviously doesn't know about the possible link between Frank Bolton and the looting. If I can prove Frank Bolton had nothing to do with it before Sally Edwards does her worst, then I will have stripped her of the hold she has over us.

My grandmother takes her gloves from her pocket. 'Anyway, I'm sorry about the diary entries – I should have made copies. I just wanted them out of the house.'

'I understand.' Sort of.

'Now, I must plant those roses before it starts raining.' She moves in the direction of the potting shed. 'I'll be in later.'

'Sure,' I say. 'But there is one more thing, and I'm afraid it can't wait. When I was tidying up in the green salon yesterday, I found a photo of Frank and two other men. This morning, it was gone. Have you seen it?'

She stops; I watch as her face turns from 'love's first blush' to 'ghost white', ending up in a shade of 'gardening glove green'.

'That photo's missing?'

'You didn't put it somewhere?'

'No.' She twists the gloves in her hand.

'No worries,' I say with a reassurance I don't feel. 'Someone probably tidied it up.'

'Let me know when you find it. I don't like the idea of photos going missing.'

'Sure. Can you tell me about it, though?'

She starts walking again, more slowly this time. I trail after her, carrying the picnic basket.

'It was one of a series taken by Robert Copthorne,' she says. 'They called him Robbie. He's mentioned in the diary. He took newsreels mostly – of ordinary people doing their bit: land girls, the home guard, the WI, evacuated children. And, of course, the devastation from the bombings. He was a master at capturing the horror of those times on film. They showed his newsreels in the cinema before each show. I think there were some old film reels of his up in the attic once.'

'Really? I'll have to look him up.'

'You should. His work was important in documenting the war. Sadly, he died only a few years after it ended. In Cambodia or Vietnam – someplace like that. A fever, I think. It was in the news at the time.'

'That's awful.' I wonder how many secrets a man like that took to his grave.

We reach the potting shed. I know I should let her get on

with her planting, but as she herself is fond of saying, 'in for a penny, in for a pound'.

'There was something written on the back,' I say. '"Flea", "Badger", and "Spider". Were they nicknames of the men in the photo?'

'I think they must be.' She sighs. 'Those names are in the diary too. Hal Dawkins was killed in the war, I think. And the other man was Jeremy Stanley.'

'Stanley? That name sounds familiar.'

She gives me a sly little wink. 'He was related by marriage to your bête noire.'

'My who...?'

'Your good friend Charles Heath-Churchley.'

'The Heath-Churchleys!' Mrs Edwards's voice rings in my head: *'He was posh. His family had friends in high places...'*

'Yes. I believe Jeremy Stanley did valuations for the auction house. His granddaughter married Charles Heath-Churchley – she was his first wife. Jeremy and Frank grew up in the same neighbourhood in London. They were friends, though Jeremy's family was well-off and Frank was a bluestocking. After the war, they went into business together briefly. But Jeremy was interested in other things. He let Frank buy out his interest in the factory.'

Relief floods through me. 'So that's where the money came from to buy the factory,' I reason. 'Frank Bolton had a rich friend who gave him the seed capital.'

'Perhaps. Though Jeremy was more like "shabby gentile". The Stanley family's house was bombed, and they made some bad investments during the war. By the end, I wouldn't have thought Jeremy Stanley had two shillings to rub together. But somehow, they managed to find the money. I guess the war provided a certain amount of opportunity for ambitious young men.'

Especially if one of them had an injection of looted cash, I don't say. My relief gives way to a new sense of dread. What am I going to tell Chris? I'd been so looking forward to seeing him again. But now, our tentative plans to see each other will have to be put on hold – possibly permanently. If I continue to assume that Frank is innocent, then there's the possibility, at least, that Jeremy Stanley could be guilty. By clearing Frank Bolton's name, I might be implicating a relation of one of Britain's 'oldest and proudest families'. And this time, it could be a lot more serious than a busted-up wedding.

* * *

I save the 'good news' for last, taking shelter from the sudden downpour with her in the potting shed. 'I've learned something else about the jewelled locket,' I tell her.

'Oh?' she says, loosening a rose from its pot.

'It might be a Fabergé – from Russia.' I wait for a drumroll and gasp that don't come.

'Really, dear? That's nice,' is all she says.

'It might even have belonged to a member of the Tsar's family.'

This time, she laughs in my face. 'Oh, Alex, what I wild goose chase I've set you on. How could that possibly be the case?'

'I don't know,' I say, a little hurt. 'But I'm going to keep digging until I find out.'

Leaving my grandmother to her plantings, I return to the house and have another look in the green salon for the photograph, then question the staff and the cleaners as to whether they've seen it, or noticed anyone lurking around. No one has. Is this another incident to chalk up to the 'uninvited guest', or just an oversight on someone's part? Without the diary entries or the photograph, how can I find out more?

I go about the morning's tasks with a tune stuck in my head: the melody from the locket. Photographs, intruders, and looters aside, the locket *is* the key to everything – I'm sure of it.

My grandmother's mother died in the bombings sixty years ago. While my grandmother has few memories of that time, Mrs Edwards, who was only a 'bun in the oven', seems so certain of her version of events. And although time is marching on, surely there are other people who lived through that time; people who might still remember.

Like the man I ran into the night of the 'bomber's moon'. For him, the horror is almost more real than his life today. What was his name? Peppercorn? No – Pepperharrow. And his little dog, Winston. It's a long shot, but who knows?

It's possible that the ghosts of East London are not completely at rest.

38

As the bus reaches the stop, I have the urge to stay put: to bury my nose in the greasy copy of the *Metro* that someone left on the seat next to me and ride back to civilisation. The door wheezes open and immediately, my senses are assaulted by the din of East London traffic, the smell of curry and car exhaust, the dull brown-grey of the buildings. A woman tries to manoeuvre a huge double pram through the door without much success. I relinquish my seat and help her lift it into the bus. Just as the door is closing, I jump off.

I wander past betting shops, hair salons, discount fabric shops, falafel and curry houses – getting increasingly wet. I recheck my *A to Z*, just to make sure my destination wasn't a one-time gateway to the past, and still exists today.

But eventually, I see the sign on the little road that seems almost like a different world from the main street. Here it's quieter, and I can no longer smell the fried chips or rubbish.

Larkspur Gardens.

I walk more quickly now, desperate to avoid running into

Mrs Edwards – or, worse still, Tim. I worry, however, because I don't know the old man's house number.

On this point, I get lucky. Halfway down the road, I spot a postman on a bicycle who tells me it's number sixty, third house from the end.

There's an air of decay about the houses in the road: cracked paint and plaster, dirty windows, tiny lawns gone to weed, overflowing bins. I stop in front of number sixty. There's a trellis in front with a scraggly climbing rose. The recycling bin out the front is filled mostly with food tins. There's a neat stack of *Daily Telegraph*s tied with twine next to the bin. The door is painted yellowish-beige. Steeling myself, I ring the bell.

There's no sound from within. I wait for a full minute, then knock again and put my ear to the door. I can just make out a shuffling sound coming from inside. All of a sudden, a dog yaps.

'Hold your horses,' the old man rasps from within.

My heart accelerates as a deadbolt *thunks*, and the door rattles and finally opens a crack. An eye peeks out below a brass chain.

'No soliciting,' he says, his shaky hand making ready to pull the door shut in my face. Winston sticks his nose out the door, sniffing the air.

'Mr Pepperharrow,' I say quickly. 'We ran into each other during the bomber's moon?'

The eye narrows sceptically. 'You should go to the shelter,' he says. 'Oh, I know there's all them people and all that pushing and shoving. But the wine cellar won't save you if the house comes down on top of you.'

'Oh.' I'm taken aback. 'Of course. I'll go to the shelter. But first I just want to talk to you for a minute. About what happened here... umm... in 1940.'

'Are you a spy? For the young whippersnapper down the

road? Never liked him, I'll tell you that for free. Too slick for his own good, that's for sure. And why didn't he join up – that's the question.'

'Yes,' I flub. 'That's the question. One of them. But actually, I'm here for a different reason.' I take a punt. 'I want to talk about the Russian lady.'

There's a sharp intake of breath and then a silence. I brace myself for the force of the door slamming in my face.

The chain jingles and a moment later, I'm inside.

Miles Pepperharrow leads the way, step by cautious step, into a sitting room. After giving my legs a cautious sniff, Winston stays close to his master's side. The room is small like Mrs Edwards's, and similarly decorated in shades of brown. But instead of ashtrays and magazines, there are books everywhere. Piled on the floor, on coffee tables and sofas, on shelves from floor to ceiling on three of the four walls. Hardbacks, paperbacks, coffee-table books, loose-leaf notebooks. All with a common theme: war. The Great War, WWII, Korea, Vietnam, Iraq, Afghanistan, the Cold War, the Wars of the Roses, the Spanish Civil War. On the shelves, the books are mostly about military history and strategy: *The Birth of the Panzer*; *Warplanes in the 20th Century*; *To fly a Poussemoth*. Interspersed on some of the shelves, serving as bookends, is a collection of model planes. Most are made from sturdy metal, lovingly painted. I pick up one of the models and run my finger delicately along one of the dagger-shaped wings. I immediately think of Chris – he would appreciate the craftsmanship that's clearly gone into them.

'That's a Spitfire,' Mr Pepperharrow says. 'Beautiful little plane; handled like a dream with those wings. But she had more than just looks – she was deadly too. She had a five-hundred-mile range, and a powerful Merlin engine. She could reach a top speed of 362 miles per hour. With eight machine guns standard, she could deliver 160 rounds per second.'

'Really?' Unexpectedly interested, I look at the model plane with a new respect.

'Yes, young lady.'

If I ever had any questions about the war, the soldiers who fought in it, or residents of Larkspur Gardens during the Blitz, I have no doubt that I've come to the right place. But what am I looking to find? The truth, or the version of it that I'm hoping for?

He sits down in an armchair by the gas fire. He's wearing plaid pyjamas with a rumpled paper poppy pinned to the collar. Winston settles on top of his slippers. 'Sit anywhere, young lady,' he says. 'I'd offer you a cuppa, but my leg's playing up like the devil today.'

'Can I make the tea, Mr Pepperharrow?' I say. 'I'm sure I can find my way.'

He peers at me. 'Fine, young lady. It's all there in the kitchen.' He gestures with his shaky hand. 'Builder's for me, please.'

'Builder's it is.'

The kitchen is decorated in shades of brown and beige. It's mostly clean, except for a pile of dishes in the sink. While I'm waiting for the kettle to boil, I squirt some soap on a sponge and give them a good washing up. On the wall near the sink is a calendar. It's this year's but the photos are all black and white come-hither pin-up shots of 1940s models: Betty Grable; Jane Russell, Rita Hayworth. I find it vaguely sweet that this probably counts as racy to Mr Pepperharrow.

I return with the tea and some Hobnobs I found in a cupboard. Mr Pepperharrow has pulled a tartan rug over his knees and turned on the gas fire – the room is boiling. Winston snores softly in doggy dreamland. I set the tea and biscuits down on the table next to the old man. 'Hobnobs,' he says, looking surprised and pleased. 'My favourite.'

'Mine too.'

I sit in the chair opposite him. On the mantel above the gas fire are some family photos. Two boys in military uniforms on the deck of a ship, an old wedding photo of Mr Pepperharrow, and, I assume, his wife. A photo of a young girl – a granddaughter maybe? – hugging a huge Pooh Bear at Disneyland.

He follows my gaze. 'Not a great world to bring a family into,' he says. 'But me and the missus, may she rest in peace, did it anyway. Two fine sons, three grandchildren. I can't say I regret it.'

I smile. 'You have a lovely family.'

'Family is important. It's the reason why we fight on. And now you've come in search of yours.'

'How did you know?'

Tilting his head sideways, he studies my face and smiles dreamily. 'You're her spitting image,' he says. 'Different hair maybe, and clothes, obviously. But the eyes – grey-blue with those amber flecks. Not many have those, I reckon.'

'Sorry,' I say, aware of my heart kicking beneath my ribs, 'who exactly are you talking about?'

'Why, Marina, of course.' He narrows his eyes like I've gone thick. 'The Russian lady. That's who you asked about, right?'

'Marina.' I say the name aloud, letting it settle on my tongue. Her eyes – the same as mine.

A cloud of scepticism crosses his face. 'Who did you say you are again?'

'I'm Alex Hart. I work at Mallow Court, up near Aylesbury. The house is owned by Catherine Fairchild. My grandmother.

She's the adopted daughter of Frank Bolton, if the name means anything.'

It obviously does mean something. A hundred emotions seem to flare up at once on Mr Pepperharrow's face. His hand trembles as he sets down his teacup on the table, the liquid sloshing over the rim onto a biography of Churchill.

'I know the name,' he says.

Afraid he's going to clam up, I turn back to the subject that got me through the door in the first place. 'I'm here to find out anything you can tell me about Marina. You see, I have something that might have belonged to her – a locket.'

His sunken eyes grow round and huge. He starts like he's going to get out of his chair, but his bad leg seems to prevent it. 'You have Marina's locket? I wondered where it got to.'

'It's with a specialist right now for repairs. Otherwise I would have brought it with me.' I shrug apologetically. 'But I don't know anything about Marina – where she came from, who she was, and why my grandmother ended up with her locket. I was hoping you could help me.'

He turns his head and stares at a clock hanging on the wall between the windows. It's a simple wooden carriage clock with a white enamel face and brass roman numerals. There's a brass escutcheon on the case for a winding key. But the clock itself is stopped, the hands pointing to 11.50.

'I told her she shouldn't be so pig-headed. It was her duty to go to the shelter.'

'Where was the shelter?'

'At the school,' he says. 'They had a deep cellar. The nearest Tube station was too far away, of course, so she was supposed to go there. But Lord Stanley had a wine cellar. Marina thought that would be safe enough.' He bows his head. 'But she was wrong.'

'The Stanleys? Was she related to them?'

'No, of course not.' He sniffs. 'They were upper class – lived in the big house at the top of the road. Marina was the cook. Lived in a tiny room on the lower ground floor just off the kitchen. Suited her, it did.' He shakes his head. 'Kept her head down in case anyone came looking for her.'

'Who would come looking for her?'

'The Bolshies. Secret police or NKVD.'

I lean forward, stunned. 'Why would they have been after her?'

'Who knows? She never talked about her time in Russia. Clammed right up.' He shakes his head. 'But I think lots of them Russians that came here were at risk. Stalin and his goons weren't ones to let well enough alone. I would have protected her, though, if she'd let me.' His eyes grow vague. 'She was twice my own age when I met her. Forty if she was a day. And with a babe in tow. But I still fancied her. It wasn't just that she was a looker. She had the voice of an angel. Used to sing the babe to sleep. Those songs in Russian – they could tear at the heartstrings even if it all sounded like gibberish.'

'I can imagine.' Those songs... words and melodies buried in the subconscious of an elderly woman who remembers little else about her early life. Mrs Fairchild is undoubtedly the 'babe in tow'. 'Who was the father?' I ask.

'Psshaw.' He waves a hand. 'She was a looker, like I said. I wasn't her only admirer.'

'So you don't know who it was?'

He looks into the blue flames. 'I didn't say that.'

'Please, Mr Pepperharrow, I know it's painful if you had feelings for her. But I really need to know.' Pieces of the puzzle swirl in my head just waiting to click into place. Was Frank Bolton an 'admirer'?

His grey eyes scan my face. 'Maybe.'

39

I sit back and stare into my teacup, finally seeing the truth – and the only logical explanation. Frank Bolton didn't just adopt a little girl with a pretty face. He sought out a very particular orphan.

'He was her father,' I say. *My great-grandfather.* A low, deep tremor passes through me. Frank Bolton. Whatever the truth is, he's part of who I am.

Mr Pepperharrow shrugs. 'Only Marina knew for sure.'

'But you believe it?'

'He adopted her, didn't he?' He twiddles his gnarled fingers. 'I doubt Frank would have done that out of the goodness of his heart.'

'Would you say Frank was... a good man?' I can't quite disguise how desperate I am for him to confirm this, especially now that I'm related to him.

'He did his bit. Norway was a bad business for all our boys. When he came back, he worked the ambulance crew. Of course, he wasn't risking his life the way those of us in the RAF were. *I* was flying Spitfires.'

'You did an amazing thing for your country.'

'Oh aye. Not that you kids these days really understand. You'd be speaking German now if it wasn't for the likes of us who fought.'

'I'm sorry to dredge all this up. It must be difficult, even after all this time.'

'I was the one who loved her – Marina, I mean. If she'd survived, and if she would have had me, I could have loved the little poppet too.'

'That's lovely.' A tear wells up in my eye thinking of how this man's love has survived all these years.

Nudging Winston off his feet, the old man gets up awkwardly and hobbles over to the broken clock. He takes out a pocket handkerchief and gently dusts the case.

'I know a man who could fix that clock for you if you like, Mr Pepperharrow. I'm sure he'd do it for free. In appreciation of your sacrifice.'

He stares at the clock, his back to me. 'I don't want it fixed. Not ever. *She* gave it to me – told me to keep it safe. So I took it to me mum's. It's not valuable, but it's special because of her. But when I returned from my mission, I found out that she was gone. The Stanley house took a direct hit, they said. The little girl survived. She stayed with Mum for a day or two. By the time I got back, the clock had already run down. There was no key to wind it. I set the hands at eleven fifty – that's when the bomb hit.' His eyes glisten with unshed tears. 'Every time I look at that clock, I think of Marina and remember.'

I wipe my eyes, unable to speak.

'It was a long time ago,' he says stoically. 'And I guess I should give you the clock if you're her great-granddaughter.'

'Please keep it,' I say. 'I can see that you treasure it, so it should stay with you.'

'Thank you, young lady.' He gazes at me with a sad smile, and I have the feeling that it's not me he's seeing, but *her*.

I gather together the empty teacups onto a tray. I'm filled to the brim with emotion, but I need to pull myself together. I came here to ask questions, no matter how difficult the answers may be to hear. Focusing on the old man's face, I take a deep breath. 'There's one other thing I wanted to ask you, Mr Pepperharrow. It's about Frank Bolton and his ambulance driver colleagues. Were you aware of any looting going on around here during the Blitz?'

His eyes narrow, seeming to sink into his face. The thin wrist leaning on his cane begins to tremble. 'I don't like your tone, young lady, or what you're implying. Back then, it was all about pulling together and keeping a stiff upper lip. We helped each other and had each other's back. Don't they teach you kids about the "Blitz Spirit" these days?'

'Yes, sir, they do.' He staggers back towards the chair and I take his arm to steady him.

''Course there were always gangs,' he concedes. 'And kids looking for coins in the gas meters. But I don't think that's what you're talking about, is it?'

'No. I'm talking about your neighbour, Sally Edwards, and her father, Harold Dawkins. He was an ambulance driver accused of looting. He was sent to the front and died there.'

'And well he should have.' He bangs his fist on the Churchill book. 'Criminals and conchies – disgraceful. When the rest of us were putting our lives on the line night after night.'

'I understand. But was Mr Dawkins guilty? It couldn't have been anyone else?'

'It was mayhem back then – absolute chaos. You have no idea. Oh, I know what they say: looting wasn't the worst thing a body could do. All that darkness, all that fear. It was a good time for criminals: rapists, murderers, black marketeers, that's for sure. Should have shot the lot of 'em, I say.'

'Um, yes. It's just that Mrs Edwards seems to think that her father was innocent, and they got the wrong man. She found his journal which implies that the looter might have been' – I hesitate, unwilling to say it out loud – 'someone else. It would be horrible if there had been a miscarriage of justice.'

'So that's what this is about? You're a friend of *that* young spiv from down the street.'

'You mean Tim Edwards?'

'Aye, that's the one.'

'I wouldn't say we're *friends*. But it was his grandmother who made the accusations. She showed me a photograph of three men – her father, Frank Bolton and Jeremy Stanley.'

He nods. 'One of Rob Copthorne's photos. Robbie was always skulking around in the darkness, that one. He saw things – oh yes, I know he did.'

'Yes, he must have. Mrs Edwards said that of the three of them, Frank was the looter. I'm sure you can understand that I need to find out the truth, one way or the other.'

'I'm afraid I can't help you with that, girl. I was flying missions. I knew Frank Bolton. I didn't like him much, but that was because of Marina. I had nothing against him otherwise. Jeremy was "out there".' He circles his finger next to his ear. 'He loved his gadgets and his clocks.' My stomach takes a nosedive at the mention of the word 'clocks'. 'I can't see him stealing anything, unless it was some old junk that nobody else wanted.'

'And Hal Dawkins?'

'I knew Hal a good long while,' he says. 'Though never well. He was a bit of a glad-hander. A chameleon. Acted like your best friend to your face. But underneath – well… I don't know.'

I stand up. 'Thank you, Mr Pepperharrow, you've been very helpful.'

I leave him sitting in his chair staring at Marina's clock. I quickly wash up the cups and the biscuit plate and put them away. As I'm about to pop my head back in the front room to say goodbye, I hear the thunking of Mr Pepperharrow's stick coming towards me.

'Young lady,' he says.

'Yes, sir?'

'Everything I did, I did for *her* – you won't forget that, will you?'

I reach out and give his arm a quick squeeze. 'I won't forget, Mr Pepperharrow. I promise. And let me know if you change your mind about wanting that clock repaired.'

40

My meeting with Mr Pepperharrow has left my emotions raw and my mind reeling. As I walk back to the bus stop, I reflect on what I have and haven't learned. The headline is that Frank Bolton is most likely Catherine's real father. *My great-grandfather.*

The pieces of the puzzle slot into place: why he adopted her, and why he left her, his eldest child, the house. Unfortunately, I'm no closer to clearing him of the accusations. Or proving who the real looter was.

And then there's the mysterious Marina – my great-grandmother? The woman with my eyes, who was always looking over her shoulder in fear, yet seemed to have had her fair share of admirers. How did she come to be in possession of the jewelled bird? Mr Pepperharrow had said she was the Stanley's cook. Could she have been a servant in Russia? Did she steal the locket from a rich employer and then flee the country? It's possible. But after so many years, how can I find out the truth that she tried so hard to keep hidden?

I take the bus west past Shoreditch and Old Street. I really should go straight home – there's lots to do before the costume exhibition opens in a few days' time. But I'm drawn by a strange magnetic force to get off near Chancery Lane and the streets that lead to Chris's workshop.

* * *

When I reach the workshop door, the chaos of ticking clocks seems disapproving and unsettling. I realise that I probably ought to have called first to give Chris the heads up that his relative is in a photograph with a would-be looter – and might even be the looter himself. I'm about to leave when I hear footsteps behind me. I turn and see Chris, along with another lithesome blond in a short skirt suit and high heels, both carrying coffees. Instantly, my stomach clenches with jealousy.

'Alex,' he says, looking surprised to see me.

'I was just leaving,' I say.

'Oh, look.' The blonde grabs Chris by the arm and thrusts her phone in his face. 'Charles Snodford paid triple the estimate for that Chippendale dining set.'

'Great,' Chris says, smiling at her. 'Dad will be pleased.'

Dad.

I go to push past them – I'm never coming here again. The blonde woman looks daggers at me, her eyes filled with judgement and dislike. I decide at that moment that I'm going to stand my ground. I stare at her and she at me. Chris glances from one of us to another, looking clueless. Then he turns to the blonde. 'Thanks for filling me in, Greta. I hope the sale goes well.'

'Fine.' Her claws tighten on his arm. 'Maybe we can do dinner later and I'll tell you more.'

With a last look at me, she turns on her heel and stalks off towards the auction house.

I glare at Chris, infinitely annoyed. 'You didn't have to do that,' I say. 'She's clearly very taken with you.'

'She's a handler at the auction house,' he says. 'It's her job to butter up the rich clients and get them to bid more.'

'I'm sure she's good at buttering,' I say.

He moves past me to the workshop door, speaking in a voice so low that I have to lean closer to catch the words. 'She and I won't be having dinner.' His breath ruffles the hair by my ears, his lips so close to my skin that I think it must be an accident.

* * *

Inside the workshop, any imagined flirtation is swiftly drowned out by the melee of the clocks chiming and cuckooing the hour. Chris sets his coffee on the desk and offers to make me one in his little kitchen. While he's boiling the kettle, I recount my meeting with Mr Pepperharrow. We chat for a few minutes about the books and the model spitfires. When the coffee's made, we return to the main workshop and I sit in the chair across from him while he fiddles with taking apart an alarm clock. I tell him about Marina, omitting one crucial fact – who she worked for.

'So Mrs Fairchild really is Frank Bolton's daughter?'

'It explains a lot,' I say. 'Like why he adopted her and why he left her the house.'

'Yes.' Chris frowns as he fiddles with removing a small bolt. 'It would seem so.'

I sit forward – I can't put it off any longer. 'There's another thing you should know, Chris. It's about that photograph. The one I couldn't find.'

'The one of Frank and two other men? Did it turn up?'

'Not yet. But I asked Mrs Fairchild about it. She knew who the third man was.' I take a breath. 'He was called Jeremy Stanley.'

Across the table, his pale blue eyes widen like pools. I feel a sudden shift in the air between us. I wish I could rewind the clock by thirty seconds; a minute. Take everything back.

'Jeremy Stanley is my great-grandfather. The original clockmaker.'

'Yes.'

His eyes sharpen. 'You knew?'

'I didn't know the exact connection. But Mrs Fairchild told me that he was connected with the Heath-Churchleys. And Mr Pepperharrow mentioned clocks.'

'Jeremy Stanley is my mum's grandfather. My great-grandfather.'

'Yes, but—'

'It looks like you have a new suspect,' he says soberly.

'Really, Chris. That's not what I'm saying. They were in a photo together and worked on the ambulance brigade. I suppose all of them were blokey – with nicknames.'

His eyes are opaque as he stares past me at the row of grandfather clocks. 'It's more than that. Jeremy and Frank were long-time friends. Didn't Mrs Fairchild tell you that?'

'Sort of...' My voice quavers.

'That's the reason Cee-Cee was having her wedding at Mallow Court. Daddy arranged it with Mrs Fairchild.'

'No,' I clarify, now on more solid ground. 'That's not right. Cee-Cee and her fiancé came to a wedding fair. I remember, because it was the first one we ever held, and I was so determined to get everything right. I met each of the couples individually. Cee-Cee complained about the size of the venue, and that's before she even looked at the catering options.' I wince at the memory. 'If I'm honest, she kind of knocked the stuffing out of me.'

'I'm sorry,' Chris says. 'She can be like that. She had her heart set on the Orangery at Blenheim Palace. That was where the first wedding was to have been held. For the second one, my father convinced her to have it at Mallow Court. He knew Catherine was trying to get the wedding business off the ground and that he could muck in. Dad may be many things, but he does honour family connections.'

'Oh.' I look away, feeling unexpectedly hurt.

'So where does that leave us with Jeremy Stanley?'

I bring myself back to the present – or, in this case, the past of sixty years ago. 'All I know is little titbits. After the war, he and Frank Bolton went into business together. Apparently your great-grandfather and mine were both into ladies' knickers.' I give a hollow laugh.

Chris doesn't smile.

'But Jeremy Stanley wasn't really a businessman, so he sold Frank his interest.'

'My great-grandfather was a clockmaker. I don't see how he could have invested any money in Frank's factory. The big house on Larkspur Gardens was destroyed, as was his shop. His father, Lord Stanley, was in banking. That took a big hit during the war, too. After the war, my great-grandfather was skint. It was the Heath-Churchleys who were wealthy. They were family friends, and Jeremy did valuations and antique restorations for the auction house. But it wasn't until Jeremy's granddaughter – my mum – married Charles Heath-Churchley that the Stanley fortunes were in any way revived.'

I'm aware of the hurt in his voice; the worry that his beloved great-grandfather might not have been the man he thought. In this case, however, I guess he'll just have to join the club. Frank and Jeremy got the money to buy the factory from somewhere. But where?

'There's nothing to suggest any wrongdoing on his part,' I say. 'And I may as well tell you the rest.'

'What, there's more?'

It's like an impenetrable wall has come between us.

'My great-grandmother, Marina, was the Stanleys' cooks. She died when their house was hit by the bomb.'

'Marina.' He speaks the name quietly, drooping his head. And at that moment, I realise with a stab of despair that whatever there might have been between us – unless that was all in my imagination too – is now at an end. I've cast new aspersions on 'one of the nation's oldest, proudest families'.

Christopher Heath-Churchley may be a black sheep...

But he's still a sheep.

'I should go now.' I drink the last of my coffee. 'The costume exhibition is opening in a few days and there's lots to do. I hope you'll come and see it.'

He nods noncommittally.

I stand up, wanting to reach out to him. But I'm too afraid – the gap between us has grown too wide.

'I should give you back the locket and the key,' he says.

Before I can respond, he turns and goes through the door to the auction house. He's gone several minutes. I look around a final time, my heart welling up with sadness.

He returns with the velvet bag and a copy of the receipt. 'Please sign here that I returned your property.'

I do so in silence, no longer taking any pleasure in the description of the item written on it – '*jewelled bird mechanical locket, possibly Russian*' – that had once filled my heart with such promise. I tuck the velvet bag in my pocket.

'Thanks for the coffee, and... um... everything.' My voice breaks. Turning, I walk down the corridor to the door, a black despair seeping into my bones. Is he not even going to say goodbye?

I reach the door; he's there behind me. We stand a foot apart, me looking up and him looking down.

'I suppose I should try to find out exactly what my great-grandfather did during the war,' he says. 'I mean, I really ought to know, shouldn't I?'

I shake my head. 'I'm sorry, Chris. None of us could have foreseen this. I've lived my whole life without knowing who my real mother was, let alone what any of my relatives did during the war.'

He leans forward and takes hold of my arms. I'm hyper-aware of every elemental particle in my body orienting itself towards him like a magnet. The incandescent heat radiating between our skin as his face comes close to mine, the delicious sharpness of his stubble on my cheek. And then his lips as they mould to mine, soft, exploratory... wanting. And I long to disappear inside of him, to give in to the rushing sensation that wants to sweep me away. My body wants to stay here, in this new alignment, this unexpected half of the same whole. But the clocks speed on relentlessly.

'Goodbye,' he whispers. He brushes his long fingers gently through my hair, then turns away and disappears back inside the workshop.

I stand in the loading bay of the auction house, willing the ghost of him to become flesh. For all this to be over – or maybe never to have begun – because right now, it's as if the wheels and cogs of the earth have ground to a juddering halt, and all I can feel is the loss of him. Our moment was sweet and beautiful, and never to be repeated.

A tear leaks from my eye as I turn back towards Hatton Garden. The Clockmaker's kiss still lingers on my lips and in my memory. As does the finality of his 'goodbye'.

41

On the train home, I grip the velvet bag in my pocket and settle into a deep state of mourning. Maybe I was deluded into thinking that Chris and I could have something between us… a future, even. But now, a long-buried past has inserted a wedge between us. I wish I could snip Jeremy Stanley out of that photograph and remove him from the fabric of that time. But the notion is silly and pointless. It's even more imperative now that I find out the truth so that everyone concerned can put the past firmly where it belongs – in the past.

Back at Mallow Court, I don't feel like speaking to anyone, so I go straight to my flat. As soon as I'm inside the door, however, I sense that something is different: a very slight, almost imperceptible scent that I don't recognise.

In the sitting room, everything is just as it was: books on the shelves, a few spread out on the table. My pictures, my sofa, the TV. The kitchen is also just the same.

At the door of the bedroom, I stop, my heart quickening. My bed is rumpled and unmade like I left it, but propped up on the pillow is a photograph in a silver frame. A photograph of three men linking arms: *Flea, Badger, and Spider*.

I run back out to the main room and grab a poker from the fireplace. Holding it before me, I check the flat: the cupboards, behind the door, under the bed. My chest pounds with panic as I check behind the shower curtain. No one.

Returning to the bedroom, I pick up the photograph, turning it over in my hands. There's no message from the 'uninvited guest' – other than the fact that he's been here. *That* message is loud and clear.

The idea that someone has violated the sanctuary of my flat makes me feel unclean and uneasy. I rush over to the main house and catch Edith on her way out. She assures me that everything has gone smoothly in my absence, and tells me that Mrs Fairchild has gone out for dinner with her friend, David.

'Thanks for letting me know,' I say. 'See you tomorrow.'

I spend the evening alone in the main house doing final preparations for the costume exhibition. If there are any intruders lurking in nooks and crannies, they graciously remain hidden.

Around ten o'clock, my grandmother returns. I've left the lights on in the great hall to alert her to my presence, and I call out to her so she's not startled.

'Oh, hello, Alex,' she says. 'Burning the midnight oil, I see.'

'I want everything to be perfect for the grand opening,' I say. 'Did you have a good evening?'

Her cheeks flush like bright apples. 'Yes, thanks. We had a lovely dinner at a new Italian restaurant in Oxford.'

'Nice.'

My grandmother yawns. 'It was, but I had a few glasses of wine. I should be getting off to bed.'

'Can I make you a cup of tea?'

'Well, I suppose.'

She follows me down the dimly lit corridor to the staff kitchen, our footsteps making the old floorboards creak grumpily. I can tell she's tired, so I immediately get down to business.

'I found the missing photograph,' I say. 'Someone left it on my pillow.'

'On your...' She raises a hand to her mouth. 'Oh, Alex. You mean they came into your flat?'

'Yes.'

'Do you think we should call the police?'

'I don't think they'll take it seriously, and besides, we do have the security company. Maybe I should get an alarm put in at the coach house.'

'Yes, do. I don't like the idea of someone lurking around.'

'Me neither, but so far it's only been mischief.' Even to me, the words sound lame and unconvincing.

'Hmm... maybe.'

I make her a cup of tea and sit down opposite her at the table. She seems pensive, staring down at the liquid in the cup before taking a sip.

'I went to London today,' I say.

'Oh? Is this about the locket again?'

'Indirectly. Have you ever heard of a man called Miles Pepperharrow? He's a neighbour of Sally Dawkins.'

She wrinkles her nose. 'I don't think so.'

'He's been living on Larkspur Gardens all his life. He remembers you and... your mother.'

'My mother?' This time, the cup doesn't make it to her mouth. She clatters it down on the saucer.

'According to him, there was a big house at the top of the road owned by Lord Stanley – Jeremy Stanley's father. They had a Russian cook who lived in a room off the kitchen. Her name was Marina.'

'Marina. The name was in the diary. She was...'

'Mamochka,' I say.

'Marina,' she repeats, lost in a memory.

'He couldn't tell me much,' I say. 'Just that she was very beautiful. I think he was a little in love with her.'

'That's nice to know.'

'But there was one other thing. He didn't have any proof, of course, but according to him, Frank Bolton was your real father.'

'My real...' She folds her hands in her lap, staring down at her cup.

I wait in silence for almost a minute while she tries to process what I've told her. Finally, she looks up. 'That would explain a thing or two, I suppose. Though' – she frowns – 'why didn't he tell me the truth?'

'Perhaps he didn't know himself? Maybe Marina didn't tell him.'

'Even if he is my... *real* father... I'm not sure it changes much.' Her sudden radiant smile belies her words.

'No. But I thought you should know.'

She takes her half-empty cup over to the sink and washes it out.

'Thank you for that,' she says. 'It really shouldn't matter after all these years. But somehow, it does.' She turns to me then, holding out her arms. I go to her and she hugs me tightly. 'But I guess you already know, Alex, how it feels to find your family at last.'

'I do, Grandmother.' I kiss her cheek. 'I know exactly.'

42

13 NOVEMBER 1940 – 5.30 A.M.

'Badger,' Spider said, his cut-glass vowels strangling from his mouth.

I knew I should comfort him, but I stayed in my chair, paralysed.

'Everything is gone,' he said. 'The house... everything.' His shoulders drooped. 'But there's worse. There was a servant. She didn't survive.'

'I know,' I said, finally coming to. 'I pulled her out. She didn't make it. But her daughter did.'

'Her daughter?' His eyes widened.

'I took her someplace safe.'

For a moment, he looked less stricken. But then he seemed to remember something else. 'And what about the clock?'

'The clock? What clock?'

'I repaired it for her. She had me... Oh God. I suppose that was destroyed too. Or stolen. The house – the wreckage – had been looted.' He shook his head violently.

'Looted? Are you sure?' But as soon as he'd said it, an image of Flea popped into my head. I tried to shake it away – how could he be capable of something like that? A day ago, I would have thought it *was crazy. But now... Images from my boyhood flashed before my eyes. Flea was always jealous of Spider. But even so...*

How would he have done it? Could he have doubled back after he dropped off the casualties? Pawed through the wreckage like a rat in the garbage? No. It's not possible.

I turned away from Spider and then, speaking of the devil, Flea walked into the room.

'Spider, mate!' Flea boomed. 'God, dreadful business – just dreadful.' Flea went up to Spider and gave him a great squeeze.

Spider flinched, drawing back. 'Were you there too, Flea?' Spider asked.

"Fraid so. Lost everything, did you? How the mighty have fallen and all that.'

'You bastard,' I said under my breath.

Flea met my eyes for a long second. 'Aren't you the pot calling the kettle black.' He turned on his heel and walked out.

'We have to do something.' I banged my fist on the table, making the coffee cups skitter. 'I'm not going to stand for this.'

Spider looked up, startled. 'What do you mean?'

'I'll explain later.' I stood. 'For now, just trust me.' I gestured for him and Robbie to follow. 'We have to stop him.'

'Hold your horses,' Robbie said softly. 'You need to think this through. Not tonight – it's almost dawn.'

'When then?' I bristled.

He shrugged in that infuriating way of his. 'Tomorrow night? Bomber's moon.'

'Check the roster,' I barked. I turned and punched the wall.

43

The day I've been preparing for for months finally arrives – the grand opening of the costume exhibition. It's been two days since the 'uninvited guest' left the photograph in my flat, and luckily there's been no further mischief.

The preparations have taken all my time over the last few days. The PR company has arranged for journalists from all over the country to come to Mallow Court to take photographs and interview the three curators from the V&A and the Costume Museum in Bath who are scheduled to come up for the day. I've also got a lorryload of champagne and a French canapé chef for the occasion. Best of all (or, perhaps most worryingly), Karen is driving up from Essex to offer me moral support.

The long gallery looks smashing – a cross between Madame Tussaud's and a fancy-dress shop. Each mannequin has been carefully costumed and posed in a tableaux. There's a group of medieval ladies listening to a lutist, a coterie of Elizabethan dancers, a group of Regency men and women playing cards, a gathering of Edwardian ladies, several 1930s women trying on hats, and my personal favourite: a group of lithesome mannequins dressed up in Mrs Fairchild's Swinging Sixties clothing for a night out in Soho.

Each piece has been carefully researched and catalogued, but I've gone one step further and written a dossier for each of the 'characters'. I've also written out a short I-spy book for children, and photocopied some pages from a fashion colouring book that I've placed on a table along with colouring pens, crayons, scissors, glue sticks, and a big box of scraps of different fabrics for them to design their own fashion masterpieces.

I'm proud of the exhibition, and I'm hoping it will double visitor numbers while it's on. I've hired in extra staff to handle the expected numbers in the café, gift shop, and the exhibition itself, and I'm relieved when they all turn up at nine o'clock sharp. Edith and the normal staff are on hand also. The house is closed to visitors for the morning and the first of the journalists is due to arrive at noon. At half eleven, I open a bottle of champagne for the staff, and together we toast the success of the exhibition.

Ten minutes before opening, I hover at the ticket desk in the great hall waiting for the first visitors to arrive. By ten past twelve, no one has come. A flicker of alarm kindles in my mind. Journalists might be fashionably late, but I had expected the women from the V&A to be on time.

At half twelve, Edith comes in. When she sees me alone, pacing back and forth on the wide polished stones of the floor, her smile vanishes. 'Where is everyone?' she says.

'I don't know. Just running late, I hope.'

'Right.' She looks unconvinced.

'No one called to cancel, did they?' I say. 'I mean, everyone knew we were starting at noon?'

'No one phoned the shop,' Edith says. 'Do you want me to check the office phone?'

'I'll go,' I say. 'The PR company handled all the invites. I've got a list of everyone – they sent it to me the day before yesterday. And I can't think what's keeping the women from the V&A...'

Edith remains behind in the great hall. I go to the estate office and see that the message light is blinking. I listen to the first message – it's from a London journalist. 'I'm so sorry you've had to delay the opening,' she says. 'Please keep me posted if the exhibition is still on.'

'What?' I say aloud, flabbergasted. My stomach clenches with dread. Picking up the phone, I ring the PR company. They came highly recommended by the V&A and the Historic Houses Association, and have already sent me a hefty invoice to prove it.

A well-spoken receptionist answers the phone.

'This is Alex Hart from Mallow Court,' I say. 'I need to speak to my account rep urgently.'

'Alex Hart?' The girl sounds confused. 'But... sorry, this is awkward. You called yesterday, didn't you? Except you were... umm... a man.'

'I didn't call yesterday,' I say. 'And I'm certainly not a man!'

'One moment please.' In a split second, I'm on hold with the normally calming strains of a Beethoven piano sonata drifting down the phone line. Just as I'm about to spontaneously combust with frustration, my mobile phone rings. It's Karen. I answer it, juggling phones with both hands.

'Alex, what the hell is up?' she yells into the phone. 'I just got to your gate. It's chained shut and there's a sign on it that says "House and Exhibition closed due to diseased livestock".'

I hold my mobile away from my ears. On the landline, the

voice of my PR rep comes on. I can't take in the panic and protestations about new receptionists and a male 'Alex' calling to cancel my event. Along with the fury germinating in my chest, there's also a tiny seed of admiration. The 'uninvited guest' has struck again, and this time he's cut me to the quick.

* * *

'Look on the bright side,' Karen says, swigging down her second flute of champagne. 'That PR agency you hired must be pretty damn efficient. Cancelling everyone at short notice like that.'

I toss the empty bottle hard into the bin. 'It's criminal,' I say. 'Identity theft.'

'Well, I assume you've got the full PR machine working on rescheduling – and at no cost to you, right?'

'The agency said they'd call everyone, but the event has been in the works for months. People can't adjust their diaries just like that.'

'Maybe not.' Karen shrugs. 'But at least the champers will keep.'

I pop the cork on a second bottle, remembering Churchill's words: *In defeat, need it...*

'The thing is,' I lament, 'how did he know which agency I was using?'

'He must have hacked your computer and then taken a punt that his bluff would work at the PR agency.'

'OK, but why?'

Over the first bottle of champagne, I'd filled Karen in on my falling-out with Tim and his nutty gran, her accusations against Frank Bolton, and the possible royal origins of the jewelled bird. Her response was predictable: 'Gosh, Alex. Since when did your life start to get *interesting*?'

I've refrained from telling her about Christopher Heath-Churchley and the feelings I'd developed for him. I don't want to relive the joy I'd felt in his presence and then explain how I haven't heard from him, won't be hearing from him, and that my family mystery has killed off something powerful.

'It all seems like a lot of mischief,' Karen says. 'At least the "uninvited guest" hasn't done any real harm.'

'No real harm!' I hug the bottle to my chest before pouring myself another glass. 'He locked me in the loo and I practically got arrested. That's false imprisonment. Then he stole a photograph and left it on my pillow. That's theft, and breaking and entering. Then he cancelled my grand opening. And then there's the diary entries that are upsetting my grandmother.'

'And you really think this Tim chap is responsible?'

'He admitted that his grandmother sent the diary entries. She and Mrs Fairchild apparently have some past animosity between them. But she can't be the intruder – you'd understand if you'd met her. So it's got to be him.'

'OK,' Karen says. 'So you need to send him a message right back.'

'How do I do that?'

'Get the police out. Let him know that you're taking things seriously.'

'No,' I say flatly. 'No police.'

'Why not, Alex? It doesn't make sense.'

'Because...' I turn the glass around in my hands, wanting to snap the stem in frustration. 'As you've pointed out, it's all just mischief. I don't want the police here, or the bad press it would lead to.'

'So you're going to sit back and do nothing?'

'I don't know!' The familiar sense of panic rises to the surface. 'I don't want to give the intruder any ammunition until

I know the truth about Frank Bolton. Once I prove his innocence, then it won't matter what anyone says. Tim – or whoever – won't have anything hanging over us. But if I go to the police, it will be in the papers. That might force his hand, and who knows what he'll do?'

'Fine, I get it. Sort of.' Karen holds out her glass for a refill. 'I just don't quite see how solving your decades-old mystery will help.'

I rub my temples, feeling a headache coming on. 'I'm sure I must be missing something. Something important.'

'I think you need to deal with what's in front of you,' she says. 'Phone this Tim chap and resort to some good old-fashioned threats if he doesn't behave.'

'Maybe.' I try to picture Tim Edwards driving boldly up to the gate, chaining it shut, and putting a sign on it about sick livestock. Or calling a PR agency and pretending to be me. 'But he's a barrister, for Christ's sake. You'd think he'd be too old – or just too damn busy – for schoolboy pranks.'

Karen gives me a sideways glance. I've unwittingly steered her back onto familiar territory.

'In my experience, men are never too old or too busy for mischief.' She raises her glass and clinks it with mine. 'God, Alex, you're making me wish I'd met your delightful Tim Edwards first. I'm a sucker for chocolate brown eyes and a devious black heart.'

44

All I can do is put on a brave face and move on. Tipsy from the champagne, I personally call a long list of people that I'd invited before the PR agency got involved and apologise for the 'unfortunate mistake'. I also reopen the house to tourists and have a trickling of visitors who haven't heard about the special event or the 'livestock disease' and are perfectly happy to traipse through the long gallery and admire the exhibition. I tell my grandmother that there was a mix-up at the PR agency without elaborating on the cause. She gives me a reassuring hug, tells me not to worry, and leaves for an early dinner with a friend.

By the end of the day, the adrenalin rush of indignation peters out, and I'm left feeling exhausted. Karen tried to persuade me to go for dinner and a catch-up, but by the time I return to the office after closing up the house, she's fast asleep and snoring on the long leather sofa in my office. She wakes up a while later, has another glass of champagne from a bottle on the floor next to the sofa, mumbles, rolls over, and goes back to sleep. I tuck a blanket around her and a pillow under her head.

I wait up until I'm sure that my grandmother has returned home safely and then leave to go home to my flat. I don't bother to set the alarm – it doesn't seem to be making the slightest bit of difference to the intruder's activities.

I sleep badly, and the next morning still feel very low. Karen comes over for breakfast, then leaves to go back to Essex where she's running a 'Forever Love and Marriage' course. Given her 'involvement' with the Churchley-Thursley wedding, the irony is not lost on me. 'Call me if there's any more mischief,' she says through the window of her Smart car as she peels away, tyres screeching.

I continue to pick up the pieces of the cancelled exhibition: giving interviews to journalists, escorting groups through the long gallery, making sure that the complimentary champagne is free-flowing. It's all very anti-climactic compared to the grand event I'd planned, but in a way, the low-key nature is a relief. As I go through the motions of my job, I ruminate over the still-unanswered questions. Could Tim really be the 'uninvited guest'? If not, then who is? As the day comes to an end, I feel light-headed, like I've been holding my breath. Waiting for something to go wrong; relieved when it doesn't. Knowing that tomorrow is another day.

* * *

Over the next few days, word of mouth spreads, several journalists come by to write their articles, and the exhibition begins to draw greater numbers. The only incident of note is a loose railing on one of the disabled ramps that causes an elderly woman's knee to buckle, and I have to get a bandage out of the first aid kit. Fortunately, the woman is satisfied with a free tea and scone for recompense. Behind the scenes, my mind jumps to the panicked conclusion that the loose railing must be the work of the 'uninvited guest', though there's no evidence of it. I call a handyman out to check every railing, stair, carpet runner, floor plank, and stone to make sure they've not been tampered with. He finds nothing amiss. Nonetheless, worries buzz in my head like angry bees.

On the fourth day after the cancelled event, I've just returned home after a long, tiring day when my mobile phone rings. I groan with irritation – there's no one I want to speak to. But when I pick up the phone and see on the screen that it's Chris calling, I experience a surge of emotion that brings me near tears. I've missed him. And whatever fledgling ideas I might have been harbouring about *us* – well, I miss those too.

I answer the phone to a cacophony of chiming of clocks that brings a sad smile to my face.

'Hi, Chris,' I say. 'How are you?'

'I've been better.' He sounds distant and strange. Though I'd no reason to hope that things could be sorted between us, my heart feels heavy with disappointment.

'What's wrong?'

'I've found something you should see. Can you come by the shop? I think it would be better than trying to explain over the phone.'

'Umm...' I picture his shop – how quaint and clever it is. Seeing it in my mind's eye gives me a visceral sensation of warmth and safety. A bubble of calm where time is suspended, the clocks acting as guardians against the outside world. A bubble that, as of our last meeting, has well and truly burst.

'I know you're busy with the costume exhibition,' he says. 'But it might be important.'

I'm a moth; he's a bright, shiny flame.

'I can come tomorrow. Shall we say eleven o'clock?'
'Fine.' The line crackles and goes dead.

45

14 NOVEMBER 1940 – 11.55 P.M.

The moon cast an eerie, rose-coloured glow as we pulled out of the dispatch the following evening. The bombs had been falling hard and fast, and I felt guilty for shirking my duty. Angry at Flea for making me do this.

'Where are we going?' Spider asked, clearly uncomfortable with my plan.

'Wherever he goes.' I pointed in front of us. I'd already told Spider what I suspected. He didn't believe me, of course. But he would – when the time was right.

'He'll be dangerous,' Robbie said, cradling his camera in his lap.

'No!' Spider said. 'We've known him all our lives.'

'Have we?' I fixed my eyes on the dark road. 'Do we really know him at all?'

'Well—'

'Let's just see.'

We followed the ambulance in front around Highbury Fields, towards Angel, then up towards Camden Town. I almost lost him as he took a sharp left through Primrose Hill, to the edge of Regent's Park. He pulled into the service drive of a newly derelict terrace of once-grand houses. The street sign was blackened over. I turned down the nearest side street and stopped the ambulance.

'Now what?' Spider said.

'We confront him.' *In my head, guns were blazing.*

'Wait a second, son.' *Robbie laid a hand on my arm.* 'Have you thought this through?'

I jerked away. 'What's to think about? We talked about this – we had a plan.'

'Assuming you "catch him" – what then? As I see it, you have two options: turn him in to the police or take over his turf.'

'What?'

He shrugged offhandedly. 'Of course, I'm sure you'll do the "right" thing – grass on your mate. Make things hard for him and his family, if he has one. I'm not sure the powers that be will thank you for it, but you'll have a clear conscience.'

'Damned right,' *Spider said.*

'Just something to think about.' *Robbie got out of the passenger side and lifted his camera.*

'You stay here,' *I said to Spider.* 'In case we need to make a quick getaway.'

'Are you sure?' *He looked relieved.*

'I'm sure.' *I turned to Robbie.* 'I'll handle this. You just stay in the background. Shoot what you can, but don't let him see you.'

He sniffed. 'I'll send you a bill for the film.'

46

As I enter the workshop, the clocks chime. This time, it doesn't sound like a greeting. Compared to the outside world, the workshop is dim and shadowy except for the circle of bright light that illuminates Chris's worktable. I blink a few times until my eyes adjust. Chris is hunched over his books and doesn't look up. I take in the planes of his face, the slight curl of the ends of his dark hair brushing the top of his shoulders. I want to go to him, mould myself to him, feel those strong arms around me and the heartbeat in his chest. Those sensitive lips on mine. But when he finally looks up and sees me, his brief smile disappears. 'Thanks for coming,' he says, his tone formal and lacking warmth.

'You said you found something.'

'Yes... maybe.' Standing up, he gathers a sheaf of papers and moves them to the centre of the worktable. I notice an absence of tools and wood and metal shavings, like he hasn't been doing much clockwork. That makes me sad – and angry too. As things seem to be over between us, if there ever was a 'thing', I may as well get it off my chest.

'You know, Chris,' I say sharply, 'just for the record, I never had any intention of dragging your family name through the mud.'

'What?'

'I guess you've got a right to be angry – me waltzing into your cosy little workshop behind Daddy's big auction house and setting a cat among the pigeons. I guess you must think I'm no better than the Edwards. Worse, probably. At least they have a wrong to right.'

'Is that really what you think of me?' His eyes darken. 'That I'm just some rich toff idling in the back of my father's work, driving fast cars and chasing women?'

'Well, you certainly do seem to have a lot of women "friends".' As soon as the words are out of my mouth, I regret them.

He moves around the desk towards where I'm standing and crosses his arms firmly over his chest. Then, without warning, he begins to laugh.

'What's so funny?' I demand.

'You.'

And a moment later, I'm swept up in those arms, and I'm drinking in his mouth, his tongue, my fingers wandering through that soft hair and down his back. I press myself against him. We stay like that for a long moment, but I can sense his hesitation and tension. I stiffen and push him away.

'This is ridiculous,' I say.

He looks down at the floor. 'You're right. It is.' He moves back around the desk.

I feel stunned and hurt, like I've just been dumped or jilted. I want to run away from this place and my own humiliation. While there might be a strong attraction on my side, at least I sense he's humouring me. And I hate him for that. I press my lips tightly together, not trusting myself to speak.

'I have some information.' Avoiding my eyes, he resumes his business-like manner. 'Do you want to know what I've found out?'

I want to cover my ears, walk out. Clearly, this is all just a game to him. But I remain there, rooted to the spot.

'I had a good snoop through the records for Churchley & Sons. I went back as far as 1960.' He points to the stack of papers. 'Remember I told you about provenance? The paper trail for every piece of art auctioned off has to be complete – i's dotted and t's crossed.' He takes a few pieces of paper off the top of the stack, each marked with a yellow sticky, and hands them to me. 'These all have the correct paper trail,' he says. 'That is, until you start looking a little more closely.'

I flip through the papers. Each one of them is a dossier for an artwork or piece of jewellery. A cover sheet charting the dates when the item was bought and sold is stapled to the carbon copy invoices backing up each entry.

'What am I looking for?'

'All these lots were inserted in the sale the day before the auction,' he says. 'The seller was a Mr D Kinshaw of Grand Cayman. We're talking fifteen different works sold between 1960 and 1980.'

'Is that unusual?'

'Not in itself. And all the invoices are there to make the provenance complete. Most were purchased in France, though a few items are from elsewhere. It's just... look at the signature.'

I can't read the scrawl across the bottom of the documents approving inclusion of the item in the auction. 'Whose is it?' I say.

'It's Jeremy's signature. Which is strange, because my great-grandfather was never directly involved in the auction business. He sometimes did repairs and valuations, same as I do. But that's it.' He taps his finger on the scribble. 'So why is his signature on these lots, and not on others?'

'I don't know.' I feel a bit thick for not grasping the significance. 'Maybe he was filling in for someone.'

'No. I think it was more than that.'

'Well... what?'

'There are no records of D Kinshaw after 1985.'

'Maybe he died?'

'That's the year my great-grandfather died.'

I shake my head. 'Sorry, but I don't understand what you're implying, Chris.' I wish I had the right to take his hand and wipe the stricken look off of his face.

'Don't you?' His pale blue eyes flash like sunlight on ice. He writes the letters D Kinshaw on the paper in front of me. 'One of my annoying little foibles, as my father would say, is that I like to take things apart and put them back together – clocks, electronics, words...'

'Words?'

'It's an anagram.'

Crossing out D Kinshaw, he scribbles: H Dawkins.

47

I stare at the pencil-written name. 'Hal Dawkins? But how can that be?'

'You tell me,' Chris says. 'I thought you said the poor bloke was sent to the front—'

'Where he was shot and killed,' I finish for him. 'I saw the telegram informing his next of kin of his death.'

'Though we're talking about criminal acts here,' Chris says. 'If Hal Dawkins really was a looter, then what's a little forgery on top? A paper trail for art, a telegram he sent himself, a mate who works at a fancy auction house...' He spreads his hands. 'The sky's the limit.'

'And how convenient if everyone thinks you're dead.'

We stare at each other like we can read each other's thoughts. But right now, all I can focus on are the permutations and possibilities.

'Maybe D Kinshaw forged your great-grandfather's signature on the auction house documents,' I say, 'to get his looted goods into the sale.'

'That seems pretty far-fetched.' Chris's shoulders droop. 'He wouldn't have had access.'

'I suppose not.'

'Another possibility is that either Jeremy or' – he winces – 'maybe Frank Bolton could have used Hal Dawkins's identity to sell their looted property.'

'Yes, but why take on the identity of a man who's dead?'

'Isn't that what criminals do?'

My brain hurts trying to process this new information. 'So you're saying that Jeremy and Frank – "Spider" and "Flea" – were looters who framed their mate Hal Dawkins, aka "Badger". Badger died at the front, and then, over a span of thirty or forty years, Spider and Flea sold their spoils though the auction house?'

'In a nutshell,' he says. 'Though perhaps Frank wasn't involved. That part, I don't know. All I have is the paperwork I've shown you.'

I shake my head. 'It just seems too improbable. And besides, the items could be legitimate. I thought you said the provenance was in order.'

'It looks that way,' he says. 'So I think the Heath-Churchleys are in the clear at least.'

'What a relief,' I say sarcastically. 'Otherwise I might have been rounded up and shot at dawn by your father.'

He nods absently, which doesn't make me feel much better. 'Here,' he says, 'I made you a copy.'

'You've thought of everything.' I shove the papers into my handbag. 'Thanks – I think.'

'And Alex...'

'Yes?'

'About what you said earlier. Do you really think I'm only

interested in protecting my family name and keeping my nice little life in the back of "Daddy's" auction house?'

'I don't know. You keep pushing me away. What am I supposed to think?'

His pale eyes penetrate mine. I wait for him to move – to close the space between us. But he doesn't.

The clocks tick on for a good few seconds before he finally speaks. 'Am I allowed to set the record straight, Alex? Would you believe me if I said that it's not about your family secrets – or mine. Honestly, I couldn't give a fig about those things.'

'I believe you, Chris.' I raise a hand, embarrassed. 'I completely understand if you don't fancy me. I mean, you're spoiled for choice, aren't you?'

'It's funny, Alex. Do you really think I'm running around with dozens of women?'

'You tell me.' Mentally, I tick off the list. 'I mean, there's your dad's blonde PA. And the other PA. And Greta – she's blonde too. And Sidney-from-the Isle-of-Wight…' I shift from foot to foot.

'It's ironic, isn't it?' he says. 'I spend my time in this workshop, practically a hermit, according to my dad. I emerge occasionally to go for a coffee, or sometimes I'm required at the auction house. Though as you can probably imagine, most of the time they try to keep me hidden away like some kind of embarrassing spinster aunt.'

I laugh. I *can* imagine.

'And you happen to run into me on the very rare occasions when I'm seeing a friend from school, or having a chat with someone from front of house.'

'I'm a woman – I see the way they look at you.'

'Well, there's nothing between me and them.'

'I'm sorry,' I say. 'I was out of line.'

He picks up a file from a roll of tools next to the lamp and begins whittling away at a tiny piece of metal. I watch him silently.

'There was someone once.' He stares down at his work. 'Someone special. We almost got married.'

'Almost?'

'In hindsight, the story is very dull. Back then, I was all about rebellion against Dad. He'd spent years parading rich girls from good families in front of me like I was some kind of pedigree hound. Hannah was just a normal, middle-class girl from up north. That's what drew me to her.' He shakes his head. 'Plus the fact that she was older than me and looked like Lauren Bacall.'

'Oh.' My self-esteem takes a swan dive.

'Dad hated her instantly, which was the icing on the cake. We got engaged. There was a huge brouhaha over announcing or not announcing it. Like I cared about things like that. Anyway, to make a long story short, Dad hired a private investigator. Turns out my "normal, middle-class girl" was a con artist.'

'Really?'

'That's a simple term for it. Dad's words were a bit more poetic. "Gold digger", "strumpet", "foreign whatnot". Turns out that her family came to England when the Berlin Wall came down. She was after a good, solid English name, and money to restore some bombed-out old schloss in God knows where.' He pauses. 'She and her husband, that is.'

'She was married?' My own inner wound begins to throb.

'Yeah.' He shrugs. 'So you can see why, after that, I decided to stick to my clocks.'

'Yes, I get it.' All of a sudden, I start to laugh.

Chris looks up, puzzled. 'OK, I guess I was a lovesick puppy back then, but it wasn't that funny at the time.'

'No, it's not that. It's just, I kind of understand.' I tell him a little about Xavier, the married poet. 'He's the reason that I swore off relationships and became a recluse in my bookish little coach house flat on the grounds of Mallow Court.'

Even though it's not funny, both of us end up laughing. Tears stream down my face as I catch my breath and gather up the papers.

'I should be getting back,' I say. 'Thank you for the information.'

He comes round his worktable; my breath catches as he stands close to me, his tall frame solid and commanding. 'When can I see you again?' he says. 'I mean... properly?'

The heat rising between us is delicious and almost unbearable. 'I'll call you,' I say, turning to leave before I can do anything that might spoil the moment. But as I reach the door, I turn back. 'For what it's worth, Chris,' I say, 'I can guarantee you one thing.'

'What's that?'

I give him a slow, languid smile. 'If you're still looking for a normal, middle-class girl – then that's me. As your dad is already well aware, I'm a "little nobody" through and through.'

48

15 NOVEMBER 1940 – 12.03 A.M.

I walked alone down the icy street. The sickly wisps of moonlight barely penetrated the gloom. The street must have once been opulent – white terraces with shiny black doors, London plane trees carpeting the pavement with orange and gold leaves. I pictured the ghosts of people walking, expensive cars purring by. A life I could only have dreamed of.

And now, the buildings were silent and dark – taped windows blacked out, some boarded up. There were no signs of life. Were the people asleep, or evacuated? Or all dead?

At the end of the terrace, one of the houses was still smouldering. It may have been hit earlier tonight, or perhaps it had been burning for a day or more. The upper floors had caved in, leaving exposed rafters to cut across the red glow of the sky.

I heard a noise then, a scraping sound, coming from around the side of the bombed-out house. I went to look. And even though I was expecting it – even though I knew what was going to happen – the moment I saw him, my stomach roiled with shock and disgust.

49

On the train home, my mind is full of Chris. We may come from different worlds, but both of us have had our hearts broken in the past. Like me, he withdrew from the world to hibernate and heal. I close my eyes and remember the feel of his lips on mine. Just a short time ago, I'd convinced myself that my life was complete and anyone who thought I was hiding away was wrong. But they were right and now, I am *so ready* to come back to life.

As the colours of the countryside blur through the window, however, my thoughts drift to the obstacles. Mr Heath-Churchley already dislikes me, and that's before I or Mrs Edwards potentially drag his family name through the mud. Plus, there's the fact that some unknown person out there is determined to wreak havoc at Mallow Court.

I take out the papers Chris gave me and reread them, trying to fit the pieces together. Could D Kinshaw and Hal Dawkins really have been one and the same? There's very little concrete evidence, but I'd expected to be able to rely on a death notice.

But what if Hal Dawkins survived the front, took on a new identity, and was alive and well in 1985?

He would have been in his sixties then, I suppose. Did he stop auctioning things the year Jeremy died because he no longer had an insider in the auction house? It's possible. Which means, it's also possible that he could still be alive now, albeit in his eighties. Could he be the 'uninvited guest'? It's much too farfetched, I decide. While we have elderly men and women touring Mallow Court on a daily basis, I just can't see how an old man making mischief would fail to be spotted.

Which brings me full circle around to the same old questions: who? Why? And how the heck am I going to get to the bottom of things?

* * *

When I return to Mallow Court, there's a silver BMW parked in a no-parking area in front of the house. My stomach roils, thinking it's Tim. But just then, Mrs Fairchild comes of the house alongside a middle-aged man in an immaculate pinstriped suit, his brown hair slicked off his forehead with gel. Together, they walk to the car.

'Oh, hello, Alex.' Mrs Fairchild looks flustered when she sees me. She turns to the man. 'As I was just saying, my granddaughter is the manager here. She's the one you'll need to speak to about the estate accounts.'

I raise a cool eyebrow. 'The accounts? They're all filed at Companies House.'

'Of course.' He gives me a coy wink, which I find distasteful. 'But how rude of me not to introduce myself. I'm Alistair Bowen-Knowles. Of Tetherington Bowen-Knowles.'

He says the name like I ought to know it, and proffers his hand. Reluctantly, I shake it.

'It's the management accounts I'd like to see.' He fiddles with a right cufflink shaped like a golf club. 'The day-to-day running of the estate. That way, a purchaser will know the turnover numbers, the employee and maintenance costs, and exactly what they're taking on.' He gives me a smarmy smile.

The bottom falls out of my heart. 'A purchaser?'

My grandmother looks at me with round, pleading eyes. 'Alex, can we discuss it later?'

'You're what, exactly?' I turn and face the man full on.

'Sorry?' His close-set eyes narrow. 'I'm Mr Bowen-Knowles. Of Tetherington Bowen-Knowles.'

'So you said. I'm afraid I haven't heard of your firm. We aren't looking to change auditors.'

'I'm an estate agent.' His obsequious manner slips, and for a second, he views me with rife hostility.

'An estate agent.' I wave a hand casually, pretending I have even the slightest clue what's going on. 'Of course you are. I'm afraid I'm not going to have any time this afternoon to go over anything with you. Can you ring and make an appointment?'

'But can't you just email me the—'

'And by the way' – I cut him off and begin to walk away, flicking a bored glance over my shoulder – 'can you please move your car? The sign clearly says no parking.'

I go inside the heavy studded doors to the great hall. Barely able to breathe, I lean against a carved wooden sideboard. My grandmother called an *estate agent* – here – to Mallow Court? A day or two ago it would have seemed unthinkable. But now...

The door opens and closes. I stand up as my grandmother comes back inside. Unwittingly, I notice the hunch to her shoulders caused by years of back-breaking work in the garden. Unwittingly, I notice that she looks *old*.

She stops in the centre of the room and stares up at the ceiling. The heraldic bosses between the geometric ridges of plaster seem to frown down on both of us, as if the house, too, is feeling the tension.

Without looking at me, she sighs. 'I'm sorry, Alex. I just couldn't bring myself to tell you.' She turns and looks at me, and I see tears running down her cheeks.

Part of me wants to rush over and hug her, but the other part... I put my hands on my hips and stare at her. 'Tell me what, Grandma?'

'Oh, Alex.' She goes over to one of the long upholstered benches positioned around the edge of the room and sinks down onto it, wringing her hands together. Her nails are crusted with dirt from the garden. Her beloved garden...

Again, I stay where I am.

'These came earlier today.' She reaches into the pocket of her cardigan and takes out a few folded pieces of paper. 'For a while, the diary entries stopped, but I knew it wasn't the end. I didn't know what was coming. But' – her voice quavers – 'now I do.'

I take the papers and unfold them, skimming quickly over the words written in a cramped hand. A diary entry describing Badger catching Flea red-handed in the act of looting. Though I've been expecting that my grandmother would be confronted with this, I'd hoped to have more time to find evidence to counter the eye-witness truth that's staring up from the page. But I'm too late.

'As soon as it arrived and I read it, I knew what I had to do. Mr Bowen-Knowles was recommended by a friend. I called him in to start the process of selling the house.'

The words are like knives to my ears.

'I've felt so muddled,' she says. 'I know it's nothing compared to what you must be feeling, and I'm sorry that things were kept from you. But now, things are perfectly clear.' She shakes her head sadly. 'It's just so hard for me to accept that my father, whom I loved so much, could have done what he did.'

'Whoa, wait a minute.' I hold up my hands. 'What do you mean, exactly? We don't know that he *did* anything.'

'Look around you.' She sounds exasperated. 'You may not believe it, but I *have* wondered before how my father, who by his own admission came from nothing, could ever have bought this house and its contents.'

'He was a self-made man. He had a successful factory. I'm sure it was possible for a young man with a grain of ambition to pick up a factory cheap after the war. Not to mention a run-down old house. He built up the business using grit and determination.'

'Grit and determination.' Her eyes darken in disgust. 'How do you think he did it? Did he rush in when all the other paramedics and emergency services were trying to save people? Did he take what he could fit in his pockets, or did he pile things into his ambulance and not bother taking casualties to hospital? Or did he pick the rings and jewellery off the corpses and remove their gold teeth, just like the Nazis did?' Her voice drips with venom. 'Or maybe he wasn't really bothered if they were dead or not. Maybe he "helped them on their way" with a hand over the mouth or a quick blow to the back of the head.'

'Grandma!' In a few strides, I'm over to her. I sit on the edge of the sofa and try to take her arm, but she turns away from me, her body shaking with sobs. She's beyond comfort, but I stay with her as she cries.

Eventually, she starts to calm down. I put my hand on her

back, letting her feel its warmth. She wipes her tears on the sleeve of her cardigan and lifts her head.

'You knew already about the looting, didn't you?' She sighs. 'You must hate the way I've dragged you into this family.'

'All I know is that I love you.' The words feel right.

'Tell me how you found out.'

Gripping her hand tightly, I explain briefly about meeting Tim and Sally Edwards, née Dawkins.

'Sally Dawkins,' she snorts. 'I tried, but I could never bring myself to like her. She had a face like a rat and a personality to match. She and her mother used to turn their back on us in the street whenever Frank took us back to his old stomping grounds. He wanted his children to know that we weren't born with a silver spoon in our mouths. I hated those trips – the noise and the smells; all those people living on top of each other.' She sighs. 'I guess I was a stuck-up snob.'

'That's not true. And I guess Sally was upset about what happened to her family. But the diary isn't conclusive proof of anything.' I squeeze her hand for emphasis. 'And I don't know what Sally Dawkins was like when you knew her, but my impression is that she's got a chip on her shoulder the size of St Paul's.'

'Maybe so. But if there's even a chance that we're related to someone who could do that...' She exhales in a gasp. 'I can't be a part of it. I can't keep living here forever wondering if the house came from ill-gotten gains. The whole thing makes me sick.'

'Me too,' I say. 'But you've stuck by Frank Bolton over all these years when he was your adoptive father. Now, it's even more important. There are lots of missing pieces: things I'm trying to find out, and things we may never know. Things that may come to light that are difficult to accept. We have to be brave.'

She sighs, glancing down at our intertwined hands. 'I was so fortunate to be brought up as a little rich girl in this pretty bubble.' She gestures with her free hand. 'But perhaps all along it was destined to burst.'

'You were Frank Bolton's daughter. His eldest child. That's why he left the house to you.'

'Maybe.' She lifts her chin. 'His sons – my brothers – were much younger than I was. Frank got married a few years after he got me from the orphanage. He told me that he wanted to give me a mum. His wife, Mabel, had a wealthy grandmother. When she eventually had children, the boys each got a trust fund. Neither of them had any particular affinity for Mallow Court. They both went off to boarding school, and then uni. After that, they both moved abroad. We were never close, though we're still in touch – Christmas and birthdays – that sort of thing. On some level, I suppose they do resent my inheritance. But they've never been short of money, and Frank Bolton's will was unassailable. He liked that I came from nowhere, just like him. "You and I come as a package," he used to say.'

'The house is yours fair and square,' I say. 'You've got a perfect right to be here.'

'Even if it came from ill-gotten gains?' Her voice rises. 'Those things in the diary?' She points at the papers. 'Don't they matter?'

'Of course they do. I feel sick too thinking that someone did those things during such a dark, terrible time. But for all the digging I've done, I haven't found anything to prove if Frank was guilty or innocent. We may never be able to prove it one way or the other.'

'The diary is pretty damning.'

'I need to read all of it. You have it back, right?'

'Yes.' She sighs. 'They're all there – the ones from a few weeks back, and the new lot too.'

'And did your policeman friend make anything of them?'

'I haven't seen him for a few days.' She turns away, clearly upset. There must be trouble in paradise.

'I'm sorry.'

'Things were moving a little fast for me.' Her laugh is hollow. 'In fact, he bought me a ring. I mean, really – at my age?'

I feel an odd mixture of panic and relief. 'Do you love him?'

'I thought I could. But this is hardly the right time, is it?'

I think of Chris – to me it feels like exactly the right time.

'Besides,' she adds, 'I'm glad he hasn't seen this new entry. He's a very moralistic person. I liked that about him.'

'No matter what the diary says, it's not conclusive,' I say. 'It lacks... *provenance*. If you want my tuppence worth, it's not enough to justify giving up everything you love. This house, your garden: the place you've lived all your life.'

'I do love it here.' She sighs stoically. 'But it wouldn't be right to keep the house if there was even the slightest question. I couldn't walk through these rooms, tend to my garden, sleep in my bed and have tea in my kitchen, with all those ghosts swarming around.' She shudders. 'When you read the diary – you'll see.'

'In that case, I'll keep looking. Dig even deeper.' I stand up. 'I just need a little more time.'

'I'm not sure how much time you'll have, Alex. Everything feels so uncertain right now.'

'I know. But we've got each other.' Reaching out, I help her to her feet. 'Let me make you a cup of tea. Surely even the swarming ghosts won't deny us a cuppa.'

'OK, that'd be nice.'

'And if I can't find proof that Frank Bolton was innocent, then by all means, call back the toff in the suit.'

As soon as the words are out of my mouth, I regret them. Have I just doomed my grandmother's beloved home to death by Tetherington Bowen-Knowles?

50

15 NOVEMBER 1940 – 12.05 A.M.

I ran over to the bottom of the ladder. 'What are you doing, Flea?' I hissed as he jumped down.

He put a finger to his lips. 'You didn't see me, Badger.' With a bold smile, he took a diamond bracelet from his sinewy finger and tossed it to me. 'Right?'

'You're a goddamn looter,' I said. 'The rest of us are out risking our necks to save people, and you're dripping with diamonds like a two-shilling whore.' I threw the bracelet into the gutter.

'What the hell?' he snarled. He grovelled around in the rubble for the glittering bracelet and slipped it in the pocket of the coat.

I turned away, my heart battering my chest, rage blinding me to any danger. But a second later, I realised my mistake. He clicked open a switchblade that was still sticky with blood.

'What's this?' I said, my gorge rising.

'Don't worry – I swear she was already dead.'

'My God. I... I don't know you.'

He laughed. 'Good ol' Badger. You know I can't let you just walk away.'

'What? Do you think I'll grass on you?'

'Do you think I can take the risk – I mean, since you "don't know me" and all?'

I laughed uneasily. 'Put that away.' I indicated the knife. My mind was tying itself in knots over what to do next. I suddenly understood that Flea would do whatever it took to make sure I kept quiet.

He took a step towards me. The knife didn't waver. It took all my courage to stand my ground. 'You won't do it,' I said.

His eyes were dark pools as he laughed. 'The problem with you, Badger, is that you're so naïve,' he said. 'You don't know what you'd be capable of if you weren't so selfish. If you had other mouths to feed.'

'Selfish?' I snorted. 'You think I'm selfish?'

'Oh yes,' he said. 'Nothing's more precious to you than your moral high ground. But if you had a child – a daughter, say – you'd do anything for her. Would you want her to grow up like we did? Stitching the crotch into some granny's knickers till her fingers crook and her eyes go square? Would you want her living in some two-bit shithole with a privy out the back and hot water every other Sunday? You want her to live where you did – with lowlife boys hanging round the corner shop whistling and waiting to pick her cherry?' He shook his head. 'Or do you want to own the factory? Set her up in a nice big house, with a bit o' garden, and fresh air. Going to church in a little white dress and satin ribbons in her hair. Saving herself for a bloke with a title – hell, maybe even royalty.'

I met his eyes over the blade of the knife. 'You're mad.'

'No,' he said forcefully. 'I'm not. I'm realistic. My girl's got one "in the oven", so to speak. I already love that little bean more than life itself. I want more for her – or him. I want everything. And if that's at the cost of some dead git's signet ring or his wife's diamond bracelet, then I'm all for it. As they say, "all's fair in love and war".'

'No – I don't believe that. It's not the war that made you a lowly, *two-bit crook.' I stepped forward until the blade was practically touching my chest.*

His laugh rang with bitterness. 'I'll be a lowly two-bit crook living in that nice, big ol' house, running my own factory. No more clocking in and clocking out, getting spittle in the face from some fat foreman with a stick up his arse.'

I shook my head. It sounded crazy – deluded. But I could feel a crack widening inside me. I thought of the girl, Catherine, catching snowflakes on her tongue amid the ruins of her life. More than anything, I wanted to take her in my arms, fill her life with happiness until there was no more room for the pain. Flea's words rang true. Where would we live? And what kind of life could I give her?

He seemed to read my mind. 'You thinking of that girl, ain't you? The one you pulled from the wreckage and pitched up on ol' Sadie's doorstep?' He gave me a look – he knew. Somehow – he knew it all. 'I went round there earlier,' he continued, 'to make sure the little mite had settled in.'

'And had she?'

'She was crying her eyes out. Kept going on about some trinket her mum gave her. Thinks she lost it. It was all she had left.'

'No!'

'Course' – he smirked – 'it could be that someone took it off o' her. You pulled her out, right? You see any of that sort around who could have done something like that? Stealing from a child who'd just lost her mum?'

It wasn't like that! I wanted to scream. But what would be the point? If I told him that I was going to give it back – and I am going to give it back – he'd just laugh in my face. He thinks I'm like him... And suddenly, the fog lifted from my mind and I knew what I had to do.

I reached out and grabbed his wrist. 'Put that knife away, Flea. Let's talk man to man.'

He tried to twist away, and I let go. It wasn't a battle of strength, just one of wills.

I looked him in the eye. 'I said... put that away.'

The change in my manner made him hesitate.

'You're right – I did take the girl's trinket. You're right about a lot of things, but not about me. You think I'm here to grass on you?'

For the first time, he took a step backwards. He tucked the knife into his belt. 'Why are you here, Badger?'

'You think I'm stupid, don't you?' I hissed. 'You offer me some goddamn bracelet when you're dripping with jewels like the Queen of Sheba?'

'Oh.' Understanding dawned in his eyes now that we were speaking the same language. 'So you do want a slice of the pie.' He chuckled. 'Just a bigger slice, is that it?'

'Bigger – yes. You could say that.' I patted the lapel of his fur coat. 'Nice, but I'm allergic to fur. You can keep the coat.'

'What? You think I'm going to give you this lot?' His hand went to the jewels around his neck. 'Why would I do that?'

I smiled slowly, thinking how satisfying it would be to walk into a police station and dump a pile of looted jewels down on the counter. Maybe I'd get a reward for turning in a thief. And for reuniting the owner with their property. But first I needed to walk away from here.

'Because I've got something you don't have,' I say, pointing to the top of the alley. 'I've got evidence.'

He turned and looked; saw the cold, unfeeling eye of the camera filming him.

'You bastard,' he hissed, reaching for the knife again. But there was fear in his eyes now. I'd won.

'Give me the lot,' I said, 'and I'll have Robbie there destroy his film. You'll walk away.'

'How do I know you'll do that?'

'You don't.' I shrugged. 'As they say, "there's no honour among thieves".'

Slowly, he uncoiled the beads from around his neck. He bared his teeth at me. 'You'll regret this, Badger.'

I smiled grimly. 'I already do.'

I untucked the knife from his belt. He handed me the jewels, including the diamond bracelet he'd offered me earlier.

'Here – you keep this.' I tossed him a plain gold ring. 'Think of it as a little gift for all your hard work.'

51

Even though I'm not one jot clearer to solving anything, I feel much happier having cleared the air with Mrs Fairchild. But there's a dagger hanging over my head ready to drop at any moment and sever my newfound connection with my grandmother, her family, and Mallow Court. A dagger in the form of a sheaf of papers, shoved into a folder. The diary entries.

That evening, the library is hired out for a small corporate drinks party. Leaving the guests in the care of the caterers, I go to the estate office and sit down at my desk with a glass of red wine from the open bar. I take a pen and notebook out of the drawer – calling it 'research' makes it easier to stay detached.

But when I start reading through the entries one by one, it's impossible to stay detached for long. With each page, I become more and more overwrought and horrified by the possibility that I'm related to someone who could have acted with such unfeeling cruelty. And not just related, but reaping the benefit of his criminal activities years later. I'm managing a house that was bought by ill-gotten gains; living in a flat on the grounds. My grandmother owns the house. Someday, I might even inherit it. The idea makes me feel sick. The more I read, the more I understand why my grandmother called in the estate agent. The foundations of the life I've built for myself have begun to shudder and crack.

I glean that Hal Dawkins, 'Badger', teamed up with the photographer, Robert Copthorne, to follow Frank, 'Flea', and gather evidence. Most likely, Flea looted the Stanley house because he was jealous of Jeremy, 'Spider', and his superior class and prospects. They followed him to another bombed-out house where he looted jewellery and furs. Though it isn't spelled out, I infer that Flea may have hacked off the wrist of a dead woman to remove a diamond bracelet. Like a rat crawling from a sewer, nothing was sacred or off limits.

Eventually, I throw down the stack of papers. I feel unclean and can't read any more. I go to the window and look out at the view – twilight is settling in over the idyllic gardens, a sliver of moon rising just above the coppice of silver birch trees. All of it seems tainted now.

I find myself wishing that Chris was here, while at the same time grateful that he's not. Anyone who read through the diary would be bound to come to the same damning conclusion. Despite his weak attempts to justify his actions to his friend Badger, Frank Bolton was a scumbag through and through.

Just as I'm about to go and check on the guests, the office phone rings. I answer it and am subjected to the cut-glass tones of the estate agent, Alistair Bowen-Knowles.

'I was hoping to speak to Catherine,' he says. 'Would that be possible?'

'She's out,' I lie.

'In that case, Ms Hart, please can you let her know that I have someone interested in viewing the property.'

'What? Already?' The words shoot out of my mouth. 'We haven't even decided to put it on the market.'

'Of course. If you could just let her know, I would appreciate it.'

Hating the man with my entire being, I slam down the phone. Just five minutes ago, I was adamant that my grandmother was right to sell the house. So why am I being so obstructive? I push the wine away. There's something niggling in my mind – something that I'm missing. I'm sure of it.

I put my head down on the desk, resting it on my arm. The sound of my wristwatch is like a time bomb ticking in my ear.

* * *

The next day is dull and rainy, reflecting my mood. There are no coaches due until the afternoon, so I use the time to get on with odd jobs, chat with Edith, and help tidy-up the back storeroom. I accomplish the tasks on autopilot, still thinking about what I have and haven't discovered and what to do next.

The answer comes to me: I need to snoop.

I wait for my grandmother to go off to her WI meeting in the village, then go upstairs and use my master key to unlock her bedroom door. Inside, the room is an odd mixture of feminine and masculine: cushions and curtains in candy floss pink, wallpaper with alternating stripes of white and China blue roses, but also heavy dark wood furnishings and a huge carved four-poster bed hung with thick draperies in nautical blue and gold. Everything is neat and tidy. I check the dressing table, the nightstand, and the closet, looking for any papers or letters that might be of interest. There's nothing. No old boxes of photographs or documents that belonged to her dead father. Inside the lining of her jewellery box, I find a single photograph of me dressed for my prom. A prickling sensation goes down my spine. Mum or Dad must have sent her the photo. How did she feel when she received it? Grateful for them to think of her, or angry that she wasn't part of my life? With a shudder, I put it back and leave the room.

Admittedly, I wasn't really expecting to find anything pertinent. The past is a painful subject to my grandmother. She wouldn't keep anything out in the open where it might be found by the staff, or... me. So where does she keep her memories?

Unfortunately, by process of elimination, I have a fair idea. I climb the back stairs to the third floor with a number of attic rooms that were once servant bedrooms. I plan to convert them in future for wedding accommodation, but for now, most of them are used for furniture storage. However, there's also a second attic above, which is not habitable, and much less pleasant. I position the wobbly wooden ladder underneath the hatch, climb up, and squeeze through. The space is cramped and stiflingly hot, with dangerous low beams jutting at every angle. I switch on my torch and crawl to the very middle where the roof peaks. I straighten up, shuddering as my hair finds a shower of dust and cobwebs. I shine the torch around. There's a colony of greenfly above one of the windows, and mice droppings that I've already crawled through. Boxes are shoved under the eaves, most labelled in black marker: books, toys, clothes, taxes. The writing is neat, and I recognise it as my grandmother's. Everything here is still too modern.

At the back of the attic is another door. I make my way over, whacking my head on a low beam and swearing. The door leads to a cavernous space that stretches the length of the long gallery. I duck down to crawl through the low door and shine my torch inside.

The room has been ransacked! Everywhere, domestic

detritus has been heaved to the side: pieces of an iron bed frame, an ancient-looking hoover, some large picture frames. Every box has been opened and tipped out: old books, trophies, horse riding gear. And papers – endless papers. With a shaking hand, I pick up a few of them. Children's drawings and old mimeographed homework, a few old bills. Someone – probably Catherine's stepmum Mabel – kept just about everything. I know for a fact that Mrs Fairchild rarely comes up to the attic, and certainly would never have left such a mess. So that means that someone else – an intruder – went through it all looking for something. My skin crawls with the knowledge that the 'uninvited guest' has clearly been making himself busy at Mallow Court without anyone's knowledge. Like a rat that crawls out from between the floorboards at night, he's been gnawing at the fibres of the past. But what was he looking for?

And more importantly, did he find it?

I rifle through more of the papers, but quickly decide there's no point. Even if I knew what I was looking for, I'm too late. I'll send one of the cleaners up here with some bin bags to clean up the mess. There's nothing else I can do.

Wiping the sweat from my forehead, I sit back on my heels. The silence is thick and cloying. The only sound is a slow drip coming from a cold water tank underneath the eaves. I crawl towards the drip and shine my torch over the black plastic covering on the tank. The last thing I need is a leak ruining the plaster ceiling in the room below.

I move the plastic aside. There's no visible leak, but shoved between the tank and the wall is another archive box with a battered top and signs of water damage on the sides. Cobwebs brush my face as I squeeze into the small space. The cardboard practically disintegrates as I pull out the box; a shower of dust and mildew sends me into a coughing fit. I'm fairly sure of one thing, though...

It's a box the intruder didn't find.

I open the battered lid and shine my torch inside. On top is something that looks like a scuba mask. But as I lift it out, I realise that it's a gas mask. In the dim light, it looks like the head of a monster designed to frighten small children. How awful it must have been to have to carry one everywhere, never knowing when it might save your life. I set it aside with a shudder.

Underneath the mask are sheaves of old papers and newspaper clippings. The damp cardboard is ready to split, so I unload some of the things, wishing I'd brought a bag. At the bottom of the box, I find a flat metal cylinder about the size of a dinner plate. I move the other things aside and pull it out. It's an old film canister for a reel-to-reel projector. Underneath are several more – I count five film canisters in all. It may well be nothing, but my pulse quickens. What could be on the films that have been preserved for so long? Family home movies of a summer picnic, a day at the beach, or excited children on Christmas morning? Or something else? Could this be what the intruder was looking for?

I pile as many of the papers and photos as I can carry on top of the film canisters. I need to put them somewhere to keep them safe. By the time I'm finally back to the hatch, I've hit my head twice and am seeing stars. But I've got an armful of treasures – or junk – to show for my troubles. I take everything down the ladder and over to my flat. Though I'm desperate for a shower to wash off the years of cobwebs and dust clinging to my hair and my skin, I want to know exactly what I've discovered. I begin sorting through the pile of papers. There are lots of old photos: men in military uniforms drinking at the pub; women in floral cotton dresses posing for the camera with smiling painted lips. A few of the photos are signed R. Copthorne with a date scribbled in pencil. Then there are the newspaper clippings: mostly headline articles mentioning various Allied victories and advances, and the occasional obituary with a name circled in red pencil. I'm about to give up when a tiny article catches my eye. I read through it, the breath catching in my chest.

Lost Romanov Jewels Hidden in London?

On Thursday night, a Russian national was washed ashore in Northern Scotland after his boat was torpedoed. Suffering from acute hypothermia, he was found by a local resident who notified the authorities. According to the resident, while in a delirious state, the man spoke of being on a mission to London to find a Russian princess who was the illegitimate daughter of Grand Duke Michael Alexandrovich, brother to Tsar Nicholas II. According to the unnamed man, the young woman escaped Russia during the 1918 Revolution with a fortune in family jewels. The man is currently in police custody after admitting to being a spy working for Soviet secret police.

In the margin of the clipping, a note is penned: *Marina?*

I flip anxiously through the rest of the clippings, but there's nothing – no follow-up article, and no more marginalia.

Marina? Could this Russian princess referred to in the article be *the* Marina that Mr Pepperharrow knew? My great-grandmother? Surely not.

Yet, I remember what he said about her always seeming frightened; how she lived her life constantly looking over her shoulder. That would have been the case for many Russians who escaped the Revolution to come to the West. Most certainly, for someone who was hiding a fortune in jewels.

A fortune in jewels?

I take the jewelled locket from my pocket and hold it in my hand along with the tiny gold key. I've bought a silver chain to wear them around my neck, and I thread it through the locket and the key. When I put it around my neck, the metal warms my skin like it contains its own life force.

No.

I fire up my laptop and do a web search for 'Marina, Russian Princess'. A few sites come up: the kind I'm afraid to open for fear they'll give my computer a virus. I then do a search on Grand Duke Michael Alexandrovich. This time, real information is more plentiful.

In a nutshell, Michael Alexandrovich was fourth in line to the Russian throne at birth, but at the time of the Revolution was third in line following his brother, Tsar Nicholas II and the Tsar's son, Alexei. Michael Alexandrovich apparently caused a scandal by marrying his mistress, Natalia, with whom he had his 'only child', George. Before that, he also had an affair with Princess Beatrice, Queen Victoria's daughter, who later married into the Spanish royal house. I swiftly jot down the main facts, specifically noting that he's not officially credited with fathering any other children. Certainly not a daughter named 'Marina'.

I learn that prior to the 1918 Revolution, Michael Alexandrovich left Russia for a time, living, among other places, at Knebworth House in Hertfordshire! Excitement bubbles in my chest. I *know* Knebworth House: we visited once on a school trip. Michael Alexandrovich apparently then returned to Russia with his family to fight in the Russian forces in World War One. But when the political situation in Russia became untenable in 1916, Nicholas II signed a document abdicating the throne in favour of his brother. Michael Alexandrovich refused to accept the honour until a provisional government had ratified his appointment – which never happened. Michael Alexandrovich was arrested by the Bolsheviks and murdered in 1918. His family, however, managed to escape to the West.

My mind is a maelstrom by the time I'm done reading. I draw out a little chart starting with Tsar Alexander III, father to both Nicholas and Michael:

Alexander III
Nicholas II Michael Alexandrovich
Marina (?) (1901–1940)
Catherine Bolton (Fairchild) (1935—)
Robin Fairchild (Hart) (1953–1972)

I can't bring myself to fill in the last blank as I stare at the family history I've made. Blood rushes to my head. I've no proof and I may never have any proof. But it's all there in black and white. I recall telling my grandmother that some of the things we discover might be difficult, and we have to be brave. For me, this is one of them.

I hold up the locket and release the catch. 'Are you sure about this?' I ask as the bird rotates and sings its song. Humming the melody that each time seems to stick in my head, I pick up my pen. Underneath 'Robin', I add my own name.

Alex Hart (1972—)

Who, by some strange twist of fate and accident of birth, might just be a real Russian princess.

52

Fate works in strange ways, and the irony is not lost on me. I'm about the last person on earth who wants to be a princess. And yet...

I tuck the locket and key inside my top, smiling to myself as I imagine what Dad's reaction would be. Disbelief, horror; he would probably disown me. Or at least make me buy every round down the pub for the rest of my natural life.

And then there's Chris. At our last meeting, I'd assured him with hands on heart that I was a little nobody. Has history made a liar of me?

I pick up one of the film canisters I brought down from the attic and turn it over. There's a faded sticker on the bottom with something scribbled on it: *R Copthorne 1940*. Could this be the proof that will settle things one way or another, once and for all?

I have to find out, even if it means signing the death warrant for Mallow Court. I take out my mobile phone and scroll down to Chris's details.

As unsettled as I feel, I'm happy for an excuse to call him

again. Not to gloat, grovel or even to share confidences. But because he's the one person I know who, in a shadowy corner of his workshop, has a reel-to-reel film projector.

Fortunately, Chris answers his phone and we arrange a meeting the following evening. I feel dizzy with excitement and fear as I hang up the phone. I put the film canisters in a rucksack along with the photographs and the newspaper article on the Russian spy and hide the bag in my dirty clothes hamper just in case the 'uninvited guest' decides to come calling.

I still feel giddy as I shower and change my clothes, then return to the main house to meet with a wedding couple. But as I'm about to enter the dining room, I overhear my grandmother, returned from her WI meeting, on the phone.

'I'm sorry she isn't cooperating, Alistair,' she's saying. 'Alex just feels this very deeply – we all do.'

I know I shouldn't listen in, but I can't help it. I know she's talking to the horrible estate agent whose emails I've tagged to go directly to my junk folder. I hold my breath as she continues on.

'But it's... nice... that someone is interested in the house already.' Her voice has a slight tremor in it. 'You should definitely bring him round for a viewing while the roses are at their peak. I'll arrange it for a time when she's out.'

Blood rushes to my head as she hangs up the phone. I hurry away down the corridor back towards the great hall. Somehow, since our last conversation, I'd deluded myself that something miraculous would happen. That I'd prove Frank Bolton's innocence in time for my grandmother to call off this plan to sell the house. But I haven't done so. In fact, I'm now holding the evidence that will likely prove his guilt.

I rush to the nearest window, fling it open, and breathe in the warm, fresh outside air. It's a hot day, the sun is out, the garden is lovely, a group of visitors are disembarking from a coach. At this moment, everything seems right – running smoothly, like well-oiled clockwork. As Karen once said: *it's practically running itself*.

But nothing can stave off the chill I feel in my heart. This time next year... will all this have come to an end?

53

As arranged, I get on the train to London the following evening. I'm still wearing the jewelled locket around my neck, tucked safely away inside my top. Whatever happens, and whatever I discover on those film reels with Chris, the locket is part of it too. All day long I've felt the weight of destiny on my shoulders. That one way or another, I'm coming to the end of my quest.

By the time I emerge from the Tube at Chancery Lane, the evening rush of commuters is nearly ended and the warren of streets off Hatton Garden seems darker and more confusing than usual. I pass the odd shady-looking character lurking in a doorway and a few drunken day traders in suits taking a shortcut to a back-alley pub. Eventually, I reach the marble monolith of Churchley & Sons Fine Art Auctioneers, glowing like a pale jewel underneath the street lights.

How many works of art auctioned off there had a dodgy past, regardless of their precious *provenance*? Art can be forged so skilfully that even the experts are fooled. So how much easier must it be to forge paperwork and records? I look up at the sky, imagining the terror of planes flying overhead, dropping their deadly cargo. How handy wars must be for people with criminal tendencies. But which of Flea, Badger, or Spider was such a person?

The alleyway is dark, but the noise of a thousand ticking clocks swarms around me like a hive of bees. The door is ajar, and behind it is a thin quadrilateral of light. Chris appears at the door, his tall frame taking up most of the space. As the clocks tick on, time seems to float in a bubble around us. We stand there staring at each other for a long moment, and then he takes me in his arms and nuzzles his face into my hair.

'Alex,' he murmurs. 'I've missed you.'

I stay there like that, breathing him in, enjoying the sense of peace and rightness that I feel when I'm with him. His heart beats against my chest, the locket sandwiched between us. He twines my hair and the chain of the locket through his fingers, as if it's somehow part of me. The clocks begin to chime the hour, first one, and then another, and then all of them together, making a right racket. We both laugh.

Holding my hand, he leads me down the corridor into the workshop. It's the first time I've been here at night. At this hour, the shop is lit by all sorts of eclectic light fixtures: an old gas street light now wired for electricity, intricate brass Moroccan lanterns hung from the ceiling, a Tiffany glass desk lamp, a dusty crystal chandelier with half the bulbs missing. The grandfather clocks cast long shadows, and in the corner, I spot the projector.

'I brought the entertainment,' I say, taking the film canisters from my bag. 'That is, assuming that works.' I point to the projector.

'I went out as soon as you phoned yesterday and got the missing part,' he says. 'It should be as good as new.'

'That's what I was afraid of.'

He laughs. 'I also took the liberty of ordering a couple of pizzas. They should be here any minute.'

'Great.'

'And I thought we could drink this.' A sheepish grin crosses his face as he holds up a bottle of red Burgundy. 'It's from Dad's cellar.' He puts a finger to his lips.

'I won't tell.' That bottle of wine is probably worth more than all my worldly goods put together. As much as the aristo ways of the Heath-Churchleys are anathema to me, admittedly even the black sheep of the family comes with his perks.

There's a space cleared on an antique oak table that's normally covered with tools and clockwork bits. Set around it are a couple of carved French chairs with mismatched upholstery. 'I found the table and the chairs in a skip,' he says, noticing my interest. 'I had to fix a few wobbles, glue some of the struts back on, and polish the top, but you just wouldn't believe some of the things that people throw away!'

'Beautiful.' I gaze appreciatively at his long, deft fingers as he removes the cork from the bottle and pours the wine into two cut-crystal glasses. The wine goes down as smooth as butter. The pizzas arrive and we eat them straight from the box, talking and laughing. Despite the secrets of the past, I'm happy in the moment just being with him. There's a definite *something* fizzing in the air between us. Every cell in my body is on high alert, just waiting for our fingers to touch as we both reach for the bottle to pour more wine, and I feel his leg brush against mine under the table.

We finish the pizzas and he removes the boxes. 'Let's start the show.' He stands up to ready the projector.

'I guess we should.' Suddenly, I'm apprehensive. We've been having such a lovely time... but will the films spoil everything? Am I ready to face what they contain?

He brings the bottle and our glasses over to a table positioned next to a blue crushed-velvet sofa with a carved wooden frame.

'Did you find that in a skip too?' I indicate the sofa.

'No.' He smiles. 'That's a nineteenth-century Louis XV divan that once belonged to the Queen Mother at Sandringham.'

I punch him playfully in the arm. He grabs me and pulls me close, kissing me everywhere on my face except my lips. My whole body sizzles like a firework.

He touches a finger to my lips. 'Hold that thought until later,' he says, stepping back reluctantly. 'Or else these film strips will never get watched.'

'You're right.' I sit down on the sofa expectantly.

Chris turns the projector on. The fan begins to hum; a bright light projects onto a white area on the wall opposite the sofa. He takes the first film from the canister and places it on the front reel, threading the loose end of cellulose through a smaller reel at the back. Finally, he flicks a switch on the wall and the other lights dim.

'OK,' he says. 'Ready to roll?'

'Yes.' I take a sip of wine to strengthen my resolve.

The white wall flickers with black and grey lines as the projector continues to hum and click. Chris turns a few knobs, adjusting the focus. As the images begin to appear on the wall, he sits down beside me, his warm solidity a buffer against whatever might be coming.

The film is mostly shots of a family playing tennis in a garden and having a picnic by the river. There's no sound, but it's obvious that they're enjoying themselves, laughing and horsing around. The images shift to another family by the seaside: playing cricket, building a sandcastle that gets washed away by a rogue wave. My hopes begins to droop. As much as

I'm glad there's nothing incriminating, I'm also no closer to the truth. Are all the reels just the home movies of a family I don't even recognise?

We watch the film to the end. The final frames are grainy and white. The images sputter out and the projector gives a high-pitched whine and seems to shut off.

'It's not broken, is it?' I say.

Chris gives the stand a kick. It hums back to life. 'All systems go,' he assures me.

The next reel shows an urban street. A group of children are standing around a man with one leg playing an accordion. Two girls toss him money, and one boy seems to be jeering at him. The impromptu 'concert' continues. I snuggle closer to Chris on the sofa, toying with the chain of the locket and the tiny gold key. If I'm not going to learn anything useful, then I may as well enjoy his company.

The reel ends with a group of uniformed men launching something large and metallic into the sky.

'What is it, do you think?' Chris asks, his hand distractingly caressing my leg.

I recall something I've seen on TV. 'I think it's a barrage balloon. To ward off enemy planes.'

'Ah. Clever girl.' His hand moves higher.

By the end of the reel, I have very little appetite to watch any more. But in an act of delicious torture, Chris gets up and puts on the next film.

This time, the frames are darker; it must have been filmed at night. There are a few shops in a terrace, and in the middle, a building that's totally collapsed. Someone runs in front of the camera. I sit forward now, my attention on the screen. More people run into the frame and past where the cameraman's standing. A woman desperately drags three children by the hand, chivvying them along. An old man limps swiftly by, carrying a cat in his arms. Then, a policeman goes past, herding stragglers. And then, the screen goes black – something has fallen from the sky, obliterating everything. I gasp, certain that the film will end there. But a moment later, the images resume, shaky now and blurry with dust. A man is rolling on the ground, his coat on fire. There are dark objects on the ground… bodies. I concentrate on Chris's hand on mine; sitting here now, I know I'm safe. But seeing the suffering before my eyes, I feel anything but.

'We don't have to watch this,' Chris whispers.

I shake my head. Whatever these films reveal, I *do* need to watch them. Sixty years later, only Chris and I are here to bear witness – to the last moments of these people's lives.

The images flicker off and back on again. This time, the camera is in a moving vehicle, racing past burning and ruined buildings at breakneck speed. The image is jerky and dizzying. The vehicle stops. The camera follows as two men in paramedic uniforms come into view. The vehicle must be an ambulance.

One of the men turns towards the camera and I jump to my feet. 'That's Frank Bolton.' I point at the fuzzy image.

'Which one?' Chris says.

'The one with the sandy hair.'

I watch rapt as Frank Bolton goes over to a body writhing on the ground. He checks the pulse and shouts to his colleague. Together, the two men lift the casualty onto a stretcher and into the back of the ambulance. Then Frank and the other men seem to be having some kind of discussion – a disagreement, maybe. Frank points at the bombed-out terrace where there are other bodies lying. The other man shrugs and gets back into the driver's seat. The ambulance roars off, leaving Frank and the cameraman. I perch back down on the edge of the sofa, barely able to breathe. The camera stays put as Frank checks each body for a pulse. He looks back at the camera and shakes his head. Then he looks up at the sky. In the light of the burning buildings all around, something on the screen begins to glisten.

'It's snowing!' Chris says. 'Look.'

I watch as Frank signals for the camera to follow him. He's clearly seen or heard something. Frank rushes towards something at the edge of the screen – a pile of debris. All of a sudden, a small girl crawls out from under the rubble, the building around her half-collapsed. She looks up at the sky and sticks out her tongue, catching the first snowflakes of winter.

'It's Catherine!' I stare at the flickering darkness, captivated and heartbroken by this moment of tragedy and hope. Frank goes up to the girl, removes his uniform jacket, and puts it around her shoulders. She points back to the rubble and Frank goes over to investigate. There's someone lying there – a woman. Her torso is partially obscured by a large timber that's lying on top of her. The girl bends over her as Frank Bolton checks her pulse and shakes his head. There's a long moment as the woman appears to speak to the girl and hands her something. The object flashes bright for a split second.

'Look!' I exclaim. 'It's the locket!' I grip the lozenge-shaped piece of silver around my neck. Chris's hand clasps over mine. The screen goes white with black and grey lines as the end of the film flicks around the turning reel.

For a long second, neither of us moves. The cogs in my mind whirl trying to make sense of what I've seen. Frank Bolton – not Hal Dawkins – rescuing young Catherine. All there in flickering, irrefutable black and white. Chris rises from the sofa and rewinds the film reel. The fan continues to run noisily.

'What does it mean?' he says.

'I think it means that the diary entries are fakes.' I stare at the white wall. 'Either that, or everyone's mistaken as to who kept the diary. My grandmother and Mrs Edwards said it was Hal Dawkins's diary. But maybe they were wrong.'

'What made them think that?'

'An inscription inside the front cover. It said Diary of Hal "Badger" Dawkins.' My brain hurts from trying to make sense of it all.

'But we already know that there was funny business going on,' Chris reminds me. 'Whoever sent the entries could have engaged in a little "misdirection" and written the inscription themselves.'

'But why? I can't see Sally Edwards doing it.'

'We'd better watch the other reels,' Chris says. 'Maybe the film tells more of the story.'

'Yes, let's.' I feel shaken to the core, but I have to see this through.

Chris puts on the next reel, and we watch with rapt interest. The image is shaky and distant, as if the photographer was trying to stay out of sight. A person in a lady's fur coat is climbing down a ladder. The light catches the flash of jewellery on her wrists and fingers.

A man steps out of the shadows. 'Look!' I grab Chris's arm. The man goes up to the woman – they're clearly arguing. A second later, the woman draws a blade.

'I don't think it's a woman,' Chris says.

'What?'

The faces turn towards the dim streetlight. The man is Frank and the 'woman' in the fur coat is... Hal.

The photographer films what is clearly an altercation between the two men. Eventually, Hal takes off the jewels he's wearing and hands them to Frank. Frank walks away. The reel flickers off.

'Unbelievable,' Chris says. He turns to me tentatively. 'Did Frank just get away with the loot?'

'In the diary it says that "Badger"– who we now know must be Frank – took the loot to the police station. "Spider" – your grandfather, Jeremy, drove Frank. He wasn't involved in the looting. The film was taken by Robert Copthorne. It must have been the evidence they used against Hal, who was also known as Flea.'

'Well, well...' Chris gives me a dazzling smile. 'It looks like you've proved that Frank Bolton is in the clear.'

'Yes.' I smile back and the world seems to close in around us. I know that there are still unanswered questions. But for now, I lie back on the sofa, enjoying the relief I feel, and the arcing of electricity in the air between us as Chris puts on the last reel.

The final reel is a victory parade – fitting under the circumstances. A huge crowd shouts and waves flags as the troops roll through the streets of London.

I lay my head on Chris's shoulder. He tilts my chin up and brushes my lips with his. His tongue explores my mouth as his hands move over my body. Every nerve ending begins to glow incandescent. I lie back as he removes my top but leaves the locket around my neck. He kisses my breasts, my throat, my stomach. And my hands caress his strong, muscular body, and I savour the feeling of him wanting me. And I sink back into the sofa that once belonged to the Queen Mother, and somewhere outside of time the clocks tick and chime. But all I'm aware of is the beating of our hearts resonating together and the soaring feeling of our bodies opening up to each other.

The film comes to an end and the screen flickers with black and white lines. And with slow and delicious deliberation, the Clockmaker takes me apart and puts me back together again.

54

Eventually I sleep, and eventually I wake. I know it's morning by the blizzard of dust motes sparkling in a shaft of light coming through a high window in Chris's workshop. My body is entwined with his and I breathe in the smell of warmth and metal and skin. I feel like I'm shimmering from inside. I lie perfectly still for a long time watching him sleep. A strange, deep-seeded contentment has taken root inside of me. It's unlike anything I've ever experienced before.

Chris murmurs and shifts. I brush my hand over his smooth chest. Without opening his eyes, he smiles. He repositions himself against me, and I can feel the desire rising in him again. He takes his time with his lovemaking, every move languorous and skilful. When I finally sink back onto the divan, happy and spent, he gets up.

'Coffee?' he says.

'Mmmm,' is all I can manage to say.

When eventually he returns with two cups of steaming coffee and a bag of assorted croissants, I'm sitting up thinking about the film strip we watched.

'So, is the mystery solved?' Chris says.

'A good part of it.' I feel like a great weight has been lifted off of me. My grandmother will be so happy and relieved that her beloved father is in the clear. But then I remember something else I found...

I swing out of bed and get my rucksack. 'You need to see this.' I rifle through the pocket and take out the newspaper clipping. I return to bed, watching his face as he reads over it, his eyes growing wider and darker. Eventually, he looks up at me, incredulous.

'Is this saying what I think it's saying?'

'Well...' I stifle a little smirk. 'It means there's a strong possibility that I might have lied to you last time. You know, when I said I was a little nobody.'

He inspects me carefully in a way that makes me blush – especially since I'm wearing only my pants, an old T-shirt of his, and the jewelled locket around my neck.

'You're a Russian princess,' he says, twining the chain around his fingers and caressing my neck.

'Well, I mean...'

I'm relieved when he begins to laugh. 'And all along you've been judging *me* for my posh family connections.'

'I wouldn't say judge, exactly...'

But he doesn't let me finish the thought – or any other thought – for a good long time.

* * *

When we finally return to reality, I suggest we leave the workshop and get a meal so that we can have a serious talk without getting distracted again. Chris puts the film reels in the safe, and we go to a little hole in the wall off Theobald's Road that serves in Chris's words 'the best bacon butties west of Hackney'.

We find a table by the window and a waitress brings us coffee. 'Let's get a few ground rules straight,' I say. 'First off – no using the "P" word.'

'Of course, "Princess".' He leans closer to kiss me over the table.

I scowl playfully. 'That's the one.' I rummage in my bag and take out the article on the Russian spy. He reads through it again, stroking the faint stubble on his chin thoughtfully.

'So assuming that the Russian "word-that-shall-not-be-mentioned" is Marina, then I suppose it makes sense that she was frightened. She was worried that the Russian secret police were after her, and it appears that she was right.'

'Yes, it makes sense.'

'And the jewelled bird – it fits too. We can surmise it may have been an imperial court piece from Fabergé that belonged to Marina or a member of her family as a girl. It's beautiful and special – just like you.'

'Don't start,' I scold.

Our food arrives. He tucks into his bacon butty like it's going out of style.

'But the article mentions jewels – plural.' He takes a sip of his coffee. 'Did Marina have more precious items hidden away?'

'I don't know. My grandmother mentioned something about a wooden box Mamochka kept under the bed. But surely that must have been lost in the bombing.'

'Probably.'

I take a bite of toast, studying him carefully. 'You don't look convinced.'

'I don't know if the jewels still exist or not. But it's possible that someone might think they do.'

'What do you mean?'

'I was thinking of your "uninvited guest"? You said he's broken in a few times.'

'Yes. And he ransacked the attic.'

'Could he have searched the entire house?'

'For what? Jewels?' I laugh. 'Or secret rooms? Hidden cupboards behind the panelling?'

'Do you have those things?'

'Of course. It's an old house. We have the odd priest's hole and a few secret cupboards.' I cross my arms in mock displeasure. 'Which you'd know if you'd bothered to take my tour.'

He laughs. 'Maybe I can schedule a private visit.' He caresses me under the table.

'Anyway, *someone* will have time to do all the searching they like,' I say. 'The estate agent said he's already got an interested buyer for Mallow Court.'

I've already told Chris about my new bête noire, Alistair Bowen-Knowles, and the firm of upper-crust estate agents, Tetherington Bowen-Knowles. Not surprisingly, he's heard of them (there was even mention of a cricket match before I cuffed him on his posh arm). His advice was to do exactly what I'm doing – ignore them.

'That was quick,' he says. 'I thought it wasn't even on the market.'

'It wasn't.' I mull this over. Trying to buy the house seems like an extreme step for an intruder to take. Unless he or she really thinks a fortune in jewels might be hidden there.

'You should talk to the estate agent again,' he says. 'Find out who the buyer is. You may not find any jewels, but you might just find your intruder.'

'Yes. I might.'

* * *

Chris accompanies me to the train station. I have a fleeting memory of a lifetime ago, when Xavier would sometimes disappear for days or weeks on end, supposedly for 'research'. I later learned he was meeting his wife for a holiday in Madrid. Each time he left, I'd feel hollow and empty, a worm of doubt gnawing at my insides. A part of me always knew that the end was just a matter of time. But that was then. This is now...

At the ticket barrier, Chris kisses me long and hard on the lips and then gives me one of his quirky, unselfconscious smiles. Instead of a worm of doubt, I feel an inner glow that, if anything, seems to be growing in intensity with every moment we spend together. Chris is real; solid. A man who makes love like a true romantic but without the drama and heartache attached. I'm more than ready for a grown-up kind of lover.

I put my ticket in the slot and go through the gate. Just inside the barrier, I turn around, lean towards him, and grab him by the scruff of his Joy Division T-shirt. A disgruntled queue of commuters grows behind me, and a few people whistle as we kiss again. 'I'll call you,' I say playfully when our lips finally part.

'You'd better,' he replies as I turn and walk towards the waiting train.

55

My glow lasts the entire train ride where I replay every moment of the last twenty-four hours, and my skin tingles with the memory of Chris's touch. When I think of my favourite things – a long, hot bath, a great novel, a glass of wine – preferably all three together, I know that I'd forego them all in a millisecond for this new pleasure. The pleasure of having a future to look forward to, a recent past that makes me happy, and a present that...

Well, nothing's perfect.

The train is crowded and the journey takes forever due to a signal failure further up the line. I use the delay to ring the awful Alistair Bowen-Knowles, but he informs me that, of course, the identity of his client is *confidential*.

'Fine,' I say, not bothering to hide my irritation. 'But don't expect me to facilitate any viewings.'

'I believe my client already has a general familiarity with the premises,' he says.

'Is that right?' Anger boils in my chest at the idea that the unnamed client might be the 'intruder' and this man won't reveal his identity.

'It *is* open to the public.'

'So it is,' I say through my teeth.

It's nearly dark by the time I reach Mallow Court. I go first to the main house to check that Mrs Fairchild is OK – I can't wait to tell her the great news that Frank Bolton is innocent. I let myself in (noting that she hasn't set the alarm). The great hall is dark and empty, and I don't turn on the lights. I go down the corridor to my office and dip inside. The message light on the phone is blinking. I set my bag down on the desk along with my research folder on the Romanovs and listen to the messages. There are several from Tim Edwards asking me to call him, and a few more from vendors and suppliers. With a sigh, I jot down the callers on a notepad. Leaving the folder on the desk, I go in search of my grandmother.

Usually she spends her evenings in the green salon, so I go there first. The door is closed, and just as I'm about to open it, I hear a sound from inside – heavy breathing. In a split second, my instincts tell me to barge in and make sure nothing's wrong. But then there's another sound: 'Catherine.' A man's voice, gasping. My heart slams to a halt.

It's one thing accepting that my newfound grandma has a 'special friend', but quite another to catch them *inflagrante*! My news will have to wait. As quickly and quietly as I can, I reverse my steps and get the hell out of there.

Though the last twenty-four hours have brought vast changes for me (and, perhaps, my grandmother too) on the romantic front, I'm relieved to see that inside my flat, at least, nothing has changed. Everything is where I left it, and there are no misplaced objects left on my pillow. Half of my heart may now reside in London, but here in my own flat, I welcome the prospect of bath, book, and bed. As I go to run the water, my phone rings.

I'm hoping it's Chris, but when I check the screen, Mum's name comes up. I answer immediately, checking that she's well.

'I'm fine, Alex,' she says. 'But do you remember that day when we talked about your grandmother? And her daughter Robin?'

'Sure. At the chippie.'

'I said I'd help if I could, though I really didn't expect it to come to anything.'

'Yes?'

'I couldn't find anything on your grandmother, so I thought I'd try Robin. I did some digging through the insurance company records. I didn't find anything, but I called a friend. Do you remember Sharon? You met her at Dad's fortieth.'

'Um, maybe.'

'She works in the NHS archives. They're computerising all the old records, tracking certain medical conditions and whatnots. But she didn't find anything either. But she called a friend of a friend who's a retired receptionist at the hospital in Aylesbury. It was a long shot, really.'

A pulse throbs in my head. 'And?'

'Well, to make a long story short... she found something. And I'm afraid it's not good news.'

'What?'

'Some old records. Robin was in and out of hospital a few times as a girl. She had a rare blood disorder. It's called haemophilia.'

'What's that? It sounds familiar.'

There's a beep on the other end of the line. 'Oh, Alex, sorry. I've got a low battery. Anyway – haemophilia. It's something to do with blood clotting. I hope it helps.'

'Yes, Mum. That is helpful. Thanks so much. I can take it from—'

The phone goes dead.

'—here.' I stare down at the phone, or rather, my hand holding the phone. I turn it over so I can see the lacing of veins on the top, some a pale blue just under the skin. The blood, pulsing inside, ebbing and flowing with every heartbeat. Something that I take for granted. But maybe I shouldn't. I hug my arms around myself, wishing that Chris was here to hold me; make love to me; brush the hair back from my face; whisper that everything is going to be fine. But what if it's not? Should I go to a doctor and get checked out? Make sure I don't have the same disorder as my birth mother? *Haemophilia.* Why does that sound so familiar?

I set my phone down on the table and open a bottle of wine. I pour the dark, burgundy liquid, watching as it splashes and fizzes into the glass. Blood...

The truth snaps into place, hard and painful like an elastic band. I suddenly remember the time I spent at the British Library researching Fabergé and the Russian Imperial Family. I read about how the Tsar's son and heir, Prince Alexei, had a rare blood disease. Haemophilia.

I rush over and find my handbag – only to realise that I've left the folder with the Romanov research in my office over at the main house. But I don't think I'd written down much except the name of the disease. I do a search on my laptop and find thousands of entries. On the NHS information website, I read that haemophilia is a genetic disorder that interferes with blood clotting. Some people are carriers of the disease and suffer no ill effects, but others are easily bruised and prone to internal bleeding. For some sufferers, a trauma like childbirth might well be...

Fatal.

Guilt and pity floods through me. Poor, stupid Robin. There are medical records of her condition, so she must have been aware of it. What were the signs? Childhood scrapes that took longer to heal, bleeding heavier than other girls with her period. And her mother must have known of it too. I think back to our conversation about Robin being a strong-willed child, but not physically strong, bruising easily. My grandmother had been reluctant to let Robin go away to study. I suppose most parents would have felt the same way. But my grandmother must have been doubly worried.

As I read on, I learn that the disease is often less severe in women. It's possible that neither Robin nor her mother realised just how serious it could be. Also, because it's a recessive genetic trait, often females are only carriers, not sufferers.

My thoughts wander back over my own life. Did I ever feel tired, bleed a lot, or bruise easily? Not that I know of, and surely Mum would have said. Maybe I've got lucky. But just to be sure, I'll make an appointment with the doctor.

I stay up half the night reading accounts of haemophiliacs and their sufferings. It's unpleasant, and yet grimly fascinating. In the nineteenth and early twentieth centuries, haemophilia was known as the 'royal disease' because it affected several of the royal houses of Europe. Apparently, the gene was passed on by two of Queen Victoria's daughters and one of her sons, who married into other royal families. Queen Victoria's granddaughter, Alix of Hesse, was a carrier of the disease, and it was she who married Tsar Nicholas II and gave birth to Prince Alexei, the heir apparent. The prince suffered from the disease, which placed many restrictions on his life. Had he survived, would he have had the wherewithal to correct the errors of the past and restore the people's faith in the Russian monarchy? Or would he have sunk into the same decadence and brutality of his father ruling a country on the brink?

History will never have an answer. Instead, he and his family were imprisoned and taken out into a snowy yard and shot. The accounts differ slightly, but one thing seems certain – they all died.

Not necessarily true, however, for their cousins, which included the child – or children – of Michael Alexandrovich Romanov, mentioned as the possible father of Marina. According to my research, he had one legitimate child – a son. But if Marina was his illegitimate child, could she have inherited the defective gene?

As I read on, a possible answer presents itself. Apparently, Michael Alexandrovich had a love affair with Queen Victoria's ninth child, Princess Beatrice. The two would have married, but were denied permission because they were first cousins. Princess Beatrice later married into the Spanish royal line, where she was the mother of several children with haemophilia.

It sounds crazy, but it explains everything. A doomed love affair that led to an illegitimate daughter – Marina. A child raised at the Russian court, who managed to escape during the revolution. Not a child of the Tsar, but a Romanov through and through, as well as a great-granddaughter of Queen Victoria. A royal child, right down to the defective gene. A gene passed on to my grandmother, who seems to not show any effects, and to my mother, Robin, who did.

I close down the website and go over to the sofa, sprawling out on it. I stare up at the slanted skylight, grey with near-dawn light. I know I won't sleep so I don't even bother to try. I feel like

I've been hit by a very large bus. I untuck the jewelled locket from my shirt and grip it tightly in my hand. I can feel the blood – pulsing, pulsing, pulsing, in my veins...

56

15 NOVEMBER 1940 – 12.14 A.M.

I turned and walked away, expecting to be knocked from behind at any moment – a blade plunged into my back. Robbie lowered his camera and moved out of the alleyway. The blood screamed in my head. He grabbed my arm to keep me upright.

'Did you get that?' I gasped. 'On film?'

'Yeah.'

His words made me stumble in relief. Spider jumped out of the ambulance – our getaway car – to help me.

'We... need...' I tried. 'We... need... to go to the police.'

As I collapsed on the seat, Robbie grabbed me by the collar. 'You sure that's what you want to do? You think the police are going to bother trying to find the rightful owner of that loot?' His laugh was bitter. 'You could put a decent little nest egg away for yourself – and your family if you have one.'

I coiled back my arm and tried to punch him. I missed, of course, and hit the dashboard instead. I put my head in my hands and began to weep. Spider, grim and silent in the driver's seat, put the siren on, and we sped away.

As we raced through the desolate city, Flea's voice drifted in and out of my head: 'All's fair in love and war', and 'I've got one in the oven'. And then I thought about the girl, 'crying her eyes out' for her trinket – that I'd taken from her. Granted, it was for her own good; I wanted to keep it safe for her. But since then, I've held it in my hands, feeling the heat of it, the power. I'd wrestled with demons inside myself. 'All's fair in love and war'... 'all's fair...'

Everything seemed unreal as we drove through the familiar streets. And then we stopped, and I was walking, though I couldn't feel my legs beneath me. Spider spoke to a man behind a desk, and we were ushered into a small room. And Robbie was talking to someone, and he gave them the film from his camera. There was a clock on the wall with a plain white face with large numerals. I watched the second hand go round and round, the minute hand jerking onwards.

Another man came in and took my statement. He frowned at me like I was the criminal. I was grassing on my friend; turning in a fellow public servant. I don't know if I was expecting some kind of reward or pat on the back, or not. Either way, I wasn't going to get it.

Eventually, it was over. I'd done my bit: turned in my friend, handed over the evidence. Robbie stayed behind, and Spider and I went to my flat. We didn't speak – we'd both lost too much. In the dingy kitchen, I poured each of us a slug of brandy. Tears ran down his face. 'They'll string him up, Badger,' he said. 'He was our friend.'

I slammed my fist on the table. 'He's a disgrace. And so is the judge who will give him a few months in Holloway, and then he'll be back out on the streets. Him and all the others like him. And meanwhile, they'll prattle on about the "Blitz Spirit" and how brave we all are. Such a crock of shit.'

I think of Marina, lying there in the wreckage. I think of a little girl... Catherine – a girl without a mother. A girl with my eyes. Suddenly, I feel weighted down. By the jewelled bird in my pocket, and...

By what I feared I might be capable of, when all was said and done.

57

It's fully light by the time I wake up, exhausted and disoriented, feeling like a too-tightly wound spring. The locket feels heavy and portentous – I'd fallen asleep with the chain coiled around my neck, the key digging into my skin. I need to tell Mrs Fairchild the good news about Frank Bolton, and the bad news about what I know about Robin and her condition. Both things are an important part of our shared history and she has a right to know. Then I remember the previous night when I'd gone into the main house and found her... I don't want to think about it. As I get in the shower, I resign myself to finally meeting her 'friend' if he's around at breakfast. Now that things are back on between them, I'll have to sooner or later.

I pass the café where Chloe's baking scones, and ask if she's seen Mrs Fairchild. I'm told that she's already up and out gardening. Reading between the lines, I conclude that the man must have left either very late the previous night or early this morning. The relief I feel makes me a little ashamed. Why can't I just be happy for her new relationship?

Chloe gives me a scone, and I savour its rich, buttery fluffiness on my tongue. Maybe I'll feel better about the whole thing when I finally meet the mystery man and start getting to know him. I'll ask my grandmother if she'll arrange it.

On my way out to the garden, I duck into the estate office to check for messages. As soon as I step inside, my heart jars out of rhythm. There's that feeling, that slight change in the current of the air that tells me someone's been here. That *he's* been here.

I rush over to my desk and start rifling through the piles of papers, but it's futile – and my own fault. I left my folder out in plain sight. It contained the newspaper clipping, my notes on the Romanovs, and the auction house records from Chris.

My skin prickles with goosebumps as I rush out of the house to find my grandmother. The 'uninvited guest' has made it even more urgent that I tell her what I've found out. The day is grey and cool with a strong northerly wind. The silver birch trees along the river bow and sway. A few early-bird tourists are browsing the plants for sale outside the gift shop, and I glimpse a coach pulling up in the car park. But for the moment, the garden seems unusually quiet. Even the bees seem to be holding their breath in case of rain.

'Grandmother?' I call out, but there's no reply. I check each of the various garden rooms, making my way through the arches in the hedges. The white garden seems wilted, but the roses in the secret garden that Mrs Fairchild keeps so carefully deadheaded are at their peak. Just beyond is the water garden. The focal point is a rectangular lily pond flanked by topiary dolphins and a curvy-backed sea monster. I enter through the arch, just in time to catch a glimpse of a person going out the opposite end – a dark blur that is quickly gone. I peer around the dolphins, expecting to see the familiar wide-brimmed hat. 'Grandmother?' I call out again. 'Are you there?'

I'm almost at the other end of the garden when all of a

sudden, I *do* spot the hat – lying on the ground behind the edge of the fountain and sprinkled with red petals. It's only then that I spot my grandmother lying motionless on the grass. My heart freezes. The petals are actually drops of crimson blood.

'No!' I scream, running towards her. I kneel down and fumble to remove her gardening glove and feel for a pulse on her wrist. There's a faint flicker beneath her blue-veined skin. A moment later, she stirs. 'Don't move, Grandma,' I say. 'I'll get help.' I grope in my jacket pocket for my mobile phone. But I forgot to put it in my pocket after talking to Mum last night.

'Help!' I yell. I check my watch. There should be some visitors wandering through the gardens by now. 'Help! I need an ambulance.'

After what seems like time immemorial but is probably less than half a minute, a couple in matching tweed hats and Barbour waxed jackets come through the arch.

'Can you go for help?' I call out frantically. 'There should be someone in the gift shop. My grandmother needs an ambulance.'

The couple goes one better. The woman takes out a mobile and rings 999. The man bends over Mrs Fairchild and checks her pulse.

By the time I've given the information to the ambulance dispatch, more people have come into the garden in response to my cries. Having got there first, the tweed hat couple take charge of the scene. 'Please keep back,' the man shoos the onlookers. 'Give her some space.' The woman helps me to a bench. From another pocket of her raincoat, she produces a small thermos of tea.

'Thank you for helping,' I half-gasp, half-sob. I sip from the cup she hands me. The tea is hot and sweet. 'I can't lose her. I just can't.'

'There, there.' The woman pats my hand. 'Us oldies are tougher than we look.'

'But there's so much blood.'

Blood. A chill wracks my body. Based on what Mum told me, I have to assume my grandmother has the gene for haemophilia. But is she a carrier or a sufferer?

'Here.' Reaching into another pocket, the woman takes out a silver flask and pours its contents into the tea. I take a sip, my throat burning from the strong taste of brandy.

'Alex!' Edith comes running into the garden, white-faced and stricken. Behind her, two paramedics in green uniforms come through the arch carrying a stretcher. 'Is she going to be OK?' Edith says.

I drown out my lack of an answer with another sip of brandy tea. Jumping up from the bench, I rush over to the paramedics and tell them my grandmother may have a blood disorder.

'Thanks for the heads-up,' one of them says. 'We'll handle her carefully.'

I hover as the paramedics load Mrs Fairchild onto the stretcher. The next few minutes are a blur of green and colour as I lead them out of the maze of bright beds and hedges around to the front of the house where the ambulance is parked, its blue lights flashing. I bend over and kiss my grandma's pale, cool cheek and summon a silent prayer from the murky depths of fear. The men load her into the back.

'Do you want to ride along?' one of the paramedics says to me.

'Yes,' I say, then hesitate as the next few hours of my life flash before my eyes. Sitting in a hospital waiting room wringing my hands; or staying here and doing my job: managing the crowds, offering everyone a free cup of tea and a scone or a slice of cake the way my grandmother would have wanted...

The decision is taken out of my hands as a police car pulls up. I turn to Edith, who has stood by me the whole time, her presence solid and comforting. 'You go,' I say to her. 'I'll need to make a statement.' *And make sure the culprit has left the premises,* I don't say. While I'm fairly sure that having accomplished what he set out to do, the 'uninvited guest' will have long scarpered, I have a duty to make sure that the visitors are safe. 'I'll come as soon as I can,' I say.

'OK,' Edith says. She climbs inside and the paramedic shuts the door.

I turn away, tears flooding my eyes. The ambulance roars off with its siren wailing.

58

The next hour is an unpleasant blur. Somehow I manage to marshal the staff together to manage all the moving parts. While the visitors are being offered free tea and 10 per cent off in the gift shop, I show the two policemen where I found my grandmother and describe the person in dark clothing whom I saw leaving the garden. As they analyse the scene and take the statements of Mr and Mrs Tweed Hat, I come clean on the fact that we've had an 'uninvited guest' about the place before.

The older officer looks at me sharply. 'And have you reported this "uninvited guest's" activity to the police?'

'No.' I carefully avoid any mention of my arrest. 'It all just seemed like mischief.' I think of the upsetting diary entries, the cancelled grand opening, the ransacking of the attic, the theft of the photo and my folder, and all the other little pranks that seemed meant to annoy, or at most, frighten us. 'Until now, that is.'

'And you have security cameras?'

'Only inside the house.'

The older policeman closes his notebook as the younger

one takes a picture of the place where my grandmother was found.

'To be honest, Miss Hart,' the older officer says, 'I don't think there's much here to pursue. It seems most likely that your grandmother slipped and hit her head on the fountain.'

'What?' I look at him, astonished. 'No. Someone hit her from behind. I told you, I saw the perpetrator leaving through the arch —'

'I think we have all we need here.'

'That's it? You're going?'

The older man nods to his colleague. 'Write this up as an accident.'

'But you're wrong!' I yell. 'If she hit her head on the fountain, then where's the blood?'

'Make a note that the scene was contaminated prior to arrival,' he says to the younger man.

'You're useless!' Fury surges in my chest. 'An elderly woman is attacked and practically murdered, and you say it's an accident? She needs to be guarded – she could still be in danger.'

'If anything else occurs, Miss Hart,' the older policeman says, 'I suggest you call us.'

'I don't think I'll bother!'

'Suit yourself.' Gesturing for his colleague to follow, he turns and walks out of the garden.

I struggle to compose myself. How dare the police be so dismissive? And what of the danger to my grandmother? I hurry back to my flat and ring Edith at the hospital.

'And they just did nothing?' she says. 'That's appalling.'

'You got that right,' I say.

She tells me that Mrs Fairchild has been diagnosed with a mild concussion. 'She woke up briefly,' she says. 'They gave her some morphine for the shock, and she's sleeping now.'

'They stopped the bleeding?'

'Yes,' Edith confirms. 'Apparently it's just a shallow wound. She's going to be fine.'

'Thank God. I'll be there as soon as I can. Probably after lunch.'

'OK,' Edith says. 'I'll call you if there's any change before then.'

I hang up, feeling a little better. Then I call Chris, needing to hear his voice, but it goes to voicemail. I leave a message asking him to call me.

At lunchtime, I cover the gift shop, answering questions about whether the nettle soap is hypoallergenic, which *Horrible Histories* book I recommend for a grandniece, and whether I can order a pair of men's Scottie dog wellies in a size 13. As I'm ringing up a Tudor-house-shaped tea cosy at the till, my mobile rings. I expect it to be Chris, or maybe Edith. Has my grandmother taken a turn for the worst?

But when I spot the name on the screen – Tim Edwards – suspicion grips me like an icy fist. Has Tim somehow heard about my grandmother's attack? Could he be the real culprit?

'Excuse me, can I have my card back?'

'Sorry.' The phone rings off. I give the customer back her card and wrap up the tea cosy with shaking hands.

Tim Edwards. I think back to the last time he came to see me at Mallow Court. He had an answer for everything; a rational explanation for why I should trust him, all reinforced by a doleful look from those big brown eyes. And then his subsequent call telling me that he wasn't going to 'let sleeping dogs lie'. All along, he's had opportunity and motive. Despite what he said about believing in his great-grandfather's guilt, it stands to reason that he could have been raised to resent Catherine Fairchild – hate her, even. So he devised a dual strategy: making mischief to try and drive her out, while in parallel, trying to win me over. Having failed so far with both, he decided to get serious and take her out with a good whack on the head. If he is the mysterious buyer for the house, what better way to incentivise my grandmother to sell up than to scare her out of her own home?

The phone continues to ring. How could I have been so swayed by appearances? Tim knew exactly how to talk to me with his 'widows and orphans' and 'us against them'. I failed to see through the amateur dramatics to the real man underneath—

'Alex? Are you OK?'

I look up. Chloe from the café leans in and whispers behind her hand. 'People are getting fed up.'

'What?' I stare at her like she's speaking Martian. Only then do I realise that there's a long queue of people waiting to buy their soaps, their tea towels, their greeting cards…

'I've got to go.' Snapping to my senses, I run out of the shop.

* * *

I jump in my car and drive to the hospital, fear pounding in my head like a brass band. Smooth-talking, soul-melting Tim Edwards. What if he's already talked his way inside the hospital to finish the job? I pull into the car park, nick a parking space and rush to the front desk and ask at reception for Catherine Fairchild. I follow the directions to the ward and burst through the double doors, expecting the worst. But instead of witnessing murder and mayhem, I see Edith sitting in the waiting area, calmly reading *Home and Garden* magazine.

'Oh, hi, Alex,' she says.

'Where is he?' I demand.

Edith's smile turns to bewilderment. 'Who?'

'Tim Edwards, the barrister. You know: tall, light brown hair, chocolate brown eyes. He and I... we dated once. I think he might be the "uninvited guest" who's out to harm Mrs Fairchild.'

'Must have been a pretty bad date.'

I almost smile. 'Yeah, I guess it was.'

'Anyway, your tall, brown-eyed man isn't here. But there is someone with her. Her policeman friend.'

'You mean the man she met at the WI meeting – the detective inspector?'

'Yes. He's called David.' She looks confused. 'You know him, right? He said he heard the news about Mrs Fairchild on the police radio and came right over.'

'We haven't been introduced.'

'What, really?'

'Really.' I shrug off the awkward moment. 'Which room are they in?'

Edith points down the corridor; I go and stand in front of the closed door. Feeling like an 'uninvited guest' myself, I knock softly. 'Grandma?' I say.

'Do come in,' a deep male voice answers.

I open the door and enter the room. My grandmother is lying propped up in the bed, a wide bandage wrapped around her head and an IV in her arm. Her eyes are closed; she's asleep. Sitting in the chair next to her bed is a man in his mid-seventies, I would guess, with a thick mop of white hair and a rugged, but surprisingly wrinkle-free, face. His eyes are large and brown and as he smiles up at me, his teeth are white and straight. He's wearing a neat pair of jeans and a blue and white striped shirt.

'Hello,' he says, a friendly lilt in his voice. 'I'm David.'

Standing up, he offers his hand. 'You must be Alex. Is it OK if I call you that?'

'Fine.' We shake hands and he offers me the chair. I'm impressed by his manners. Oozing with polite, old-school charm, he's just the kind of man my grandmother should have to keep her happy in her old age. I want to like him – I mean, it's churlish not to. When I saw them together having the picnic, she looked so happy. And based on the shenanigans I overheard, whatever rift there was between them must be well and truly patched up. My grandmother mentioned something about a ring. My eyes dart to her hands. Nothing on her fingers...

I glance at him again, narrowing my eyes. On the day of the picnic, I was too far away to get a good look at him. But now that we're here in the same room, something about him seems familiar.

'I've been looking forward to meeting you,' he says. 'Catherine has told me so much about you. I just wish it hadn't been' – he glances worriedly at Mrs Fairchild – 'like this.'

'Me too.'

'Anyway, I expect you want some time with her alone.' He goes to the door. 'You must have been so worried.'

'Thank you.' As much as I want to 'vet' him some more, now isn't the time.

Whistling softly, he goes out of the room, closing the door behind him.

59

'Grandma,' I whisper, sitting down in the still-warm chair. I take her hand in mine and trace the veins with my finger. I sit there with her, tears filling my eyes.

After a few minutes, she stirs in the bed.

'Oh, Alex, I'm so sorry.' She squeezes my hand weakly.

'Shh, Grandma, it's OK. How are you feeling?'

'I've been better.' She manages a little chuckle. 'My head hasn't hurt like this since last time I went clubbing in Soho.'

I laugh, glad that she's taking it on the chin. 'Can you tell me what happened? The police think you fell and hit your head. But it seems obvious to me that you were attacked. Can you remember anything?'

The heart rate monitor blips faster; I worry that my questions are too much for her. 'I was trimming the grass around the base of the fountain,' she says. 'It hadn't been done all summer, and it was starting to look unkempt. I really must speak to the gardeners...'

'Yes?' I urge.

'I was humming. Some song from the sixties that came into my head. I can't remember the words.'

'And then...'

'Then I woke up here.'

'That's it?' I struggle to hide my disappointment. 'So you don't remember anyone sneaking up on you and hitting you over the head?'

'No, Alex. Nothing like that.'

'So it *is* possible that you could have fallen?'

'I... I don't know.'

'Either way, I was so worried. You could have been killed. I know that Robin suffered from a disease called haemophilia. It interferes with blood clotting. I was worried that you might have it too.'

She shudders visibly. 'As you can see, the wound has stopped bleeding. I can't tell you how many times in my life I wished that I could be the sick one, not my daughter. I tried to bargain with God, to ask him to take everything from me, but just make her well. But in the end, it didn't work. All it did was make her think I was an overprotective, interfering, and annoying mother of the worst kind. We loved each other, but she wanted to make her own mistakes. So I tried to let her. She was so young when she died,' she sobs. 'Not even twenty.'

'I'm so sorry,' I say.

'Just after you were born, I told your father straight away. That what killed Robin could be genetic. He took you for a screening test when you were little – I'm not even sure Carol knew about it. So as far as I know' – she smiles – 'you're OK.'

I'm OK. Despite the fact that I ought to feel aggrieved for yet another thing that I should have been told about, the words wash over me like waves lapping a beach. I'll get my own test done, of course, but it seems that neither I nor my grandmother are affected.

'That's good to know.'

'And genetic disorders aside, if someone meant to kill me, then they made a mess of it, didn't they?' Her tone is brisk. 'Lying here, I've been doing a lot of thinking. About the offer on the house and all.'

'The offer?' I say. 'I didn't know. I guess you didn't want to tell me.'

Her smile is brittle. 'The house isn't officially on the market – not after you told the estate agent where to go. But someone approached my solicitor and got the estate agent's details.'

'That sounds very odd.'

She shrugs, wincing at the pain of physical movement. 'It was all very sudden. I said I'd need time to think about it. Which is what I've been doing.'

I grip the edge of the chair, knowing full well what the outcome of that thinking must be. How on earth can I blame my grandma for wanting to sell Mallow Court when her life is in danger because of it? And yet—

Her laughter startles me. 'The funny thing is, Alex, that before this little incident, I might have come to a different conclusion. I might seriously have considered selling. But now...' She shakes her head. 'That house is your inheritance, just like the locket. There's no way I'm going to be bullied by anyone into selling it. I never should have let it cross my mind.'

'Really?' My heart does a flip. 'But what about the danger?'

'I don't think there's any real danger. As soon as I'm well, I'll go and see Sally Edwards. Try to make things right between us, if I can. If not, then she can do her worst. If she has proof, then she should take it to the police. If Frank Bolton was a looter and there are any victims out there who want restitution, then the law can deal with it. That's the right way to go about this, not veiled threats and subterfuge. And whatever comes, we'll manage it together.'

'We won't have to, Grandma.' I squeeze her hand firmly. 'Because Sally Edwards has got the wrong end of the stick. When I found you in the rose garden, I was coming to tell you the good news. I've found evidence – real evidence – that clears Frank Bolton.' I take a breath. 'Frank wrote the journal, not Hal Dawkins. Frank's the one who pulled you from the wreckage.'

She gives a little start, but sinks back weakly into the pillow. 'But I saw the inscription. Are you absolutely certain?'

'Yes. Frank Bolton is innocent. It's even caught on film.' I give her a shortened account of the box with the film canisters that I found in the attic (though I decide not to tell her that someone had ransacked the place).

'I... I don't remember that night,' she says, shuddering. 'Though when I read the account in the journal, I almost imagined that I did. All I know was that it was dark and cold. I was so scared...' A tear rolls down her cheek. 'And I lost Mamochka.'

'I'm so sorry,' I say. 'Sorry that it happened, and sorry that you had to relive those memories.'

'Actually, I think it's been a good thing. All these years there's been a little part of my mind that's been fenced off from the rest. It's been hard, of course, confronting what's inside. But it's freeing too. And it's my duty to remember her, along with the rest of my loved ones who have gone before. If I don't, who else will?'

'There is someone else who remembers Marina.' I remind her briefly of Mr Pepperharrow. 'Which reminds me – I found something else up in the attic.'

I tell her about the newspaper article about the Russian princess, and the note written in the margin: *Marina?*

My grandmother is understandably dismissive. 'A princess?' she tsks. 'I thought you said she was a cook.'

'But we know nothing of her life in Russia, isn't that right?'

'Correct.'

'Well' – I spread my hands – 'maybe someday, I'll go to Russia and try to find out more about her.' It's the first time I've imagined doing such a thing, but the idea sounds exciting and right.

'Yes.' She brightens. 'It would do you good. When all this is over...'

'There's one other thing I want to clarify. Other than the locket, did Marina have any other jewellery?'

Her eyes close and I fear my question is one too many. I hold her hand as she inhales deeply. When she speaks again, her voice sounds far away.

'She had a gold ring she wore sometimes,' she says. 'And then there was the box under the bed. The wooden box with the face and the key. The lock was broken and she asked the man upstairs to fix it. He fixed clocks. That's the only time I ever caught a glimpse inside.' Her lips blossom into a beatific smile. 'It was full of shiny things.'

I brush a strand of white hair from her forehead and sit back in the chair, holding her hand. Less than a minute later, her grip slackens, and she's asleep.

60

16 NOVEMBER 1940 – 9.24 A.M.

One by one, the dominos began to fall. Flea was arrested when he returned to Sadie's house. I heard about it the next day when there was a knock at my door and a policeman was standing outside.

'What about the girl?' was all I could say when he told me about the arrest. 'She was there with his landlady.'

He shook his head. 'The landlady took the girl to the church. From there, she was evacuated to a home for orphans.'

'No!'

The policeman shrugged.

'I need to find her.'

'You've got to come with me first,' he said.

'What? Why?' My hands were clammy with fear. Had Flea somehow managed to turn the evidence around? Had he mentioned the jewelled bird?

'There's someone who wants to see you in person,' he explained.

'Who?'

He looked me over – I was still wearing the same tattered trousers, sweat-stained shirt and blood-crusted shoes from the night before. 'You'd better shave first and put on a suit,' he said, frown-

ing. 'And for God's sake, let's see some spit and polish on those shoes.'

* * *

The dark-wood corridor smelled of varnish and cigar smoke; my feet sank into the plush carpet runner. A woman in a prim grey suit led us to a door at the end of the hall. She knocked softly.

'Mr Churchill?' she said.

Blood thrummed in my ears. The next thing I knew, I was standing inside a vast office, all leather, chrome, and wood. But my eyes were drawn to the man standing at the window, his hands in the pockets of his trousers, his large frame blocking out most of the light.

When he turned towards me, it was like all the air in the room was sucked in his direction. He commanded the space and everything in it.

'Sit down, sir.'

As he greeted me, I was struck by the look on his face. Disgust, plain as the jowls under his chin. Disgust with Flea, of course, but just as strong was his distaste for me. A grass. A snitch. My words snuffing out the Blitz Spirit like a humidor for his fat cigar.

I sat down. He remained standing, and didn't offer to shake my hand. There was a rumbling sound like the distant drone of the bombers. It was his voice, resonating through the hollow of my skull. I tried to focus on what he was saying...

'Our duty is to preserve public morale during these desperate times.'

I nodded vigorously, though I can honestly say that I didn't understand.

'I can assure you, the matter is being dealt with.' His lip curled in disgust. And then he called for the secretary to escort me out.

Looking at the floor, I followed her towards the door.

'One more thing.' He stopped me with his voice; I raised my eyes to his. *'You will say nothing. We never had this conversation, and you know nothing of this. And if you ever violate this mandate, then you will be dealt with in the most severe manner. Do you understand?'*

I nodded again. The secretary escorted me out and the door closed behind me. It was over almost before it began. And later on, as I write these words, the memory seems like a bubble frozen in amber. I replay his words in my head, trying to remember every second. But it's no use. I'm struck not by the things the great man said – but by what he didn't say.

He never said 'thank you'.

61

I hold my grandmother's hand as she sleeps, watching the rise and fall of her chest and feeling the slow coursing of her pulse. I think about what she said – how she has a duty to preserve the memory of those who came before and bear witness to those terrible times. I think how close the 'uninvited guest' came to being able to rewrite history to serve his own purposes.

But as much as I've learned, I still don't know what exactly he was after. The films? The jewels? The house?

I kiss my grandmother on the forehead and return to the waiting area. Edith is drinking tea from a plastic cup.

'How is she?' she asks.

I slump into the chair beside her. 'Asleep. Is David still here?'

'No, he had to leave.'

'Oh really? What did he have to do that's so pressing?' Maybe it's my prejudice against him, but it's almost like he's avoiding me.

'I don't know. He said he'll come back later, and that he'll swing by Mallow Court and pick up some of her clothes and books.'

'I could have done that.'

'Sorry, I'm just relaying what he said.'

'I didn't mean to snap at you.' I've given Edith the third degree because there's no one else. Other than the odd doctor or nurse, there's no one to keep guard over my grandmother if the police happen to be wrong.

'I feel a bit bad for earlier,' Edith says. 'It didn't even occur to me that you hadn't met David. I assumed she'd introduced you.' She gives a little laugh. 'I remember that time when I saw him in the stockroom and thought he was a burglar.'

'What?' I straighten up. 'He's the man you saw?'

'Yes. It turns out that he was helping out an old woman who was looking for the loo and got lost. He's such a gentleman.'

'Yes,' I say drily. 'He seems it. Maybe I should ask him if he knows who locked me in the loo – that same day, remember?'

'Was it?' Edith frowns. 'You think David had something to do with it?'

'He's a dark horse, isn't he? Turning up at a WI meeting and sweeping my grandmother off her feet. He even offered her a ring, did you know that? But she turned him down. Maybe he thought he'd convince her by a blow to the head.'

'Come on, Alex. That sounds a bit preposterous. I mean, why would he do that?'

'I don't know. But I'd really like to ask him. Except…' I stare towards my grandmother's room. 'Someone needs to stay here in case she's in danger.'

Edith shakes her head. 'I know you're strong, Alex. And independent too. But you can't distrust everyone.'

'Right now, I'm struggling with that.'

'I know, and I care about your grandmother too. If you really think she's in some kind of danger, then why don't I call Paul? He could send someone from the police to keep an eye on things here. Not the local police, but someone from his station in Oxford.'

'That'd be good,' I say. 'I'd feel a lot better.'

'And I could get back to work.'

I check my watch. It's nearly four o'clock. 'You should go home, Edith – you've been such a great help today.' I give her the warmest smile I can muster. 'Thank you so much.'

'No problem.' Edith stands up. 'But are you going to stay here?'

'For now. I don't want to leave her alone.'

'Here, take these.' She hands me her stack of magazines. 'I bought them earlier in the shop. Everything in the waiting room was either medical or out of date.'

'Thanks.'

'I'll call Paul now. And if there's any change with Mrs Fairchild, ring me right away, OK?'

'Of course.'

'And Alex...' She purses her lips. 'You will be careful, right?'

'Right.'

* * *

Time ticks on. Chris finally calls me back, apologising that he's been at an antiques fair all day with his dad. I tell him what happened as best I can – in between his bursts of anguish that he wasn't there for me.

'God, Alex, I can't believe this. Is she going to be OK? How are you doing? Let's see – I'm driving up from Portsmouth now and I need to swing by my workshop. I can be with you by nine maybe. I'm so sorry. This is just awful...' I let him gabble on for a minute.

'I miss you,' I say. 'And if you could come tonight it would be good. I just feel so... tired.'

'I'm sure. Damn it! This traffic is terrible. I'll be there as soon as I can.'

We ring off and I feel better knowing that I'll be seeing Chris later. Then Edith calls and tells me that her boyfriend will send someone round. I read the magazines that she left from cover to cover. There's an article about a house in London where three teenage girls found an unexploded bomb in the back garden and managed to save their father, who was about to dig it up. There's also a news item about a Georgian house near Bath that's about to be opened to the public. It makes me think about how I felt when Mallow Court had its grand opening: proud that I'd got everything ready in record time; scared that something would go wrong; and above all, determined to make it work.

And I have. Now that I've cleared Frank Bolton's name and my grandmother has agreed to keep the house, I feel a renewed energy. It's a new start. But there's a niggle in my head that won't go away. Does my new start involve staying on as manager of Mallow Court, or turning the job over to Edith and going in a whole new direction?

I shift in the uncomfortable chair, my eyelids growing heavy. In my mind's eye, I picture a young girl standing in front of the Winter Palace in St Petersburg – its elegant green and white facade and hundreds of windows dwarfing her as she stares at it in wonder. She cranes her neck upwards as snowflakes begin to fall, lightly at first, and then in a flurry. Something drones in the air above: planes. She stands paralysed as silver bombs begin to rain down all around her. And the sky shimmers with jewels and bombs and snow and the world is burning and freezing and exploding all at the same time, and I open my mouth to scream and the whole world shifts on its axis around me.

'Alex Hart?'

My eyes snap open, the terror of the dream dissolving into the dark maze of memory. My heart is galloping in my chest and I breathe deeply until the panic subsides.

'Sorry,' I say to the uniformed police officer standing in front of me. 'I must have nodded off.'

'No problem,' he says. 'Paul asked me to hold the fort here. So you can go home.'

'Thanks.' I rub out a crick in my neck. 'What time is it anyway?'

'Just gone half seven. Sorry I couldn't get here earlier. Had to help give the baby a bath.'

'No worries.' I stand up, my right knee feeling like a rusty gate hinge. 'How long can you stay here?'

'Well...' He hesitates. 'I checked the file. The lads who visited the scene said it was an accident.'

'Look,' I say firmly, 'I know that's the official line, but can you stay here a few hours until I sort things out?'

'Of course.'

'Give me your number, and I'll ring you when it's OK to leave.'

'Fine.' He takes out his phone and I copy down the number. 'But you're not going to do anything daft, are you?'

I think back to Mrs Fairchild's brave statement about needing to confront the danger head on. She said that once she was well, she would go and visit Mrs Edwards and try to make things right. But with everything that's happened, I can't wait until my grandmother finds the time to confront Sally. Not now that I've learned the truth about the diary. Frank Bolton's diary, not Hal Dawkins's. I need to know exactly how Sally Edwards came by it. It has to be Tim – it just *has* to be. And if not... My head aches as I put two and two together and feel a little closer to getting four.

I give the officer my meekest smile. 'Whatever gave you that idea?'

* * *

I leave my grandmother under guard at the hospital and drive to the station. The London train is delayed, and as I wait on the platform, I take out my mobile phone. Four missed calls: three from Tim, and one from Chris.

I press play, determined to listen dispassionately to anything Tim has to say, and forward anything important to Edith's boyfriend.

'Alex, it's Tim here. Please can you give me a call? I think you might be in danger. I'll explain more but we need to talk. Can you meet me?'

Beep.

'Alex, please call. I heard what happened to Mrs Fairchild and I think I know who did it. Seriously – you won't believe it. Give me a call.'

Beep.

'Hi, Alex, it's Chris.' My stomach flutters like a bird at the sound of his voice. 'Traffic is awful. I'm not even back in London yet. I'm so sorry I haven't been there for you today. Shit – idiot!' In the background, a horn honks. 'Sorry about that, I—'

Beep.

'Alex – Tim. Listen, I know you don't want to talk to me, but it's important. I'm at Gran's house. Give me a call as soon as you can.'

Beep.

I quickly call Chris back and get his voicemail. 'Listen, Chris, there's been a change in plan. Don't go to the house. I'm coming down to London. The train's delayed, but call me when you get back to your shop.'

Hanging up, I scroll to Tim's number. Should I call him back and arrange to meet him? Or just turn up at his gran's and confront him? Obviously, I shouldn't go there alone, even though I still can't believe in my heart of hearts that he's responsible for knocking my grandmother on the head. A part of him, at least, is a competent, professional barrister with a lot to lose from shenanigans like that. Could he really be the clever arch villain that I've conjured in my mind? What does he, or anyone, have to gain from all of this? It's not like there's a fortune in Romanov jewels hidden somewhere that managed to survive the London Blitz.

Or is there?

The train limps into the station, grinding to a halt at the platform. I climb aboard and move through three carriages until I finally find an empty seat – a middle seat occupied by a handbag, the owner of which is none too pleased when I ask her to move it so I can sit down. Ignoring the sharp elbows on both sides, I continue my speculation.

What if the 'uninvited guest' assumed that Marina had given the jewels to Frank Bolton, the father of her child, to take away for safekeeping? It makes sense that he might have used a few of them for 'seed money' to buy his factory and hidden the rest at Mallow Court. Is that why the intruder is so desperate to get rid of Mrs Fairchild? Is he biding his time until he can buy the house and do a proper search? It seems like an extreme measure for something so speculative. But who knows what lengths a criminal might go to?

The train crawls along, punctuated by frequent announcements from the guard apologising for the delay due to a stalled train down the line. My mind races onwards. Everything hinges on what happened on a bombed-out London street in November 1940. A girl crawls from the wreckage as it begins to snow. A man rescues her, but can't save her dying mother. A mother gives her daughter a jewelled locket...

The jewelled locket. I'm still wearing it, tucked under my shirt, with the small gold key dangling from the chain. I no longer feel it's weight – it's part of me now.

Later on, the girl's rescuer adopts her. He gives her a nice life, a nice family, and a beautiful house. He's also a hero in another way: he informs on a colleague who's abusing his position on the ambulance service to loot corpses and bombed-out buildings. The looter's actions are hushed up without a trial, and the culprit is sent to the front lines to die. His daughter grows up bitter and hateful of the little girl pulled from the wreckage. She finds a journal somewhere – I'm still not sure where she got it – that seems to clear her father's name. But the journal wasn't written by her father at all. This is proved by the film hidden in the attic.

My head hurts with the effort of trying to put the pieces together. As the train trundles along, I check my phone again, but neither Chris nor Tim has called back.

The train comes to a dead halt at another station. My heart revs with tension at the delay. I stare out the window at the people on the platform: some looking angry, most looking resigned. The guard makes another announcement – we'll be stuck here for ten minutes. *Ten minutes*. I glance at an old-style clock (one with hands and numbers) hanging on the platform next to the electronic board. I've been on the train for almost forty-five minutes. I stand up, feeling like a caged animal. I could abandon my quest and return home, but those trains aren't running either. With a sigh, I sit back down and look at the platform clock again. It still says 8 p.m. The second hand isn't moving. It's broken, just like the bloody train down the line. A stopped clock...

I reach for the chain around my neck and feel its pulsing, elemental electricity. There's a rumbling sound as the train lurches slowly forward. But my mind is racing like a bullet train. The tiny key... I hold it up to my eyes. A key that unlocks the answer to the mystery.

A jewelled bird, a wooden box, my great-grandmother, Marina, a Russian princess, who fled the revolution with a treasure trove of jewels.

And I know where they are...

62

I curse, I cajole, I silently *will* the train to move forward more quickly and reach its destination sometime this century. Another twenty minutes feels like twenty years. And just as we're finally pulling into the platform at Euston, my mobile rings.

It's Chris. All of a sudden I want nothing more than for this all to be over so we can snuggle up on his old sofa, watch more films on the reel-to-reel, and take all the time in the world to explore each other's bodies the way we already seem to know each other's souls. With the two of us together, I feel like anything might be possible. Possible, that is, once my murky, star-crossed past is finally resolved into something coherent.

'Hello,' I say breathlessly.

'I just got your message. I'm at the auction house. Are you in London?'

'Just got here,' I say. 'I'm on my way to East London.'

'No, Alex.' He whispers into the phone, sounding panicked. 'Don't go there. Not alone. I've found out something else.'

'What?' I say, worried by his tone.

'I had my dad's PA check through all the records up to the present. Just three months ago some pieces were listed: three American impressionist paintings and some items of jewellery.'

'And?'

'They were put into the auction by a D Kinshaw of Grand Cayman Island.'

The train judders to a halt and the world tips on its axis. The truth, or the version I wanted to believe, turns on its head. The other people in the train carriage hurry to stand up and get off the train, but I sit still, unable to move. 'D Kinshaw' aka Hal Dawkins is alive. Hal Dawkins is still engaging in mischief and criminal activities all these years later. Still creeping out of the gutter to exploit and ruin people's lives, and 'help them on their way' as necessary. And this time, those people are my grandmother and me. He messed with her house, her head, and her heart. But what I find completely infuriating is that he didn't even bother to change his first initial.

'D Kinshaw'.

David.

'Alex, are you still there? Do you think he could be your "uninvited guest"?'

'Thanks, Chris,' I say. 'That's really helpful.'

'OK. Can you come here—?'

I end the call and join the queue to get off the train, my pulse drumming in my head. As I'm rushing through the crowded station, the phone rings again. I press the reject button on Tim Edwards's call and switch off the phone.

63

I don't bother with the Tube or the bus. Outside the station, I get a taxi directly to Larkspur Gardens. My head is galloping as we drive past crowds of pub-goers in Shoreditch and continue east to the wilds of the city. I phone the policeman at the hospital and tell him that if my grandmother's 'boyfriend' turns up, he should arrest him. As the cab reaches the top of Larkspur Gardens, I hang up, pay the driver and get out. Right now, the element of surprise is my only advantage.

Pulling the hood of my jacket up over my head, I walk to the end of the road. There's a light on behind the brown curtains in the Edwards's window and I can hear the noise of the television from several houses away. Tim's message said he was at the house. I could go there, knock on the door, ask to see Sally like I'd originally planned to do. But I might well be walking into a trap. Instead, I detour up the narrow walkway that leads to Mr Pepperharrow's house. My stomach plummets when I see that the windows are dark. How can he not be at home? Where on earth can he—

A sharp bark startles me. 'Down, Winston,' a voice says from behind me.

I turn. 'Oh, hello.'

Mr Pepperharrow frowns at me. 'No soliciting.' He points a finger to the sign next to the door.

'It's me, Alex Hart,' I remind him. 'Marina's great-granddaughter.'

The old man takes a pair of glasses from the breast pocket of his coat, wipes them, and puts them on. 'My apologies, young lady. I didn't recognise you with the hood.'

'Sorry.' I take it down, glancing furtively up and down the road to make sure no one is following me.

'One can't be too careful these days.' He takes out a set of keys and unlocks the two deadbolts on the door. 'There are Bolshie spies everywhere.'

I seem to have caught him in one of his 1940s fugue moments, and I'm unsure how much to play along. It's a relief when he holds open the door so I can enter. Winston gives me a good sniff in the narrow hallway, but I seem to pass muster. He wags his tail; I pat his head. Mr Pepperharrow sends the dog off to the kitchen and closes the door.

'I thought you'd be back again, young lady,' he says. 'At least, I hoped so. My old eyes have seen things you can never imagine. I've got pictures burned into my brain of terrible things. Pain, suffering, and so much death. But when I look at you...' He ushers me into the sitting room. 'Those things are wiped away. Erased. I can see *her* once again.'

Smiling sadly, I stare at the books, the model airplanes, and ultimately, the plain wooden clock on the wall, its brass hands frozen at a moment in time, its springs wound down, its pendulum hanging limp.

'You told me before that Marina gave you that clock, didn't you?' I walk over and stand in front of the boxy wooden case, examining the brass escutcheon and the dark, empty keyhole.

He stands next to me. I can sense his hesitation – and his regret. 'I did,' he says.

'Did she have it on the wall when you knew her, or did she have it hidden away? Under the bed, maybe?'

He shrugs but doesn't respond.

'Do you have the key to the case by any chance?'

He's silent for a long moment. 'No,' he says finally. 'I think you do.'

Nodding, I remove the key from the chain around my neck. He gives a little gasp at seeing the locket. I hold the key in my palm; the metal grows warm against my skin. 'Before you left for your mission, you put the key inside the jewelled bird,' I say. 'You wanted to help Marina keep it safe.'

'I didn't put it there,' he says. 'I told her to take it to Jeremy Stanley. He was into fixing things. I asked him to sort it for her.'

He moves away from me, lowering himself into the armchair. 'Marina confided in me. Told me who she really was; that she grew up in a palace. But then the world went to hell. She had loyal servants who helped her escape. One of them had relatives in England and helped her start a new life.'

'So she was royalty.' The excitement I feel at having this confirmed is tempered by sadness at the loss and the waste. 'She could have relied on her connections to the British throne and lived here as a princess in exile. Why didn't she? She might have survived.'

He shakes his head. 'Don't think I didn't tell her that. I pleaded with her to go and claim her rightful place. But she wasn't interested in fancy clothes and garden parties and balls.

Those things were the cause of everything she'd lost: her family, her homeland, her way of life. Instead, she dedicated herself to the care and protection of the few things she had left. Her daughter, whom she loved dearly, and the few treasures she'd brought with her. It was a hard life, but she was quick to laugh, and quick to love – maybe too quick. But Marina was happy, in her own way. Maybe you can tell your grandmother that...' He wipes a tear from his eye.

'She'd like to hear that.' I smile. 'And maybe I can arrange for you to tell her yourself.'

'Little Catherine – such a wee mite she was then. I kept tabs on her from afar, you know. I never wanted to make myself known. Didn't want to upset her nice life.' He frowns. 'Maybe that was wrong.'

'I'm sure she would love to know you. When this is all over.'

'Aye.'

Moving closer, I take his arm, feeling a strong connection with this man who helped my great-grandmother. For them, there was no happily ever after. On a dark London night, their love died a cruel death. But when he smiles at me, I can see happiness and relief in his eyes, because something of her lives on in me.

'Can I have a look at that locket?' he says. 'It was Marina's favourite. She used to sing the words to the song it played. Her voice, it was so beautiful. Deep and pure.' He dabs his eyes with a handkerchief.

I withdraw the locket and undo the clasp. The bird flips up onto its perch and begins its slow rotation. The jewels glitter in the light; the music box makes its melodic tinkling sound. Mr Pepperharrow watches, mesmerised, humming softly under his breath.

'She was so...' But he doesn't finish the sentence. Winston lets out a whine and a bark from the kitchen. From the hallway just outside the door, there's a sound of soft clapping. I turn as a figure appears in the doorway. My heart bangs in my chest.

A man holding a gun.

64

'Hello, David,' I say. 'Or should I call you Hal?'

'Such a touching sight.' When my grandmother's erstwhile boyfriend sneers, his smooth, tanned skin cracks into a mass of wrinkles. Instead of looking early seventies like I'd originally thought, he's definitely older than that. 'But then,' he says, 'it's always nice to see people on the side of the angels. So sorry to break up the party.'

I stare down at the hard black metal of the gun, knowing I should be feeling desperately afraid. But it's like the curtain has come up on some kind of surreal pantomime. At least while this man is here, my grandmother is out of danger.

Mr Pepperharrow leans forward, rigid in his chair. 'Harold Dawkins.' He grimaces as he says the words. 'It's an evil day when the dead start to walk again.'

'Especially someone who deserved his punishment,' I say, looking from Mr Pepperharrow to Hal. 'Frank Bolton gave evidence against you, but your case was hushed up. You were sent to the front. Where you obviously didn't die.'

'You worked it out then. Now, where are Marina's jewels?' His question is punctuated by a wave of the gun in my direction.

My heart sprints in my chest, but I stand my ground. 'I assume they were destroyed in the bombing. Why would you think any differently?'

'They weren't destroyed. That pretty bitch was too smart for that.'

'I hope you're not using that language to refer to my great-grandmother,' I say. 'Because that might make me angry.'

He laughs. 'You know, Alex Hart, I like you. You have spirit. And I liked Catherine too. Sometimes, I almost wish things had been different.'

'What?' I snort. 'That you weren't a lying thief who's pretended to be dead all these years, and who wormed his way into my grandmother's life and heart so that you could search her house?'

'That's one way to put it.' He shrugs. 'You young people are so cynical these days.'

Mr Pepperharrow makes a move to stand up, his hand shaking atop his stick. 'Can someone tell me what is going on here? Why is this scoundrel, this sewer rat, in my house?'

The gun swings towards the old man. I press him on the shoulder so that he sits back down. I don't want him to endanger himself. I've done enough on that score already.

'For Mr Pepperharrow's benefit and my own,' I say, 'let me make sure I've got this straight. It was Mallow Court you were after all along, right? You suspected that Marina had a treasure trove of Romanov jewels with her when she came to London, and she'd hidden them somewhere. When the house on Larkspur Gardens was bombed, you searched and looted the wreckage but found nothing. You assumed that she'd given the jewels to Frank, the father of her child.'

'That's where you're wrong.' He laughs. 'I didn't know about any jewels until you started asking Catherine about them, and I saw the article in your office. So, thanks for putting me onto that.' His lip curls. 'And for your information, it was the house I was after. Frank's house that should have been mine. And his life. A nice life in a pretty place with lots of green, and a factory where I was the boss, not the lackey. The life that my girl should have had, not his. I was the one who put the idea in his head, you know?'

'So?'

'I know what Frank thought, with his highfalutin morals. He'd turn me in, and I'd cool my heels in Holloway a few months having learned my lesson. But he was wrong, wasn't he? Sent me off to die; and I'll have you know, I almost did.' He turns to Mr Pepperharrow. 'Shot in the back when I was doing my bit.' He grins. 'Just didn't hit anything vital.'

'Despicable,' Mr Pepperharrow mutters.

Hal's face twists into a snarl. 'Shut up, Miles. You always were so *small*.'

Mr Pepperharrow clenches his gnarled fists. I put my hand on his shoulder to keep him in the chair.

'So when you searched the attic of Mallow Court,' I continue, 'you found Frank's diary, is that right?'

'God, Frank and his pretty words,' he rails. 'I was gonna use it as kindling. But then I saw he'd only used our nicknames from when we were kids. They called me Flea because I was always scratching. Frank was Badger because he saw one in the rubbish bins once. And Jeremy was Spider because he once kept one as a pet in a jar under his bed.' He laughs. 'Frank was such a sentimental fool back then thinking we would always be friends. But I saw how I could use it. I wrote my name in the front cover and sent photocopies of some of the entries to my

Sally. Nice girl, but not the sharpest knife in the drawer. She put two and two together and got five.'

I roll my eyes in disdain. 'You fuelled your own daughter's anger against Mrs Fairchild. You involved her in your little scheme: she was the one who called the police pretending to be Catherine, and I got arrested. Then you searched the house again. Were you looking for the film reels?'

'They were the only thing that could disprove my "little scheme", as you call it. The only real evidence. I knew Frank would have kept them. But I didn't find the damn things.'

'The films made for interesting viewing; though I'm not sure the fur coat suited you.'

Hal snorts. The gun doesn't waiver.

'And when Sally eventually came to her senses and stopped sending the diary entries,' I continue, 'you took over yourself. And you decided to make some "mischief". That would surely do the trick. And it almost did, didn't it? My grandmother called in an estate agent. She was serious about selling. You may not have a conscience yourself, but you're a damn good judge of character. Her weakness was that she was a good person – perfect for exploitation. In fact, so perfect that you decided to try a dual approach. You waltzed into her life like a fake-tanned, face-lifted prince charming. You told a cock and bull story about being an ex-detective inspector and swept her off her gardening clogs.'

'She was up for it, believe me.' He sniffs. 'And for your information, I was a DI in the Caymans.'

'So why attack her? If your plan was working so well.'

Hal ignores my question. 'Do you know, I actually proposed to her? I had a ring and everything: the ring I took from her mother's finger, all those years before. I thought it was a nice gesture my giving it back to her. But that daft cow said she didn't want to marry again. Said she had a granddaughter now, and that was enough. Told me that things between us were "a bit of fun" but nothing more. I realised it had all been a waste of time.'

I shake my head. 'Shame on you.'

'Shall I get down on my knees and say I'm sorry?'

'That'd be a start.'

But I've gone too far. He takes a menacing step towards me, holding the gun just inches from my chest. 'That's enough chat, clever clogs. You've obviously got everything figured out. So now you're going to do two things. First, you're going to give me that pretty pendant around your neck. Frank stole it, you know. He took it off the neck of his own child while she was asleep. If it wasn't for me, I doubt he would have given it back.'

'He would have and he did.' I cover it protectively. 'Frank wasn't like you.'

'Ha! You just keep on believing that.'

I gasp as he lurches towards me, grabs the chain and yanks hard. For a split second I think the links are going to cut through my neck. But it breaks in his hand. He bends down and picks up the locket.

'Like candy from a baby,' he says with a sneer. 'And secondly' – straightening up, he presses the gun sharply into my chest – 'you're going to tell me where the rest of the jewels are.'

65

It may be a surreal pantomime, but the pain is real as the gun presses against my ribcage. I wish fleetingly that everything didn't depend on my dubious acting ability. I've got two choices – one: to collapse in a cowering heap, whimpering protestations of innocence; and two: think of something else. I punt for option two. Lifting my chin, I stare Hal Dawkins in the eye and lean forward into the barrel of the gun.

'Read my lips, Hal – I. Have. No. Idea... You scumbag!'

Maybe that last bit was too much, but I'll never know. Winston starts to bark again and the door bursts open. A cricket bat appears, held by the trembling hands of Tim Edwards.

'Put the gun down,' he bellows in his 'court voice'.

'Well,' Hal sneers, 'if it ain't "widows and orphans boy" come to save the day.'

'I mean it, Great-Granddad. It's over.'

Suddenly, the pressure is released from my chest as Hal wheels around and points the gun straight at Tim. 'You little pussy,' he says. 'If you hadn't made a right muck of everything from the start, then we'd be living the high life by now. But no, you had to go and spring her out of jail. Get her snooping around and asking questions. Taking her to meet Sally and all. Where were you when the brains were handed out, boy?'

'I had no idea what was going on,' Tim says. 'Gran started going on about an old friend – someone she had a score to settle with. I worried she might get herself in trouble. You told her you regretted not being in her life, but really, all you wanted to do was involve her in stirring up trouble.' He shakes his head. 'You should have stayed away – left well enough alone. Stayed put on your sunny island with the women and the daiquiris. Instead, you're here waving a gun around looking for some treasure that doesn't exist.'

'What do you know about it?' Hal snarls. As the two of them stand off against one another, I look around for something I can use as a weapon – a letter opener or a fireplace poker. But all Mr Pepperharrow has in his sitting room is a whole lot of books. My eyes come to rest on something else: the model Spitfire that's propping up a section of books on the Great War. I inch over towards it but it's too far away. Too far away unless I can keep him talking.

'You're grasping at straws,' I say. 'If the jewels did exist – and that's a huge *if* – then the most likely scenario is that they were buried or destroyed when the house was bombed. You've never had any reason to think anything different.'

'You didn't know Marina.' He swings the gun back at me. 'She would have made sure they were safe – she was like that. I reckon those jewels were her insurance policy. The only proof she was royalty, like that article said. And who knows? If she'd lived, one day she might have been first in line.'

I inch closer to the shelf. 'And what about Jeremy Stanley? Was he in on it with you?'

'Spider?' Hal laughs. 'He had his arse stuck up a clock; he

weren't interested in anything else. He wouldn't have gone to the police. And later on, I took a chance – that he'd feel sorry for poor old Flea, banished and exiled. Asked him if he couldn't help a poor bloke sell a few whatnots he'd picked up in France. He did it too, through that fancy auction house.' His laugh turns hollow. 'And I've got a strange suspicion it weren't the first time.'

'What do you mean?'

With the hand not holding the gun, he reaches into his pocket and pulls out a few loose sheets of paper. 'The final diary entries. Don't you want to know how Frank's story ends?'

'That's enough!' Tim says. 'This needs to end once and for all.' He reaches out and grabs the pages in his great-grandfather's hand. Hal jerks his hand away. There's the sound of ripping paper. Hal is left with a fragment of a page in one hand, and a gun in the other. He levels the gun at his great-grandson, looking murderous.

I move within touching distance of the Spitfire. It's made of metal – simple, but strong. Just like the real plane would have been.

All of a sudden, there's the sound of running footsteps outside. 'Alex!' a voice calls out. I freeze in horror. I may have absolutely no control over the situation, but I can take care of myself. But if Chris gets hurt or killed, I'll never forgive myself.

The front door bangs open. Hal cocks his gun.

'Alex!' Chris calls out again.

Taking advantage of the distraction, I grab the spitfire and jab the point of its nose into Hal's arm. The world seems to shake on its axis, shuddering into slow motion as a gun goes off in a deafening explosion. 'No!' I scream. At that moment, I know that Chris has been hit, and he's dead, and my life is over... And that knowledge gives me superhuman strength. I leap at Hal and wrestle the gun from his fist. It explodes again and there's a crack of wood splitting open and something heavy showering to the floor. And the pain blooms under my skin and my ears are ringing so much that I can hardly hear the sirens outside and the armed police unit rushing in and taking over the scene. I feel like I'm running through water as I try to reach Chris but instead find myself tumbling to the ground over the clock that's been shot open and fallen to the floor. Marina's clock. And there before my eyes, the world begins to sparkle and glow in the colours of shimmering jewels – red, green, blue, gold, silver. And the snow begins to fall, light and crisp in front of me, and I shiver in the cold and stick out my tongue to catch the crystalline flakes as everything around me fades to black...

PART V

The strongest of all warriors are these two – Time and Patience.

— LEO TOLSTOY, WAR AND PEACE

66

1 DECEMBER 1940

I've done what I've done. The bombs keep falling, people keep dying. I go to work each night, swallowing back the same fear over and over again. But there's a new fear too. Fear of seeing the light go out in Catherine's eyes when she looks at me. She... who has become my everything.

I tracked her down – it wasn't hard. Most of London's orphans had been evacuated. I found her in a beast of a place out Essex way. Cold, grey: a building that might benefit from being levelled by a bomb.

When the matron brought her to me, I wanted to shout that she'd got the wrong girl. I didn't recognise the dull, sallow skin, the dank yellow hair, the slump in her shoulders. Or the eyes, hollow and haunted. She'd been crying; they told me she'd skinned her knee. My fist itched with the urge to punch the matron and everyone else who'd put that look on the girl's face. But instead, I knelt down and brushed the tears from her cheeks. I made the decision then and there – the right decision. I couldn't believe I'd wavered even a little...

I reached into my pocket and touched the heavy locket on the chain. As I drew it out, her eyes changed: growing animated and starting to glitter with life.

'Oh!' she cried, putting a hand to her mouth. She took the locket and held it up to her face and kissed it. 'You found it?'

'Yes.' I ruffled her hair. 'I found it. And it's yours always.' I swallowed back a tear as somewhere inside me, a tiny spark of hope flickered to life. 'And I'm yours too, if you'll have me.'

* * *

I signed the adoption papers and we left the building hand in hand. 'Today is the first day of the rest of your life,' I said.

She looked at me with eyes the colour of a summer sky. 'Thank you,' she said, 'for everything.'

Not everything, I wanted to say, but instead I just squeezed her hand.

67

I wake up in my bedroom – not the bedroom in my flat in the coach house, but in my childhood bedroom. I'm lying under the glow-in-the-dark stars that Dad pasted up on the ceiling the summer I turned ten. When I try to turn my head, it feels like cement. Mum is there, sitting in a chair reading a novel. A mug of tea steams on the bedside table.

'Mum?' I say groggily.

'Alex! You're awake!' She puts down the book and picks up the mug. 'Here, drink this.' She holds the cup up to my mouth and I take a tiny sip. 'It's builder's with two teaspoons of sugar,' she whispers. 'Dad said I should give you chamomile or lemongrass. But what he doesn't know won't hurt him.'

'Thanks, Mum.' The room spins as I try to sit up. 'And how is' – my heart seizes with worry – 'Chris?'

'He's fine, and so is your grandmother.' She smiles reassuringly. 'One of the neighbours – I think her name was Sally Edwards – called the police.'

'She did?' It's too much to take in. 'And how did I get here?'

'Your friend Chris called an ambulance. You were in

hospital for two days. They had to operate to remove the bullet in your shoulder.'

Oh. So that's why everything hurts.

'If the painkillers are wearing off, I can get you another dose. But I insisted that you come home.'

'Thanks, Mum.' As I reach for her hand, a sharp pain shoots from my shoulder all the way down my arm.

She brushes the hair away from my face. 'I can't tell you how worried I was when they phoned. I thought...' Her voice quivers away to nothing.

'I'm so sorry for putting you through that.'

'I'm just glad it's over.' She hesitates. 'It *is* over, isn't it?'

'Yes, Mum,' I say. 'And it's quite a story. I'll tell you all about it... another time.' The stars begin to swirl above me. 'Right now, though, I need another little sleep.'

* * *

Hours later – or maybe it's days – I wake up still in pain, but slightly less hazy. This time, it's Dad sitting in the chair next to my bed. 'Alexandra,' he says solemnly. 'How are you feeling?'

'Like I've been shot in the shoulder.'

He takes my hand in his. 'Think of the pain as a balled-up fist. Then think of the fist releasing and the pain and tension drifting off into the universe.' He traces a circle on my palm.

'Um, yeah. Are there any more of those painkillers?'

'Yeah, sure. They're around here somewhere.' With a grin, he rummages in the drawer of the bedside table.

'Did they get him?' I ask. 'The man who shot me – Hal Dawkins, aka David Kinshaw.' Just thinking about the smug look on Hal's face as he levelled the gun in my direction brings a fresh wave of pain to my shoulder.

Dad chuckles as he takes out a blister of tablets. 'You wounded him badly enough to put him in A&E. They took him into custody from there. When you're up to it, they'll come and take your statement. What was it you stabbed him with? A model Spitfire?'

I nod.

'Glad to see our good old British planes saved the day again. Did you know, Alex, without people like your friend Miles Pepperharrow, we'd all be speaking German today?'

I raise an eyebrow at Dad's uncharacteristic show of patriotism. 'Or Russian,' I can't resist adding.

'Yes, well...' Dad looks a little sheepish as he hands me two tablets and a glass of water. As I swallow them, his tanned brow furrows, like he's trying to figure out if he knows me.

'I'm sorry, Dad,' I say. 'About... who I am, you know?'

To my surprise, he laughs. 'I guess having a daughter who's *actual royalty* is my comeuppance for not telling you about your birth mother. The world works in mysterious ways.'

'It sure does.' I smile. 'So you're not... disappointed?'

He ruffles my hair. 'How can I be? To me, you'll always be the daughter of Rainbow and your mum. Not to mention, yours truly.' He points to his chest. 'It's the best combination of nature and nurture I could imagine.'

I laugh. Humility was never Dad's strong suit.

'Though,' he muses, 'I hear your young man is quite the toff. Not sure I approve of that.'

'But Rainbow was...' I trail off as the painkillers start to kick in and my eyelids grow heavy.

'Yes, Alexandra. Come the revolution we'll all have a lot to answer for.'

* * *

The sky is red, the buildings black. I look up at the bomber's moon darkened by arrows of planes flying across. I brace myself for the flash, the earth-shaking blow. But all of a sudden, clouds appear, and the planes scatter without dropping their deadly cargo. Rain begins to fall, washing away the sins of the past. Dawn breaks over the horizon and I hear music. Humming; words in a strange language, low and powerful...

'Alex?'

I blink awake. My grandmother wipes away the tear that's fallen onto my cheek as she leans over and kisses my forehead.

'Grandmother,' I say. 'Are you OK?'

She laughs and cries and smiles, all at the same time. She squeezes my hand like she'll never let it go. 'Oh, Alex, I'm fine. It's all over now... isn't it?'

A torn piece of paper in his hand.

'Yes, Grandmother. It's over. I'm so sorry about your friend David.'

'As it turns out, he was just too old for me. But when I visit him in jail, I must get the name of his plastic surgeon if I ever need a little nip and tuck.'

I laugh. My good, sunny, happy grandmother. She's back.

'Also, I had a long chat with Sally Edwards. She's mortified by the whole thing. When her father waltzed back into her life about six months ago, she thought he was Lazarus returned from the dead. Gave her a line about taking care of her, getting to know her and Tim after all these years. But she didn't tell Tim he'd returned – not until after the incident that put me in the hospital. She wanted you to know that Tim was as in the dark as the rest of us.'

'Hmm.' I'm noncommittal. 'But why did Hal come back after all these years? Why now?'

'Turns out he'd made a nice life for himself in the Caymans

with his ill-gotten gains. He really was a police inspector there for a time. But he was homesick for England, and the money was running low. He heard that I was a widow, and a plan formed in his mind.'

'Gosh,' I say. 'To think he's been out there all this time.'

'Anyway, Sally's come to her senses now. She's younger than me, though you might not know it to look at her. She wasn't even born until after her father was sent away. We're going to meet again for coffee and get to know each other.' Her face colours. 'I told her I'd got used to having a man about the place again. She mentioned this new thing they're doing in London – speed dating. We might give it a try.'

'Speed dating? With Sally Edwards?'

'Well, Alex, I've learned that you only live once.' Her smile fades suddenly. 'And something tells me that you may not be at Mallow Court forever – not now that you've got yourself a young man.'

I think of Mallow Court and the affinity I've had since the first moment I came there. It's only now that the ties of family and history connecting me to the place have become visible. Could I really leave now after all I've discovered? I shift in the bed. On the other hand, even if I do move on at some point, those ties will remain. It's comforting to know that if I leave the nest, I'll always be able to fly back again. And although I still don't feel completely comfortable with my 'upper-crust' roots, hopefully Chris can help put me at ease.

Chris... Maybe it's the painkillers, but a vision pops into my head. Him working in this shop taking things apart and putting them back together, me with a little desk set up in the corner doing research and writing articles. Learning more about art and my Russian history. Maybe even travelling there together...

She brushes her hand over my forehead. 'Anyway, Alex, you

don't need to figure it out now. Just rest and get well. You've had quite a shock. We all have. But what's most important now is that we have each other. Family...'

She takes something out of the pocket of her cardigan. A piece of paper yellowed at the edges.

'What's that? Another journal entry?' Alarmed, I try to sit up.

'No.' She smiles sadly, patting my shoulder. 'This was inside the clock along with the jewels. I'd like to read it to you.'

'OK.'

Holding the paper close to her face, she reads:

My darling Dochka,

I am penning these lines in haste so that I may give them to Miles on his leave and he can keep them safe. I no longer trust in anything I do, and will rely on him. He is the best of men, and I love him dearly. He would have been willing to raise you as his own if I had let him. But I know that he is destined for a better life than he could have with me. I am not strong, and my time may be short.

Your father is a man called Frank Bolton. Also a good man, and he was a comfort to me in my loneliness before I met Miles. But I have not told him the truth of you. He would have wanted to 'do the right thing', and would have married me out of obligation and duty, not out of love. And love – of you – is the sole ray of light in this life of mine. And so we will muddle along, you and I, for as long as the fates, and our enemies, allow.

Yes, my darling, I am sorry to tell you that our enemies are many. In another life I was a princess like in one of your story books. I had gowns and jewels and horses and servants. I did not ask for these things, nor did I value them.

Above all I valued my father, and my cousins and relations, though I was not officially acknowledged as their kin. That hurt, as did the fact that I was never allowed to know my mother. But it hurt less than what came after. There was... so much death.

I was lucky, or so I was told, to have escaped to this dull, grey island. Miles told me I should seek out my relatives, claim what was rightfully mine. But I didn't listen. I saw what having such things did to my family while the people starved – it got them killed, including my beloved father. But I was too vain and greedy to give up all my treasures. And this has placed our lives at risk.

There are people seeking me. People from the darkness of that glittering past. So I have remained hidden in the trappings of the simple life of a servant. If I am jumping at shadows, looking over my shoulder, it is to protect you. Because they would not hesitate to take away everything I love.

And so, little daughter, let me end with the words to the song played by the bird so beloved of you.

> *Fly, little feather, through the sky*
> *And float away my sorrows.*
> *Open my heart with your voice*
> *And turn into my wing.*

Your loving mother... Marina

She stops reading. I pull her close to me and we cry together over poor, troubled Marina, blood of our blood, who, in fleeing one war, came to a tragic end in another.

'I'm sorry...' I say, over and over.

'Don't be, child.' My grandmother smiles like the first ray of sunlight after a fresh, spring shower. 'I have a few small memories of her, and now I have her words.' She folds the paper. 'It's enough. My only regret is that I didn't meet that lovely old man – Miles Pepperharrow – sooner.'

'You've been to see him?'

'Yes. Just after I saw Sally Dawkins. I showed him this letter.'

'It must have meant everything to him.'

'Yes, it did. I've invited him up to the house for tea. He says he'll come – next time he "has leave from the RAF".'

I laugh. 'Great.'

She reaches into another pocket. 'And he gave me this – I think you dropped it in all the kerfuffle.' She holds up a shiny jewelled locket on a broken silver chain.

'I'm so glad it's safe!'

She stares at it, mesmerised, as she flips open the catch and the bird pops out, singing its song, the precious stones on its wings glittering in the light. Then she closes it again.

'Here.' She places it in my hand. 'It's yours. All this princess business… well… I'll leave that up to you.'

'Thanks, I think.'

She laughs. 'Now, you need to get some rest, and I need to get back to my garden. Those roses aren't going to deadhead themselves.'

I reach out for her hand at the same time as she reaches for mine. She leans in and gives me a gentle kiss on the forehead.

* * *

Voices filter up from the spiritual garden; laughter and lively conversation. Clearly life – and yoga class – must be going ahead. I prop myself up on my elbow and manage to look out the window. I can just see Dad sitting at the responsibly sourced teak table with a Raku cup in one hand and a beer in the other. His visitor leans forward, coming into view, and my whole body starts to fizz. They laugh again, clearly hitting it off. Then the visitor stands up and shakes hands with Dad, who gives him a hard pat on the back.

Frantically, I try to finger comb my hair and pinch my cheeks to add some colour. Not that I've looked in a mirror for days, but I can only imagine how awful I must look. I glance around the room: there's an old Duran Duran poster up on the wall next to a print of the Chi Ro page from the Book of Kells. There are a number of photos tacked onto the bulletin board: mostly unflattering family shots of me with big hair and acne. But as Chris Heath-Churchley enters the room, I don't feel self-conscious at all. I feel happy.

'Alex – are you OK?' His smile lights up the deepest corners of my soul. He comes over to the bed and gives me a melting kiss.

'Yes,' I say. 'Better now that you're here.'

'I'm sorry I didn't come up sooner. I had some important business to conduct.'

'Oh?' I pretend I didn't see him talking to Dad. 'And what might that have been?'

'I had to convince *someone* that I'm not some kind of irritating toff. That I'm a down-to-earth-guy. I wore my John Lennon "Imagine" T-shirt just for the occasion.'

I admire the contours of his chest just visible underneath. 'Good move.'

'And after that, I had to ask that same someone for his blessing to "court" his daughter, who happens to be royalty.'

'Sounds daunting. And how did you get on?'

'Not so well on the blessing bit. Turns out he's an atheist.'

I raise an eyebrow. 'And the daughter?'

'Don't even get me started. There was lots of talk about heads rolling "come the revolution" and things like that. Mostly mine if I ever did anything to hurt a hair on her royal head.'

I laugh so hard that my shoulder starts to throb.

'But all in all' – his pale eyes twinkle – 'it went rather well. Now there's just one thing left to do.'

'Oh?' I shiver. 'And what's that?'

He reaches into the front pocket of his jeans and pulls out a velvet bag. 'I know it can't compare to the amazing jewels that you found,' he says, sitting down on the bed. 'But this belonged to my mum. It has sentimental value.' He takes out a gold band set with pavé diamonds and a trefoil of seed pearls and sapphires in the middle. 'It's a medieval style, I think.' He scratches his head. 'Come to think of it, I'm not sure where she got it – she loved trolling around little antique stores.'

'Sounds like another mystery.'

'Yes, it does.' He takes my hand and stretches my fingers out. 'So all that's left then, Alex Hart, is for me to ask you if, at some point in the near future, you might consider riding away with me on a white horse into the sunset?' He smiles, and I feel like I'm shimmering all over.

'Of course, Chris. As long as you're there to give me a leg up into the saddle.'

He slips the ring on my finger and caresses the top of my hand. As he's bent over me, I give in to the feeling of rightness and desire. I pull him down and our mouths lock together, not so gently this time. We stay like that, entwined together on my single bed as the day turns to night and the fluorescent stars on the ceiling above begin to shine and glow.

68

25 DECEMBER 1944

Catherine plays on the floor, twining her jewelled locket around the neck of the doll I bought her for Christmas. I close the newspaper and crumple it up in a ball.

I have sent a man to his death.

I toss the ball of paper into the fire, but the words leap from the flames and brand themselves behind my eyelids. The name in the obit column: Harold Timothy Dawkins, private. Killed in action. Many men would have wanted that kind of death, I suppose. But not Flea. He would have wanted his life. I took that from him.

'Look, Daddy, she's dressed for town.' She holds up her doll. In addition to a tiny handbag and red velvet hat that matches her coat, the doll has a miniature gas mask cut out of paper. It's a gruesome reminder that although the daily bombardments have stopped since Jerry invaded Russia, in the streets outside of this cramped, dingy flat, the war rages on.

Maybe it's the boys who hang out by the corner shop whistling at every girl that walks by. Maybe it's the thin broth she's forced to eat because I don't have time to stand in line for rations. Maybe it's this decrepit, soul-destroying neighbourhood, a flat with a privy out the back and hot water every other Sunday. Maybe it's life on the wrong side of the tracks that will eventually drain the colour from her hair, the laughter from her face, and the hope from her eyes. And when that happens, what will I have to show for my selfishness? My high-falutin morals?

'She looks lovely,' I say. 'What's her name?'

'Robin,' she says. 'Because of her red coat.'

'What a lovely name. Have you ever seen a real robin?'

'No.' She shakes her curls. 'Have you?'

'No – I don't think so.' *My voice catches; she cocks her head sideways to consider me.*

'Are you crying, Daddy?' *she says.*

I blink hard and smile. 'No, darling. It's just a bit dusty in here, that's all.'

'Oh.'

'In fact, now that Robin's dressed, why don't you get your coat on too. Let's go out and get some fresh air.'

She jumps up excitedly. 'Where are we going?'

'You'll see.' *I stand up and put on my coat.*

Flea's gone. He's really gone – his name was there in black and white.

She puts the doll in its pram and gets herself ready. I check the pocket of my coat to make sure the advertisement is there: the particulars for the property auction to be held the following week. Among the lots is a partially derelict textile factory in North London, and a sixteenth-century country house in Buckinghamshire in need of refurbishment...

69

MAY 2001 – MALLOW COURT

One year later...

It's the perfect day for a wedding. The wisteria twining around the arbour is in full bloom; the sprigs of white roses hand-tied with lavender silk ribbons have a hint of dew on their petals. The weather is warm with a slight breeze that ruffles the organza chair bows. Wisps of clouds decorate the sky like celestial confetti. Bees hum in the borders and an iridescent butterfly floats from flower to flower. Daisies and buttercups dot the field where the marquee has been erected amid grazing sheep.

Perfect.

Most importantly, from the perspective of the wedding planner hired by the Heath-Churchleys, at least, the posh Portaloos, the five-tier cake, the sushi chef from Nobo, and a whole lorryload of Pol Roger arrived early this morning, right on schedule. And I made sure that our chosen vicar, Karen, was kept far away from the village pub where the groom and his party were staying.

Or at least, was supposed to be staying...

I roll over and nestle into the warmth of Chris's back. I kiss the place between his shoulder blades and he begins to stir. Some brides might be superstitious spending the night with the groom before the wedding, but not me. Life is short, and I want to enjoy every moment.

'We'd better get up,' I whisper into his soft hair.

He nuzzles my neck, sending bolts of lightning through my body. 'I feel a little bad, but it's the right thing, isn't it?'

As he caresses me, I think back to last night, when Chris had turned up at the door of my flat about 10 p.m. looking positively green.

'What's wrong?' I'd said, my heart in fight or flight mode. Immediately, I knew the truth – he didn't want to go through with it. My future flashed before my eyes: the future we'd been planning together. I'd spent the last several months curating an exhibition on the life and work of Robert Copthorne: my last contribution at Mallow Court before Edith takes over as manager. After the wedding, it was arranged that I'd move to London with Chris. We'd start out in his little flat near the British Library, and look together for a bigger flat or a house once we'd saved up enough for a deposit. I feel sad leaving Mallow Court, of course, especially now that it's truly become my family home. But it's only a train ride away, and Chris and I are looking forward to striking out on our own, without the help of our families. In that regard, I've even managed to line up a few job interviews: it seems that my credentials as a manager at a historic house count for something among independent art foundations, museums, and historic home associations. It had even crossed my mind that I might finish my long-abandoned thesis and see where that might lead. But the most important thing – the thing that I'd thought we'd both wanted – was just to be together.

But as he stood there before me, I felt like a child holding a snow globe, watching it slide from my hands and smashing to the floor in a million glittering pieces. I forced myself to meet his eyes. Whatever he had to say, he'd have to say it to my face, no holds barred. I just couldn't believe it, though. We were so in love... I thought...

'Umm.' He shifted from foot to foot. 'There's something I didn't tell you.'

'What?' I'd braced myself for the worst, knowing that as long as he still loved me, nothing else mattered. 'Is it your family?' I knew full well that some feathers were still ruffled. I'm hardly 'Daddy' Heath-Churchley's ideal daughter-in-law-elect. After Chris brought the dodgy auction records to his attention, Mr Heath-Churchley called in a firm of independent auditors, who undertook a thorough investigation into the connection between Churchley & Sons, D Kinshaw/Hal Dawkins and possible looted artworks. There were several nail-biting weeks on the home front as boxes of records going back sixty years were checked and rechecked with a fine-toothed comb.

Unsurprisingly, nothing conclusive turned up. The official position of the auction house was that the listings signed off by Jeremy Stanley were 'a failure of risk management at the time that allowed a few isolated rogue acts' – the subtext being that Jeremy was 'not quite right in the head'. There were a few negative articles in the press, but these were overshadowed by positive press engendered by several hefty donations given to charities for war veterans, the elderly, and an East London teen centre. In the end, the house of cards remained standing. That made it a little bit easier for me to look my future father-in-law in the eye (he even gave me a brusque apology, once Chris advised him of my true origins), but only just.

'No, nothing like that.' Chris's shaky smile gave me little

comfort. He sat down beside me on the settee. 'It's just... kind of embarrassing.'

I braced myself for a new worst: he'd caught a loathsome disease, he'd slept with the vicar, he and Tim had exchanged identities...

'It's OK.' My spirits sunk like lead. 'Whatever it is, I'll try to understand.'

He enfolded my hand in his. 'I really, really love you, Alex, and I really, really want to marry you.'

'OK...'

'But in truth, the thought of getting up in that church in front of all those people and being the centre of attention is making me feel positively ill. I've got terrible stage fright.' He hangs his head sheepishly. 'Always have, I guess.'

I stopped his words by leaning forward and kissing him hard on the mouth. 'Look, mister, you scared me there for a second.'

He ran his fingers through my hair. 'I don't want to ruin your special day. I know you've been so busy making preparations.'

'You know none of it was my idea. Your dad and stepmum have had their hand in everything. I thought it was what *you* wanted. I mean' – I gestured at his Kraftwerk T-shirt – 'not wanted, exactly. More like, were tolerating on their behalf.'

'You mean you really don't mind?' There's a flame of hope in his eyes.

'No.' His return kiss took my breath away. I reassured him with my lips, my hands, and finally, my words. 'I feel the same way,' I said. 'This big wedding isn't "us". I want our families to be happy, but at the end of the day, shouldn't we get the final say?'

He lifted me onto his lap, using all of his considerable powers of persuasion to reassure me that he agreed completely.

* * *

A while later, a knock on the door startled me. I hurriedly made myself decent, looking around in vain for a place to hide the groom. 'Who's that?' I said worriedly.

'Umm,' Chris said, 'I took the liberty of asking your friend Karen to come over.'

'What? Why?'

Warily, I got up from the sofa and opened the door. Karen was standing outside at the top of the narrow staircase, wearing her dog collar, a smart black suit jacket, and a less intelligent black micro mini-skirt.

'Hey ho, Alex,' she said. 'Happened to run into the groom down the pub. But don't worry' – she gave me a wink – 'I've learned my lesson, and nothing untoward happened!'

'Come on in,' I said. 'Glass of wine?'

'Oh no.' She waved her hands. 'Lots to do before the wee hours. He told you, right?' She eyed me and my swiftly reassembled clothing critically. 'Or... not?'

Chris took my hand. 'I was just about to.'

'Never mind,' Karen said. 'The thing is, Alex, as your friend and vicar, it's my duty to ask if this wedding business is what you want.'

'You know it isn't. I wanted a small ceremony – just family.'

Chris gave Karen a thumbs up. She walked over and plopped a few sheets of stapled papers onto my lap.

'What's this?'

'Your new itinerary. You'll have time early tomorrow morning for a quick wedding ceremony – just your parents, your grandmother, Miles, and Chris's mum. Then it's off to the airport with you.'

'Really?' I looked at Chris.

'I moved our flights forward. Hope that's OK?'

He looked so sheepish and quirky, and drop dead sexy. I launched myself forward into his arms. 'Yes, it's fine. It's brilliant.'

'Whoa, tiger.' Karen tugged me away from him. 'Are you all packed?'

'Yes, I think so.'

Chris held me at arm's length, his eyes shining. 'Thank you, Alex.'

'You're welcome.' I stood on tiptoes and kissed his neck just below his chin. 'But you're sure you don't want your dad at the ceremony as well? Won't he be angry?'

'I think we'd better leave well enough alone.'

'I agree,' Karen said. 'I'll break the news to him that another one of his children won't be attending their own wedding reception at Mallow Court.'

'Thanks.' I hugged her swiftly.

'No problem. God forgives a multitude of sins. But for everybody else, I find that free-flowing champagne helps a lot.'

70

ST PETERSBURG, RUSSIA

May 2001

The midnight sun dances orange on the rippling current of the river. The view – from the Peter and Paul Fortress on the opposite bank to the elegant bridge, slowly lifting up to let the night boats float underneath – literally takes my breath away.

Holding me close with his arm around my back, Chris, who, as of a lovely private ceremony early this morning, is now my husband, senses my overwhelm. 'Are you OK?' he says.

'I'm fine. I just can't believe we're here – it's so amazing.'

The bridge lifts further and for a second the sun glows behind it. As the tresses continue to move, the sun reappears; it's as if someone up in the sky has given us a great big wink. Maybe it's my fated ancestors or maybe just a trick of the light. Either way, Chris and I plan to spend at least six months here so I can learn about my history and pick up a bit of my 'mother tongue'.

I turn and look towards the Winter Palace, now the Hermitage Museum; its long, elegant facade and hundreds of windows dominate the waterfront. On the second floor, ten windows in, is a small gallery where the recovered Romanov jewels are on display – beautiful, precious objects, several by Fabergé. When the discovery first came to light, Chris's dad got involved. He recommended a lawyer friend to help me sort out the ownership. But after a heart-to-heart discussion with Mr Pepperharrow, my grandmother, and Chris, we decided that they rightfully belonged to the people. I had the lawyer draw up a bequest to the Hermitage, setting out certain conditions, including that they allow the jewels to be displayed at certain English venues, including Mallow Court. But one piece was kept out of the bequest – the jewelled bird. For now, at least, that's going to stay in the family.

I reach up to my neck and draw out the locket on the heavy chain that Chris repaired after I was shot last summer. The little gold key is reattached to the chain. Marina's clock, however, shattered by Hal Dawkins' bullet, was beyond even his skills to salvage. Chris brushes a windblown strand of hair from my cheek as I undo the clasp and the bird springs up on its perch, its jewelled feathers glimmering in its native light. Together we watch as it begins its slow, mesmerising rotation to the tinkling melody. As usual, Chris's eyes light up like a kid in a candy store.

'Do you believe in genetic memory?' I ask.

'What do you mean?' His hip presses against mine.

'When my grandma was in hospital, I dozed off in the waiting area,' I say. 'I dreamed of a little girl standing here, in this spot. Bombs were falling, and then snow.' I shudder. 'Maybe that girl was me, or my great-grandmother, Marina, or some member of my family before me – I don't know. But I've got this weird sense of déjà vu. That I've been here before.'

He covers my hand with his and closes the locket. The skin

on my neck tingles with electricity as he tucks it back inside my shirt, caressing me with his finger.

'I don't know if I believe in that or not,' he says. 'I never found a lot in common with most members of my family, except my great-grandfather, Jeremy. I wish he'd kept a journal too – he must have known about Marina, or at least guessed. But I do know that you've been through an awful lot. What was it that Hal Dawkins said in his statement about the diary? That it was so vivid, he almost convinced himself that the memories were his.'

I nod, the memories still raw. In this case, not all of the 'bad' ended up 'unluckily'. Following his arrest, Hal Dawkins managed to get himself a good lawyer – his great-grandson Tim. I've come to terms with the fact that Tim isn't really a bad apple; he simply got swept up in the murky depths of his own family history, same as I did. And while his wily great-grandfather isn't exactly one of his usual 'widows and orphans', Tim did his job well enough to get him released on bail. It may have come as a surprise to the court, though not to me, that Hal didn't turn up for his trial. Once more, he disappeared into thin air.

Unfortunately, not completely. A week before our wedding, a brown envelope arrived postmarked Grand Cayman. It contained an unsigned compliments slip with a one-line message: 'A wedding gift – this is the original' and a ripped piece of paper – the final diary entry that got torn the day I was shot. I read it many times – the final part of Frank Bolton's story. Eventually I plucked up the courage to show it to Chris so there would be no secrets between us. He suggested that I bring it here. I take it out of my pocket now, staring down at the words on the paper.

'Did I do the right thing? Not telling my grandmother, I mean?'

'I think so.' Chris steadies me with a hand on my back. 'I can't see what good it would have done. Not after so long. None of them were saints – they were just human beings living in unimaginable times.'

'Maybe by adopting Catherine, Frank was trying to atone for what he did.' I sigh. 'I hope that by donating the jewels, I've done the same.'

A tear rolls down my cheek as I tear up the paper and throw it into the dark waters of the River Neva. The tiny pieces eddy and swirl, and gradually sink away. A secret lost to all but memory.

'I would have liked to have seen him brought to justice,' I say.

'You mean Hal?'

I sigh. 'Yes. Him too. But in some ways, I think Hal did get his comeuppance – living most of his life in exile from his family and his English homeland. Just like my great-grandmother, Marina, was exiled from hers.'

Chris puts his arm around my shoulder and pulls me close. 'Hey, it's going to be all right. It's a powerful feeling, being here.'

'It is.' I lay my cheek against his chest, listening to the sound of his heart, steady and regular like clockwork. And I know that whatever happens – whatever emotions I still have to process in order to come to terms with the past – he'll be at my side every step of the way.

'I guess history is written by the survivors,' I say.

'Sometimes.' Chris nods. 'But I think equally, the truth has a way of coming to light. I mean, just imagine. Never in my wildest dreams did I, a lowly clockmaker, guess that I'd be here in St Petersburg standing next to a Romanov princess!'

'Hey.' I nudge him with my elbow. 'You're forbidden to use that word, remember?'

'Yes, your highness.' He gives a mock bow.

'That's it then – you're toast!' I raise my fists so that he has to grab them and pull me close. His kiss is overwhelming, and I can feel my body mould to his and begin to glow, luminous, as the love sparks and flows between us.

He takes me by the hand, and together we begin to run – away from the river and towards our suite in the Astoria Hotel. And the city blurs before me, and the last year flashes before my eyes. And I realise that although I'm the same Alex Hart that I always was, I'm also so many more things than I'd ever dreamed was possible. In finding the secrets of the past, I've created my future, too. *Our* future. And in the end, isn't that what matters most?

EPILOGUE
25 DECEMBER 1944 (FRAGMENT)

'Please, Daddy,' Catherine says. 'Tell me where we're going.'

I laugh at her spirit. 'We're going out for cake and hot chocolate.' I ruffle her soft hair. 'Just after we stop by Uncle Jeremy's, OK?'

'Oh good!' She pushes the doll's pram across the small room and opens the door.

I pick up the advertisement for the auction of the factory and skim over it again. I've already told Jeremy what I need him to do. I need cash – and he has friends in high places.

On my way out, I go to the kitchen and reach into the flour tin, drawing out a small velvet bag. Through the cloth, I feel the hard stones of the diamond bracelet that Flea stole that night. Silently, I mouth a prayer. God give me the strength not to do this thing I'm about to do.

'Come on, Daddy,' my daughter shouts.

As I join Catherine outside on the grey, filthy London pavement, I know that this time, my prayers have fallen on deaf ears...

'Come on,' I say. 'Let's go.' I shove the velvet bag into my pocket.

After all, he's dead and gone, and no one will ever know...

A LETTER FROM LAUREN

Thank you for reading *The House of Hidden Secrets*. If you enjoyed this book, please can I ask that you leave a review. It really helps other readers find my books and might help someone discover their perfect next read. If you want to keep up to date on my new releases, or are interested in becoming a beta reader for my books, please sign up at the following link. Your email address will never be shared and you can unsubscribe at any time.

https://www.laurenwestwoodwriter.com

This book is a work of fiction; however, it does have a basis in historical fact. The period of intense German bombing known as the London Blitz began on 7 September 1940. For the next fifty-seven days and nights, German bombs fell on London and other cities, with attacks continuing until May 1941, when the Luftwaffe was redeployed to attack Russia. While there were countless acts of bravery and self-sacrifice, unfortunately, the Blitz did create many opportunities for criminals.

Looting was carried out in the aftermath of air raids by civilians, gangs of children, and occasionally even by public service workers. Incidents ranged from stealing WWI medals and coins from gas meters to a notorious incident following the bombing of a popular London nightspot, the Café de Paris, in March 1941, when looters cut off the fingers of the dead in order to steal their rings and jewellery.

One early incidence of looting took place in October 1940, when six London firemen were accused and convicted of looting from a bombed-out shop. Winston Churchill himself ordered that the conviction be 'hushed up' in order not to damage public morale.

There are many excellent books and articles written on this period of history, and it is thanks to writers like Gavin Mortimer, Joshua Levine, Juliet Gardiner, and others that many eye-witness accounts and anecdotes have been recorded and preserved. I have consulted books by these and other authors, and any mistakes and embellishments in my descriptions of events from this period are purely my own.

The other historical event that I refer to in this book is the murder of Tsar Nicholas II, his wife Alexandra, and their children Alexei, Anastasia, Olga, Maria, and Tatiana. The execution was carried out by Red Army soldiers in the basement of a house in Ekaterinburg on the night of 17 July 1918. The alleged reason for the death order was the strong following that Nicholas (who had already abdicated the throne) still had among Lenin's White Russian opponents. There is anecdotal evidence that not all of the family members died swiftly due to the bullets ricocheting off jewels sewn into their clothing.

Through the years, there were rumours that one or more of the royal children had escaped execution, and several 'pretenders' claiming to be the Grand Duchess Anastasia surfaced over the years. While this notion may be poetic, unfortunately it is not based in fact. Five bodies were exhumed from the main grave site in 1991, but it wasn't until 2007 that the last two bodies – of Prince Alexei and one of his sisters – were discovered nearby. DNA testing has shown that all of the family members (and a number of their retainers) are accounted for.

That said, many members of the extended Romanov family did survive. A large number escaped Russia to Europe and beyond, and indeed, Prince Phillip and the current line of heirs to the British throne have Romanov blood. Among the escapees in 1918 were the wife, son, and stepdaughter of Grand Duke Michael Alexandrovich Romanov, the younger brother of Tsar Nicholas II. While Michael Alexandrovich did not manage to escape (he was executed by the Bolsheviks on 13 June 1918), his family was smuggled out to safety.

During the nineteenth and early twentieth centuries, haemophilia, known as 'the royal disease', affected several lines of European royalty. The carriers were several of the children of Queen Victoria who married into European royal houses in Germany, Russia, and Spain. Among them were Queen Victoria's granddaughter Alexandra Feodorovna ('Alix of Hesse') who was married to Tsar Nicholas II of Russia, and mother to Alexei, who suffered from the disease. Another carrier was Princess Beatrice of the United Kingdom, the ninth child of Queen Victoria, who passed the disease to several of her children via her marriage into the Spanish royal line. Prior to her marriage, she did have a love affair with Michael Alexandrovich, but the couple was not allowed to marry due to the fact that they were first cousins. My character Marina, who is purported to be a child of these two royals, is completely fictional, and I have also taken some liberties on the manner of genetic inheritance. The disease is now considered to be extinct among European royalty.

Finally, while the jewelled bird is (alas!) also fictional, the treasures created by the House of Fabergé are truly spectacular works of art. This seminal firm of Russian jewellers was founded in St Petersburg in 1842 by Gustav Fabergé. While the firm is best known for making jewel-encrusted Easter eggs for the Russian imperial family, they also created a full range of other decorative items and jewellery, and at their height in the early twentieth century, employed over 500 craftsmen. Although the firm was nationalised by the Bolsheviks in 1918, Carl Fabergé went on to found other branches of the company in Paris and elsewhere. The brand has since changed hands a number of times, but the Fabergé jewellery and egg-making tradition has recently been revived.

Today, treasures made by the original house of Fabergé can be worth millions, and some large collections have reportedly been sold for hundreds of millions. For the rest of us mere mortals, we are fortunate that despite the vicissitudes of war and history, many beautiful Fabergé pieces and Romanov treasures still survive, and many can be viewed today in museums such as the Hermitage in St Petersburg and the Victoria and Albert Museum in London.

I would like to thank my family for their continued love and support. I would also like to thank my readers for choosing this book. I am very privileged as an author to find an audience for my characters and stories. It is you who truly brings them to life.

Lauren Westwood

Surrey 2024

ABOUT THE AUTHOR

Lauren Westwood writes about old houses and quirky historical mysteries. She is also an award-winning children's author (Laurel Remington), a mother of three, and works as a lawyer in renewable energy. Lauren is originally from California, and now lives in the UK, in an old house built in 1604.

Sign up to Lauren Westwood's mailing list for news, competitions and updates on future books.

Visit Lauren's website: www.laurenwestwoodwriter.com

Follow Lauren on social media here:

- facebook.com/Lwestwoodbooks
- instagram.com/lwestwoodwriter

ALSO BY LAUREN WESTWOOD

Secrets and Love Series

The House of Second Chances

The House of Hidden Secrets

The House of Love and Dreams

Letters from *the past*

Discover page-turning historical novels from your favourite authors and be transported back in time

Join our book club Facebook group

https://bit.ly/SixpenceGroup

Sign up to our newsletter

https://bit.ly/LettersFromPastNews

Boldwood

Boldwood Books is an award-winning fiction publishing company seeking out the best stories from around the world.

Find out more at www.boldwoodbooks.com

Join our reader community for brilliant books, competitions and offers!

Follow us
@BoldwoodBooks
@TheBoldBookClub

Sign up to our weekly deals newsletter

https://bit.ly/BoldwoodBNewsletter

Printed in Dunstable, United Kingdom